Meant to Be Immortal

BY LYNSAY SANDS

HIGHLAND TREASURE

LOVE IS BLIND

HUNTING FOR A HIGHLANDER

MY FAVORITE THINGS

A LADY IN DISGUISE

THE WRONG HIGHLANDER

THE HIGHLANDER'S PROMISE

SURRENDER TO THE HIGHLANDER

FALLING FOR THE HIGHLANDER

THE HIGHLANDER TAKES A BRIDE

TO MARRY A SCOTTISH LAIRD

AN ENGLISH BRIDE IN SCOTLAND

THE HUSBAND HUNT

THE HEIRESS • THE COUNTESS

THE HELLION AND THE HIGHLANDER

TAMING THE HIGHLAND BRIDE

DEVIL OF THE HIGHLANDS

THE LOVING DAYLIGHTS

Meant to Be Immortal

An Argeneau Novel

Lynsay Sands

HARPER LARGE PRINT

An Imprint of HarperCollinsPublishers

MEANT TO BE IMMORTAL. Copyright © 2021 by Lynsay Sands. All rights reserved. Printed in the United States of America. No part of this book may be used or reproduced in any manner whatsoever without written permission except in the case of brief quotations embodied in critical articles and reviews. For information, address HarperCollins Publishers, 195 Broadway, New York, NY 10007.

HarperCollins books may be purchased for educational, business, or sales promotional use. For information, please e-mail the Special Markets Department at SPsales@harpercollins.com.

FIRST HARPER LARGE PRINT EDITION

ISBN: 978-0-06-309046-0

Library of Congress Cataloging-in-Publication Data is available upon request.

21 22 23 24 25 LSC 10 9 8 7 6 5 4 3 2 1

Meant to Be Immortal

Prologue

Mac had just finished setting up his centrifuge when he caught a whiff of what smelled like smoke. He lifted his head and inhaled deeply; there were the astringent cleaner he'd used on the counter surfaces, various chemical and other scents he couldn't readily identify that were coming from the boxes he had yet to unpack, and—yes—smoke.

A frisson of alarm immediately ran up the back of Mac's neck. Where there was smoke there was fire and fire was bad for his kind. It was bad for mortals too, of course, but was even worse for immortals, who were incredibly flammable.

Straightening abruptly, Mac stepped over one un-opened box and then another, weaving his way out of the maze of unpacking he still had to do and to the stairs leading out of the basement. He took them two at a time, rushing up the steps to the special door he'd had installed several days ago. It blocked sound, germs, and everything else from entering the lab he was turning his basement into. He'd also had the walls sealed and covered with a germ-resistant skin. Apparently, his efforts had been successful. Even at the top of the stairs, he was only able to catch the slightest hint of smoke in the air, yet when he opened the door he found himself standing at the mouth of hell. The kitchen on the other side of the door was engulfed in flames that seemed almost alive and leapt excitedly his way with a roar.

A startled shout of alarm slipped from his lips as heat rushed over him, and Mac slammed the door closed at once. He nearly took a header down the stairs in his rush to get as far away from it as he could and crashed into a box as he stumbled off the last step. Pausing then, he stopped to turn in a circle, a mouse in a blazing maze, searching for a way out.

His gaze slid over the small half windows that ran along the top of the basement wall on the back of the house, skating over the flames waving at him from the burning bushes outside, and then he turned toward the rooms along the front of the house and hurried to the door to the first one. It was a bathroom, its window even smaller than the others in the main room. It was also covered with some kind of glaze that blocked the view. Even so, he could see light from the fire on the other side of it.

Rushing to the next door, he thrust it open. This was an empty room about ten feet deep and fourteen wide, with two half windows that ran along the back of the house. Mac stared with despair at the flames dancing on the other side of the glass. He was trapped, with no way out . . . and no way even to call for help, he realized suddenly. There was no landline in the basement, and he'd left his cell phone upstairs on the kitchen counter to avoid interruptions while he set up down here.

I'm done for, Mac thought with despair, and then glimpsed a flash of red light beyond the flames framing and filling the nearer window. Moving cautiously forward, Mac tried to see what was out there, and felt a bit of hope when he spotted the fire truck parked at the top of the driveway and the men rushing around it, pulling out equipment. If he could get their attention, and let them know where he was . . .

Turning, Mac rushed back into the main room, wading through the sea of boxes until he spotted the one he wanted. He ripped it open and dug through the bubble-wrapped contents until he found his microscope. It was old and heavy, and Mac pulled it out with relief and then tore the bubble wrap off as he moved back to the empty storage room. He didn't even hesitate, but crossed half the room in a couple of swift strides and simply threw the microscope through the nearest of the two little windows. Glass shattered and Mac jumped back as the flames exploded inward as if eager to get in. They were followed by rolling smoke that quickly surrounded him, making him choke as he yelled for help.

He was shouting for the third time when dark figures appeared on the other side of the fire now crowding the window. He thought he could make out two men in bulky gear, what he supposed was the firemen's protective wear, and then someone shouted, "Hello? Is there someone there?"

"Yes!" Mac responded with relief. "I am in the basement."

"We'll get you out! Just hang on, buddy! We'll get you out!"

"Get somewhere where there's less smoke," someone else shouted to him.

"Okay!" Mac backed out of the room, his fascinated gaze watching the fire fan out from the window as the drywall around it caught flame. It would spread quickly now that he'd given the fire a way in, he knew. The smoke was already filling this room and pouring out into the main room, but he could deal with that. Smoke couldn't kill him. Fire would.

Cursing, he turned abruptly and returned to the bathroom next door. There was no fire or smoke in the small room yet, but would be soon enough. Moving to the cast-iron claw-foot tub he'd had refinished before moving in, Mac plugged in the stopper and prayed silently as he turned on the taps. Relief slid through him when water began to pour out. The fire hadn't stopped the water from working yet, and the taps and faucet were old enough not to have an aerator to reduce the speed at which the water jetted out. It gushed from the tap at high pressure, filling the tub quickly, or at least more quickly than his tub back in New York would have filled. There it would have taken ten or fifteen minutes to fill the tub; here it took probably half that, but they were the longest minutes of his life and fire was beginning to eat through the wall between the bathroom and the storage room before it was quite finished.

Mac didn't wait for it to finish filling, but stepped into the quickly heating water in his pajama bottoms and T-shirt when it was three-quarters full, and submerged himself up to his nose. Smoke was coming into the room now, pouring through the air vents, making breathing hard, and the water was hotter than hell, the fire heating it in the pipes on its way to this room and the tub. But it was only going to get hotter. The one wall of the room was now a mass of flames, and the fire was eating its way into the two connecting walls as well. The linoleum tile on the floor was catching flame and curling inward toward the tub. The water he was in would be boiling soon, by his guess. He now knew how lobsters felt when dropped in boiling water. It was one hell of a gruesome way to die . . . But it wouldn't kill him. As long as he didn't catch fire, he would survive, but Mac suspected he'd wish he was dead before this was over.

One

The reception room of the police station was empty when CJ entered. Not a big surprise. Small-town police stations usually had minimal staff at night. The counter that ran along the back of the room had a bell on it, but she didn't end up having to use it. Even as she started toward it, an older man stuck his head out of the door behind the reception counter and raised his eyebrows at her.

"CJ Cummings?"

CJ nodded. "Captain Dupree?"

"That's me," he assured her, and then added with no little bit of irritation, "I've been waiting on you."

CJ allowed her eyebrows to rise slightly, but merely said, "It's not quite midnight. We agreed I should be here at midnight when Jefferson got off shift."

"Yes, we did," Dupree acknowledged testily. "But when we made that plan, I didn't know some firebug would take it into his head to burn down one of my citizen's houses while he was still in it. Had I known that was going to happen, I'd have gotten a contact number from you. I've been stuck here waiting on you before I could go out there and walk the crime scene."

CJ's eyebrows had risen higher and higher as he spoke. Now she said, "I don't really see why you felt you had to stay here, Captain. It's Jefferson I'm here to interview. You don't need to be present for that."

"I may not need to be, but he's one of my men and I intend to be," he told her firmly. "But that's no never mind anyway since Jefferson is the one who caught the call about the fire on his way back to the station. He's out there now waiting for us to join him."

"Us?" CJ echoed with surprise.

"Us," he said with a firm nod. "I need you there."

"Why?" she asked at once.

"You're a detective, aren't you?" It wasn't a question and he didn't wait for an answer, but continued, "Well, I was a detective before I was captain, but that was twenty years ago. Evidence gathering may have changed since then. This is the first murder Sandford has seen, and I don't intend to mess it up."

"Surely one of your men—" CJ began, only to be interrupted.

"My only detective dropped dead of a heart attack last month. I haven't hired a replacement yet, and while one of my younger fellows is taking a training course in detective work, he's just started that. I need someone who knows their business out there to help with evidence collection. So—" he paused and raised his eyebrows "—I figure you can come tell us what to collect and how to bag it and ask Jefferson your questions while you're at it."

CJ was shaking her head before he'd finished speaking. "Captain, I'm not a cop. I'm with the Special Investigations Unit; we're a civilian organization. We investigate cops; we aren't one of them. I've got no business being at a crime scene," she said firmly.

"You may not be a police officer now, but you used to be," Captain Dupree said with unconcern.

CJ's eyes narrowed at these words, and only continued to do so as he proved he'd looked into her background by adding, "In fact, while you started out on patrol like my boys, you moved up to homicide detective before shifting over to CSIS, the Canadian Security and Intelligence Service. I gather there you were blazing a fine trail of successes as one of the best detectives they had before you switched over to the SIU."

He didn't say "and became a traitor to the boys in blue," but CJ could hear that in the words. Investigating the police for corrupt or illegal activity did not make you a lot of friends. At least not with the police. They tended to see CJ and the people she worked with as traitors to fellow officers. As far as other police officers were concerned, the members of the SIU were one step up from slugs. Or maybe one step down.

CJ didn't particularly care. She had at first, but she'd gotten used to it, and what she did was important. To her mind, a good cop was worth their weight in gold, but every profession had their bad apples, and bad cops could do more damage than your average dirtbag criminal. She felt no regret or guilt over what she did.

"Well?" Dupree snapped. "Are you going to step up and help out here or what? If you don't, we'll have to wait for a detective from the Ontario Provincial Police to come help us. That could take days and evidence has a tendency to walk away or get trampled on if not gathered right away."

CJ knew that when it came to fires, a lot of evidence was unavoidably damaged by the firemen as they fought to put out the fire anyway. But it was always better to collect whatever wasn't damaged as quickly as possible.

"Sure," she said finally. "I'll help. But I can't collect or bag evidence. That would affect your chain of custody."

"You won't have to. You just tell Jefferson what and how and he'll do it," he assured her, some of the stiffness sliding from his shoulders now that he had her agreement. He immediately came around the counter to hand her a slip of paper with an address on it. "That's where the fire is. You'll want to take your own vehicle so you aren't stuck there until one of us is ready to go. You have GPS?"

CJ nodded as she glanced down at the address.

"Good. I'll—"

"Captain!"

Irritation flickered over his face at that shout from somewhere toward the back of the building, and then Captain Dupree started to back away, saying, "You head on over there. I'll follow in my squad car."

He didn't wait for a response, but turned and hurried around the counter and through the doorway at the back of the room, disappearing from sight just as someone shouted for him again.

CJ folded the slip of paper and headed back out to her car. This wasn't how she'd planned to start her investigation, but that didn't bother her. Investigations rarely went according to plan. Hell, neither did life for that matter, and she'd learned to roll with the punches that came at you. Still, being roped into a police investigation was a bit unexpected and, in this case, not something she was looking forward to since it involved a crispy critter. Her nose wrinkled at the term they had used on the force to describe murder victims whose remains had been burned. They'd had lots of nicknames for victims. Civilians probably would have thought them heartless and cruel for the most part, but when you investigated the atrocities people committed on each other, you had to find a way to separate yourself from it emotionally or it would tear you apart. Nicknames were just one of the ways they did that.

Sandford was a relatively small town of 12,000 people. That might not seem small to some. There were much smaller towns, but 12,000 was small for having its own police department. Most towns in Ontario that were that size, and some with even larger populations, had given up the expense of running their own department in favor of contracting out to the Ontario Provincial Police. Sandford had avoided that so far. But while the town wasn't all that large when it came to population, it was much larger in physical size thanks to being a farming town and it took nearly twenty minutes to reach the address the chief had given her, which ended up being on a rural route lined with large fields and the occasional farmhouse.

CJ was able to see the house from several minutes away, or at least the fire raging through it. The building was an old brick farmhouse and the fire was still roaring, despite two fire trucks and more than a dozen men fighting valiantly to put it out. CJ pulled in behind a long line of pickups—volunteer firemen was her guess—parked on the grassy verge of the extremely long driveway and made her way up the gravel drive toward the chaos of bodies moving around the blaze. She was about halfway up the driveway when she heard the "whup whup" of the ambulance and saw it heading toward her. CJ had to step onto the grass to make way for it to leave, but then continued forward, heading for the only man in the mass of people ahead who was wearing a police uniform.

Pain, pain, pain. That's what woke Mac. Every bit of his body was in agony, from the tips of his toes, to the top of his head, and every inch of his skin felt like it was afire. A scream of agony was rising up in his throat when voices pierced the cloud of suffering, distracting him.

"My God."

"What is it, Sylvie? Is he dead? Should I turn the lights and siren off?"

"No, Artie. He's still alive, but he's—well, he's healing."

"What?" Artie asked. "What do you mean, healing?"

"He's healing," Sylvie said with something like awe. "The blisters are— You need to see this, Artie. This isn't normal. Pull over and—"

The woman's words died when Mac finally managed to push his eyes open.

"Your eyes," she breathed with amazement as the ambulance began to slow. "They're silver."

"What was that?" Artie asked from the front of what Mac now realized was an ambulance. The woman's uniform and the gurney he was lying on gave that away.

Which meant he was on his way to the hospital, Mac realized, and knew that couldn't happen. Rising up on the gurney, he sunk his fangs into the female EMT's neck, and began to drink.

I think that's it," CJ said as she watched the officer bag the cigarette butts she'd spotted. They'd started the search over an hour ago, using a grid-work pattern to cover the outer edges of the property first, and then moving slowly inward. Fortunately, by the time they'd reached the area around the house itself the fire had been all but out, the firemen concentrating on the interior.

"Yeah. I think we've covered everything outside," Officer Simpson agreed, closing the evidence bag and straightening next to her.

CJ nodded absently, her attention on the farmhouse. They couldn't look inside yet, but she doubted that would be necessary anyway. Gasoline had been used for the accelerant. She'd been able to smell it as she approached. That and the melted remains of three empty gas cans that they'd found on the edge of the fire had given it away. Two of the three plastic cans had just been melted lumps, but the third one had only been partially melted, and the handle and cap had remained. It might be a lucky find if the arsonist hadn't used gloves. The cigarettes might be helpful too if they belonged to the arsonist. They might get some DNA off them.

"What now?" Simpson asked.

CJ turned to Officer Simpson. Not Jefferson. Simpson. Officer Jefferson had left about ten minutes before she got there. Simpson had told her that after introducing himself, explaining that Jefferson had been called away to handle a situation downtown. CJ suspected it was the same situation that'd had someone back at the station shouting for the captain as she left, because he had never shown up here either.

"I think that's it for the night," CJ said, and wasn't surprised by the obvious relief on Simpson's face at her words. It was nearly 2 A.M. and she suspected the younger man probably worked the same shift as Jefferson, and should have been off at midnight. He was probably ready to go home to bed.

"Will we need to go through the house itself?"

CJ eyed the charred remains of what had once been a charming old Victorian-era farmhouse. The fire was out, but a couple of firemen were still running a spray of water over the smoking ruins to make sure there were no embers that might spark up later. She knew from past experience that no one would be allowed inside for a day or two, if at all. An inspector would have to check to see that it was safe to enter and floors wouldn't collapse underfoot. If there were still floors inside the brick exterior, she thought, but said, "Not tonight. Maybe in a day or two . . . if it's even necessary," she added. "I don't think the arsonist bothered to go inside to set this fire. It looks to me like he just poured the gas over the front porch, back porch, and the bushes around the house and lit it up."

"Yeah. It does," Simpson agreed, contemplating the house as well.

"We can come back and check inside in a couple days if we have to, or whenever the fire chief says it's safe to enter," she said. "Will the body be examined here in town, or will they have to send it to the city?"

"The body?" Simpson asked, turning to her with a frown.

"Captain Dupree said the homeowner was in the house when it was set on fire and this was the town's first murder," she explained.

"Oh." Simpson nodded, his gaze sliding toward the vehicles in the driveway. "Yeah, the guy who lived here was trapped in the basement until the firemen were able to beat back the flames enough to go in through a basement window and get him out. I guess they found him in a tub in a bathroom down there. He'd filled it with water and submerged himself." Grimacing now, he added, "They said the water was boiling by the time they got to him. He was alive still, but barely. I didn't see him when they brought him out, but Jefferson said he was red as a lobster, parboiled with huge bleeding blisters all over." He shuddered at the thought of it. "They rushed him to the hospital just before you got here, but the EMTs didn't think he'd even survive the ride."

"Yeah, the ambulance passed me on their way out," CJ murmured, her thoughts now consumed with the shape the man must have been in. Boiled alive didn't sound any more pleasant than burned alive to her.

"I wonder why they're back," Simpson said suddenly.

Eyebrows rising, CJ followed his gaze to where an ambulance was parked on the lawn next to the fire trucks. It was quite a distance away, but she could see that the back doors of the ambulance were open, and there were a couple of people inside, hovering around the gurney.

"Do you think one of the firemen got hurt?" Simpson asked with concern.

"That or they found someone else in the fire," CJ said, and set out across the yard toward the vehicles, with Simpson at her side.

Several firemen and a woman in a paramedic's uniform were gathered to the side of the trucks and CJ wasn't surprised when Simpson veered off toward the group rather than heading straight to the ambulance. She assumed he was going to ask them what was going on rather than bother the EMTs working in the ambulance, so she followed him. But while he stopped briefly, and opened his mouth as if to ask something, he then snapped his mouth closed without saying a word, and turned abruptly to continue on to the ambulance.

CJ stared after him with surprise, and then followed. But when he started to climb into the back of the vehicle where a male paramedic and a fireman were bent over someone sitting up on the stretcher, she caught his arm to stop him.

"They're working on the man—wait here and give them room," she admonished when he turned a blank face her way.

Officer Simpson didn't respond, even in expression. That remained blank, she noted, and CJ was about to ask if he was all right when movement in the ambulance drew her attention. The fireman had straightened as much as he could and was moving toward the open doors with the paramedic following. Both of them were walking slightly bent at the waist to maneuver the cramped space.

"Is this a second victim, or did one of your men get hurt fighting the fire?" CJ asked as the fireman stepped down from the ambulance. Much to her amazement, he didn't even slow down or glance her way to acknowledge the question. Expression oddly blank, the fireman simply walked past her to join the group of people several feet away.

"I was the only victim."

CJ tore her surprised gaze away from the rude fireman and turned back to the ambulance at that announcement. She couldn't see the speaker at first—the paramedic was now stepping down from the ambulance, his bulk blocking her view—but once he was on the ground and following the fireman, CJ was able to get her first good look at the speaker. A lack of light in the ambulance affected visibility, but he was a big man, with wide shoulders. She suspected he would be tall once he was standing. His hair was short and appeared dark, while his skin was very fair, but looked blotchy to her in the poor lighting. Although that could have been due to the shadows cast in the ambulance, she thought, and then asked, "I'm sorry, did you say you're the only victim?"

The man was silent so long she didn't think he was going to respond, but finally he said, "Yes. I live here alone. Or I was supposed to. I guess I shall have to find somewhere else to live now."

"Then who did the first ambulance take away?" CJ asked with confusion.

"The first ambulance?" The question was sharp, with an undertone of concern.

"There was an ambulance leaving when I arrived," she explained.

"Ah," he said with understanding, "you must have arrived as they were heading for the hospital with me. Fortunately, I regained consciousness before they reached town and convinced them I was fine, so they turned around and brought me back."

CJ's eyebrows rose at that. "I was told the tub of water you were in was boiling by the time they got to you. Officer Jefferson told Simpson here that you were red as a lobster, parboiled and covered with large blisters. They didn't expect you to survive."

"Where is this Jefferson?" the man asked at once.

"He left before I got here," CJ answered.

The man clucked with annoyance, and then pointed out, "Well, obviously this Officer Jefferson was wrong, was he not? Maybe all the flickering lights from your emergency vehicles played havoc with his eyes. But I assure you I am fine."

CJ didn't respond at first. He certainly sounded fine, but she couldn't see him well enough to be assured that he really was. The interior lights in the ambulance had no doubt been on earlier, but were now off. They'd probably turned them off when they realized there was nothing that needed doing for him, if he really wasn't injured. But then what had the men been doing in the ambulance when she and Simpson had approached? And why hadn't they taken him to the hospital? He'd said he'd regained consciousness before they reached town. Something must have caused his unconsciousness. Probably smoke inhalation, she thought. In which case they definitely should have taken him to the hospital to at least be checked out. The man had barely escaped being burned to death, not to mention boiled alive, and rather than allow them to take him to the hospital, he'd made the paramedics bring him back to his burning home? "Mr.—"

"Argeneau," he said when she paused expectantly.

"Mr. Argeneau," she started again. "You really should go to the hospital. You've been through a traumatic experience, and could be suffering from shock or smoke inhalation. You should be treated for that."

"They gave me oxygen here," he announced. "I am fine."

"Smoke inhalation is a serious business, sir," she said firmly. "They don't just give you oxygen for a bit and call it good. They give you humidified oxygen, bronchodilators . . . sometimes they even have to use suction and endotracheal tubes and—"

"I have no need for any of that," he interrupted her.

"You don't know that," she responded at once, and lectured sternly, "You should have your lungs checked. You might think you're fine, but you may have suffered some thermal damage to your lungs or throat. If so, you could go into bronchospasm, or your lungs could become infected, swell, and fill with fluid restricting your air supply, and if that happens you could suffer brain damage or even die."

Rather than be dismayed by her words, she was quite sure the man smiled faintly as if amused by her concern before he asked, "So, you're a doctor?"

"No," she said with irritation. "I'm with the SIU."

"Ah, a police officer," he said with a nod.

"No," she corrected quickly. "I'm not police."

"Does SIU not stand for Special Investigations Unit?" he asked with surprise. "I thought from the TV shows I have watched that it was an arm of the law."

"It might be in some parts of the world, but here in Canada we are a civilian-run organization that investigates the police," she said stiffly. "I'm not a police officer anymore. I'm just helping out here tonight because the local police department recently lost their only detective, and I have some training in that area."

"Ah." Nodding, the man suddenly swung his legs off the gurney and stood up as much as he could in the cramped space, then made his way toward the back of the ambulance to get out. Once he was standing in front of her, she saw that he was indeed tall. The man was a good six inches over her own 5'11", and while she'd thought his shoulders wide from a distance, they were wider still once they were right in front of her, blocking out the world. The man now stood uncomfortably close, so that she had to tip her head back quite a bit to meet his gaze.

He clearly had no concept of personal space, CJ thought, and scowled at him, but didn't step back as she wanted to do. She wasn't the sort to back down from a challenge, and that's what it felt like to her, like he was trying to intimidate her.

"You smell good," he said suddenly, a smile definitely curving his lips.

CJ stiffened at the unexpected comment, and snapped, "You smell like smoke, which your lungs are probably full of. Now get back in the ambulance and let the paramedics take you to the hospital."

"My lungs are fine," he assured her with amusement.

Irritated by his attitude, she threw his own question back at him. "So, you're a doctor?"

"Yes."

CJ blinked at his answer, the steam running out of her like air out of a balloon as she squeaked, "You are?"

"Yes," he repeated, grinning widely now. "So, I can assure you with some authority that I am fine."

"But the fire—"

"Smoke rises," he interrupted the argument she'd been about to give him. "Unfortunately, I was working in the basement when it started and didn't realize there was a problem until the whole upper story was ablaze and I was trapped. I let the firemen know where I was and took shelter in the bathroom, filled the tub with cold water, and submerged myself to wait for them to get in and rescue me."

He paused briefly, and then repeated, "As I said, smoke rises and I was as low as I could get in the house lying in that old claw-foot tub, so I inhaled a minimal amount of it at best. My lungs are fine."

CJ's mouth compressed at this news and she turned to glance toward Simpson, which also served to give her some space from the man. She'd lied when she'd said he smelled like smoke. He didn't. In fact, he smelled good, like spices and the woods mixed together. It was a potent aroma that was playing havoc with her thought processes, and she was grateful to suck in a breath of some good clean, smoke-tinged night air to wash his scent away.

She was less pleased to see that Simpson had slipped away to join the circle of firemen and paramedics. His presence would have made a helpful buffer between her and this man. Aside from that, though, Simpson was the police officer here and should be the one questioning the man as to what had happened. Apparently, that hadn't occurred to him yet, and the fact that it hadn't made her wonder just how much of a rookie the kid was.

"Simpson," she called with exasperation.

The patrolman turned a blank face her way, and then left the group to rejoin them. When he then just stood there, she asked pointedly, "Don't you have some questions for Mr. Argeneau?"

"No." The word was said without any inflection at all.

CJ gaped at the young officer briefly, and then shook her head and snatched the small notepad and pen out of his front chest pocket where she'd seen him place it earlier. She quickly flipped it open to the first clean page, and turned to Argeneau. "Can you give us your full name, Mr. Argeneau?"

"Macon Argeneau," he answered easily. "But my friends call me Mac."

CJ quickly wrote down *Macon (Mac) Argeneau*. "No middle name?"

"No."

CJ nodded. "Birth date?"

"June 21," he answered.

"Year?" CJ asked as she wrote down what he'd said, and then glanced up when he hesitated. Raising her eyebrows, she repeated, "Year?"

"You tell me yours, and I shall tell you mine," he said lightly, but when CJ stared back at him, unimpressed, he sighed and said in a questioning tone, "1985?"

It was almost as if he were testing to see whether she would believe him, CJ thought, and since he looked about twenty-five and being born in 1985 would place him around her own age of thirty-six, she didn't believe it. She didn't say as much, though, but merely raised one eyebrow and asked, "Is that a question or the year?"

"The year," he decided.

CJ nodded and wrote it down, but put a question mark beside it. She suspected he was lying about his age, which raised red flags in her mind. Someone had set his home on fire and he was lying about his age. Was he even giving his real name? She'd ask for ID, but since he was standing there in pajama bottoms and a T-shirt and his house had just burned down with everything in it, she doubted he'd have any to provide. She'd check his info when she got back to the police station, CJ decided as she asked her next question. "And where do you work?"

"From home," he said at once.

CJ lifted her gaze to his, her pen poised over the notepad, but not writing. "You said you were a doctor."

"Yes." He nodded.

"And you work from home?" she queried doubtfully.

"I started out a physician, but then went back to

school to study hematology and now I work with, and study, blood in the lab."

"From home?" she repeated dubiously. That seemed even more unlikely than running a doctor's office from home.

Mac shrugged. "I prefer to work from home, and fortunately the company I work for allows it."

"And who is that?" CJ asked at once, and then clarified her question. "The company you work for?"

"Argentis Inc."

CJ wrote it down with a question mark beside it. She'd never heard of it and would be looking up the company later too. If she got lucky, they'd have an employee listing online. Some companies did, and sometimes even had photos of the individuals. Although usually it was people in leadership roles, and she doubted Argeneau was a manager or other leader if he was working from home.

Lifting her head, she eyed him solemnly for a moment, and then said, "You mentioned that you were working in the basement when you smelled smoke. So, you were working with blood?"

"No. I was unpacking boxes and setting up my lab," he corrected, and then added, "I only just moved in yesterday."

CJ had lowered her head to write down his answer,

but jerked it back up at that. She blinked briefly as she absorbed the fact that his home had been burned down directly after he'd moved in. She cleared her throat and said, "It's 2 A.M. on Saturday morning now. Are you thinking it's still Friday night and you moved in Thursday, or do you mean you moved in Friday?"

"I arrived at about eleven on Thursday night. The movers got here about ten minutes after that and worked through the night to move everything in, finishing about nine thirty or ten Friday morning," he explained, getting more specific.

CJ turned to peer at the house. It wasn't overly large. She would have guessed it was a three-bedroom, which she estimated would normally take five to seven hours to move, not the nearly eleven he was claiming it had taken. But if he had a lot of lab equipment, maybe it would take longer.

"They were a full-service mover," Mac said, obviously sensing where her mind had gone. "They had a crew of six, but set everything up in the living areas, placing the furniture where I wanted it, putting the beds together, and even making them. They also placed the books on the bookshelves, etc." He shrugged. "They would have set up the lab if I'd wished it too, but I wanted to do that myself. Which is what I was doing tonight when the fire broke out."

CJ nodded, but asked for the name of the movers. She intended on checking out everything this man told her.

"The movers were hired through Argentis Inc.," he said with a slight frown, and then shrugged apologetically. "You shall have to check with them to get that information."

CJ hid her expression as she wrote that down. If he wanted her to call the company, he was probably telling the truth, after all. Which was surprising to her. She would have sworn he wasn't, and her instincts were usually pretty good about these things. It was why she'd been such a good detective. Her old partner used to say that she had an incredibly sensitive bullshit meter that always went off when something wasn't quite right, or someone was lying to her. It usually worked great. But for some reason this guy was throwing her off.

CJ glanced over what she'd written and then peered at the house again before turning back to Mac and saying, "So, you moved in Thursday night/Friday morning and were working down in the basement last night/this morning, setting up your lab when you smelled smoke and realized the house was on fire?"

Mac nodded.

"Did you hear anything prior to smelling the smoke?" she asked. "Someone moving around outside or upstairs, maybe?"

"No." He shook his head firmly. "I didn't hear a thing from outside, and I know they weren't inside."

"How can you be sure?"

"It's an old house. The main floor is hardwood and creaks like crazy when someone crosses it. I noticed that when I was directing the movers on where to put the boxes in the basement. I heard every step the others took upstairs from down there. I even heard them going up and down the upper stairs to the second floor from down in the basement." He shook his head again. "Whoever set the fire definitely did it from outside and did not enter the house or I would have heard it and gone to investigate."

It was exactly what CJ had suspected, but she was glad to have verification and made a note in the pad before looking up to ask, "Can you think of anyone who might want to kill you?"

It was a blunt question meant to catch him by surprise, and hopefully shock an honest response from him. Instead, it made the man smile.

"I've hardly been here long enough to make enemies," he pointed out with amusement. "I haven't even met my neighbors, let alone annoyed them enough to make them set my house on fire."

CJ merely nodded. "Where did you live prior to moving here?"

"New York City."

She stiffened at that and raised her eyebrows. "You're American?"

"No. But I lived and worked in New York for the ten years preceding my move here," he answered.

"So, you're Canadian?" she questioned, and her eyes narrowed when he again hesitated before answering.

"Yes."

CJ considered him briefly, quite sure he was lying, and then asked, "Why move here?"

"To be closer to my father and sister," he said at once, which suggested he hadn't been lying about being Canadian, after all. If his family was from here, then he probably was too.

CJ shook her head as she wrote down his answer. He had again set off her bullshit meter, and then made her think the meter was wrong with his next words. It was more than a little frustrating.

"So," she began after considering what he'd said, "you grew up here in Sandford and your family still lives here?"

"No."

CJ glanced at him sharply. "No what?"

"No, I did not grow up here and my family does not live here," he answered helpfully, but not helpfully at all.

"But you just said you moved here to be closer to your family," she pointed out a bit irritably.

"Yes. I moved to Canada to be closer to my family. But my father lives in Toronto and my sister lives in Port Henry so I wanted someplace that would make visiting either of them easier. Sandford seemed a nice little town and is about halfway between the two," he pointed out.

CJ was writing down the info when he added, "My sister is Katricia Argeneau Brunswick. She's a police officer in Port Henry. Her husband, Teddy, is the chief of police there."

Her handwriting slowed at this news, but she finished it, and then peered up at the man speculatively. He wasn't from the town, had only been here a little more than twenty-four hours, and someone had set his house on fire . . . with him in it, which was usually an attempt to kill the individual inside. But as he'd said, he hadn't lived here long enough to make enemies in Sandford.

"Any enemies back in New York?" she asked abruptly, considering the possibility that the trouble had followed him.

"No-ooo."

CJ's eyebrows rose at his response. Initially, the answer had come out quickly as if he didn't have to think about it, but then had drawn on and ended on an uncertain "o" sound as if something had occurred to him.

"You don't sound too sure," she pointed out.

"Well, I cannot think of anyone I have pissed off lately, but someone did set my house on fire . . . with me in it, which suggests I must have someone who wants me dead," he reasoned, his mouth twisting wryly as he spoke. Glancing from her to the burned-out shell of a building, he continued, "I suppose that means they might try again when they find out the fire did not succeed in killing me." Turning back to her, he added, "I guess that means you shall have to take me to a safe house and guard my body until this whole thing is resolved."

CJ blinked once and then again at his words. Guard his body? That was pretty much all that her mind had registered, or at least all that it was focusing on. Guarding his body. It wasn't really a crazy suggestion if someone had tried to kill him. Hell, come to that, whoever set the fire could be around here somewhere and already know he wasn't dead, she realized. Arsonists did tend to like to watch their handiwork, she recalled, and turned to Simpson to say, "Take pictures of the area in all directions. The road, the field, the yard, and everyone in it. And try to get pictures of the license plates on the vehicles in the driveway as well."

Pleasantly surprised when the man didn't argue or ask questions, but immediately pulled out his phone to start taking photos, she glanced around briefly in search of anyone who stood out, or didn't seem to belong there. But while her eyes were searching the surrounding area, CJ's brain seemed stuck on Mac's comment about guarding his body. He was right, of course, someone was going to have to stick close to this man day and night, watching over him while he slept, showered, and shaved. Much as she disliked admitting it, under normal circumstances, she might not have minded such a chore herself. It wouldn't have been a hardship. At least not on the eyes. The flashing lights of the fire truck were strobing over him occasionally, giving her a better look at the man. It hadn't escaped her notice that he was a beefcake. His hair and clothes were still a little damp from his time in the tub, and his cotton T-shirt was clinging to his chest, emphasizing his muscular physique, while the pajama bottoms were clinging to other more interesting bits with enough intimacy that it wasn't hard to tell that his chest wasn't the only thing that was big on the man. Of course, that could just be a trick of the flickering shadows being cast by the lights on the ambulance and fire trucks. It didn't really matter, though; these weren't normal circumstances, because her life wasn't normal and hadn't been for three and a half years.

Besides, none of this was her problem, she acknowledged. In fact, her assistance here was no longer needed. She'd helped with what she'd agreed to and could leave.

"I'm heading out," she announced, loud enough for Simpson to hear, and then told Mac, "Stay close to Officer Simpson. He'll keep you safe."

"You're leaving?" Mac asked with a combination of dismay and a tone that was almost accusing.

He made it sound like she was abandoning him, CJ thought, but merely nodded, and said, "Simpson is in charge here. He'll drive you back to the station where I'm sure Captain Dupree will arrange some protection for you, Mr. Argeneau."

"I want you."

Two

I want you. The words echoed in CJ's head, sounding really suggestive to her. It also sent a strange shiver through her body that she had absolutely no desire to analyze. She had no interest in men, and the chaos and mess having relationships with them caused. CJ had learned her lesson well during her marriage. Men were bad news. Really bad news. She'd learned that lesson so well she'd resigned herself to living her life alone. Not a big deal. Get a dog for companionship, and buy a vibrator to deal with sexual tension, and you were pretty much covered if you knew how to change tires and fix leaky taps yourself. Fortunately, CJ knew how to do both.

"He's right. We should keep him close for his own protection," Simpson said suddenly, and CJ turned to him with surprise. The man hadn't said a word while she'd asked questions, and *now* decided to join the conversation? Apparently, he was finished taking the photos she'd requested. Although he couldn't have got each of the license plates on the vehicles in the driveway, but probably planned to get that on his way out, CJ decided. But she merely smiled grimly at his comment as she closed his notepad and slid it back into his front chest pocket along with his pen. Patting the outside of the pocket then, she said easily, "Yes, you should. You'd better take him back to the station and see what Dupree wants to do about that, then."

CJ had already started to turn away when Simpson said, "I don't have a vehicle."

Pausing, abruptly, she swung back around. "What?"

"I was riding with Jefferson," Simpson explained, his face still oddly devoid of expression. "He left me and the evidence-gathering kit here, but took the patrol car to go on another call. I was hoping to catch a ride back to the station with you."

Which meant letting Mac Argeneau into her car too, CJ thought, and found herself really reluctant to agree to that. She had no idea why. It was just a car. She'd ridden in lots of cars with lots of victims over the years. Although usually it was criminals she'd ridden with, and they had been handcuffed and behind the steel mesh cage or bulletproof glass that was installed be-tween the front and back seats of police cars. She didn't have either in her own car, because she wasn't meant to be transporting criminals . . . or victims. But she couldn't see a way to get out of it, so muttered, "Let's go, then," and realizing how ungracious that sounded, she added, "I'm ready to call it a night and go back to the bed-and-breakfast where I'm staying. I'll take you two to the police station first."

CJ didn't look around to be sure Simpson and Mac were following her as she headed for her car. She just hurried down the driveway, eager to get out of there. It wasn't until she'd reached her vehicle and peered back that she saw she was alone.

Huffing out an exasperated breath, CJ propped her hands on her hips and scanned the distance. The fire was out, but even without it adding to the illumination, the scene was somewhat lit by the headlights of the many vehicles scattered around the property. While a long line of pickups bordered the driveway, there were also several on the front yard itself, along with the two fire trucks and the ambulance. There were still dark spots, and strange shadows here and there, but she had no problem making out the group of emergency work-ers still moving around. Or standing around, really, she thought, noting that the only ones actually moving now were two men working the hose to continue wetting down the interior and exterior of the house.

Her gaze slid over the people gathered by the ambulance, but they were in one of those shadows and she couldn't tell who made up the group, so she let her eyes shift over the rest of the yard until she spotted Simpson with what looked like a large fishing tackle box but she knew was actually his evidence-gathering kit. She'd forgotten all about that, CJ realized, and relaxed a bit, some of her annoyance sliding away. He might have forgotten about questioning the victim, but at least he hadn't forgotten the evidence. That was something, she supposed as she watched the young officer walk over to the group by the ambulance.

Once he reached it, a large figure stepped out of the center of the crowd and joined him. Macon Argeneau, she realized as the pair started down the long driveway, stopping at each vehicle so Simpson could take a photo of the license plate.

Argeneau moved like a panther, she thought as she watched the two dark figures make their way along the driveway. He was all sleek muscle, and smooth movement, which she found ridiculously attractive. CJ could have stood there watching him walk for hours, but then realizing just how much she was enjoying surveying his body as he approached, she turned abruptly and got into her car.

"Men," she muttered to herself as she slammed her door closed. CJ didn't have the time or patience to deal with them. She liked her life just the way it was: nice, peaceful, no drama. She didn't need some strutting male stud rampaging through her life, waking up desires she hadn't felt in years. Not that Mac Argeneau had done that, she reassured herself. So . . . he was attractive. She could appreciate that without it meaning anything. Hell, she thought Rodin's *The Thinker* was beautiful too. Didn't mean she wanted to sleep with the statue.

CJ tapped one finger on the steering wheel as she tried to figure out how long it would be before she could go to bed and get some sleep. She was obviously tired. That was probably why she found Mac attractive: exhaustion. She'd rectify that quickly. She'd take Officer Simpson and his arson victim to the police station, and check in to see if Jefferson was still around. If he was, she would question him. If he wasn't, she'd find out when his next shift started and flee to the safety of the bed-and-breakfast where she was staying.

Jefferson was the reason she was here, CJ reminded herself. She was going to handle her investigation as quickly as she could and get the hell out of Dodge—or Sandford as the case may be—and drive straight back to Mississauga to present her findings to her superior. Then she would forget all about Macon (hot as hell Mac) Argeneau and get on with her nice, quiet, peaceful life where her hormones played hide-and-seek with her instead of running amok at the smell of woods and spice.

The front passenger door opened and that very scent rushed into the car and straight up her nose to make the synapses in her brain start firing like a roll of caps lit on fire. Blinking her eyes open, CJ ignored the sudden chaos in her head, and watched Mac settle in the front seat next to her.

"I hope we did not keep you waiting long." He offered her a smile that she saw only briefly before he closed the door and the car's interior light went out again. Even that brief view was enough to have her pulse fluttering like a Victorian virgin at the threat of being ravished. It had left an imprint in her mind, an impression of his face, and what a gorgeous face it was: piercing silvery blue eyes, full pink lips, sharp cheekbones, firm chin, and a nice straight nose under dark brown hair. But dark brown was too pedestrian a description of the hair color she'd glimpsed; it was mostly dark brown but streaked with every color in the brown spectrum from pale beige sand to the dark brown of coffee beans, and even a few splashes of red strands thrown in. The man could have been a model with his looks, CJ thought, and then the back door opened behind her and the light flickered on again.

"Sorry. I had to get the evidence kit," Officer Simpson explained as he slid in with his tackle box.

"It's fine," CJ growled, and started the engine as he closed the door. The car radio immediately began to blast classic rock and she reached quickly to turn it off, recognizing even as she did that the song playing was Pink Floyd's "Comfortably Numb" . . . which was something she was well acquainted with. Comfortably numb was pretty much how she'd been going through life the last few years. It was a state she'd embraced, but one she feared she'd have trouble holding on to with Macon Argeneau around. Thank God he wouldn't be in her car, or her life, for long.

Twenty minutes, she told herself. That's how long the ride back to the station would be, and then she wouldn't have to worry about, or see, Macon (sexy as hell Mac) Argeneau again. Just one twenty-minute silent car ride. She could handle that, she reassured herself. Just concentrate on the road and don't look at the man.

"So, you aren't from Sandford?"

CJ blinked at the man, noting that the lights from

the GPS screen and various other dials and whatnot in the car all seemed to be glowing on him so that she could see him quite well. Dear Lord he was gorgeous.

"You mentioned staying at the bed-and-breakfast," he explained, apparently thinking she was gaping at him from surprise rather than simply goggling at his male beauty. "I assume that means you aren't from town."

His comment served to bring her out of her momentary fog of lust, and CJ forced her gaze back to the road ahead and nodded. "Yes. I mean, no, I'm not from Sandford."

She didn't expand on that, but clenched the steering wheel and told herself to keep her eyes on the road. Safety first, she reminded herself, and it was definitely all kinds of safe for her to concentrate on driving and ignore the man next to her. She managed to do that for the forty-five seconds he let pass before speaking again.

"You're here to help the police?"

CJ was silent for a minute, her mind taken up with the way he slid in and out of formal speaking. Sometimes he used contractions sounding much more informal, and sometimes he didn't. It was kind of weird, she decided. She'd only seen that in people who learned English as a second language.

"Ms. Cummings?" Mac asked when she didn't respond.

His words managed to pull her from her thoughts, but then dropped her into a new one, and that was to wonder how he knew her name and why it sounded so naughty when he spoke it. Simpson must have told him, she decided, and forced herself to the topic at hand, but it was oddly difficult. It took her a full minute to recall his earlier question.

"Right. Helping the police," she muttered, and then shook her head. "No. Definitely not. I'm here to investigate them. I only agreed to help out tonight because they were in a pinch."

There, that sounded perfectly normal, she reassured herself, not at all like she was a drooling idiot preoccupied with wondering how his soft lips might feel on her body.

"Wow! Where did that come from?" she muttered to herself with dismay.

"What?" Mac asked. "Where did what come from?"

CJ was so surprised by the question and the fact that it meant she'd apparently spoken out loud that she glanced over at him askance. Fortunately, he was busy peering worriedly out the front window, apparently trying to see what might be ahead. Mouth tightening, she forced her attention forward again and said, "Nothing. A deer just ran across the road."

A complete and utter lie, she acknowledged, but better than admitting she had been talking to herself. Out loud. About this sudden lust she had for him. Puffing out an exasperated breath, she reached over and turned on the radio. At least they couldn't talk that way, which seemed the safer bet.

"Perfect," she breathed unhappily as "Burnin' for You" by Blue Öyster Cult filled the car. Obviously, the universe *was* laughing at her, because that was a pretty good description of how she was feeling at the moment. But at least with the music on she could pretend she was alone and ignore the man seated beside her. Or try to. He was hard to ignore. CJ was aware of every movement he made as he shifted to a more comfortable position. She was also aware that he was watching her. She could actually feel his eyes on her skin. Or it felt like she could, and she wanted to yell at him to keep those silver-blue orbs to himself. Instead, she just straightened her shoulders and stared grimly ahead for the next seventeen and a half minutes until they'd reached the police station.

Mac shifted uncomfortably in the passenger seat, trying to take pressure off his backside. He didn't know why, but while the rest of him was mostly healed, that area seemed to have been left for last. He was pretty sure the blisters were gone but there the area was still tender. The only thing he could think was that since it was mostly cushioning and wasn't as important as his hands and feet, the nanos hadn't considered it a priority. It was seeming like a pretty important priority at that moment, though, as pain vibrated through him from sitting on it, but since there was nothing he could do about it, he resigned himself to the discomfort for the duration of the ride. Once at the police station, Mac hoped to be able to get the blood he needed to finish the healing, and supposed he should just be grateful that he had managed to heal as much as he had before CJ Cummings had appeared at the back of the ambulance. Had she arrived even twenty minutes to half an hour earlier, she would've seen the evidence of those blisters and lobster-red skin that Officer Jefferson had mentioned.

That thought reminded Mac that he still had work to do tonight before he could retire. He needed to find this Officer Jefferson, and erase the memory of what he'd seen from the man's mind. Mac hoped that was the only person he'd missed but couldn't be sure. He'd thought he'd got them all before CJ had mentioned Jefferson.

Turning to CJ he tried again to read her mind, but he was just as unable to penetrate her thoughts now as he had been when she'd first approached the ambulance, and he suddenly wondered, why her? The question made him look her over more carefully. He hadn't seen her in what most people would consider proper lighting, but with his eyesight it didn't matter. He could see her as well as he would have in a lit room. CJ had intelligent green eyes, full lush red lips, and a slightly tipped-up nose in an oval face framed by long blond hair. She was an attractive woman. But he'd seen more attractive women in his life, women so beautiful they could almost have been a work of art, and yet not one of them had stirred him the way she did, and had from the moment he'd first spied her approaching the back of the ambulance. Tall, slim, with long legs and a confident stride, there had been something about her that had drawn his interest right away.

Still, it had been a shock when he hadn't been able to read her mind and control her as he had everyone else tonight. Before he'd realized he couldn't control her, Mac had thought he had two more blood donors to help him heal, and two more memories to rearrange. Up till then he'd been putting the thoughts in the paramedics' and firemen's minds that the house fire had been a result of faulty wiring, and that he hadn't been injured. But once he'd realized that he couldn't do that to her memory and that she and Officer Simpson had already found proof that the fire had been deliberately set, he'd had to change his plans. While Simpson had gone to collect his evidence kit, Mac had quickly gone into the minds of the firemen and paramedics again and changed their memories to arson, but left the part about his escaping without serious injury.

Of course, Mac had been annoyed at having to do it. A nice, naturally caused fire from electrical issues or something would have been less memorable and therefore more preferable. His kind did not like attention, and arson would invariably draw that. But now, as he watched the way CJ was studiously ignoring him, and speeding in what he could only assume was a desire to be rid of him as quickly as possible, Mac couldn't help thinking that perhaps having to go with arson might be a good thing, after all. Because CJ Cummings was showing a dismaying resistance to his inimitable charms.

Oh, he could tell she was attracted to him. The way her face flushed, her eyes dilated, and her heart rate sped up when he drew near told him that. But those were all physiological signs that were automatic and involuntary. And, unfortunately, they were also immediately followed by protective, closed-down responses like averting her eyes, tightening her jaw, and hunching her shoulders slightly to draw her arms in closer to her body. Ms. Cummings's body might want him, but her mind definitely wasn't in agreement. If he hoped to get anywhere with the woman, he'd have to find some way to stay close to her, because he was pretty sure her plan was to dump him at the police station and avoid him like the plague from that moment on.

It was starting to look to him like the act of arson at the house he'd just rented and barely moved into might be his only hope of keeping close to her. The problem was how to work it. She wasn't a police officer, although from a couple of things said tonight, he was pretty sure she had been at one time. He'd read Officer Simpson's mind to learn more about her, but Simpson hadn't known anything about her other than her name, that she was in Sandford for some sort of investigation into an arrest that had gone bad for another officer, and that, as she had said, she was just helping them out in a pinch at the fire site.

His gaze slid over her tense shoulders and stiff jaw, and Mac considered that her not being a police officer here in town presented a problem. It meant there was no reason for her to be the one to guard him and have to stick close to him at some sort of safe house . . . unless he could make sure there was no one else to do it and that she had to continue to help in this pinch.

If that failed, he could always rent a room at the bed-and-breakfast, Mac supposed. That would put him close to her at least some of the time. She must be staying at Mrs. Vesper's, he knew. It was the only B and B in town. Mac had stayed there himself when he'd been scouting towns, and then again when he'd come to see about a house to buy, but there hadn't been anything on the market in Sandford. He'd almost given up and decided to try another town when Mrs. Vesper had told him that the owner of an old farmhouse outside town wanted to rent.

Mac hadn't been too keen on the idea of renting at first, but as the dear old woman had pointed out, it would give him a chance to see if he liked it in Sandford before he actually purchased, and if he did, she suspected the homeowner would be willing to sell somewhere down the line if he was patient. So, Mac had contacted the homeowner via an email address Mrs. Vesper had given him, and arranged to rent the house.

It had all happened quickly after that. Mac had used e-transfer to send first and last month's rent to the homeowner and made arrangements for monthly withdrawals to cover future rent. He'd then arranged for the renovations he'd wanted for the basement so that it could be used as a lab. Once the renos had been finished he'd flown back to New York to arrange for his house there to be packed up and sent north. Then he'd flown back and booked into the bed-and-breakfast again to wait for his belongings to be driven up.

Mac had only expected to be at the bed-and-breakfast one night this time. He'd flown straight up the evening that they'd finished packing up his things, but the truck wasn't going to leave until the next morning. He'd expected it the next night, Wednesday, but it had been held up at customs for more than twenty-four hours, and hadn't arrived until nearly midnight on Thursday . . . and now, here he was with everything he owned burned up along with his new rental, and nowhere to go except to the bed-and-breakfast where CJ must be staying. But Mac could only think that might be helpful for him. He needed to spend time with the woman to woo her, and he needed to woo her to convince her to be his life mate.

Mac savored the words in his mind. *Life mate.* The one thing every immortal yearned for. The one person who could beat back the loneliness every immortal invariably suffered thanks to their need to protect their thoughts from older immortals, and block out the thoughts of younger immortals as well as mortals. But that wasn't necessary with a life mate, which was a gift. Having to constantly guard your thoughts could be exhausting, and often led to his kind avoiding others to avoid the need to do it . . . and that could lead to madness and going rogue.

Mac didn't think he'd been in danger of that quite yet, but he *had* waited a long time to finally meet his life mate. So long that he'd begun to think it might never happen . . . and now here she was. She'd just walked up to the ambulance in his darkest hour, changing what had seemed like one of the worst days of his life into the best damned day ever.

Mac smiled faintly at the memory. Her arrival in his life had been so normal that, at first, he hadn't recognized that his very existence was about to change, or that she was about to become the most important person in his life. CJ had just been a tall, slender stranger walking toward the ambulance in a white blouse and dark business jacket that contrasted wildly with the jeans and cowboy boots that finished off the outfit. Everything about her had been surprising, but he thought she should have had a spotlight on her, and been accompanied by a symphony, or a choir singing "Hallelujah!"

Mac smiled at the thought, and then turned his mind to more pragmatic matters . . . like that he had to contact the local Enforcers and bring them in on the case. If someone was trying to kill him, they needed to know. Not only so that they could try to sort out who it was, but because they'd have to do damage control when it came to the mortals in the area and any official reports the case generated. He would have preferred to let it play out as a simple fire caused by electrical issues as he'd originally intended. Being an old farmhouse, no one would have questioned that, and it would have got little attention at all that way. But not being able to control CJ had put paid to that plan and now they'd have to try to manage the situation.

Mac also needed to arrange for more blood to be delivered to him wherever he ended up. A safe house would make that difficult if CJ was the one guarding him. Hell, even in the bed-and-breakfast it would be difficult, but he needed more blood, and soon. While the blisters were gone and he looked mostly healed on the outside, his body was still repairing the internal damage and was quickly using up the blood he'd managed to acquire from the various firemen and paramedics at the scene. Mac was already feeling the gnawing ache that came when his body was in need of more blood. Not really a surprise. He'd pretty much been parboiled in that tub by the time the firemen had managed to beat back the flames enough to make a path in to get him out. The water had been bubbling around him, scalding him alive, and it had taken every ounce of self-control he possessed to keep from leaping out of the water. The only thing that had kept him from doing so was the sure knowledge that he would be dead in seconds if he got out. His body could repair almost any damage done to it, but nothing could bring an immortal back from ash and that's what he would have been had he got out of that tub, because the one weakness immortals had was being incredibly flammable.

Pushing away the unpleasant memories of his time in the tub, Mac turned his thoughts to how he was going to make the calls he needed to. His phone, along with everything else he owned, had been destroyed in the fire, and the calls he had to make could not be done in front of others. He needed a phone and privacy for at least a few minutes, and was considering how to manage that when the loud music that had been playing since they left the house suddenly died.

Glancing around, Mac saw that they'd arrived at the police station. He turned back to CJ, his mouth opening and then snapping shut with alarm when he saw that she was already getting out of the car. Quite sure that if he let her out of his sight she'd never give him the chance to see her again, Mac quickly unsnapped his seat belt and scrambled out to follow.

Three

"So, what does 'CJ' stand for?"

CJ's jaw tightened as that question told her that her attempt to escape Mac Argeneau hadn't worked. She hadn't moved quickly enough to leave him behind. Although she had managed to lose Simpson, she saw with a quick glance back. The officer was still scrambling out of the car with his evidence kit. Turning to face forward again, CJ didn't respond to Mac's question, but suggested, "You should really wait for Simpson, Mr. Argeneau. If someone is out to kill you, you'll need him to keep you safe."

"I am sure you can keep me just as safe as he could," Mac said with unconcern.

"I don't have a gun, he does. Stick with Simpson," she said firmly, and reached for the glass door of the police station, only to snatch her hand back to avoid touching his when it got there first.

"Allow me," he said courteously.

Biting back her irritation, CJ muttered, "Thank you," and hurried inside, very aware that he was directly on her heels.

The reception area was just as empty now as it had been when she'd arrived earlier. This time, however, no one stuck their head through the back door to greet them.

"Charlotte Jean?" Mac said suddenly.

CJ turned to frown at the man with confusion. "Who's Charlotte Jean?"

"Not you apparently," he said with a faint smile, and then tried, "Christine Joan?"

Realizing he was trying to guess what her initials stood for, CJ turned abruptly, moved around the reception counter, and through the door Captain Dupree had poked his head out of earlier. She wasn't surprised to find herself in a large bullpen office with four desks set up in each corner, leaving a small aisle running up the middle.

"Catrina Jacqueline?" Mac tried again, pausing beside her.

CJ ignored him to glance around the large open office space, noting the filing cabinets and cupboards running the length of all four walls, absent only where doors were. There were seven doors: the one she and Mac had just come through, three in the wall to their left, two on the right, and one in the back. Both doors in the right wall were open. Through one she could see a large table with several chairs around it that she guessed would be a conference room or the morning meeting room where the captain addressed his men. The other open door on that side led into a large, well-appointed office that had to be the captain's. It was empty now.

"Cherry Juice?" Mac guessed next, and CJ finally turned to look at him.

"Cherry Juice?" she echoed with disbelief.

"It's possible," he said defensively. "I met a girl once with that name."

"I'm going to take a wild guess here and say she was a stripper," CJ suggested dryly.

"No," he said at once, and then frowned, and reluctantly admitted, "Actually, I could not say. We merely shared an elevator in a hotel I stayed in once. She was quite chatty, but did not mention what she did for a living and I never asked."

"With a name like that she was probably a prostitute," CJ muttered, and turned to glance to the doors in the wall on their left. Two of them were open, the first and last, while the door in the middle was closed. The open doors revealed small rooms with a single table and two chairs in each. She recognized right away that they were interview rooms, which meant that the middle room between them was probably fitted with two-way mirrors and a sound system where interviews could be observed and recorded. They were as empty as the bullpen and the other two rooms, and CJ frowned at the deserted state of the place.

"I really think if you are going to be guarding me that I should at least know your name."

"Trust me. I will not be guarding you," CJ assured him grimly. She started toward the door in the back wall when it suddenly opened and a short, middle-aged woman in a loose, rumpled pink velour jogging suit entered. The woman was staring blearily down at the cup of coffee she was stirring as she walked.

CJ stopped abruptly at the sight of her. The lady had bedhead, her salt-and-pepper hair standing up in all directions. Her eyes were bloodshot from lack of sleep and she was wearing absolutely no makeup. She looked like someone who had just been rumbled from her bed in the middle of the night and dressed quickly.

"Oh!" the woman gasped, and paused when she lifted her head and saw she had company. For a moment, she looked as if she wasn't sure whether they were friend or foe, or what to do, but then Officer Simpson entered behind them, and the woman relaxed with relief. "Michael! Thank goodness!"

Simpson came to a halt next to CJ and Mac, surprise covering his expression as he stared at the little woman. "Mrs. Dupree! What are you doing here?"

"Oh, Charles asked me to come in and cover for a bit," the woman said wearily.

"Cover?" Simpson glanced around at the empty bullpen with a frown. "Where is everyone?"

"Charles and Steve are at the hospital," she explained anxiously, her gaze sliding to CJ and then away. "And everyone else is out on calls."

"Everyone?" Simpson asked with amazement, moving to the nearest desk on the left and setting the evidence kit down before turning to concentrate on Mrs. Dupree.

Mrs. Dupree nodded. "I don't know what's going on tonight. Maybe it's a full moon, but Dandridge is handling a break-and-enter at the pharmacy, Owens is at the scene of a pretty bad car accident, and Brown and Jamieson are at a domestic dispute. Brown went on that call alone originally, but I guess there was trouble and he called in for backup. Jamieson was the only one here so Charles called and asked me to come man the phones so Jamieson could go help Brown." Her eyes skittered to CJ and away again before she added, "And, of course, you were covering the fire with the lady from the SIU."

"Ah, yes." Simpson glanced to CJ with an apologetic smile. "Ms. Cummings, this is Captain Dupree's wife, Audrey Dupree. Mrs. Dupree, this is CJ Cummings from the SIU."

"Ma'am," CJ murmured politely, offering a pleasant smile and nod.

"And this is Mr. Argeneau," Simpson added quickly when Audrey Dupree's eyes narrowed unpleasantly on CJ. When that didn't draw the woman's angry glare away from CJ, he added, "It was his house that was set on fire tonight. He nearly died."

That did manage to get the woman's attention off of CJ. Blinking in surprise, Audrey Dupree turned to Mac with amazement, her gaze sliding over him in his now dry pajama bottoms and T-shirt as she set her coffee on the nearest desk and rushed forward to take his hands. "Oh, my goodness, Mr. Argeneau. Are you all right? Should you be up and about? Charles said you were trapped in the house and they didn't expect you to live, but you look fine. What—?"

"Yes, I was trapped in the house, but the firemen got me out in time and I *am* fine," Mac assured her soothingly, interrupting her torrent of words, and then, smiling wryly, he managed to retrieve his hands and gestured to himself. "Not well dressed at the moment, but alive and well."

"Well, you come sit down and I'll fetch you a sweater or something," Mrs. Dupree said at once, tugging him toward a chair. "I can't imagine how frightening it must have been to be trapped in a fire like that."

"Did the captain tell you when he expected to be back from the hospital?" Simpson asked as Mrs. Dupree tried to steer Mac toward the nearest desk chair. "I need to get this evidence logged, but I want to call him and tell him that Mr. Argeneau is alive and ask what to do about protection for him."

"Protection?" Mrs. Dupree asked with surprise.

"Well, someone tried to kill him tonight," Simpson pointed out gently. "He was in the house and—"

"Oh, good Lord, yes!" Mrs. Dupree said with dismay, and then turned a pitying look on Mac before saying, "I'll call Charles after I get Mr. Argeneau a sweater. I want to talk to him anyway and see what's happening at the hospital. You go log your evidence."

"There's really no need to fetch me a sweater," Mac protested, resisting the older woman's efforts to get him to sit down. "Really, I am fine, Mrs. Dupree."

"You might think you're fine, young man, but you've been through a traumatic event," Audrey remonstrated firmly. "You just sit down and I'll fetch you a sweater."

She started away before adding, "And maybe a cup of coffee with some whiskey in it to settle your nerves. Yes, that should do."

CJ watched the woman hustle away through the open door of the captain's office and then turned to peer at Mac, only to find him looking back. Shifting uncomfortably under his penetrating eyes, she immediately turned to Simpson and asked abruptly, "Where is the ladies' room?"

She'd needed to go to the bathroom for the last hour at least, but had been unwilling to squat in the trees that lined Mac Argeneau's driveway, which was where the firemen had been relieving themselves, she knew. The benefits of having a penis, she thought on a sigh.

"Follow me," Simpson said, scooping up his evidence kit and heading for the door at the back of the room.

Uncomfortable at the idea of leaving Mac alone when someone had so recently tried to kill him, CJ hesitated, her gaze immediately going to him, but he smiled and waved her off. "Go on. Mrs. Dupree will keep me safe."

When CJ raised one eyebrow dubiously, he added, "I saw those glares she was casting at you. The lady has a mean streak. I suspect everyone in Sandford knows that and few would cross her. I should be safe enough with her."

The words made CJ's lips twitch with amusement and she quickly turned to follow Simpson to hide it from Mac.

A hallway stretched out ahead of them once she followed Simpson out of the bullpen. The first door on the left led to a large room fitted out with a kitchen and three round tables for eating at. The door on her right was labeled Men. The next door on the right, though, read Ladies.

"There you are." Simpson nodded to the door and then simply continued down the hall to the next one on the left. When he turned in there, CJ supposed it must be the evidence room, but her attention was on a metal door she could now see at the end of the hall. It had a very small glass window that she could see bars through. The cells, she realized, and turned to slip into the ladies' room.

She wasn't surprised to find it was a one-person bathroom. This wasn't a huge police station, and as far as she could tell there weren't a lot of females in it. The only one she'd seen so far was the captain's wife, though there might be a secretary or receptionist during the day. There may even be at least one female officer. She supposed she'd find out eventually if that was the case.

Locking the door behind her, CJ tended to her business, washed her hands, and then took a minute to check emails and messages on her phone. She even quickly answered an email from her mentor at the SIU to let him know how things were going. She had started to answer another from a friend when she realized she was just delaying having to go back out to the bullpen until she was sure she wouldn't be alone with Mac. CJ was finding herself distressingly susceptible to his cheerful charm, but didn't like to think of herself as a coward, and that was what she was being right then.

Stopping in the middle of the second email, she saved it to Drafts and put her phone away. She then paused just long enough to take a deep breath, before leaving the ladies' room and heading back up the hall to the bullpen.

CJ had expected Simpson and Mrs. Dupree to be back from their tasks when she entered the bullpen, but neither of them were, although Mrs. Dupree had obviously returned at some point. Mac was still seated in the desk chair the older woman had insisted he settle in, but now had a heavy woolen cardigan draped over his shoulders and a steaming cup of coffee in his hands. CJ could smell the whiskey in it from ten paces away. It didn't look like he'd had any of it yet. He was just holding it in front of his face, allowing the whiskey-infused steam to fill his nostrils, a miserable look on his face as he peered down into the liquid. He cheered, though, when he saw her walking toward him.

"I thought you'd slipped out the back door to avoid Mrs. Dupree," he teased in a low voice when she stopped in front of him.

"Everyone in the business is a Mrs. Dupree when it comes to SIU agents. I'm used to it," CJ assured him, and then glanced around before asking, "Where are Mrs. Dupree and Simpson?"

"Mrs. Dupree is in there," Mac said, nodding toward the office she'd guessed was the captain's. "As for Simpson, I think he left."

"Left?" CJ asked with alarm.

"I think so," Mac answered with a shrug. "He came back, went into the office, and then left with Mrs. Dupree shooing him off like he was a kid who'd stayed up past his bedtime. She told him to . . . 'skedaddle,' I believe was the word."

CJ was trying to absorb that when he added, "He only left a minute ago. I am surprised you did not pass him in the hallway on the way back from the bathroom."

CJ was moving before he finished speaking, heading back the way she'd come. Simpson was the only officer here. He was the only protection Mac had from whoever had set his house on fire. The man couldn't leave. Well, she supposed he could, but it would leave her as Mac's only protection, and while she didn't mind helping out in a pinch, she'd be damned if she was going to be roped into playing bodyguard to a man like Macon Argeneau. He was just too damned handsome and charming for her own good. Besides, she wouldn't be much protection. She didn't even have a gun, for heaven's sake!

The hallway leading to the back of the building was as empty now as it had been when she'd returned from the bathroom moments earlier. CJ peeked into each room as she rushed past, even opening the doors to both the men's room and the evidence room for a quick look around, but there was no sign of Simpson, so she continued on.

The door to the cells was the very last door in the back wall, but as she reached it, she noticed a small narrow hallway leading to the left to what was obviously an exterior door. CJ immediately turned down it and jogged to the exit. The exterior door opened easily, and she stepped out to peer over what was obviously the parking area for police cars and any vehicles they impounded. She was just in time to see a white pickup roll toward the parking lot exit.

CJ let go of the door and took several steps forward, shouting and waving her arms in an effort to get Simpson's attention. She could've sworn the man peered toward her as he stopped at the road to look both ways, but if he did, he ignored her and simply pulled out onto the street and drove away.

"I don't think he heard you."

CJ turned to find Mac standing in the open back door of the police station. The sweater that had been draped over his shoulders was gone, but he was still carrying the cup of whiskey-laced coffee. He was holding it under his nose like it was smelling salts and he was a Victorian miss feeling faint. Never one to let something go to waste, CJ snatched the cup out of his hand as she walked past him back into the building.

"Thirsty?" Mac asked dryly, letting the door clang shut behind him as he followed her.

"You didn't look interested in drinking it," CJ said, slowing to glance back at him in question.

"I'm not."

Nodding, CJ immediately raised the cup to take a drink herself, but stopped when he added, "Because, I thought, since someone appears to be trying to kill me, it might be good to keep my wits about me."

CJ lowered the cup, irritation rushing through her even before he added, "And since you are supposed to be guarding me, it might be good if you avoided drinking as well."

She spun on him abruptly at that, her eyes wide. "What?" she asked with amazement, and then started shaking her head. "I'm sorry, Mr. Argeneau, but as I told you, I am not guarding you. That's why I was trying to stop Officer Simpson. As the officer in control of your investigation, he should have seen to your safety before leaving."

"But he didn't," Mac pointed out with a shrug. "I guess that leaves you."

"The hell it does," she exclaimed with dismay. "I'm not a police officer anymore."

"But you used to be, and you did agree to help out tonight," he pointed out. "Besides, there is no one else." Arching an eyebrow, he added, "Surely you wouldn't just leave a poor defenseless citizen to be killed? I mean, how would that look?"

CJ opened her mouth, closed it, opened it again, and then narrowed her eyes briefly on the man. She recognized manipulation when she saw it, and Mac wasn't even trying to be subtle about it. She got the feeling he wasn't really worried about an attack, or at all sorry Simpson was gone. She was getting the distinct impression that, for some reason, he just wanted to keep her close, and making her responsible for his well-being would definitely do that. She could hardly leave him here alone with Mrs. Dupree as his only protection.

Someone had set his house on fire. If they'd stuck around the scene as arsonists tended to do, they'd know he still lived and might try to finish the job when he left here. On the other hand, if he didn't leave the police station, he'd probably be safe enough, she thought. The trick was keeping him from leaving.

"You're absolutely right," she said suddenly. "You are the victim of a violent crime, and despite the fact that I'm not a police officer, I used to be, and your safety should be my main priority. I don't know what I was thinking."

"Well, it is late and no doubt you have had a long day," he said sympathetically. "I am sure you simply were not thinking clearly."

CJ's jaw clenched at the words, her annoyance ratcheting up another notch even as she agreed. "Yes. Still, that's no excuse for losing track of my priorities." Spinning on her heel, she led the way out of the narrow hall. With Mac following, she turned left, and pushed her way through the large metal door with the little window in it as she added, "I mean, what if I abandoned you here unprotected and went off to go over the notes of the case I'm actually on? And what if something happened after I'd left you alone? Dear God, the guilt I'd feel at leaving a poor defenseless citizen to be reattacked by his attacker."

"Well . . ." She could hear the frown in his voice even before he assured her, "I am not *completely* defenseless."

"Of course you are," she argued, leading him along the row of cells in this room. There were eight altogether. Four on each side. The first four actually had occupants in them. By her guess, the inhabitants of the first cells on either side of the aisle were both sleeping off an overindulgence in alcohol. One looked like a homeless man, the other was dressed in a slightly rumpled suit, but they were both snoring up a storm on their cots, and smelled like a dive bar's floor.

The next two cells both held young men in jeans and T-shirts. Judging by the bruises on their faces and the way they were scowling across the aisle at each other, CJ would guess they'd been brought in for brawling. Moving past the occupied cells, CJ continued, "You're an unarmed civilian with no self-defense training, weak and unskilled." She clucked her tongue sadly. "Helpless as a baby, really."

Pausing at the open door of the first empty cell, she turned back to see that her words had made his mouth turn down with displeasure. Judging by the way he scowled, the pitying look she now gave him did not improve his mood. He definitely didn't care for the idea of her seeing him as weak and feeling sorry for him, she decided when he straightened abruptly, and assured her, "I am not helpless as a baby."

"Of course not," she agreed easily, turning to lead the way into the cell. "But as a civilian . . ." Pausing, she turned sideways to watch him walk past her and then took several steps back toward the cell door as she added, "You're like a turtle on its back. All soft flabby skin, just waiting to be sliced and diced."

"Flabby!" he squawked. "I am not flabby. In fact, it's impossible for me to be flabby. I'm all sinewy muscle and—" Halting as he reached the cot attached to the wall several feet in front of her, he whirled back and suddenly yanked up his T-shirt almost all the way to his neck, saying, "Look!" He smacked the hard stomach he'd revealed and growled, "I am not soft and flabby."

CJ *was* looking, and stared hard at what was revealed. She'd heard of the hallowed six-pack. Mac didn't have that. It looked more like an eight-pack to her. Good Lord! The man could have been mistaken for a marble statue. Her eyes slid over his pale, muscled skin and she actually had to fight the urge to fan herself as she was hit by what she could only think was a premature hot flash. Instead of fanning herself with her hand, she used the cell door, swinging it closed firmly enough to create a slight breeze that fanned over her even as the metal door clanged shut.

Mac blinked in surprise at her through the bars now between them, and then his gaze moved down to the square metal panel holding the lock to the cell she'd led him into while distracting him with her words. Raising wide eyes back to her face, he asked with amazement, "What are you doing?"

"Leaving you in protective custody where you'll be safe," she said easily, giving the cell door a tug to be sure the lock was engaged. "This is the safest place for you until Captain Dupree can arrange someone to guard you. Maybe even until he finds out who tried to turn you into a shish kebab with that fire. Please enjoy your stay."

Turning then, CJ headed back along the cells, a smile sliding over her lips as she ignored his shouts for her to return and let him out.

"Hey! Come back here! Let me out!" Mac shouted, his gaze dropping to CJ's behind as he watched her walk away. Realizing what he was doing, he jerked his eyes up to her shoulders instead. It was his staring at her ass as he'd followed her inside that had landed him in the cell. He'd been so busy ogling her legs and butt and even her cowboy boots that he hadn't paid attention to where she was leading him until she'd distracted him with that flabby turtle business and then had closed the cell door between them. Now he was stuck in the cell. At least temporarily. The moment anyone entered, and surely someone would enter eventually, he would take control of them and make them let him out. As long as it wasn't CJ who returned, of course. Her, he couldn't control.

"Women, eh?"

Mac glanced to the man in the cell next to his and quickly read his mind. He'd been pulled in for drunk and disorderly after getting in a scrap at a bar with the man in the cell across from him. Both men were pickled, which was a shame. He might have been able to feed off the one in the next cell if he weren't. A little mind control on him and the man across the way, draw his neighbor's hand through the bars, and he could have fed from his wrist. However, alcohol made the man's blood pretty useless to him. It would just leave him more depleted. He'd have to wait for one of the officers to return and check on him, he supposed, and settled on the hard bench in his cell with a sigh.

CJ was still smiling at what she'd done as she strode up the hall toward the bullpen. In fact, it wasn't until she was crossing the bullpen itself that her smile began to fade and her footsteps to slow as guilt started to worm its way up through her.

Mac Argeneau had endured a hellish day. He'd nearly died in a fire, had lost everything he possessed, and now she had just rounded out his evening by locking him up in a jail cell.

Poor bastard, she thought guiltily. How cold was that?

Sighing, CJ shifted on her feet, her gaze moving longingly to the door to the reception area and the exit beyond. She wished she could just leave, go back to the bed-and-breakfast, go to sleep, and forget the man and his troubles altogether. But she just didn't have it in her. CJ's conscience wouldn't let her leave him in that cell. But once she let him out, she'd have to keep him safe, and she didn't want to hang out here either. Maybe she could take him back to the bed-and-breakfast with her? She was pretty sure he'd end up there anyway. The town only had one hotel and it was presently closed for renovations. That was how she'd ended up at the bed-and-breakfast. So, whoever ended up guarding him would either have to take him to their home, or a room would have to be booked for him at Mrs. Vesper's bed-and-breakfast. She might as well escort him there, get him a room, and sit around in the common area to be sure no one came in and tried to finish the job they'd started with the fire. At least until one of Captain Dupree's officers got free and could come take over the job.

Hopefully, that wouldn't take long, CJ thought grimly, and turned, intending to go back and release the annoying man from the cell she'd put him in. But she paused when Mrs. Dupree appeared in the door to the captain's office and announced imperiously, "My husband, *Captain* Dupree, wants to talk to you."

The little woman made the announcement as if CJ *had* to "jump to" and take the phone. She nearly disabused the woman of that idea and refused to speak to the man, but then had second thoughts as it occurred to her that she could dump Mac in his lap if she spoke to him.

Nodding abruptly, CJ changed direction and strode to the door of the captain's office, vaguely amused at the way Mrs. Dupree backed warily out of the way to let her enter.

"Where is Mr. Argeneau?" Mrs. Dupree asked as CJ crossed to the desk to pick up the phone receiver.

"I put him in one of the cells," CJ answered, knowing it would upset the woman and rather enjoying the idea.

"You what?" Mrs. Dupree gasped with horror.

CJ ignored her and picked up the phone. The moment she said, "Captain," into the receiver, Mrs. Dupree rushed from the room, muttering under her breath about "*uppity SIU people.*"

"You put the fire victim in a cell?" Captain Dupree snapped in response.

"Well, Simpson didn't stick around to see to his safety and it seemed to me there was nowhere safer for the man to be than in a jail cell. I consider it protective custody," CJ said mildly, settling herself on the corner of the captain's desk and grinning as she watched Mrs. Dupree bustle through the bullpen. She suspected the woman didn't often move that quickly.

A moment passed where she could hear the captain breathing heavily, and then he cleared his throat and said, "Unfortunately, my wife sent Michael—Officer Simpson—home."

"Uh-huh," CJ said in her most disinterested voice. She'd already known that from what Mac had said.

"Audrey sees my men as family members," he explained, sounding uncomfortable. "Like adopted sons. She fusses over them," he admitted unhappily, and then growled, "Problem is, they don't want to upset her and listen to her like she's their gosh-darned mother."

"Uh-huh," CJ repeated.

"I tried to call Simpson the minute Audrey told

me what she'd done, but I can't reach him on his cell phone," he said grimly. "So now we're in a pickle."

"*We're* in a pickle?" she queried gently, and heard the long sigh that traveled down the phone line.

"Ms. Cummings, I appreciate your help out at the fire tonight, I really do," he said solemnly. "And I really hate to trouble you for more help, but I'm still at the hospital with Jefferson, and my men are all presently on calls." He paused, and cleared his throat in what she suspected was the hope that she'd jump into the silence with an offer to help so he didn't have to actually ask for it, but she kept her mouth shut and simply waited. The man had not proven overly helpful up until now when it came to her interviewing Jefferson. He'd found every excuse in the book to put her off until tonight, and then she'd arrived to find the interview delayed again. She felt she had to help whether she liked it or not, but she expected his cooperation in return. So, she waited.

Finally, he sighed and said, "I'd really appreciate it if you could see your way clear to helping out just a little bit more. Nothing big," he hastened to add. "But I know you must have a room out at Mrs. Vesper's, and I was thinking maybe you could just drive Mr. Argonauts out there, stay with him while he rents a room, and then see him safely into it and keep an eye on him for a bit. I promise the very first man who returns to the station will head straight there to take over from you to guard him."

CJ didn't bother to correct his mispronunciation of Mac's name; she simply waited patiently, allowing the silence to draw out. She was rewarded for her patience.

"And, of course, in return, I'll make sure Jefferson is available tomorrow afternoon at whatever time you want for that interview you need," Captain Dupree said finally with resignation. "I'll escort him to the bed-and-breakfast, or wherever you want, so you can talk to him."

CJ smiled, but kept her tone mellow as she said, "One of the interview rooms here will do just fine, or even your meeting room. He starts his next shift at 4 P.M. tomorrow, so let's set the interview time for 3 P.M."

"Fine," Captain Dupree grunted resentfully. "So, will you look after this Mr. Argonauts for a bit? If you aren't comfortable taking him to the bed-and-breakfast, you could always wait there at the station with him. I just thought—"

"I'll take Mr. *Argeneau* to Mrs. Vesper's," CJ interrupted at once, emphasizing his correct name. "As you said, he'll probably end up there anyway."

"Argeneau. Right. Good," Captain Dupree muttered. "Thank you. I appreciate your help."

"No problem, Captain," CJ said magnanimously, and then since she felt he would feel he owed her, she asked, "Why are you and Jefferson at the hospital? Was he hurt? Are you?"

There was a moment of silence, and then Captain Dupree said, "Oh, here's the doctor. I have to go."

The words were followed by the dial tone, telling her he'd hung up.

Four

C J set the receiver down with a shake of the head. She was good at her job, and the captain's reluctance to answer her questions just made her more determined to find out what had happened tonight. She wouldn't bother except that it involved Jefferson and he was who she was here to investigate. The captain's avoiding her questions just made her suspicious and annoyed. But she'd find out what had happened. Eventually. It was hard to keep secrets in a small town.

Sliding off the corner of the desk, she walked out of the office to find Mrs. Dupree had freed Mac and was trying to urge him into a desk chair again.

"Time to go," CJ announced, bringing a halt to Mrs. Dupree's nattering.

"Go?" the woman echoed with dismay. "Go where?"

Even as she did, Mac was sprinting to CJ's side, asking cheerfully, "Where are we off to now?"

CJ hesitated, but then ignored his question in favor of asking Mrs. Dupree, "Is there a spare coat and hat here to disguise Mr. Argeneau for the walk to my car? Just in case the arsonist is out there watching for him to leave," she added when the captain's wife continued to simply glare at her.

The last comment worked. Mrs. Dupree's eyes widened, the glare dropping away at once, and she whirled and rushed into the captain's office.

"Surely a disguise isn't necessary," Mac muttered as they watched the lady bustle out of sight.

"Better safe than sorry," CJ said simply, and was relieved to see the captain's wife return quickly. She was carrying an officer's dress coat and cap—probably the captain's, was CJ's guess, but she didn't ask and simply waited for Mac to don them both. Once he'd finished, they both looked him over. He looked ridiculous, of course. The jacket was tight across the shoulders, but far too large at the waist, and his checkered, flannel pajama bottoms just did not go well with the fancy dress jacket and cap.

"Just let me get the pants," Mrs. Dupree said suddenly as she rushed away again.

Mac shifted his shoulders in the jacket and made a dissatisfied face, but neither of them spoke as they waited for Mrs. Dupree. She returned a moment later, carrying the outfit's matching dress pants still on a hanger.

"They'll be a bit large for you, but at least they'll fit over your pajama bottoms," Mrs. Dupree said as she reached Mac's side and tugged the pants off the hanger. "You might have to hold them up though."

Mac sighed, but accepted the pants and pulled them on over his own clothes.

"Do you have twist ties?" CJ asked Mrs. Dupree as she watched Mac clutch the pants in hand to keep them from falling down once they were up.

The captain's wife nodded and hustled off again, this time disappearing through the door that led to the hallway to the kitchenette and cells. When she returned, she had several large green twist ties, probably from a package of garbage bags.

CJ murmured, "Thank you," took one, and moved to Mac's side to quickly slide the tie through three belt loops of the dress pants, then twisted it closed and stepped back to survey her handiwork. When Mac released them and the pants were still loose and nearly fell, she accepted another twist tie from the lady and walked around to Mac's other side to gather two more loops with it. This time when she stepped back and he released his hold on the pants, they stayed in place.

"I look ridiculous," Mac said, scowling down at the bunched-up pants.

"The coat will cover it," CJ assured him, before adding, "And it's dark out. It'll be fine."

Mac grunted, but let the coat drop to cover the top of the pants, and then surveyed himself briefly, before nodding and holding one arm out to her in a courtly gesture. "Shall we?"

CJ stared blankly at the offered arm, but didn't take it. Instead, she snorted and swung on her heel to lead the way out of the bullpen.

Mac followed silently until they were crossing the front reception room, and then he said, "Catherine Jane."

"Oh, good Lord! Don't start that again," she snapped with irritation.

"It seems to me I should get to know the woman who is going to guard my body," he responded lightly.

"Not necessary," she assured him as she pushed the front door of the station open and paused to glance around, looking for cars in the parking lot, or anyone who might be watching. She didn't see anyone, but that didn't mean there wasn't someone there.

"Keep your head down so no one can see your face,"

she instructed as she started forward again, allowing him out of the building.

"You must really hate your names," Mac commented as he followed her to the car.

CJ looked over her shoulder to be sure he had his head down, but didn't acknowledge his words. She merely took his elbow to hurry him along to the car. She hit the button on her key fob to unlock it as they approached, and then opened the front passenger door, scanned the empty parking lot as she waited for him to get in, and then closed it for him once he was seated before hurrying around to the driver's side.

"Well, this is strange," Mac commented as she slid behind the wheel and pulled her own door closed.

"What is?" she asked absently, her eyes dancing around the parking lot as she buckled up and started the engine.

"You seeing me into the car," he explained. "I am usually the one who does that when with a lady."

"I'm not a lady. I'm your bodyguard," CJ reminded him grimly as she shifted gears and backed out of the parking spot. "Do up your seat belt and keep your head down."

He did as instructed, and then remained silent as she steered them out of the parking lot and onto the road. Much to her surprise, he stayed silent even after that as she divided her attention between driving and watching the rearview mirror for anyone who might be following them. This late at night, or early in the morning as the case may be, there weren't a lot of people out driving around, and no one seemed to be following them. Still, CJ drove twice around the block where the bed-and-breakfast was to make sure they didn't have a tail before pulling into the driveway and steering her car around to the small parking area behind the old Victorian house.

"I feel bad about having to wake up Millie at this hour to rent a room," Mac murmured as they got out and headed for the back door of the house.

"Yeah," CJ breathed, a frown taking over her face. Millie Vesper was a widow in her late sixties whose children had grown up and moved to the city, leaving her alone in the town where she'd grown up, married, and raised her own family. Apparently, her children had wanted to sell her house and move her to a seniors' home in the city to be close to them, but Millie had refused and had turned her home into a bed-and-breakfast instead. CJ suspected the woman had done it for company rather than out of any need for money. The woman had chatted away nonstop to her every chance she'd got. CJ had only arrived a couple of hours before she'd headed to the station and had spent most of that time listening to the chatty, but dear, lady tell her about the town of Sandford and its inhabitants. CJ now had the lowdown on who was sleeping with whom, and who wasn't getting along in their marriage. At least she knew the names of the troubled and misbehaving individuals, but since she didn't know anyone in this town, she didn't have faces to put with them.

CJ had listened with polite interest to what had amounted to a soap opera of the goings-on in town, but it wasn't until she was driving to her appointment at the police station that she'd considered that she should maybe ask Mrs. Vesper about the people there, and Jefferson in particular. CJ suspected the woman would have an earful to tell her, but wasn't sure if that would be a good thing or not. She was supposed to investigate objectively, and she worried Mrs. Vesper's bias might influence her.

"A light just came on inside."

CJ followed Mac's gaze to a window at the back of the house, and noted the light now shining through the curtains. The sound of the car engine must have woken the old lady, CJ supposed, but it could only be a good thing. It meant they wouldn't have to knock on her door in the middle of the night.

"Goodness! Aren't you two a sight for sore eyes!"

CJ glanced around with surprise at that greeting as she ushered Mac into the house. They hadn't had to knock. Mrs. Vesper had left the door unlocked. Spotting the lady now rushing down the hall toward them in a terry cloth robe, CJ offered a smile and pushed the door closed, then locked it as she murmured, "I'm sorry if we woke you up, Mrs. Vesper."

"Nonsense, who could sleep with all the goings-on tonight?" she said promptly, her footsteps taking her straight to Mac, who she grasped by the hands and then dragged in for a hug. "You poor dear boy. I heard about the fire and have been worrying about you."

"I am fine, Millie," Mac said reassuringly as he awkwardly returned the woman's embrace. "I am afraid your friend's house and my things are a loss, but I am well."

"And that's all that matters," Mrs. Vesper assured him, pulling back to meet his gaze straight on as she said it. She then clucked and added, "But I am sorry about your things. And you'd just moved in too." She shook her head and clucked some more, then pulled Mac in for another hug before leaning back to take in the overly large uniform he was wearing. "The captain's?"

"Yes," Mac admitted with distaste as he removed

the captain's hat. "I had best take it off so it doesn't get wrinkled or dirty."

"Take it off?" Mrs. Vesper asked with amazement, and then breathed an understanding "Oh" when he next shrugged out of the jacket and dress pants, revealing his T-shirt and pajama bottoms underneath. As he folded the dress uniform and set it on the hall table next to the hat, Mrs. Vesper turned toward the kitchen. "Well now, you two could probably do with some nice soothing tea, and maybe some cookies."

She bustled off before either of them could protest.

"Looks like we're having tea and cookies," Mac said softly when CJ didn't immediately follow.

Giving up any hope of thinking up an excuse to avoid it, CJ nodded and headed after the older lady with a sigh.

"Now," Mrs. Vesper said as she began to pour tea into their cups a few minutes later. "You'll have to tell me what happened, dears, because the grapevine was all a-tangle tonight. First Jeannie called saying the house was on fire and you were dead," she said with a glance to Mac. Her gaze then switched to CJ and she added, "And then Joan called saying she'd heard from Amelia that you were kind enough to help out at the fire since Charles was without a detective." Her eyes slid back to Mac. "But that you weren't actually dead yet. You were boiled alive in a tub of water in the basement, but still breathing when you left the house in the ambulance. They didn't expect you to survive long enough to make it to the hospital though."

She didn't wait for a response, but went on. "And then Margaret called and said John—that's her husband," she explained. "He's a volunteer fireman and went out to help at the fire." When they both nodded their understanding, she continued, "Margaret said John said you were fine. You were in a tub of water, but the firemen got you out of the house in time and you didn't even have to go to the hospital to be checked over. That you'd left with CJ and little Michael Simpson to go to the police station."

CJ had to cough to cover the burst of laughter that tried to slip out of her mouth at the mention of *little Michael Simpson*. Mrs. Vesper made it sound like the man was four years old when he was about twenty-eight or so, tall, and rather well put together. Though not as well put together as Mac, she admitted to herself, mentally comparing the two.

"So?" Mrs. Vesper set down the teapot to eye them both expectantly. "What happened?"

"Joan and Margaret got it right," Mac told her when CJ didn't respond. "I was trapped in the basement, got in the tub, and fortunately the firemen got me out in time. The EMTs started to take me to the hospital but turned back when they realized I was fine, and then I left for the police station with CJ and Officer Simpson."

"Oh," Mrs. Vesper breathed, and shook her head. "Well, this has been an awful start to your move here."

"It was not the best start, no," Mac agreed with a wry twist of the lips.

"Well, have a cookie, dear. Cookies always make everything seem better," Mrs. Vesper assured him. "You too, CJ. Have a cookie."

CJ reached for a cookie, and Mac followed suit, but while she immediately took a bite of hers, he just turned his over in his hands, eyeing it as if he'd never seen one before.

"Are you just going to hold that like you did the coffee at the station?" CJ asked with amusement. "If so, give it to me. Mrs. Vesper's cookies are too good to waste."

"He's probably a dunker," Mrs. Vesper guessed, and then tsked as she glanced down to see the three full cups still sitting in front of her. "Goodness, I poured them and then didn't give them to you. Here you are, dears."

"Thank you," CJ murmured as she took the teacup the older woman now held out. Setting it on the table in front of her, she added cream and sugar and then pushed the sugar bowl and cream toward Mac. He immediately added a teaspoon of sugar and a dollop of cream just as she had done, but he didn't dunk his cookie in his tea; he simply took a bite and chewed it experimentally, his eyes widening as he did.

"This cookie is really good, Mrs. Vesper," he complimented the minute he'd swallowed. "Delicious. It has been millennia since I've had anything so tasty."

The older lady beamed under the exaggerated praise, and then said, "Now aren't you sorry you wouldn't have them when you stayed here?" Turning to CJ she added, "I couldn't get this boy to eat a thing when he was staying with me. He ate out for every single meal."

"I stayed here for a week or two last month while I searched for a house in the area," Mac explained to CJ. "At first, I hadn't settled specifically on this town and was doing a lot of driving around, both here in Sandford and farther afield." He shrugged. "A lot of the time it was just easier to stop at whatever restaurant was nearest and eat there rather than rush back for meals."

"You didn't have that excuse when you stayed here Tuesday and Wednesday night this week, though," Mrs. Vesper pointed out with a bit of asperity and told CJ, "He was only supposed to stay Tuesday night, but the moving truck was held up at customs and he stayed

Wednesday as well." Head swiveling back to Mac she added, "And you didn't eat a thing then either."

Mac nodded solemnly. "But I assure you I certainly shall not make that mistake this time now that I know what a fine cook you are."

Mrs. Vesper started to smile, but then blinked. "This time?" she asked with alarm.

Mac nodded, his mouth full of cookie again, and it was CJ who explained. "He needs a room now that his house has burned down."

Mac swallowed so that he could add, "One next to CJ's room if that's possible." He winked at the older woman and confided, "She's guarding my body."

"Guarding your body?" Mrs. Vesper echoed, her wide eyes turning to CJ.

"It will be fine, Mrs. Vesper," CJ assured her. "I suspect it will turn out that Mac's house burning down was just a firebug who thought it was still empty. After all, he's just moved in and hasn't lived in Sandford long enough to have made enemies."

"Oh, goodness, no, dear, he hasn't," Mrs. Vesper agreed.

"But until we know for sure, we have to at least take precautions to ensure he's safe from further attacks," CJ pointed out. "Just in case. But I don't want you to worry. You are in no danger. No one knows he's here, and I took precautions leaving the police station and on the drive to ensure no one followed us," she assured her. "And, no doubt, Captain Dupree will make arrangements for him elsewhere after tonight."

"But my dear, you work for the SIU," Mrs. Vesper pointed out with a slight frown. "Why are you guarding his body instead of one of our town's police officers?"

Good question, CJ thought dryly, but said, "I'm afraid all of Dupree's officers are busy at the moment, so he asked me to keep an eye on Mr. Argeneau until one of his men becomes available."

Mac nodded solemnly. "So, I'll need a room close to hers. In case there's trouble."

CJ narrowed her eyes on the man. There was just something about his expression and tone of voice . . . She got the feeling he wasn't worried at all, but was happy to use the excuse of his safety as a way to stick close to her, though she couldn't fathom why. They were virtual strangers.

"Oh, dear," Mrs. Vesper said unhappily, drawing CJ's attention back to the older woman as she confessed, "I'm afraid that won't be possible."

"It won't?" Mac's smile slipped.

"No," she said apologetically. "I'm all full up, you see."

"Really?" CJ asked with surprise. "I was your only guest when I left tonight."

"Well, yes, but then the Wilkersons showed up."

"The Wilkersons?" CJ felt sure the lady had mentioned the name once or twice while she'd been chattering away before CJ had left for the police station, but she hadn't been paying that much attention then.

"Yes, dear. You remember, I told you that Ned and Mary Wilkerson's three sons and their wives and kids were coming," Mrs. Vesper said, and then turned to Mac and explained, "You see Cindy Wilkerson is getting married, and her brothers and their wives are in the wedding party, as groomsmen and bridesmaids. And then Bobby, the oldest Wilkerson boy, well, his four-year-old daughter, Nina, is the flower girl, and she is the sweetest little thing." Mrs. Vesper shook her head with wonder. "A pretty sprite with big blue eyes and long, curly blond hair. She's going to look adorable walking up that aisle. Yes, she is." She sighed at the thought, and then seemed to realize she'd gone on a tangent, and quickly said, "But anyway, the wedding is tomorrow. Well, today now, I suppose, and they're staying until Sunday."

She huffed out a breath, and then turned back to CJ. "They all moved to British Columbia for university, one after the other, and ended up settling there. Cindy's the only one who stayed in the area. Well, the boys and their families flew in on the same flight and were supposed to land in Toronto at eleven. I expected them here shortly after you left for the station, but their flight was delayed a couple hours. They only got in about forty-five minutes ago. The whole lot of them were exhausted. I'd just got them all settled and managed to climb into bed myself and turn off my light a minute or two before I heard your car pull in, so I got back up to let you know so the noise of kids and others wouldn't startle you in the morning." She shook her head unhappily. "Between you and them every room is full up. I simply have nowhere to put another person."

"Oh, I see," CJ said with a frown. That was a problem.

"Except perhaps with you," the old lady added thoughtfully.

CJ gaped at the suggestion. "Mrs. Vesper!"

"Well, dear, your room does have the salon attached," she pointed out, and then said to Mac, "It's the room you were in when you stayed here."

CJ felt her heart sink at Mrs. Vesper's suggestion. Her room was actually a suite with a bedroom and attached salon that was a small sitting room with a dining table and chairs set up at one end by a large picture window, and a couch, coffee and end tables, as well as a TV set up on the other end closest to the entry. CJ had paid extra money to get the suite with the salon so that she could use the table to make notes after her interviews, and would have somewhere to relax at night other than the bed. She had not rented it expecting to have a roommate.

"And I do have a lovely little cot, very comfortable. I'm sure Mac would be happy sleeping on it in the salon. And this way, you will be better able to guard him than if he was in another room altogether," she pointed out.

"Well, if that's the only solution to this problem, I suppose we'll just have to make do," Mac said cheerfully.

CJ scowled at the man with irritation. Of course he was fine with it. He was taking over her room. As the one under threat, he'd be safest in the inner room, the actual bedroom, with the bed. She'd be the one stuck on the cot in the sitting room of her own suite, between him and the entry. Bastard, she thought with a sort of amused disgust. She couldn't decide if he was the luckiest son of a bitch alive, or she was the unluckiest. She supposed that was probably an odd thought considering his home had just burned down, but he'd survived, which was pretty damned lucky to her mind, and now he was getting her bed. Bastard.

"You know," Mac said suddenly. "I feel safer already just at the idea."

"I'm sure you do," CJ said, rolling her eyes.

"Well, it's all settled, then," Mrs. Vesper said happily. "I'll just get that cot, shall I?"

"Don't be silly, Mrs. Vesper," Mac protested, jumping to his feet when the old lady started to get up. "You can't possibly carry the cot. Just show me where it is and I shall fetch it back."

CJ watched the older woman lead Mac away, and then stood up with a sigh. She started to head toward the stairs, only to turn back for her half-empty teacup and a cookie. After a hesitation, she then grabbed two more cookies to take with her as she left the kitchen to go to her room.

CJ had never been the neatest person on the planet. Okay, the truth was she was a slob, she admitted to herself. It was hard not to admit it when she stepped into her room and saw the mess she'd left behind when she'd headed out earlier. CJ had driven down here in jeans and a T-shirt, but had decided to change to a more professional look before heading to the police station. She'd changed her mind at least three times about what to wear, tossing her clothing about as she pulled them on and stripped them off. In the end, she'd decided on a white blouse, dark blue pantsuit jacket, jeans, and cowboy boots. Not everyone's idea of a professional look, she was sure, but that was one of the things she liked best about the SIU: they weren't stringent when it came to a dress code. At least her boss wasn't.

After years of climbing in and out of her police uniform, a more relaxed dress code was something she enjoyed. For the most part. Right now, though, CJ almost wished the SIU had a standard uniform as well. At least then she wouldn't have such a mess to clean, she thought as she set her cookies and tea on the table in the sitting room of her suite and then rushed about, gathering her bra and panties, jeans, her T-shirt, and two different pantsuits. She was just rushing toward the double French doors leading into the bedroom when the door to the hall opened.

Hoping that neither Mac nor Mrs. Vesper had spotted her and her stack of clothes, she tossed them into the open suitcase on the bed and quickly zipped it closed. She then carried it out to drop next to the table where her laptop sat open, before turning to watch Mac wheel in an ancient cot. Honest to God, it looked at least fifty years old. It was one of those rollaway beds, where the ends folded up for easy storage. Closed as it was right now, she couldn't see the whole mattress, but what she could see didn't look promising. It had definitely seen better days, and CJ bit her lip, worrying over just how comfortable it would be.

Not that it mattered, she supposed. Comfortable or

not, she was stuck with it, so CJ gave in to the inevitable and hurried over to shift furniture so that the cot would fit in the room. In the end, she didn't have to move much. Shifting the couch and end tables toward the dining table a bit left enough room for the cot to be positioned in front of the door. Although it only left a couple of inches for the door to be opened before it would hit the side of the bed.

"There," Mrs. Vesper said with satisfaction as Mac straightened from setting up the cot. But her smile disappeared nearly as quickly as it had appeared when she saw the stained mattress. "Oh, dear, I suppose you will need sheets," she muttered, and turned to the door, only to find it didn't open enough for her to slide out.

"Just a minute, Mrs. Vesper," Mac said, and quickly closed the rollaway bed again so she could get out.

"I'll be right back," she assured them in a whisper, presumably to avoid disturbing the other guests, and then she slipped out into the hall and hurried away.

CJ eased the door shut behind her and then turned to survey the room. Even with the rollaway bed closed, the room seemed much smaller than it had without it. Or maybe it was Mac having that effect. The man was large too, she acknowledged, and moved around him to take up the seat in front of her laptop at the dining table. She then picked up her tea and started to sort through her emails, ignoring Mac until he asked with interest, "Are those cookies?"

"Yes," CJ answered as she quickly grabbed them up to keep him from taking any.

"Not the sharing sort, I see," Mac said with mild amusement.

CJ scowled. "Not when it comes to homemade chocolate chip cookies. And definitely not when it comes to someone who is stealing my bed."

"Ah. Yes, well, they *were* good," he acknowledged. "I— Wait, what do you mean stealing your bed?" he asked suddenly, a frown curving his lips down. "I'll take the cot."

CJ turned on him, one eyebrow arched. "I'm guarding your body, remember? That means putting myself between you and trouble. You're safest in the bedroom with me between you and the entry."

"But—"

"Besides," she added, cutting him off, "the bed in there is queen-sized. Might be a bit tight but should fit two men fine if one of the officers shows up. He can sleep in there with you."

"What?" he squawked with alarm.

CJ smiled at him sweetly, and then glanced to the door as it swung open and Mrs. Vesper hurried in with a stack of pink sheets in her arms.

"Here we are," she said in a soft voice as CJ set down the cookies and jumped up to take the linens from her. "I'm afraid I only had pink ones left, but I know you'll be the one on the cot since you're the one guarding. I was hoping that would be okay."

"It's fine," CJ assured her. She didn't care what color they were.

"Well, then, I'll leave you and go find my bed. I have to get up early to make breakfast for everyone tomorrow." She followed the admission with a slight sigh, but then straightened her shoulders, gave them a smile and a cheery "Sleep tight," and sidled out of the room.

CJ immediately set the sheets on the couch, and then moved to the door to lock it. Once that was done, she opened the cot and quickly riffled through the sheets until she found the bottom one.

"Let me help," Mac offered, grabbing one end of the bottom sheet.

"Thanks," CJ said easily. Working together, the bed was made in no time. They both turned to look at the pillowcase still on the couch.

"I'll check the closet in the bedroom," CJ said, and hurried out of the room to do so. Not that she had to go far; it was perhaps twelve steps from the end of the cot to the closet in the bedroom. Much to her relief, there were two spare pillows and even a couple of blankets on the shelf above the clothing rod. CJ grabbed all four items and carried them back out to the sitting room.

"There were two blankets," she announced as she set her burden on the bed. "I took both, but if you get cold in the night and want one of them, just let me know."

"I'm sure I'll be fine," Mac said, but didn't head into the bedroom. Instead, when CJ moved back to the table, he followed and settled across from her.

CJ hesitated, and then raised her head and arched an eyebrow. "Not tired?"

Mac shook his head. "I suppose I should be after the fire and all, but I work nights as a rule and only got up at nine o'clock last evening. It's still early for me." He hesitated and then offered, "But I'll go sit in the bedroom if I'm bothering you."

"You're not bothering me," CJ lied, and proceeded to ignore him as she opened her emails on her computer. After a moment, though, she growled, "Stop staring at my cookies, Argeneau."

"Sorry," he chuckled. "They just look so good. I wonder if Mrs. Vesper left the other cookies out."

CJ hesitated, and then sighed and stood up. "Fine, I'll get you some cookies."

"Don't be silly, you're busy," Mac said, getting up as well. "I can go get my own cookie."

"You aren't going anywhere," CJ announced abruptly.

"I'm supposed to be guarding you. I can't guard you if you're wandering around the house on your own."

Mac scowled, but then said, "Fine, then we'll both go, because you're not waiting on me."

CJ didn't comment; she simply led the way to the door, only to pause at the foot of the cot. They'd have to close the cot to get out. CJ bent to start to do so, but Mac said, "Hang on."

Moving away, he quickly shifted the couch and end tables to the left several more inches, then stepped back to the cot to shift it as well. When he finished, he'd managed to make a good foot of space between the cot and the door. It couldn't open all the way, but it was enough to let them out without having to suck in their guts.

"Thanks," CJ said, but raised a hand for him to stay where he was as she cracked open the door to peer briefly out into the hall. Finding it empty, she gestured for him to follow and stepped out. CJ normally wouldn't have locked the door for such a short trip, but there was a possible threat to Mac's life, so she took the time to lock the door before escorting him downstairs to the kitchen.

Five

Mrs. Vesper hadn't only left the cookies out, the pot of tea remained on the table as well and was still warm. CJ fetched a fresh teacup while Mac emptied his now cool drink from earlier and then they poured themselves tea, doctored them, and put the cream in the fridge before grabbing several cookies each and heading out of the kitchen. They'd nearly made it to the stairs when they heard a car pull into the driveway.

CJ set her tea and cookies on a small table by the stairs, gestured for Mac to stay where he was, and then moved to the back entrance that overlooked the small parking area. Tugging the curtain aside a bit, she peered out at the vehicle parking in the only empty space next to her own, and then relaxed. It was a police car. Her replacement was here, or her backup, she supposed, since they'd have to share her room for tonight at least. It was just too late to bother to find somewhere else for Mac to stay. But tomorrow she would pester Captain Dupree into making alternate arrangements, CJ thought as she unlocked the back door, opened it, and watched the officer who got out and started toward the house.

He was an older man, tall with a slight stoop to his broad shoulders, and a bit of a gut. Not a huge one, but one that suggested he liked his beer after work. His walk was confident, his hands loose at his sides, relaxed but ready to retrieve his gun if necessary.

"Ms. Cummings?" he asked as he mounted the steps.

CJ nodded, but placed one finger to her mouth in the sign for him to lower his voice. She didn't want to disturb Mrs. Vesper or her guests, so waited until he was in the house and the door was closed again before holding out her hand and saying softly, "Pleasure to meet you, Officer . . . ?"

"Dandridge," he answered at once.

CJ nodded and then gestured to Mac as he came to join them, "This is Mr. Macon Argeneau."

"Sorry to hear about your troubles, Mr. Argeneau," Dandridge said as he shook his hand. "Looks like I'll be guarding you for the rest of the night."

"Yeah, I'm not too sure about that," Mac replied, and when Dandridge showed surprise, he added, "No offense, but you're a big guy and I just can't see you and me fitting into a queen-sized bed together."

"What?" Dandridge asked with amazement.

CJ rolled her eyes with exasperation, locked the back door, and simply said, "Come." She then led both men back to the stairs, pausing long enough to collect her cookies and tea before leading the way up to her bedroom suite where she had to hand Dandridge her tea so she could unlock her door. She then gestured for both men to wait in the hall briefly while she slid inside to perform a quick search to be sure the rooms were still empty. She wasn't really expecting trouble, but it was better to be safe than sorry as the saying went. Once assured that no one had entered while they were gone, she returned to the door and waved the men in.

"Your tea," Dandridge said, offering her the steaming cup when she turned from locking the door behind them.

"Thanks." CJ took the cup and carried it and her cookies to the table, murmuring, "I was supposed to bring Mr. Argeneau here, wait while he rented a room, and see him safely to it," she explained as she set her goodies next to her computer. Turning back to the man, she continued, "I then probably would have waited in the hall for whoever Dupree sent to take over watching him. Unfortunately, Mrs. Vesper had no more rooms."

"Ah, damn," Dandridge murmured.

"Yeah," CJ agreed.

"Fortunately, CJ had rented the suite with the sitting room," Mac put in.

"Salon," CJ corrected with wry amusement. She had called it a sitting room several times after first arriving, only to have Mrs. Vesper correct her repeatedly. It was *the salon.*

Mac must have experienced the same thing when he had rented the suite, because he grinned with commiseration and said, "Yes, of course, *the salon.* But as Mrs. Vesper pointed out, this setup works better for my safety anyway. With the cot in this room with CJ in it, and me in the bedroom, she stands between myself and anyone who might try to enter."

"Right." Dandridge nodded, and then glanced to CJ. "Well, I'm here now. I'll take the cot and you can go."

CJ stared at him with disbelief. "Go where exactly, Officer Dandridge? This is my suite of rooms, and there isn't another one available."

"Shit, right. I mean, shoot. Sorry," he muttered, and then, obviously flustered, gave his head a shake as if to clear his thoughts. "Well, this is a problem."

"I would say so," Mac agreed.

"I wouldn't," CJ countered at once. "You two get the bedroom. I get the cot. Seems simple to me."

"I won't be sleeping. I'm on shift," Dandridge pointed out, and then shrugged. "I'll just hang around out here . . ." His voice trailed off as his eyes landed on the rollaway bed and he apparently recalled what Mac had said. "Oh. You're sleeping out here?" he asked CJ.

"Well, that was the original plan," CJ admitted. "But now that you're here, I guess I can sleep in the bedroom and Mac can sleep on the cot while you sit on the couch . . . watching."

"I'm not going to be able to sleep with him staring at me," Mac said.

"I won't stare," Dandridge promised him.

Mac snorted and assured CJ, "I will not sleep."

CJ threw her hands up with exasperation. "Fine, I'll sleep on the cot and he can stare at me."

"The hell you will," Mac snapped, suddenly annoyed. "I wouldn't be able to sleep knowing that he was here staring at you either. Besides, this is completely unnecessary. I would be perfectly safe here alone with you. There probably won't be any trouble anyway."

"Probably not," CJ agreed, and then pointed out, "But if there is trouble, I don't have a gun and Dandridge does. You are not safer here alone with me. Hell, I'm not safer here alone with me if there's trouble. We'd both be safer with Dandridge and his gun here with us."

Mac frowned at her words, and then suggested, "What if he watched the house from outside and we pushed the cot up against the door, blocking it? That way no one can enter, and he can see and stop anyone who approached the house. It's doubly safe."

CJ stared at him blankly for a moment, bewildered by how tangled this was all getting. She had only agreed to watch him until one of Captain Dupree's officers was free to do so. But now, thanks to a lack of rooms, she was getting roped into watching him *with* the police officer. This wasn't her job!

"That sounds like a fine idea to me," Dandridge said, turning to the door with obvious relief. "I'll be in my car if you need me."

The man was obviously eager to escape the discussion. He was out of the room almost before he finished speaking.

"There," Mac said with satisfaction. "Now we can have our tea and cookies."

CJ turned to stare at him with disbelief, but what could she say? Besides, now that he'd reminded her of the cookies, she was hungry. Shaking her head, she locked the door again, pushed the cot up against it, and then walked to the table where Mac was already pulling her chair out for her.

CJ wasn't at all comfortable with the courtesy. Mostly because she didn't know how it was supposed to go. Was she supposed to sit on it and make him push her and the chair in? Or was she supposed to lift her bottom and balance in a semi-squatting position, pulling the chair even as he pushed? In the end she went with the second option, a very awkward maneuver. But if she did it wrong, Mac didn't comment and simply walked around to settle in the chair diagonal to her own; they enjoyed a brief silence as they started to eat the cookies and drink the tea.

After a moment, Mac asked, "So . . . CSIS, huh?"

CJ glanced at him sideways, one eyebrow rising as she guessed, "Mrs. Dupree?"

Mac nodded. "Apparently, Captain Dupree has a friend on the force in Toronto who filled him in on your history, he talked about you at home, and she decided to share with me."

CJ grunted at this news. She'd suspected it was something like that when Captain Dupree had proven that he'd looked into her. Now she wondered just how much of her history the man had learned.

"So?" Mac said. "First a police detective, then a detective with CSIS, and now a detective with the SIU. An interesting career trajectory."

"Not really. It's all investigative work," she pointed out, and then sat back in her seat and eyed him solemnly. "Speaking of investigative work, have you come up with anyone you pissed off enough that they'd follow you here to Canada to kill you?"

He frowned at the question, and actually looked thoughtful for a moment as if considering the possibility, but then shook his head. "No. I cannot imagine anyone wanting to kill me. I'm really a very agreeable fellow."

CJ felt her lips twitch with amusement at the claim, but pressed, "No jealous husbands or jilted ex-lovers?"

"I would never take on a married lover," he assured her stiffly, a scowl claiming his mouth at the suggestion.

CJ merely shrugged and asked, "What about ex-lovers or even present lovers, then?"

"No," he responded at once.

"No what?" she asked.

"There are no present or past lovers," he said quietly, and when her expression turned doubtful, he added, "I have been concentrating on work and avoiding entanglements of such a nature for quite some time."

CJ relaxed and nodded, but wondered how long "quite some time" was to this man. A year? A month?

A week? Telling herself it wasn't really her business, she wasn't with the police anymore, and this wasn't her problem to solve, she withdrew a notepad and pen from the computer case she'd left leaning against a leg of the table and handed them to him, suggesting, "Well, perhaps it would be a good idea to make a list of past girlfriends you've had over the last couple years, with how long ago you broke up, and whether it was amicable or not."

The moment Mac accepted the notepad and pen, she turned her attention back to her computer. Or tried to. While she was staring blindly at the screen, she was aware that he had merely set the pad and pen on the table and wasn't writing anything, but was staring at her instead. She did her best to ignore it and tried to actually read the email she had opened, but the man was very distracting and she was almost relieved when he asked, "What does your family think of your choosing such a dangerous career?"

CJ kept her gaze on her computer and shrugged mildly. "I don't have a family."

"What?" he asked with disbelief. "Everyone has family."

"Not everyone," she assured him with a faint smile. "I don't . . . and neither do most of my oldest and dearest friends."

Mac was silent for a moment and she could feel his

eyes on her as he considered what she'd said and then he guessed, "Orphanage?"

"Good guess, but not quite. Foster care," she told him, and then glanced his way and added, "I don't even think they have orphanages anymore, do they?"

"Perhaps not," he allowed solemnly.

Noting his expression, she clucked her tongue with exasperation and turned back to her computer again as she said, "Don't give me that look."

"What look?" he asked at once.

"The sad-eyed, pitying thing," she explained. "You're feeling sorry for me now, but there's no need. I had a great childhood."

"Really?" His tone didn't suggest he believed her.

"Really," she assured him, and then noted his still doubtful expression and sighed. "I know there are bad foster parents out there. People just interested in the money they get for it, or predators looking for easy victims, but I was one of the lucky ones. A wonderful pair of foster parents took care of me like I was their own from the time I was about six weeks old, until my teens. After that I lived with a lovely lady named Sue Miller until I finished high school and went off to university at seventeen."

"Seventeen?" He didn't hide his surprise. "Isn't that young for university in Canada?"

"Maybe," CJ allowed, and then gave up staring at her screen and raised her gaze to him. "Yes, all right, it was young. I took summer courses and even a couple of web courses to graduate early so I could move to campus and start university."

"Why? To get away from this Mrs. Miller?"

"No. I told you she was lovely and she was. Besides, technically, I was still under Mrs. Miller's care until I was eighteen."

"But you no longer lived with her," he said slowly.

"I visited on weekends about once a month, though," CJ told him.

"Only once a month?" he asked. "Did you not get along with the other kids?"

CJ wrinkled her nose with irritation at the question. The man was nosy and annoying, but after a couple of moments of his expectant silence, she gave in and said, "I got along fine with the other kids. In fact, I'm still friends with three of them all these years later. I just . . ." She hesitated briefly, and then admitted, "I wanted my independence. I already planned to be a police officer, had researched and found out what I had to do education-wise to become one, and just wanted to get it done with and start my career."

"Ah." Mac nodded with an understanding smile. "Once I knew what I wanted to do I was eager to get the education part done and move on to the actual doing as quickly as possible too."

"You started as a physician and switched to hematology," she remembered, and then raised her eyebrows. "That's a jump in profession."

"Not really," he assured her. "As a physician I tried to work out what was wrong with patients to heal them. As a hematologist I do the same, but just work more specifically with blood to try to heal people." He pursed his lips briefly in thought, and then said, "When you think about it, both professions involve a certain amount of detective work too."

CJ didn't agree, instead asking, "But why would you switch out to hematology of all things? I mean, blood is . . ." She paused and shuddered as she made a face to show that she found it gross herself.

Mac chuckled at her antics and argued, "Blood is fascinating: the viscosity, shear rate, tissue perfusion. It's all . . ."

He paused, searching for the right word to describe something when she hadn't understood much of what he'd already mentioned, and CJ interrupted with, "All right, Dexter, I get the idea. You're into blood."

"Dexter?" he asked blankly.

CJ tilted her head and eyed him with disbelief.

"Surely you know who Dexter is? The forensic guy who specialized in blood splatter?" When he continued to stare at her blankly, she added, "He was a serial killer on TV?" When that got no response, she tsked with exasperation. "I thought everyone in the world either watched or at least had heard of that show. Although it ended back in 2013 or something, and you were probably ten back then and not allowed to watch it," she added dryly, her gaze sliding over his facial features. The man had skin as pure as a four-year-old girl's. The pores were nonexistent. She'd originally thought he was probably around twenty-five, but she was now reassessing that.

"I am much older than I look," Mac said, sounding a touch irritated. "I have two doctorates, for heaven's sake. That takes a lot of schooling. Speaking of which," he added before she could respond. "I need to call Bastien."

CJ had no idea who Bastien was or what Mac's doctorates had to do with the man, but waited with interest to see what would follow.

"My phone's back at the house," he pointed out when she just stared at him.

"It's probably ruined, then," she said mildly.

"Yes," he agreed unhappily, and then glanced around

the room, presumably in search of a landline. But there wasn't one. She wasn't at all surprised when he asked, "May I borrow your cell phone?"

The words had barely left his mouth before his eyes dropped to the phone she was already holding out.

"Oh. Thanks." He accepted it with a smile and then stood and started toward the open double doors to the bedroom of the suite. At the threshold, he paused to explain, "I'm just going to make the call in here. I'll be quick."

"Take your time," CJ said easily, her focus already on her computer as she closed her emails and opened Google instead. She had a pretty good memory and remembered pretty much everything Mac had told her back at the fire. She might as well check out what she could while stuck guarding the man, she thought, and typed in "Argentis Inc."

While CJ had never heard the name before Mac had spoken it, there were several companies with Argentis in the title and it took her a minute to find the one she wanted. At least she thought it was the one she wanted. It had offices around the world, including Toronto, New York, and Europe, and seemed to be the mother company of a bunch of different enterprises: blood banks, courier services, transportation, construction, scientific exploration . . .

Good Lord, it was very diversified, she thought as she scrolled through the website. There wasn't really very much to see at the site though. Any time she clicked on one of the sublevels on the menu, a box popped up asking for a membership number, and then said if you didn't have membership to click here to enroll. Not wanting to enroll, she went to the bottom of the first page and clicked on the contact tab, then quickly wrote down the number to call in New York for information. She'd have to call and ask about Mac and his working history and so on. It wasn't really her job. Simpson should be doing this, but she suspected he was probably sound asleep in his bed right now, and judging by his less than stellar performance at the fire tonight, she wasn't counting on his following up on gathering information on Mac himself tomorrow.

That thought had her next typing "Macon Argeneau" into the search engine, but nothing much of interest came up there, just Macon, Georgia, and some fiction series that she'd never heard of that was apparently about a family named Argeneau. Next, she tried "Macon Argeneau, Hematologist," and got a lot of hits for various hematology centers, so she started to go through the listings in case his name was farther down on the list of headings that popped up.

Six

"Yes, Bastien, I said fire. The house I just moved into burned down. The whole place went up in flames. And that would have included me if I hadn't filled the tub with water and submerged myself until the firemen could get me out," he announced, still a little shaken at how close he had come to becoming one dead immortal.

"And you are sure the fire was deliberate?" his cousin asked, concern in his voice.

"Yes. I read from the minds of a couple of the firemen while I fed off of them and I gather they think gasoline was splashed around the house and poured through the mail slot of the front door," he said grimly.

"You fed off the hoof?" Bastien snapped with alarm.

"I did not have much choice," Mac said stiffly. "My

blood supply went up with everything else in the fire and the situation was desperate. I was boiled alive, Bastien," he announced grimly. "It was a most unpleasant experience and left my skin a mottled mess of pussy blisters and—" He broke off, not wishing to recall the shape he'd been in when they'd finally dragged him out of the tub of boiling water and carried him from the house. He'd been conscious when they'd entered the bathroom, spraying their icy water everywhere. Mac had leapt to stand in the tub the moment the nearby flames were extinguished. But that was as far as he'd got before he'd started to lose consciousness.

Fortunately, two of the firemen had reached him before he'd passed out and fallen back into the boiling water in the tub. The pain their grasp on his blistered parboiled arms had caused had pushed him briefly back to full consciousness and he'd roared in pain and then the world had gone black.

"I fed from every one of the couple of dozen firemen there and it wasn't enough to fully heal me," he finished, rather than further describe the state he'd been in.

"All right. I get it. It was an emergency situation," Bastien said suddenly, drawing Mac's thoughts back to the conversation he was having with his cousin and the head of Argentis Inc.

"Yes," Mac breathed unhappily.

"Are you all right now?" Bastien asked after a hesitation that told Mac it was only one of many questions the man had and he'd had to take a moment to prioritize them in his mind.

"A little low on blood still," Mac admitted. "And not completely healed, but well enough I look fine on the outside. At least where my clothes aren't covering me."

"Right. I'll have blood delivered to you right away. It should be there in an hour or so depending on how far you are from the nearest Argeneau blood bank."

Mac licked his lips at the thought of it, but then breathed out with frustration and said, "That might be a problem."

"Why?"

"Because . . ." He paused and turned to look toward the closed French doors to the salon, before continuing the turn until he was facing the window in the room. Walking to it, he checked to see that it would open, winced when it squealed in protest, and let it ease back down. He wasn't surprised when there was a knock at the bedroom door and CJ asked, "Mac? Are you all right?"

"Fine," he assured her. "I was just checking that the window locks."

There was a moment of silence, and then she said, "Okay," and he heard her footsteps move away.

"Who was that?" Bastien asked in his ear.

Mac sank to sit on the window ledge and admitted, "The problem. Her name is CJ Cummings. She's a detective with the SIU in Mississauga. She was helping collect evidence at the fire and got roped into guarding me for the night. She's presently in the next room, between me and the suite's exit, and I can't read or control her. It will be impossible for me to get out of the room and meet with the courier."

Bastien blew a soft whistle down the line. "You have met your life mate."

"Yes," Mac breathed, a soft smile struggling to spread his lips.

"Did Mom suggest you rent a house in Sandford?"

Mac frowned at the odd question. "What? No. She suggested I look for a house or cottage on Pelee Island," he answered. "Why would you ask that?"

"Oh, it is just that she has a tendency to hook up immortals with their life mates lately, and I wondered— Never mind," he interrupted himself. "Obviously she had nothing to do with it this time."

"No. She didn't," Mac assured him.

"Right," Bastien murmured. "I am guessing you have not told this CJ Cummings about us?"

"Hell, no!" he said with exasperation. "That's not something you spring on a woman on first meeting,

Bastien. I need to gain her trust and interest before I even broach that subject."

"Yes. Of course. Well, do not worry. I shall make sure to send an immortal with the blood delivery. He can control Ms. Cummings for you so that we can get you the blood you need. And I will call Uncle Lucian and apprise him of the situation. He shall no doubt have Mortimer send a couple of Enforcers down to investigate and sort out who tried to kill you."

Mac grunted at that. Mortimer was the head of the Immortal Enforcers, basically the police for his people. They were a necessary group. Mortal police certainly couldn't manage their kind and ensure they followed immortal or even mortal law. Mac's kind called themselves immortals, but most of humankind who did not carry the nanos that kept them alive and well and unaging would call them vampires. They certainly resembled the vampires of lore. They didn't age, didn't grow ill, were extraordinarily strong, fast, and able to see well in the dark. They also could read the minds of, and control, mortals and even immortals younger than themselves . . . and they needed more blood than their bodies could provide to satisfy the nanos that worked so hard for them. That meant feeding off of mortals with the fangs the nanos had given them. At least it had before the development of blood banks. Now they were supposed to feed only from bagged blood except in an emergency like the one he'd encountered tonight. But their depending on bagged blood, and the nanos behind their extraordinary abilities, were the only real difference between immortals and vampires . . . and the fact that they were all alive. They were not the dead soulless creatures of myth. Merely enhanced humans, really.

"Is there anything else you need?"

Mac pushed his thoughts away and shook his head. Then, realizing the other man couldn't see it, he said, "No. Thank you. I— Wait, I need clothes and a tooth-brush, hairbrush, a razor. Basically, I need everything, and I'd buy it all myself but all my ID and credit cards went up in the fire."

"I'll take care of it and get you new ID and bank cards," Bastien assured him.

"Thank you," Mac said sincerely, and then cleared his throat before approaching work matters. "I'm afraid this will set my work back a bit. It will take some time to find another house and arrange for new lab equip-ment and such."

"You might as well leave that until you sort out this life mate business," Bastien suggested.

"What?" Mac said with surprise. "Why?"

"Because if you are able to claim your Ms. Cummings

as a life mate, you might wish to live in Mississauga. It's where you said she was from," he pointed out. "There's no sense setting up a lab there, just to have to set up another one in Mississauga."

"Oh. Yes," Mac agreed thoughtfully.

"So, I'll just consider you on temporary leave until you sort out your personal life," Bastien said now.

"All right," Mac said quietly, and felt weird doing so. He hadn't taken leave in a long time. A very long time. He didn't even take vacations. It wasn't because he needed the money; he had more than enough to last several mortal lifetimes. The truth was, while he technically worked for Argentis Inc., he had a lot of freedom. He worked when and how he liked, but he'd made work his whole life the last several centuries. It was the only thing that had interested him, and he couldn't even imagine what it would be like not to be tinkering about in his lab with his experiments. It was definitely going to be interesting.

Distracted with these thoughts, Mac was only half-aware of Bastien's words as he said he'd call later to check on him and said goodbye. It was the absolute silence in his ear that made him finally pull the phone away and look at it to see that the call had been ended.

Grunting at the realization, he stood and then turned to peer out the window. It faced the front yard and the street beyond, but there wasn't much to see at this hour. Just the other houses on the block. They were all dark. Everyone was asleep, and the street was empty, with not a car in sight. At least not a moving one. He briefly considered closing the curtain, but left it open in the end and went back out into the sitting area of the suite.

"**All done?**" CJ asked when Mac came back into the room.

"Yes. Thanks." He set the phone on the table next to her hand and then settled into his chair again. "It was long distance, so I'll give you some money when I have access to it again."

"No worries," CJ assured him solemnly. "Family is important."

He appeared a bit confused, but murmured, "Yes. Family is important."

CJ tilted her head and eyed him briefly. He didn't seem sure why she'd said that, so she asked, "That's who you called, right? Bastien is your father and you called him and your sister so they wouldn't worry if they saw the story about the fire on the news."

"Oh." He looked blank-faced now, and then shook his head slowly.

"No?" she asked with surprise.

"No. Bastien is my boss," he explained. "He's also

my cousin, so I'm sure he will let my father know what is happening here. Or really, I suppose, my uncle Lucian will probably be the one to do that," he added almost thoughtfully.

CJ stared at him with disbelief. "Don't you think your family would want to hear about it from you rather than another relative? Just so they can talk to you and find out for themselves that you're really okay?" She might not have a family now, but she did remember what it had been like with Marge and Johnathan Cummings. They would have wanted to talk to her themselves after hearing she'd been caught in a fire, and wouldn't have stopped fretting until they had. But then she realized—

"Oh, I suppose you didn't want to wake them up at this hour, and plan to call them in the morning." Which wasn't far off, she thought as she noted it was closing on 4 A.M.

"No, my calling wouldn't have woken them," Mac said with a faint smile. "They're night owls like me. My whole family works nights. I just figure Bastien will give them the necessary information and— Who are you calling?" he interrupted himself to ask with surprise when she picked up her phone with an exasperated tsk and started to punch in one of the phone numbers she'd written on a notepad on the table next to her computer.

"Your sister," she answered abruptly as she finished entering the numbers for the Port Henry Police Station and heard the first ring. She'd planned to wait until morning to call Mac's sister and verify he was who he claimed to be, but if the woman worked nights—

CJ's thoughts died as the phone was answered and a professional-sounding female voice answered. "Port Henry Police Station. How can I help you?"

"May I speak to Katricia Argeneau—" she glanced to the paper and finished "—Brunswick?"

"Speaking," the woman on the other end of the phone said, sounding curious now.

"Why are you calling my sister?" Mac asked with amazement before she could say anything.

CJ waved him to silence, but the woman had obviously heard Mac speak, and recognized his voice, because she said, "Is that Mac I heard?"

"Yes, it is, Ms. Brunswick," CJ answered in her best professional voice even as she scowled to keep him from speaking again. "It's him I'm actually calling about. He is your brother?"

"Yes," the woman said at once.

"And he lives at—" She read the address of the farmhouse from her notepad. CJ had copied it from the piece of paper Captain Dupree had given her.

"I'm not sure," the woman admitted slowly. "I

know he rented a house in Sandford, but I don't have the address with me at the moment. That sounds right though."

"And he worked in New York previous to this, for ten years or so?" CJ asked, noting the way Mac's eyebrows rose as he realized she was verifying the information he'd given her.

"Yes. At Argentis Inc.," Katricia Argeneau Brunswick said, sounding more professional now as she too cottoned on to what CJ was doing. "In fact, he still works for the company. He simply moved to Canada and will work for them from here."

CJ took a moment to think if there was anything else she needed to verify, but while there were loads of things she'd like to ask, none of them were really pertinent to the case of his house being burned down.

"Who am I speaking to?" Katricia asked suddenly, and CJ grimaced as she realized she hadn't identified herself.

"I'm sorry," she apologized politely. "My name is CJ Cummings. I'm an investigator with the SIU." As a police officer, Katricia would know what that was and probably wouldn't like her any more than any other officer usually did, so CJ rushed on to explain, "I came to Sandford to interview an officer here, but got roped into helping at a fire instead. The fire was at your brother's home. He is fine," she added quickly as the woman sucked in a gasp of air. "In fact, I'll pass the phone to him now so that he can reassure you of that himself."

CJ held out the phone to Mac, and then got up and moved to stand by the window and look out at the road as he began to talk to his sister. She was trying to give him privacy, but it was hard not to hear him reassure Katricia that he was fine and explain what had happened.

"Yes, Katricia, she called to verify my information," he said after a moment when his sister apparently spoke. "No, I couldn't," he said, sounding cheerful. Curious, she turned to see that he was grinning and staring right at her while he did.

CJ turned back to the window abruptly, fighting the urge to blush for some reason.

"Yes, she is," Mac said now. "Yes . . . No, I do not need help. No. Really, Kat, I do not want help. Dammit! Sisters," he muttered suddenly with exasperation, and she heard a clatter that made her glance around. He'd tossed her phone back on the table, and was now scowling at it with displeasure. The phone call was apparently over and had not ended the way he would have wanted.

"Problem?" CJ asked mildly, moving back to her seat.

"She has decided she should come here to help," he said with disgust.

CJ's eyebrows rose at this news. "I somehow don't think Captain Dupree will appreciate help with his investigation."

"Not with the investigation, with y—" He stopped abruptly, and then asked, "Why would he not appreciate help? He requested *your* help."

"Only because he lost his detective last month," she responded. "Besides, I suspect that was as much to make it look like he was trying to be cooperative while not really being cooperative at all."

"You told my sister you were here to interview an officer," he recalled.

CJ nodded.

"What about?"

CJ opened her mouth, and then closed it again, and simply shook her head. She couldn't talk about it with him. It was official business.

"Time for bed," she announced abruptly, and grabbed the handle of her rolling suitcase as she stood. "I'll use the bathroom first."

She left him at the table and walked through the bedroom and into the suite's small bathroom, pulling her case behind. The other guests in the house didn't have their own bathroom, but shared a larger one upstairs and another downstairs. Mrs. Vesper called this the honeymoon suite. She had told CJ that it used to be the master bedroom and bath when Mr. Vesper had still been alive, with the bedroom taking up the space that was now both the bedroom and salon. But Mrs. Vesper had given it up for a smaller bedroom when her husband died and then had hired contractors to divide the huge master bedroom into the two still-large rooms. She said it was the best thing she'd ever done and that she had regulars who rented the suite for their anniversaries and special occasions through the year.

CJ was grateful for the setup right now, especially with the bathroom being inside the room since the cot was now up against the door to the rest of the house again. Otherwise, it would have been a bit of a pain if Mac needed to use the facilities while she was sleeping. He would have had to wake her so they could move the cot and so on, but its position was an added safety measure to block the door. It would help keep anyone out and away from Mac, and that's why they were supposed to be there.

Although, in reality, CJ wasn't expecting trouble. If she was, she wouldn't have brought Mac here. She would never willingly put Mrs. Vesper or anyone else in danger. But between the disguise worn out of the police station, and her circling the block a couple times to be sure they weren't followed, CJ was pretty sure no one knew he was here. Tonight. The next night might be a problem, though. She suspected the town's grapevine would spread the news of his survival and whereabouts by then. But she would leave that problem in Captain Dupree's hands. In fact, she planned to drop it in his lap the minute they reached the police station the next day. And then she would make sure the captain kept to his promise to arrange the meeting with Jefferson. She'd definitely gone above and beyond the call of duty tonight in helping him out, and she expected a little payback for it. If he didn't arrange the meeting with Jefferson as he'd promised, she would be calling her boss and letting him bring the hammer down.

Knowing she wouldn't be able to sleep if she started fretting about that, CJ pushed those thoughts from her mind as she prepared for bed. She normally slept in an oversized T-shirt and panties, but tonight she added a pair of joggers to the ensemble. If something did happen, she didn't want to be running around in panties.

It was while she was brushing her teeth that it occurred to her that Mac didn't have a toothbrush . . . or anything else here with him. She briefly considered making a run to a local drugstore, but then shook the thought away. First, she didn't know if there was a twenty-four-hour drugstore in the small town, and second, it was just too damned late to be bothered. She'd offer him the use of her mouthwash and hairbrush, and they'd get whatever he needed in the morning, she decided, and finished her nightly ritual of cleaning her face and brushing her teeth. CJ then closed her suitcase and headed back out, her footsteps faltering when she saw that Mac had moved into the bedroom and was now lounging on the bed with his ankles crossed and his hands under his head.

CJ eyed his relaxed pose briefly, and then cleared her throat and said, "I just realized you don't have a toothbrush or anything else with you. There's nothing we can do about that at the moment, but I left mouthwash and my hairbrush in there for you, and we'll make a run to the drugstore in the morning, and maybe to Walmart for some clothes," she told him as he sat up and slid his legs to the floor to stand. CJ heard his "Thank you" when she finished, but was already hurrying out of the room and pulling the double doors closed between them.

Pausing in the middle of the salon, CJ pressed her free hand to one cheek and closed her eyes. She'd rushed out of there like her butt was on fire, and all because he'd stood up. But the man had the most bizarre effect on her. The moment he'd stood, the room had suddenly felt tiny and hot and he'd seemed much closer than he had been while lying down. Worse yet, she'd wanted to get closer still and had actually started to take a step toward him before she'd caught herself and turned to leave instead, hurrying for the door with a loud alarm ringing in her head.

Damn. She didn't need this complication, and would be glad to be relieved of the man. Why on earth had she offered to take him to Walmart in the morning? The drugstore had been bad enough, but Walmart? Compassion was the answer. Seeing him there stretched out in his pajama bottoms and T-shirt had made her realize those were his only clothes too, and compassion had made her offer to help rectify that.

Shaking her head at her own stupidity, CJ promised herself to can the compassion and think before she spoke in future. Otherwise, she'd never be rid of the man. Tomorrow, after taking him shopping, he would be Captain Dupree's problem and she could concentrate on talking to Jefferson and arrange to meet up with Keith Kaye, the young man who'd launched the complaint against him. Then she'd get the hell out of Sandford and head home and never have to see the man again.

"A good thing," CJ assured herself in a whisper.

Ignoring the disappointment that part of her felt at the very idea, she set her suitcase aside, made sure the cot was right up against the suite door, and climbed in. The old mattress wasn't as uncomfortable as CJ had feared, and much to her surprise she was soon drifting off to sleep.

Seven

It was a child's laughter that woke CJ in the morning. The high, light sound was followed by a soft shushing and a deep voice admonishing the child to be quiet or she'd wake up the other guests.

It was too late to prevent that. CJ opened her eyes to glance around the salon. Morning sunlight was pouring through the large window by the table. It was enough to make her cast a quick look at the wall clock, which told her that it was a little after nine o'clock in the morning. CJ almost groaned and rolled over to go back to sleep, but the bang of a screen door closing changed her mind. Tossing the sheet and blanket aside, she got out of bed and then stood there to stretch and yawn before turning in a small circle to consider what to do first.

Normally, she would head straight into the bathroom, but that option was out today. She wasn't willing to try to sneak through the bedroom and risk waking Mac.

Blowing her breath out on a sigh, CJ ignored her body's needs and quickly stripped the small cot, folding the blanket and sheets as she removed each. She then folded the cot itself up into its storage state, retrieved her suitcase, grabbed her keys off the table, and slipped from the room. She had to go to the bathroom badly now, and since she wasn't willing to wake Mac up to do it, she'd have to use one of the other bathrooms in the house.

CJ took the time to lock the bedroom door and then headed down the hall to the other bathroom on this floor. She didn't encounter anyone on the way there, though she could hear the low murmur of voices from somewhere downstairs. Much to her relief the bathroom was empty when she reached it, though there was evidence it had been well-used. Toiletries and several wet towels gave that away.

CJ turned on the water in the shower to let it warm up while she relieved herself, then hopped under the spray and—aware that she was leaving Mac alone and unprotected in her room—took the quickest shower she'd had in her life. Truly, she washed her hair, barely ran soap over her body, rinsed, and got out. She dried even more quickly, and was probably more wet than dry as she slid into clean clothes. That was followed by a swift brushing of her teeth with one hand, while running a hairbrush through her wet tresses with the other, before rinsing her mouth, spitting, and quickly tying her hair back in a ponytail using a scrunchie.

CJ stopped a moment then to consider her reflection in the mirror and moaned aloud. Her skin was pale and splotchy from the hot shower she'd taken, except under her eyes where dark smudges attested to her lack of sleep. Muttering under her breath, she took another moment to apply a bit of concealer under each eye to make herself look less like a raccoon and then paused to stare at herself again.

Some part of CJ wanted to pull out all her makeup and give herself a good going-over—blush, eyeliner, the whole nine yards—but in the end, she merely ran a pale pink lipstick over her lips and called it done. She wasn't trying to impress or attract anyone, so this would do, she lectured herself as she put everything away and left the room, dragging her suitcase behind her.

There was no one in the hall. CJ made her way back to her suite and was unlocking the door before she realized that the murmur of voices below that she'd heard earlier was gone. That made her stop to listen, but then the bedroom door was pulled open and she whirled to see Mac standing there, a questioning expression on his face.

"I heard the key in the door, but it did not open," he explained when she stared at him blankly. "Is your key not working?"

"Oh." CJ gave herself a shake and forced a smile. "No. I just . . ." She waved vaguely along the hall, but stepped inside and closed and locked the door. "I could hear people talking downstairs when I left the room, but just noticed I couldn't hear it anymore on my way back," she explained, and realized that probably made no sense, but he apparently understood.

"Two or three vehicles left a few minutes ago," he told her.

Probably while she was in the shower, CJ reasoned, and relaxed as she looked over Mac. His hair was ruffled and morning stubble covered his cheeks, but while he'd got no more sleep than her, he didn't have dark shadows under his eyes. He did appear pretty pale, though, deathly so in comparison to her, she thought, but he'd been pale since she'd met him. Besides, even pale as death he looked adorable, she acknowledged, and then pushed the thought from her mind.

"Well, I just slipped out to use the bathroom down the hall rather than wake you, so the bathroom here is all yours if you want to take a shower or something.

Then we can we go downstairs for coffee and whatever delight Mrs. Vesper has planned for breakfast."

Mac ran a hand down the dark stubble on his cheeks and made an expression of distaste, but shook his head. "Showering and then putting on these clothes again would be a waste. I will wait on that. But I do need a moment."

"Sure," CJ said agreeably, and watched him retreat to the bedroom and the bathroom beyond.

While she waited, CJ recalled her phone and walked over to pick it up and check it for messages. There were none, but the battery was also low, she noted, and scowled as she realized she'd forgotten to plug it in. Hopefully, she wouldn't have any calls to make, she thought as she slipped it into her purse. Slinging it over her shoulder, she walked to the window and peered out at Mrs. Vesper's front yard. The house was probably built around the same time as the farmhouse Mac had rented . . . maybe a hundred years ago or so. A fancy black wrought iron fence surrounded it, and a two-foot-deep garden filled with flowers of every variety followed the fence all the way around the yard except where the gate was. The flowers weren't separated in any way. It wasn't like there was a patch of roses here and a patch of something else next to it. It was as if Mrs. Vesper had bought twenty different varieties of flower seeds, mixed them in a bowl, and then just sprinkled them around and through the garden. It was something CJ had never seen before. It was beautiful chaos.

"All set."

Turning, CJ smiled faintly at Mac. He looked the same as when he'd left except that his hair was a little smoother and damp in spots. He'd obviously run wet fingers through it to try to tame it. He'd also used her mouthwash, she noted as she joined him to leave the room, and smelled the minty freshness of his breath. That made her realize that she hadn't used mouthwash. She almost turned back to go give her mouth a rinse, but in the end decided she'd brushed and that was good enough.

"There you are!" Mrs. Vesper greeted them cheerfully from her position at the stove as they joined her in the kitchen moments later. "I thought I heard you two moving around upstairs, so I started making your breakfast. And you will eat it, young man," the older woman said firmly, glaring at Mac. "You look ready to faint on us. Sit down."

Much to CJ's surprise, Mac obeyed and sat at once, positioning himself at the opposite end of the table, about as far away as he could get from the older woman and CJ, who had approached her. She'd meant to ask what she could do to help, but instead found herself frowning as she looked Mac over. She'd noted upstairs that he was pale this morning, but now she saw that his hands were balled into fists and his jaw was clenched. Both were signs of either anger or pain in her experience. In this case, she suspected pain.

"Are you all right?" she asked, leaving Mrs. Vesper's side to move toward him.

"Yes, I just—" He lunged out of his seat, backing away from her, as he finished, "I just need some air."

In the next moment, he'd turned on his heel and walked out of the kitchen. CJ followed in time to see him walk out the back door, but when he made a beeline for the police car parked beside her own vehicle, she decided Dandridge could keep an eye on him, and returned to the kitchen to see if Mrs. Vesper needed any help.

"I think that boy is anemic," Mrs. Vesper announced as CJ rejoined her. "That or he didn't get out of the fire as well as we thought. Maybe his lungs were damaged by the smoke and he's not getting enough oxygen."

"Hmm," CJ murmured. "He *is* pale this morning."

"Pale?" Mrs. Vesper gave a bark of laughter. "He's whiter than that bread. Speaking of which, dear. Throw those last four slices in the toaster for me, will you, please? This is almost ready."

CJ moved to the plate of bread in front of a four-slice toaster and did as requested as she said, "I think I'll talk to Dandridge and have him take him into emergency on the way to the police station so they can check him over."

"You aren't taking him in yourself?" Mrs. Vesper didn't hide her surprise.

"No. Really, he's the responsibility of the police now," CJ answered, saying what had only occurred to her moments ago, and then to distract her, asked, "Does Sandford have a hospital, or will Dandridge have to take him to a bigger town?"

"Oh, yes. We've had a hospital since 1951," Mrs. Vesper assured her, and then smiled faintly and explained, "I know that because I was one of the first babies born there and my mother was glad not to have to rely on a midwife or go to the city to have me. She always said the new hospital was finished just in time for my birth."

CJ smiled at this bit of the woman's history, and then picked up the butter knife Mrs. Vesper had left next to the plate and began to butter the toast when it popped.

"Perfect timing," Mrs. Vesper crowed, bustling to a cupboard next to the sink to fetch a large bowl. Returning to the stove she set the bowl down, and began to shift the scrambled eggs she'd been cooking into it from the frying pan. She carried the pale-yellow mixture to the table while CJ finished buttering the toast, and then returned and opened the stove to retrieve bacon and hash browns that she transferred to the table as well before returning to open the stove yet again.

"Just put those on here, dear," Mrs. Vesper instructed as CJ finished buttering the last slice.

CJ glanced over to see that she'd retrieved a plate already stacked high with buttered toast from the oven where it had been keeping warm.

"Good heavens, Mrs. Vesper!" she said with amazement as she transferred the new toast to the stack the older woman held. "We won't eat all this toast."

"Well, then I'll make French toast tomorrow morning out of whatever's left over," she said complacently. "Now go tell that young man that breakfast is ready. Maybe we can put some color into his cheeks."

Mac withdrew his fangs from Officer Dandridge's neck and straightened in the passenger seat the moment he heard the squeak of Mrs. Vesper's porch door opening. He remained facing the man, though, as he quickly wiped his mouth to be sure there was no blood on it, and released the police officer from his control. Only then did he turn to peer out the car window to see CJ crossing the porch to the steps. She stopped, though, when she saw him look, and waved him over, calling, "Breakfast is ready."

"Coming," Mac called out, then glanced back to Dandridge and rearranged the man's thoughts so he'd think they'd been discussing the house fire and the captain's plans for him. Mac then got out of the car and made his way to the porch.

"Well, Mrs. Vesper will be relieved," CJ said with a faint smile, stepping back as he mounted the porch stairs.

Mac raised his eyebrows as he stepped up next to her. "About what?"

"You looked ready to drop dead on us when you left the kitchen. Now you have a little color in your cheeks," she explained, turning to lead him to the door.

"Oh. I just needed fresh air," he lied, following. The truth was, he'd needed blood. Badly. Mac hadn't slept a wink after CJ had gone to bed last night. Instead, he'd paced the room, his gaze moving repeatedly to the window in the hopes of seeing a vehicle approaching. But the courier Bastien had promised would be there in an hour or two had not shown up.

By the time Mac had heard CJ slip out of the room this morning, he'd been desperate for blood and in pain with it. Just having her back in the room with him had been torture, but being in the kitchen with both women had been worse. He'd known he wouldn't last long without snapping and feeding on the pair of them. Not willing to risk that, he'd headed outside to feed on Officer Dandridge instead, and didn't regret it a bit. Mac hadn't taken a lot of blood, just enough to tide him over and make him less dangerous to be around. Aside from which, this was still an emergency situation since his courier hadn't shown up.

That thought made him wonder where the hell the man was. Bastien would not have forgotten to arrange a delivery. It would have been a priority. Leaving an immortal without blood when he was healing from something like what Mac had gone through was just not an option. It was too risky. The injured immortal might run amok and attack someone, drawing attention to the presence of their kind in the world, and that was something they avoided at all costs.

"It smells delicious, Mrs. Vesper."

Mac looked around at CJ's words as they entered the kitchen and inhaled deeply. While he was sure CJ was referring to the odors of cooked food in the air, all he smelled was blood with an undertone of bacon. Obviously, he hadn't had enough blood, Mac realized unhappily, and looked around for CJ's purse. Spotting it on the counter, he started toward it, asking, "CJ, can I use your phone again? I need to call Bastien and check on the arrival time of that courier he was going to send. He should have been here by now and I am beginning to worry that he may have had a misadventure."

"You can use the house phone," Mrs. Vesper offered, and then added, "After you eat."

Mac turned to face the older woman with surprise. "But—"

"After you eat, young man," Mrs. Vesper said firmly, carrying coffees to the table. "I did not go to all the trouble of cooking this food so that you could let it go cold while you yap on the phone. The courier will get here when he gets here. Now sit down and eat."

Mac nearly took control of Mrs. Vesper and made his call anyway. The problem was, he couldn't control CJ and she would consider the older lady's sudden about-face odd at best. Besides, Mrs. Vesper reminded him so much of his mother in that moment that he couldn't help but smile. He hadn't been a child for well over a thousand years, but that didn't stop his mother, Mary Delacort, from treating him like a ten-year-old when she felt the occasion called for it. Biting back his smile, Mac settled at the table. He could control himself for the length of time it would take to eat. He hoped.

"Well, dig in," Mrs. Vesper said happily once they were all seated.

Mac began scooping food onto his plate, taking a

healthy portion from each offering despite being unsure whether he would enjoy it. He was hungry, which was a new experience for him. Mac hadn't eaten in more than a millennia before the cookies he'd had last night, not even at family parties and such where most immortals ate out of politeness. Food simply hadn't held any appeal for him. Not until now. But then that was one of the signs of meeting a life mate: a sudden hunger for pleasures that had not tempted the immortal in ages, food and sex being the two most notable among them.

"This is very good, Mrs. Vesper. Thank you," CJ said suddenly, and then added with concern, "I hope you didn't have to cook twice. First for the others and now for us."

"No, no. They were going to a special wedding party breakfast after the rehearsal so I didn't have to cook for the others at all," Mrs. Vesper assured her. "A bit of coffee and they were off."

"Isn't it usually a rehearsal dinner the night before?" CJ asked with surprise.

"Yes, but since most of their wedding party wouldn't be arriving until late last night, they arranged it for breakfast this morning," Mrs. Vesper explained. "Fortunately, the church was available for an early rehearsal, and the wedding is late afternoon, so they planned a fifteen-minute to half-hour rehearsal, followed by breakfast, and then the girls are heading to the local spa for manicures, pedicures, and to get their hair and make-up done, and so on. No doubt they'll be there right up until it's time to dress for the wedding."

"And what will the men be doing?" CJ asked.

"Why, golfing, of course," Mrs. Vesper said with amusement, and both women laughed, although Mac noted that the tone of their laughter was rather dry. He supposed it had to do with the fact that the women would spend the better part of the day having to primp for their roles in the wedding, while the men would relax on the golf course, probably having a couple of beers along the way, and then spend ten minutes in the shower, shave again if they had five-o'clock shadow, and then dress and head for the church.

It did seem unfair sometimes that women were expected to do so much to be considered attractive while men pretty much just had to show up. At least that's what his sisters told Mac. He'd always responded that if they didn't like it, then women could simply stop all the added primping. Since that usually resulted in one of them throwing something at him, he supposed he shouldn't share that thought with CJ and Mrs. Vesper. He also supposed he shouldn't share that, to his mind, the men would have the better day. He didn't expect that would please them much either, so he simply concentrated on the food on his plate. It was all really delicious, an explosion of different tastes on his tongue that made him wonder why he'd lost interest in food for so long.

"I suppose what with helping out with the fire and all that you didn't get to interview Officer Jefferson?"

Mac stopped eating and glanced up sharply at that question from Mrs. Vesper, his eyes sliding between the two women as CJ turned a startled gaze on the older woman.

"How did you know I was here to interview Officer Jefferson?" CJ asked with surprise.

"My friend Amelia Fairly is also friends with Audrey Dupree," she explained. "And for weeks now Audrey has been complaining to anyone who would listen about—as she put it—*some upstart agent from the Special Investigation Unit wanting to grill poor Jefferson over that little incident with that young ruffian Keith Kaye.* So, when you said you work for the Special Investigation Unit, I knew it must be you."

"Is Keith Kaye a ruffian?" CJ queried.

Mrs. Vesper considered the question seriously. "According to Audrey, Jefferson says he is and that he's always up to no good. But no one else has said anything of the like that I know of."

"I see," CJ murmured, and picked up her coffee for a sip, her expression thoughtful.

"So?" Mrs. Vesper prodded as CJ set her coffee cup back down. "Were you able to interview him or will you be staying another night?"

Mac watched as CJ struggled briefly with her conscience, but finally she sighed and admitted, "No. I wasn't able to speak to him last night. When I got to the police station he was supposedly at the fire, which is what Captain Dupree used to convince me to go help out there. He suggested I could ask him questions while I assisted in evidence collection. Which—" she added grimly "—would have been next to impossible if I didn't want to risk missing evidence." CJ shrugged. "But it didn't matter anyway since he'd left the site by the time I got there."

"Why are you investigating him?" Mac asked with curiosity.

CJ's gaze shifted from Mrs. Vesper to him and she frowned. He was positive she was too professional to answer, so wasn't surprised when she started to shake her head.

The moment she did, though, Mrs. Vesper explained, "Because a month back Officer Jefferson beat the hell out of Keith and put him in the hospital with a broken arm and whatnot. Jefferson says Keith was resisting arrest and got injured in the struggle to subdue him. But Keith says Jefferson pulled him over for no reason and just went off on him and started beating him up when he challenged him about pulling him over without cause. He lodged a complaint, and said he had a witness who could back up his version of the story."

Mac ignored the frown CJ was casting Mrs. Vesper and raised his eyebrows. "A month ago? And it took this long for the SIU to send someone here to investigate?"

"The complaint only crossed my boss's desk two weeks ago," CJ explained, turning her frown on him now at the implied criticism.

"Hmm," Mrs. Vesper grunted, and then told them, "Keith lodged a complaint with the captain first, but when the boy realized the captain wouldn't do anything about it, he did some research, found out about the Special Investigation Unit, and sent his complaint to them."

"Did he?" CJ murmured with interest, and judging by her expression, the fact that the captain hadn't passed on the complaint was a bad thing.

When Mrs. Vesper nodded in response to her question, CJ frowned.

"So, your boss assigned it to you two weeks ago and

you are just now getting around to speaking to him?" Mac had no doubt the question would piss her off, but he also knew the truth of the matter. However, he knew it from reading both Mrs. Dupree's and Simpson's minds, and he wanted her to say it out loud because she would never believe that Simpson had told him all of what he already knew. He didn't want to slip up later and say something in conversation that might have her questioning the source of his knowledge.

"He assigned it to me and I called and talked to Keith Kaye right away to set up an appointment," she assured him grimly. "But Keith ended up telling me his version of events over the phone. I still plan to see him in person, but it isn't really necessary until I talk to Jefferson," she explained. "Only Officer Jefferson wouldn't even take my calls when I phoned his cell. When I called his home, his wife always answered and claimed he was out, and I wasn't getting anywhere with the police station either. I would call and they'd say he was unavailable."

CJ heaved out an irritated breath just at the memory of the runaround she'd been given, and then said, "In the end, I resorted to calling Dupree, but it didn't get much better. He hemmed and hawed and put off setting up an appointment at first. When he finally agreed to one, it was canceled the day before, rescheduled, and then canceled again. I had to resort to threats at that point to make them cooperate."

"What kind of threats?" Mac asked with interest.

"I said that if Officer Jefferson wasn't going to talk to me, I'd just have to base my evaluation of the case solely on Keith Kaye's statement and that wouldn't go well for Jefferson," she told him with a slow, satisfied smile. "That's when last night's appointment was finally set up. I suspect the captain suggested midnight on Friday night in the hopes that I'd refuse and he couldn't be blamed for another delay."

"But you said yes," Mac said with a slow smile of his own.

CJ nodded. "I didn't care when it was. I live alone and am not a partier. It doesn't bother me to work at midnight on a Friday, so I said yes." She shrugged. "Of course, I got here to find Jefferson was out at a fire, and then got to the fire to find he'd left for another call, so I still haven't had the interview."

"What are you going to do?" Mac asked at once.

"What do you mean?"

"Well, I know you probably have a plan. You are not just going to return home and try calling to arrange another appointment and go through that nonsense again."

CJ smiled faintly at his certainty, but nodded. "You're right. I'm not."

"So? What are you going to do?"

CJ hesitated, but then admitted, "I got the captain to agree to make Jefferson available for a 3 P.M. meeting today. But I found out Jefferson's work schedule from Simpson, so if the captain and Jefferson find a way to weasel out of this afternoon's appointment, I'm going to follow him around and hound Jefferson until he speaks to me."

Mac's eyebrows rose. "The kid just told you Jefferson's shifts?"

"Well, I didn't ask him outright," she admitted. "I asked if he and Jefferson are always partnered up, and he said not always, they usually ride alone. But they worked the same shifts, so if partners were needed, they were often put together."

"And then you asked Simpson what his hours were," Mac guessed with amusement.

CJ nodded. "I left the subject alone for a while, but then, yes, I asked him about his hours—if they were swing shifts, or if he was always on evenings. When the shift would change again and so on." She shrugged. "I'll use that to my advantage if I have to."

Mac nodded, but was thinking he should take control of Jefferson and make the man more cooperative for CJ. His very next thought was that he shouldn't. CJ would no doubt leave town the moment she'd finished her interviews. The longer Jefferson delayed, the longer she would stay, and Mac wanted her to stay. He couldn't woo her if she wasn't here . . . unless he followed her back to Mississauga or wherever she lived.

His thoughts were distracted when the sound of an engine caught his ear and movement outside the kitchen window over the sink caught his eye. That window overlooked the driveway that ran along the side of the house, and the movement that had drawn his attention was a large RV . . . one he recognized by the design on the side. Mac was on his feet at once.

"What on earth is that?" Mrs. Vesper gasped with surprise as she too looked out the window.

"My delivery," Mac announced to reassure the women as he headed out of the kitchen.

Eight

By the time he stepped out onto Mrs. Vesper's back porch Mac's tongue was practically tingling at the thought of the blood he hoped to soon be consuming. He watched as the RV lumbered into view and parked next to the police car. It now completely blocked Dandridge's view of the house, he noted, and wasn't surprised to hear the man shout out an angry protest from the other side of the large vehicle.

"That is not a courier truck."

Mac had been about to start down the porch steps to approach the RV, but paused when CJ suddenly spoke and gripped his arm to stop him. Tamping down at the impatience that wanted to claim him, he turned to offer what he hoped was a reassuring smile. "No. That's my aunt and uncle's RV. They must have offered to bring me what I needed, which explains why it's taken so long," he added dryly. "My aunt is late to everything."

"I resent that, Macon Argeneau."

He and CJ both turned to stare at the woman standing in the now open side door of the RV. With long auburn hair, and a wide smile, Marguerite was beautiful, even with a stomach big enough that she could have had a beach ball under the pale blue sundress she was wearing, Mac thought with amusement as the woman waited for the RV steps to finish dropping into place and then gingerly descended them.

"The only reason it has taken so long to get here is because you did not bother to tell Bastien the address you were at, and the phone you called from showed Private Caller so he couldn't call back to get the address from you," the very pregnant woman announced with a hint of exasperation as she crossed the backyard to the stairs. "Julius and I have been hanging about for hours while Bastien tried to sort out where you were. It was not until we went to the police station here in Sandford that we were able to find out that you were at the local bed-and-breakfast and get the address."

"Marguerite?"

Mac had opened his mouth to respond to his aunt, but stopped and turned sharply to CJ when she said her name. He hadn't introduced them yet, or mentioned her name. Yet, CJ apparently knew it, and judging by the growing pleasure on her face, she knew her personally as well.

"Why, CJ Cummings," Marguerite said now, beaming at the younger woman and hurrying awkwardly up the stairs to hug her. "How delightful to find you here." Pulling back, she then grinned at Mac as she admitted, "Although I had a feeling we'd meet here in Sandford."

Mac's gaze immediately narrowed on his aunt.

"Why would you think we'd meet here?" CJ asked with obvious surprise. "I live in Mississauga and told you that when we were on Pelee Island."

"Ah," Mac breathed as his conversation with his cousin, Bastien, ran through his mind. *"Did Mom suggest you rent a house in Sandford?" "What? No. She suggested I look for a house or cottage on Pelee Island,"* he'd answered with surprise, and then had asked, *"Why would you ask that?" "Oh, it is just that she has a tendency to hook up immortals with their life mates lately, and I wondered— Never mind,"* Bastien had interrupted himself. *"Obviously she had nothing to do with it this time."*

After Marguerite's suggestion, Mac had actually looked into Pelee Island as a possible home base. But it was much farther away from his father and sister, and necessitated a boat ride in the summer, or a plane ride in the winter when the lake was frozen and unpassable. Aside from that, though, everything would have had to be flown out to him in the winter, which had seemed somewhat inconvenient, not to mention expensive, since he received almost daily deliveries of items needed for his experiments.

Marguerite distracted him from his thoughts when she answered CJ's question with, "Because you have been on my mind a good deal this morning. That usually means I'll see the person soon, and since I plan to be here for a while, that would mean I'd see you here."

"Oh," CJ laughed at her words. "I have a friend who's like that with money. Well, not like that exactly. She swears that any time she has trouble sleeping, a check shows up in the mail the next day."

"Well, then, for her insomnia pays," Marguerite said, and both women laughed.

"Well, goodness, I guess I'd best put on more coffee."

Mac glanced around at that comment from Mrs. Vesper to see that she had joined them on the porch, but it was CJ who held out a hand to the woman and waved her forward, saying, "Oh, no, Mrs. Vesper. First come and meet Marguerite. Marguerite, this is Millie Vesper. Mrs. Vesper this is Marguerite Notte. I met her and her husband—" Head swinging back, she asked, "Julius is here too?"

"Yes. He and the boys went around to talk to that nice officer in the police car about where to move the RV to. I gather it's blocking his view," Marguerite explained, but Mac noted that her gaze was focused on Mrs. Vesper with great interest. Perhaps that's why he wasn't overly surprised when she said, "My goodness, Millie, you have interesting energy about you. It makes me think of someone else I know."

"Marguerite Argeneau Notte, I told you to wait for me to escort you."

Mac glanced toward the RV in time to see Julius Notte rushing toward them around the front of the vehicle with Justin Bricker and Mac's cousin Decker Argeneau Pimms on his heels. He also noticed that, while Marguerite's husband's voice might have sounded sharp, his expression was pure anxiety.

"I'm fine, it's fine," Marguerite said breezily, waving away his worry.

"It is not fine, my love," Julius countered at once, his voice an odd combination of exasperation and affection. "What if you had fallen or—"

"Darling, I'm pregnant, not crippled," Marguerite said with a laugh, sliding her hand through the man's arm as he reached her. "You worry too much."

"You make me worry too much," Julius countered, retrieving his arm from her hold to slide it around her waist and press her to his side. "You are none too steady on your feet lately."

"Are you saying I'm clumsy?" Marguerite asked with affront.

"No," he assured her. "I am saying you are simply not used to this new distribution of weight you are having to deal with."

"So, you're saying I'm fat," Marguerite suggested, eyes narrowing.

"No, no, I would never," he said at once, his expression becoming alarmed. "You are not fat, my love."

"I am so fat," Marguerite argued unhappily. "I'm big as a barn."

"*Si*, but with my child and I love you for it," Julius argued at once, and seemed to realize his mistake at once when Marguerite's eyes narrowed on him. "I mean, no. Not as big as a barn, my love. Just round like ripe fruit."

"Round?" Marguerite asked with dismay.

"Lush, I meant lush," he backtracked quickly.

"Give it up, Julius," CJ said on a laugh. "You're just digging yourself a deeper hole."

Julius Notte turned to blink at CJ and then smiled widely in greeting. "CJ Cummings!"

Mac watched with amazement as CJ's face bloomed with a wide, joyful smile that turned her from simply attractive to stunning, and then Julius stepped forward to give her a quick hug of greeting and Mac scowled. He wanted to slap the man's hands off of her and push him away, but Justin Bricker distracted him by saying, "Marguerite, I thought I heard you say this lovely lady's energy reminds you of someone else as we came around the RV? Did I hear that right?"

At Bricker's question, Marguerite turned to peer at Mrs. Vesper again and smiled faintly. "Yes, you did, and she does."

"Huh," he said dryly. "Then yet another one bites the dust."

"Another two," Decker corrected.

"*Si*, you must include Mac," Julius pointed out as he released CJ.

"Yeah," Bricker said with a grin. "We drop like flies around Marguerite."

The men all grunted agreement at that.

"I'm sorry, am I missing something? Who's biting the dust?" CJ glanced around the group with confusion.

"No one," Mac said quickly.

"It's just a family joke," Decker added, and then his attention shifted to Mac and he raised his eyebrows. "We have the things you requested in the RV for you if you'd like to go take a look."

Knowing the things Decker was referring to were clothes, credit cards, ID and—most importantly—blood, Mac nodded.

"We'll be in the RV," Decker announced as he turned to lead the way toward the large vehicle.

Mac didn't follow right away, but glanced to Julius instead, to find the man hesitating, his gaze sliding from Marguerite to the RV. He obviously wanted to go too, but was torn at the idea of leaving his very pregnant wife. Fortunately, CJ waved him off, saying, "Go on. I'll keep an eye on Marguerite."

"I'm not a child," Marguerite said with exasperation. "No one needs to keep an eye on me."

Ignoring his wife, Julius murmured, "Thank you, CJ," and joined Mac to follow Decker and Bricker to the RV.

"My goodness, that husband of yours is a considerate fellow," Mac heard Mrs. Vesper say as they walked away.

"Yes," Marguerite said. "And handsome too."

"My dear, all of them are handsome," Mrs. Vesper said with a delighted laugh that made Mac smile. He liked the lady. So much so that she was part of the reason he'd settled on Sandford as the place to live. If Marguerite thought she might be a life mate to one of their kind, it would be a fine thing in his book.

"So, someone set your new house on fire," Julius commented as they entered the RV and closed the door behind them. "Who have you pissed off this century?"

Mac gave a faint laugh and shook his head. "That was one of CJ's first questions too."

"Your life mate?" Julius asked, and then answered the question for himself. "Yes. Definitely your life mate. You are older than me by a good five hundred years, and I have never been able to read you. Yet right now I can read you as easily as young Justin here."

"So can I," Decker announced cheerfully.

"I can read you too," Justin Bricker added.

Mac stiffened at this news. Old as he was, there were few immortals who could read him. Knowing that all three men could now do so was more than a little discomfiting.

"But I have to say," Bricker said suddenly, "it's kind of disappointing to be able to read you since all you're thinking about at the moment is blood. Normally new life mates are all about the partner and sex."

"There is no sex to think about yet," Mac said with irritation, and then asked, "Where is the blood?"

"There may not be sex yet, but there should be sexy thoughts running through your head about what you want to do with her, and sex dreams that you should have shared last night. But there's nada. What's up with that?" Turning to Julius, Bricker raised his eyebrows. "Are you sure they're life mates?"

"I did not sleep last night," Mac said irritably, but was now worrying about whether CJ was really his life mate as well. He hadn't had any sort of sexy thoughts about her yet. He thought she was attractive, but he hadn't thought anything like Bricker was suggesting.

"Yes. They are life mates. He simply has not had a chance to get close enough to touch her yet," Julius said slowly, his gaze focused on Mac's forehead as he riffled through his thoughts.

Mac could feel him in there poking around. It too was discomfiting.

"She is keeping you at a distance," Julius said now, and then added, "I am not surprised. She has some issues. I read that from her on Pelee Island when we encountered her there back in May."

"What issues?" Mac asked at once, forgetting about the blood he wanted so desperately.

"That is for you to find out," Julius said solemnly.

"It would be easier if you just told me," Mac snapped, quickly losing his patience. He wasn't getting blood, and he wasn't getting information.

"This is something I think it is better you learn from her," Julius said quietly, heading into the bedroom at the back of the RV. "You might be tempted to use the knowledge as a shortcut to convince her to turn rather than wooing her, and then you would be cheating her, and yourself."

Mac was frowning over that when his uncle reached into what looked like a cupboard, but was obviously a refrigerator made to look like a cupboard, because he pulled out a bag of blood and turned to toss it to him. Mac caught it and slapped it to his already dropping fangs as his uncle turned back to retrieve several more bags of blood. These ones the man carried back and set on the small dining table next to him, then urged him to sit.

"Relax," Julius suggested mildly. "You need at least six bags and then you need a shower. You smell like death."

Mac grimaced around the bag at his mouth, but settled on the seat as the men began to describe their efforts to find him in more detail.

"Mac said his aunt and uncle own the RV." The words slipped out of CJ's mouth as the RV door closed behind the men. Now she turned to Marguerite with confusion, her gaze sliding over the lovely young woman she'd met while relaxing at her cottage on Pelee Island in May. Marguerite Notte and her husband had taken their friend Ildaria to the island for a weeklong get-away before she started summer classes at a university in Toronto. She'd guessed at the time that the trio were in their mid-twenties. That would still be her guess looking at Marguerite now, and surely that was young for them to be Mac's aunt and uncle.

"Mac is my nephew by marriage," Marguerite explained easily. "His father was brother to my first husband, Jean Claude Argeneau. I believe I mentioned the last time we met that my first husband was much older than me," Marguerite reminded her.

CJ nodded slowly. Yes, she had. Marguerite had also said her first husband had been controlling and abusive and she'd been glad to see the back of him.

"Mac is your nephew?" Mrs. Vesper asked with interest.

"Yes." Marguerite beamed at the woman. "Is he not a charmer?"

Mrs. Vesper was quick to agree. "Yes, indeed, he is. Makes me wish I was fifty years younger."

"Well, he has an older brother who is just as charming, and I think the two of you would get on famously." Marguerite smiled and locked arms with her to urge her toward the door of the house. "I do not suppose you have tea, Millie?"

"As a matter of fact, I do. Would you like some, dear?"

Mrs. Vesper asked as CJ opened the door and stepped to the side to allow the other two women to enter first.

"I would love one," Marguerite assured her. "I can smell coffee and it does smell delicious, but I fear the caffeine overstimulates me."

"I don't have that problem, but I do prefer tea myself," Mrs. Vesper said lightly as CJ followed them into the house and down the hall to the kitchen.

"Why don't you two sit down and I'll see about the tea," Mrs. Vesper suggested.

"Nonsense. I'll help. I'm not one of your guests," Marguerite said at once.

"Well, I am, but I'd like to help too," CJ said. "What can I do, Mrs. Vesper?"

"Sit and finish your breakfast," Mrs. Vesper said firmly as she retrieved CJ's still half-full plate from the oven. Mac's and Mrs. Vesper's plates were both in there too, she noted before Millie closed the oven door and carried the plate toward her. Obviously, the older woman had stopped to put their plates in the oven before following her and Mac outside when the RV had arrived.

Thinking of the RV made CJ recall her first meeting with the woman now chattering away with Mrs. Vesper as they gathered cups and filled the teakettle. Marguerite and Julius had been staying in the RV on Pelee Island, renting space on her neighbor's property, when she met them there in May. CJ had gone to the island intending to see what needed to be done to the cottage before she could sell it. But she'd returned home having changed her mind and determined to keep it. Marguerite and Ildaria had been a big part of that decision. Despite being more than a decade older than the pair, she'd got along quite well and become fast friends with both women and even Julius. She'd really enjoyed her stay on the island thanks to the trio. It had reminded her of why she'd always loved the island and why she'd refused to sell it years ago when her now ex-husband had tried to get her to.

Of course, he'd never thought much of the island himself. Too boring, he'd claimed. But then there hadn't been any prostitutes or drug dealers there to ratchet up the excitement for him. One of the hazards of working in drug enforcement as her ex had done, she thought bitterly. He'd found normal relaxing pastimes too sedate and had seemed to constantly be jonesing for the adrenaline rush he was used to on the job. Of course, she hadn't realized that at first.

"Oh, dear, why is Officer Dandridge leaving? He's supposed to be guarding Mac."

CJ stood and moved to the window at Mrs. Vesper's gasped words. She was just in time to see the patrol car heading out of the driveway.

"Oh, it's fine," Marguerite said soothingly. "That's what Bricker and Decker are here for."

"What?" CJ asked with surprise, turning to the woman.

"They are here to guard Mac and look into the fire," Marguerite explained.

CJ stared at her blankly, and then asked, "What are they? Some kind of private security sent out by the company he works for?"

"How clever of you to guess that," Marguerite congratulated, not actually saying that was the case, but implying it. "What made you think of it?"

"Well, the only person Mac called was his boss," CJ pointed out, returning to her seat.

"Yes. Bastien." Marguerite smiled affectionately as she spoke the name. "He's Mac's cousin, and the reason Julius and I came to Sandford. The minute he mentioned the trouble Mac had run into and that he'd encountered his life m—you, we offered to bring Justin and Decker so they had somewhere to stay while here." Turning, she smiled at Mrs. Vesper. "I gather your beautiful bed-and-breakfast is full up," she said, and then added, "I can see why, Millie. This is a delight."

"Thank you," Mrs. Vesper said, a blush of pleasure rising on her cheeks.

The warmth in Marguerite's smile ratcheted up a

couple of degrees at her reaction and then she turned to CJ to ask, "So, what were you and my nephew planning for the day?"

The way she said it made it sound like they were a couple and CJ was about to protest that she hadn't planned anything to do with Mac, but in truth she had, so she admitted, "I had thought to take him out to get a few necessities: toothbrush, hairbrush, shaving stuff, and clothes. But now that you're here—"

"Oh, thank goodness for that!" Marguerite exclaimed with happy relief, cutting her off. "Of course we brought him a toothbrush, ID, money, and such. But I have no idea what size Mac wears in clothes, so we could not take care of that for him. I decided we would go shopping when we got here, but I forgot we were in the RV." Turning to Mrs. Vesper, she told her with a wry smile, "The RV is handy for staying in. Quite lovely for it, really. Like a house on wheels. But it does drive like a little house on wheels too. Big, and awkward, and my goodness does it guzzle gas, which is just horrible for the environment, of course. Not something you'd want to go shopping in." Turning back to CJ, she reached out to squeeze her hand with gratitude. "How lucky we are that you are offering to take him in your car."

"Oh, I . . ." CJ frowned. She'd seen freedom on the

horizon, thinking their arrival meant she could be rid of Mac, and suddenly that freedom had just been snatched away. She couldn't even dump him on Dandridge now that the officer was gone. Hell, she thought with irritation. It was like the universe was doing everything it could to ensure she wouldn't be rid of the man.

"You finish your breakfast and I shall go tell the boys to get ready to go shopping," Marguerite said now, getting up from the table.

"The boys?" CJ echoed with confusion.

"Well, Justin and Decker will have to accompany the two of you. They are here to protect Mac, after all," Marguerite pointed out as she headed out of the room. "I shall be right back."

CJ heaved a defeated sigh as she heard the screen door squeal open and clang shut, then turned to Mrs. Vesper and forced a smile when she noted the woman's amused expression. "It would appear I'm going shopping."

"Yes, dear. It seems so," Mrs. Vesper said sympathetically, and then added, "It will be fine. Mac is a lovely young man. I know he'll appreciate your help in the matter."

"Yeah," CJ murmured, and lowered her gaze to her plate. Oddly enough, she wasn't hungry anymore.

Nine

Mac finished tucking in the clean T-shirt he'd just donned, and then took a moment to run his fingers through his still damp hair to smooth down the disorder that pulling the cloth over his head had caused. He'd had six bags of blood, taken a shower, shaved, and was now dressed in lovely clean clothes and ready to begin his wooing. He felt much better than he had before his aunt Marguerite and uncle Julius had arrived. Actually, he felt great now. He was clean, well-fed, and had met his life mate.

Life was good, he decided, winking at himself in the mirror before bending to scoop up the pajama bottoms and T-shirt he'd stripped out of to shower. He considered them briefly, and then simply tossed them in the small garbage bin next to the toilet before opening the bathroom door and stepping out into the equally small bedroom.

Mac heard Marguerite's voice as he passed through the bedroom to the main part of the RV, which was a compact combination living room/dining area. Still, while he knew she was there before he stepped out of the bedroom, he was completely unprepared for her to gasp with horror and immediately start shaking her head when she saw him.

"No, no, no! Take those clothes off and put your pajamas back on," she ordered, hurrying to his side.

"What?" he asked, dumbfounded.

"Take them off!" she insisted, jerking his T-shirt out of the jeans and starting to wrench it up his chest.

"Marguerite!" he protested, trying to grab at the cloth to pull it back down, but he was too slow. She was already jerking it off over his head, forcing his arms up as she did. "What are you doing?" he muttered with bewilderment through the cloth while it was temporarily covering his face.

"I am trying to prevent you making a huge mistake, Macon," she said as she managed to get the cloth off his head. "I am helping."

"Hey!" he roared, grabbing her hands to stop her when she started to work at undoing his jeans. "What the hell, woman?"

"I think he can manage the rest on his own, darling," Julius said with gentle amusement as he slid an arm around her waist and drew her away from Mac.

"Yes, I can," Mac said, scowling at her, and then he added, "Or I would if I knew why the hell I should take off the nice clean clothes I just put on."

"I told CJ I did not know your size and could not bring you clothes," Marguerite said abruptly, looking like she was ready to burst out of Julius's arms and start undressing him again. "You cannot let her see you dressed in the clothes we brought you."

"I will just tell her that Bastien sent them with Bricker and Decker and you didn't know it," Mac assured her with a small frown, not sure why the woman had bothered to lie at all, but not wanting to reveal that she had if he could help it.

"You cannot do that," Marguerite said with exasperation. "If you have clothes, there would be no need for her to take you shopping."

"So?" he asked with bewilderment.

"So, I've read her mind, Macon. If she is free of the need to take you shopping she will abandon you here and go find and interview Keith Kaye in person, and you will not get the opportunity to woo her," she said grimly.

"Who's Keith Kaye?" Justin Bricker asked with curiosity.

"Some kid who got beat up by a police officer during an arrest. CJ is here to investigate the matter on behalf of the Special Investigations Unit," Mac explained, frowning now as well. It was CJ's job to interview both Keith Kaye and Officer Jefferson, and she probably would take off and get to it if he didn't have an excuse to keep her near.

Cursing, he turned on his heel and headed back to the bathroom to change back into the pajama bottoms and T-shirt he'd just thrown out. He'd been relieved to get out of them. After the fire and his being boiled in the bath, followed by hours sitting, pacing, then tossing and turning in them while he'd tried to sleep, they had started to look sad and smell even worse. At least to him, and probably any other immortal around. An immortal's sense of smell was as keen, or keener, than a dog's thanks to the nanos circulating through their bodies. But hopefully his clothes didn't smell as bad to mortals, because he wasn't going to get far wooing CJ if he smelled bad.

Muttering under his breath, Mac snatched his previous clothes out of the garbage bin, and grimaced at their wrinkled and now damp state thanks to his stepping on them when he'd got out of the shower. Sighing in resignation, he removed his clean jeans and quickly shook out and then pulled the unclean clothes back on.

He did not remove his boxers first, though. To hell with that. He'd just showered. He wanted something clean between himself and the material that still had bits of his dead skin attached to the inside of the cloth. The material had apparently melted to his skin in places in the boiling water, or perhaps his skin had melted to the material. Whatever the case, while a lot of it had fallen out when he'd removed the clothes, and again when he'd just shaken them out, not all of it had.

"Disgusting," he muttered to himself as he finished dressing. This time when he took a moment to look in the mirror and smooth his hair, Mac didn't feel nearly as good as he had the first time.

Life, he decided, had an interesting way of kicking you in the balls just when you thought things were going your way. Of course, there was the other side too. Just when you were experiencing the very worst day of a long and event-filled life, you met your life mate, turning it into the best day of your life. Basically, it seemed to him that when it came to life, you just had to roll with it and wait to see what happened next.

"Better?" he growled in question as he stomped back out to join the others.

"Perfect," Marguerite said with a pleased smile.

"Perfect?" Bricker asked dubiously. "He smells. How is he supposed to woo her while he stinks like death?"

Mac's shoulders slumped at the words. It was a question he was wondering himself.

"You will not smell to CJ," Marguerite said soothingly to him. "She is mortal, and—" she rushed to the back of the RV and the bathroom he'd just left, and came back just as quickly with what he could only presume was Julius's cologne in hand "—this will help," she finished as she began to spray him with it. "Now go before she thinks of a way to get out of taking you shopping."

Mac led Bricker and Decker to the door, even as she ordered, "And take your time about shopping, then take her to lunch. And you boys give them some space. Watch, but from a distance so he can woo her."

"Aunt Marguerite seems eager to help you claim your life mate," Decker commented with mild amusement once they were out of the RV and crossing the backyard.

"Hmm," Bricker grunted in agreement when Mac didn't comment. "She's certainly more helpful than you bastards were with me and Holly."

Mac glanced at Bricker and raised an eyebrow in question when the comment made Decker laugh.

The younger immortal scowled at Decker for his amusement, but then told Mac, "Decker and Anders did their best to screw with me when I met my life mate, Holly, telling me she liked things she hated and a bunch of junk like that. It was a shit show."

"We were just paying you back for the stuff you said and did when we met our life mates," Decker said, still chuckling. "You deserved it, man."

"Yeah, yeah," Bricker muttered. "Maybe I did, but I already had it hard with Holly and you guys just made it worse." Turning to Mac, he explained, "Holly was married when I met her."

Mac winced at the words, knowing that would have been a serious problem. Immortals were not supposed to interfere with a mortal's marriage. Ever. "How did you claim her if she was married?"

"Well, see," Bricker began, and then paused when the porch door clanged shut and CJ jogged down the steps to approach them.

"If we're going shopping, let's go," she said a touch shortly as she walked past them, heading for her car.

Mac and the other two men stared after her briefly, then hurried to catch up.

"Right now?" Mac asked, once they'd closed the distance between her and them.

"Yes. I have a job to do, and the sooner we get started, the sooner we'll be done and I can do what I'm here for," she said firmly, and then stopped abruptly to ask, "Or would you rather wait until later? Mrs. Vesper says there is a taxi service in town. She has the phone number. She'll give it to you if you want—"

"No, no. Now's fine," he assured her.

"Great," CJ growled, not sounding like she thought it was great at all. Turning abruptly on her heel, she continued around the RV to her car. Hitting the button on her fob to unlock the doors, she said, "Get in."

Mac claimed the front passenger seat as she slid behind the wheel. Bricker followed him around to the passenger side and took the seat behind him while Decker got in behind CJ.

The first part of the drive was extremely quiet. Exceedingly so. CJ obviously wasn't happy with this chore. Mac tried to think of something to say to break the silence and hopefully ease the mood, but couldn't seem to come up with anything. In the end, it was Bricker who broke it by saying, "Hey, Mac, you should probably introduce us, don't you think?"

Relieved to have been handed an opening gambit, Mac said at once, "Yes, of course. CJ Cummings, this is Justin Bricker and Decker Argeneau Pimms."

"Most people call me Bricker," Bricker put in even as Decker said, "Nice to meet you, CJ."

"Pleasure," CJ said politely, and then commented, "So, Mac's boss, Bastien, sent you, right? You guys are security working for Argentis Inc.?"

A moment of silence followed as Mac turned in his seat to cast an alarmed gaze on the two men in the back. For a moment he was afraid they'd say no, but he needn't have worried; immortals quickly got used to having to lie to people. They could hardly go around telling the truth. If mortals knew they shared the world with what they would consider vampires, who fed off of them, they'd most likely hunt them down and try to kill them.

"Bastien thought we should come check out things and keep an eye on Mac, yes," Decker answered, and Mac was actually impressed that he'd managed to answer without lying. Because while Bastien had thought someone should look into the matter, he wouldn't have been the one to send Decker and Bricker. Mortimer was in charge of them.

"Are you both American, then?" CJ asked next.

"No," Decker answered even as Bricker said, "Yes."

"Uh-huh. Which is it?" CJ asked dryly.

"Bricker was born in California and his family still lives there, but he lives in Canada now," Decker explained, and then added, "And I mostly live in Canada, but my wife and I have been known to travel for work."

"So, you weren't sent here from New York?" CJ asked, and Mac tensed at the way her eyes narrowed at this news.

"No. Toronto," Decker answered. "Argentis has offices there too, and it was more convenient to send us than drag a couple guys up from New York."

CJ relaxed a bit and nodded.

"So, what do your initials stand for?" Bricker asked after another moment of silence.

"My first and second name," CJ said in a tone that made Mac think she'd given that response so many times she didn't even think about it anymore. He was disappointed, though. For a moment he'd hoped he'd finally learn the answer to that himself.

"Shall we guess?" Justin asked with amusement.

"Only if you feel like walking the rest of the way to Walmart," CJ said, and this time her voice was cheerful, as if the thought of that made her happy.

Mac chuckled softly at her response, but was surprised when Bricker showed his amusement too by protesting on a laugh, "Stop! You remind me of my sister with your hard-ass talk. You're making me homesick for California."

Mac peered over his shoulder at the man. He had no idea if Bricker had a sister or was just using that line as a way to make CJ talk, but that's what it did. He saw her gaze shift to the rearview mirror to look at Bricker and then she asked, "How long have you lived in Canada?"

"Oh, years now," the Immortal Enforcer said evasively, and followed up quickly with, "Where are you from?"

"Who says I'm not from Sandford?" CJ asked rather than answer.

"You're staying at a bed-and-breakfast," Bricker pointed out. "That kind of suggests you're maybe not from around here."

"Ah, right," CJ said on a little sigh, and admitted, "I'm from Mississauga."

"But you met Marguerite and Julius on Pelee Island?" Bricker asked.

Mac watched with fascination as CJ actually smiled. Her voice even went soft as she said, "Yes. I have a cottage there and went down on my vacation. I went to the tavern for dinner the first night and ran into Marguerite, Julius, and their friend Ildaria. We shared a table and had a nice night. When I woke up the next morning their RV was parked on my neighbor's yard. They were renting space off him while on the island and none of us even realized it when we were talking the night before," she said with a laugh.

Mac exchanged glances with Bricker and Decker. None of them believed for a minute that Marguerite, Julius, and Ildaria had been renting a spot there before they met CJ. It had no doubt been arranged after Marguerite realized CJ might be a life mate for Mac.

"Actually," CJ added, "now that I think about it, it's kind of weird. I never would have even imagined my neighbor, George, would rent space to anyone, let alone allow them to hook up to his power and water. He's a grumpy old bastard who doesn't generally even seem to like people, let alone want to have them around." She pursed her lips briefly and then said, "Not sure how they ended up there. I wonder how that came about," she added thoughtfully. "I should ask Marguerite."

"Sounds like you had fun with them, though," Decker commented, and one look at the concentration on Decker's face as he stared at the back of CJ's head told Mac the Enforcer was reading CJ's mind and memories.

"Oh, gosh, yes," CJ said with a grin. "We got on like a house on fire. I spent my whole vacation hanging out with them. Took them to Lighthouse Point, showed them Flat Rock, had bonfires, barbecues, went swimming. I even took them fishing. We had a blast. It reminded me of my childhood," she added, her voice turning reminiscent. "My foster parents originally owned the cottage and left it to me. We used to go down every weekend during the summer, plus usually three weeks to a month straight into June or July. Our trips to the island make up some of my best memories."

"It sounds idyllic," Mac murmured.

"Yes," she agreed with a faint smile.

"Ah," Bricker said suddenly with understanding, and when CJ raised her eyebrows in question at him in the rearview mirror, he explained, "When you first started talking about a cottage on Pelee Island, I wondered why you wouldn't have got one up Muskoka way. It's closer to Mississauga, I think. But if you inherited it . . ." He shrugged.

"Yeah." Her smile suddenly faded, as if Bricker's words had made her think of something unpleasant, and then she flicked on the blinker and announced, "Here we are."

Turning his head, Mac saw that they'd arrived at Walmart. Time for shopping, he thought with an inner sigh. He hated shopping.

"Well, Mac, so far you're doing a bang-up job of wooing her," Decker commented dryly fifteen minutes later. "You hardly said two words to her in the car and now you're sitting out here with me while Bricker is inside shopping with her."

Mac turned to give the man a scowl, but didn't tell him to shut up like he wanted to. Everything Decker had said was true. He'd let the other two men carry most of the conversation on the drive over, and now he was sitting out here on the hood of her car waiting for

CJ and Bricker to return with a pair of shoes for him to wear into the store.

Mac looked down at his bare feet, hardly able to believe he'd left Mrs. Vesper's place barefoot. It was, of course, how he'd been carried out of the burning house last night and how he'd been walking around ever since. He'd got so used to it that he hadn't even noticed that he didn't have shoes on until the door greeter inside Walmart had politely explained he couldn't enter barefoot. Now CJ and Bricker were inside buying him shoes so that he could shop for clothes he didn't really need just to spend time with her. So far, he wasn't acing this wooing business.

"She's very guarded," Decker said suddenly.

"I had noticed," Mac said wearily.

Decker nodded and then added, "She's going to be a hard sell."

Mac looked at him worriedly. "Do you know what the issue is that Julius mentioned?"

Decker shook his head. "Nothing has popped up on the surface of her thoughts yet."

"Hmm." Mac turned to look back toward the store entrance and said impatiently, "What the hell are those two doing in there? How long does it take to buy a pair of shoes?"

Ten

"I really can't see Mac wearing those," CJ said, eyeing the paisley-patterned, plastic purple flip-flops Justin was holding up with the disgust they deserved. Good Lord, she wouldn't even make Captain Dupree wear the ugly things, and he was in her bad books right now.

"Yes, well, it seems to me he doesn't have much choice since we don't know his shoe size," Bricker pointed out.

CJ frowned. He was right, of course, but still . . . The flip-flops were really ugly, and she was quite sure he'd never wear them after today, if they even managed to get him to wear them into the store. She debated the matter briefly and then heaved out a sigh and shook her head. She simply could not do it. Especially not when he had so much that he had to replace at the moment.

"No. It would be a waste of his money," she said finally, and started to dig in her purse for her phone, only to stop when she recalled she'd forgot to charge it. Letting her purse drop back to her side, she asked, "Can I use your phone?"

"My phone?" Bricker echoed with surprise.

"Yeah. Mine is dead or so close to dead it might die mid-call and I want to call Decker," she explained.

"Decker?" Bricker said dumbly.

"Well, Mac doesn't have a cell phone. I presume Decker does?" she asked, and when he nodded, she arched an eyebrow. "So? Let me call him on your phone so I can have him ask Mac his shoe size. Then we can at least pick something he might wear more than once."

"Ah." Bricker nodded, but looked slightly disappointed as he set the purple flip-flops back and handed over his phone after opening it to Decker's number. CJ got the feeling he'd really liked the idea of making Mac wear the ugly things.

Boys! she thought, shaking her head as she tapped the green phone symbol and placed the phone to her ear.

Decker answered after the first ring with, "Hope you are nearly done, Bricker. We are sitting out here in the sunlight waiting on you two, and you know that isn't good. We should have brought a cooler with us."

"A cooler of what?" CJ asked with amusement. "Cold water or beer?"

"CJ," Decker said with obvious consternation. "Sorry, I just assumed it was Bricker."

"No. I borrowed his phone to call and find out what size shoe Mac wears," she explained. "And maybe his clothing sizes too."

"Right. Hang on," Decker said, and then must have pressed the phone to his chest because she heard a rustling and his muffled voice followed by what she was sure was Mac's. A moment later, Decker rattled off Mac's shoe size, shirt size, and pant size and then asked to speak to Bricker. CJ thanked him, and handed the phone to Bricker, silently reciting the sizes in her head as she walked along the row of shoes, examining the ones in the size Decker had mentioned.

In the end, she settled on some black Rockport slip-ons that looked comfortable but could pass for both casual and dressier. The man had lost everything in the fire and items that could do double duty seemed a good idea to her.

Of course, now he needed socks. Leaving Bricker to follow, she headed for the men's clothing section. CJ found herself stopping to examine a pair of faded, straight-leg jeans along the way. After the barest hesitation, she selected a pair in the size Decker had given her, and slung them over her arm. She passed through shirts next, where a bright blue polo shirt caught her eye. It joined the jeans and then she continued on to the socks.

"CJ," Bricker said, hurrying up to her a moment later. "None of us thought to mention it, but Mac and Decker are both allergic to the sun. Maybe I should—"

"What?" she interrupted, turning with a pair of black socks in hand. "Allergic to the sun?"

"Well, their skin is sensitive to sunlight," he said slowly, his gaze moving over the clothing she was holding. "Holy crap, woman! Are you done already?"

CJ looked down at everything she held and shrugged. "I guess I am. Except for underwear," she added with a frown. "He probably needs underwear too."

When she hesitated, frowning at the idea of picking out something so personal for Mac, Bricker caught her arm and urged her along the aisle to the underwear. Releasing her there, he eyed the selection and then picked up a pack of boxer shorts and another of boxer briefs and held them up. "Which ones?"

CJ glanced from one to the other and then pointed to the briefs and Justin nodded and tossed the others back. "We're done. Let's go."

"So, Mac and Decker are both sensitive to sun-light?" she asked as they got into one of the long lines at the cash registers. It was surprisingly busy. Well, not really surprisingly, she supposed. It was Saturday and Saturdays were always busy at Walmart.

"Yeah. It's a family thing. Runs in my family too," Bricker muttered, drawing her attention back to him. She saw his gaze slide impatiently over the people in line in front of them as he added, "We all avoid the sun as much as possible because of it."

"That explains why you're all so pale," CJ commented. Bricker didn't respond. In fact, his attention had settled on the woman in line in front of them. He was staring at the back of her head with a concentration that seemed weird to her. Trying to distract him, she asked, "So what happens when you guys are out in sunlight too long? Do you break out in a rash or something?"

"Or something," Bricker said evasively, and urged her forward as the customer in front of them suddenly took her cart and left the line. CJ thought the woman must be going back to find something she'd forgotten, but she simply pushed her cart to the next line and took up a position there.

CJ pursed her lips, and glanced between Bricker and the woman, wondering if the shopper had sensed his concentrated glare on her back and left because he was making her uncomfortable. She'd barely had the thought when the next customer in front of them suddenly took his few items off the conveyor belt and walked to another line as well.

"That's weird," CJ said with a frown as Bricker started taking the items she was holding and setting them on the conveyor belt. "Both customers just up and moved to another till."

"People are weird," Bricker muttered, pulling out his wallet to retrieve what looked to be a company credit card.

"Yeah, but the guy would have been next to be rung up. He already had his stuff on the belt," CJ pointed out, eyeing the man with curiosity. As tall as Bricker, but with arms as big around as her thighs and covered in tattoos, the guy didn't look to be the type who might be intimidated by someone glaring at him.

"Maybe he's here with his wife and she ran back for something and he was afraid he'd get rung up before she returned," Bricker suggested.

"I don't know. He— Yes, that's probably true," CJ found herself saying, and was suddenly quite sure that was the case. In the next moment, she'd forgotten all about both customers and their unusual behavior. In fact, she found herself oddly unconcerned about anything as the cashier finished with the customer in front of them and started to ring up their order.

"Damn," she murmured as they stepped outside moments later and she saw Mac and Decker sitting on the hood of her car. "I forgot I locked the doors. I should have given them the keys so they could sit inside with the air conditioner on."

"Yeah," Bricker murmured, some concern in his own voice. "They shouldn't be sitting out in the sun."

He began to move more quickly then. The man had long legs and was moving so fast she would have had to run to keep pace with him. Deciding she wasn't in the mood for that, she let him run ahead with the shopping bag.

CJ was still a good distance back when Bricker reached the other two men and Mac took the bag. She saw him riffle through it, and pull out the shirt she'd picked. Her steps slowed and her eyes widened, though, when he then stripped off the shirt he was wearing.

She'd recognized that the man was well put together when he was wearing the T-shirt, but without it . . . Good Lord in heaven, Mac was beautiful, his chest wide and sculpted in a way one wouldn't expect from a geeky scientist type. He was a marble statue come to life and she definitely felt heavy disappointment when he covered up all that male beauty with the new shirt she'd picked out. That disappointment turned to shock, though, when Mac followed that maneuver with suddenly pushing down the pajama bottoms he'd worn since she'd first met him. CJ stopped walking altogether, her eyes nearly falling out of her head when he then stepped out of them, leaving him only in the polo shirt and tight white boxer briefs that revealed more than they covered.

"Oh, my God," she muttered, and turned abruptly to walk back to the store entrance. She could feel that her face had gone hot with embarrassment, and peered around to see if anyone else had witnessed Mac Argeneau stripping in a parking lot. Much to her amazement, no one had. Part of it was because she'd parked at the back of the lot, a habit she'd taken up several years ago to get in extra steps during her day. The other part was just human nature, she supposed. CJ had come to realize through her years as a detective that people just weren't very observant anymore. They walked around with their cell phones out and their gazes locked on them, even when walking to their cars in a busy parking lot. They didn't know what they were missing. The man shirtless had been a wonder, but without his pants and in only a pair of tight boxer briefs and his shirt . . . well, CJ had never really thought of the male body as beautiful, but Mac's was. It was a sight she wouldn't soon forget. She was quite sure it was burned onto her retinas.

Shaking her head, she risked a glance back over her shoulder, and was just in time to see Mac pulling on the new jeans she'd picked out. CJ turned forward again at once.

Taking deep breaths, she kept her gaze forward until she reached the covered area in front of the store entrance, and then she stopped and turned back the way she'd come to see what was happening now. She was more than a little surprised to see that not only was Mac now fully dressed, including socks and shoes, but that the men were less than half a dozen steps behind her and closing quickly.

Spotting the Walmart bag Mac was carrying, CJ asked, "Do you want me to unlock the car so you can stow your bag in there?"

Mac shook his head. "Thank you, but no. I'm done with these," he assured her, and proceeded to drop the bag in the garbage bin next to her, before offering her his arm. "Shall we?"

CJ eyed his offered arm with distain. "What do I look like? An old lady who needs help crossing the street?" Snorting, she walked around him and into the store, leaving the men to trail her as she made a beeline for the men's section.

What followed was the most amusing couple of hours CJ had enjoyed in quite a while. Justin Bricker was an enthusiastic shopper, choosing items and insisting Mac try them on for them to judge. Unfortunately, Bricker's taste ran to floral-patterned short-sleeve shirts, and Mario Brothers–themed T-shirts. These he liked to pair with orange or green shorts or joggers. CJ had to bite her lip several times to keep from laughing at Mac's irritation as Bricker pointed out his finer qualities in the horrid outfits. Things like while the floral pattern might be a bit much, the blue flowers did bring out the color of his "gorgeous silver-blue eyes." Or that maybe the orange shorts were ugly and far too tight, but they did show off his fine legs and generous "package." A comment that had embarrassed her enough that CJ had decided the fun was over and it was time to intervene. She'd taken over the picking out of outfits then, selecting several nice plain T-shirts in solid colors without sayings, images, or comments on them, and a few dressier shirts both long- and short-sleeved also in solid colors. She'd also picked jeans rather than shorts, and a pair of black dress pants. Bricker had said his skin was sensitive, after all, so pants were probably better than shorts for him. It was certainly better for her not to be staring at his bare legs in shorts.

Mac liked everything she selected. He didn't seem

to want to try anything on, and she—more than happy to speed this shopping trip along—didn't suggest he should. She also left the underwear shopping to him. They hit the shoe section after that, and then the pharmacy section to pick up personal items before taking everything up to check out.

The lineup was even worse than it had been when she and Bricker had purchased the clothes Mac was now wearing. CJ resigned herself to waiting, but glanced around as they did. Like Bricker and Decker, she had been on the alert the entire time they'd been shopping. Not expecting trouble, just keeping an eye out for it. They were doing the same now, but as CJ took note of the other shoppers in line, she couldn't help noticing the looks the other female shoppers were giving the men. It made her take a real good look at the three of them.

They were all tall, all well-built, and all good-looking. But while Justin and Decker were looking dangerous and sexy in black T-shirts, black jeans, and black boots, Mac was more approachable in the jeans and shirt she'd picked out.

Even so, CJ thought as she examined them, they were all incredibly . . . hot. Almost unnaturally so. Seriously, there was just something about them . . . She looked each man over more slowly, trying to figure out what it was. Each was handsome, sure, but they were all also pale. Not sickly looking as Mac had appeared that morning, just pale like someone whose skin had never been touched by sun. That pale skin was flawless though. The pores so tiny they weren't visible. Each had dark hair, but in slightly varying shades. Each was tall too, and well put together with wide shoulders and slim hips. Still, their attraction seemed to stretch beyond that. It was almost irresistible.

Like they were charmed, CJ thought suddenly, and smiled crookedly at the thought. She'd read a story once about a witch who had created a charm that made her irresistibly attractive to the opposite sex, and that was what had just popped into her mind. It was like they each had a charm like that fictional witch had possessed.

"Ridiculous," she muttered to herself, and turned her attention to watching the people around them again until it was their turn at the till. Despite the amount of time it had taken them to shop, Mac hadn't bought much: a pair of dress pants, a couple of pairs of blue jeans, several T-shirts, two short-sleeved dress shirts, one long-sleeved dress shirt, running shoes, and sport sandals. He'd also bought deodorant, toothpaste, a toothbrush, a hairbrush, bar soap, and shampoo. That was about it, though, and once they were being rung up, it didn't take long. Thanks to the shoeboxes they ended up with five bags to carry.

"You shouldn't be bogged down with bags if you're on bodyguard duty," CJ pointed out, taking the bag Decker automatically reached for. When he nodded and stepped back, she took another bag, leaving the other three for Mac to carry, and they headed out of the store.

"I'm hungry," Bricker announced as they stepped outside.

"Funny you should say that," Mac commented as he and CJ followed Bricker into the parking lot with Decker at their back. "I was just thinking we should take CJ to lunch to thank her for bringing us shopping."

CJ glanced toward him with surprise, and opened her mouth to say that wasn't necessary, but before she could, Mac added, "Besides, your arrival this morning interrupted our breakfast and I didn't get to finish. I'm kind of hungry too."

"Me too," Decker admitted. "We were too busy trying to track you down to have breakfast ourselves."

CJ closed her mouth and swallowed back her instinctive protest. She'd feel like an ass if she refused now. Instead, she checked her wristwatch, half hoping it was late enough that she would have to say, "No, I'm sorry. I have that meeting with Jefferson and can't be late." Unfortunately, it was barely noon. The meeting wasn't for a good three hours. She had no excuse to avoid lunch.

"How about it, CJ?" Mac asked now, smiling at her. "Can I buy you lunch?"

"If you're hungry, we can stop for lunch," she said carefully. She wouldn't let him pay for her meal, but she would take them to a restaurant and sit with them, although she wasn't hungry herself. At least, she wasn't until they walked into the Sandford Pub and Grill and the delicious smell of steak, burgers, fish tacos, and fries hit her. CJ's appetite immediately roared to life.

A waitress was at their table almost before they finished taking their seats, and if the woman had smiled any harder or giggled any more as she handed out menus and took their drink orders, CJ was quite sure she would have vomited right there at the table. Not because not one of those smiles or giggles were directed her way and she was treated like she was invisible, but because the woman was all over the men, especially Mac. The waitress was practically cooing at him and rubbing up on his arm and shoulder like a cat in heat. She leaned her hip into his shoulder when she was standing straight, and when she found an excuse to bend over the table, she did so in such a way that she could use her breasts to their best advantage. While passing out the menus, she leaned across Mac to pass one to Bricker, who was sitting kitty-corner to him and across from CJ, and if Mac hadn't leaned back and to the side toward CJ in response, she was pretty sure he'd have ended up with the woman's breast in his mouth.

It wasn't just nauseating to witness; it was really kind of embarrassing too. CJ had seen obvious women before, but this was something else entirely. It was like Mac was catnip and their waitress was one big feline who wanted to roll all over him.

"Maybe you should have kept your pajamas on," Bricker said with amusement when the woman finally went away to get their drinks.

"What?" Mac asked, turning to the other man with surprise. "Why should I have kept my pajamas on?"

CJ grinned at Bricker with amusement and answered for him. "You might have been safer."

"Exactly!" Bricker agreed at once. "Our waitress would have thought you were a weirdo and given you some space. I swear she was trying to put her breast in your mouth with that one move," Bricker said with a shake of the head.

"Hmm," CJ murmured, thinking it was like the man had plucked the thought right out of her head. Instead of admitting it, though, she said, "The woman seems to have a balance issue. She was constantly leaning into Mac while standing next to the table. I'm just concerned she might lose it altogether and drop the drinks in his lap when she comes back. It would be a shame to ruin his new clothes."

"If she does drop the drinks in his lap, it would only be so she had an excuse to mop his crotch," Bricker said with amusement.

"No doubt," CJ agreed, and burst out laughing at Mac's horrified expression.

"Yes, fine, laugh it up," he said. "I don't know why you're picking on me. She was leaning into Decker too."

"Only at first. Then she noticed the wedding ring on his finger and shifted all of her attention to you," Bricker pointed out, and then glanced at Decker when his pocket began to buzz, and he pulled out his phone.

"It's Dani," Decker announced. A grin curving his lips, he answered and said, "Hi, beautiful. Hang on just a minute." Pressing the phone to his chest, he stood, saying, "I'm going to take this outside. If the waitress returns before I do, order me the steak, rare, with fries."

When they all nodded agreement, he returned the phone to his ear and walked away talking into it.

"Dani's Decker's wife," Bricker announced as they watched him push his way through the glass doors to head outside.

CJ merely nodded as she turned back to the table. She'd gathered as much, but it was good to have it verified that the guy wasn't a douchebag who would talk openly with his girlfriend in front of others.

"My wife's name is Holly," Bricker added, and then continued, "Mac's single though. What about you?"

CJ stiffened, but answered, "Divorced and completely off men."

"Well, that sucks," Bricker commented, his expression going solemn for the first time since she'd met him that morning. The man had been teasing and laughing throughout the shopping trip and the drive in the car. Now his face was grim as he said, "He must have been a real douche to turn you off men."

CJ just shrugged, not willing to be drawn into a conversation on that topic. Fortunately, the waitress arrived then with their drinks and the subject was dropped as they gave their orders, including Decker, who returned before they'd finished and was able to give his own.

"Dani good?" Mac asked as the waitress left them.

"Good," Decker said with a nod, and then took a drink of his iced tea before adding, "But she's got a serious case of baby fever. Which reminds me, Mac, she wanted me to ask how your research is going. Whether you're getting close or we should consider a surrogate."

CJ's eyebrows rose at that. "I thought your area was blood, Mac. What's that got to do with infertility?"

She didn't miss the glances exchanged between the men. It seemed to be some kind of silent communication. Whatever it was that passed between them, Mac narrowed his eyes, shook his head slightly at the other men, and then turned to her and explained, "Decker's wife has a pathogen in her blood that could be passed on to her child."

"A pathogen?" CJ asked slowly.

"A pathogen is a bacterium or microorganism."

"I know what a pathogen is," CJ assured him. "But what—?"

"Holly's got baby fever too," Bricker announced. "I blame it on the Port Henry babies. They see them, hold them, and want them."

CJ bit her lip briefly as it occurred to her that asking what pathogen Decker's wife had would have been rude. It was really none of her business and she supposed she was lucky Bricker had spoken up before she could finish putting her foot in her mouth. Now, she said, "What exactly are Port Henry babies? I mean, I know Port Henry is where Mac's sister lives, but—"

"It is just the babies born in Port Henry," Mac said

simply. "Except that several members of our . . . family and friends there had children around the same time five years ago or so, and another group had babies again just recently. My sister was in the group that had them five years ago. There were three or four children born weeks apart. That round of kids is now in kindergarten. The latest group was just a couple months ago." He shrugged slightly. "They call them the Port Henry babies because they're having them there in groups instead of one or two."

"Hmm," CJ murmured, and just shook her head. She didn't really understand why three or four kids born weeks apart would be worthy of such a distinction like "Port Henry babies." Surely there were children born in Port Henry every year, maybe even every month or week depending on the size of the town.

"So, CJ," Bricker said suddenly. "Mac mentioned you used to work for CSIS?"

CJ glanced at him and nodded mildly. "For three years before switching to the SIU."

"That's like what?" Bricker asked. "The Canadian version of the CIA or something? You were a spy?"

CJ's mouth twitched with amusement at his eager expression and voice, but she said, "It's like any other job, not nearly as exciting as it sounds. I mean, anything gets to be boring and commonplace when you do it all the time."

"Yeah, I can see that," Bricker said solemnly. "I mean, look at James Bond, having to visit casinos, drive fast cars, sleep with gorgeous women, and shoot the bad guys all the time. After the third or fourth movie it's just like, yeah, so you have to save the world again. Big deal."

CJ burst out laughing at his sarcasm and shook her head. "Yeah, well, I did visit a casino on one assignment, but I did not drive fast cars or sleep with gorgeous women, and I only shot one bad guy, so . . . yeah, I wasn't Jane Bond, and I'm pretty sure nothing I did saved the world." She shrugged. "Sorry to disappoint."

"I'll get over it," Bricker assured her, and then grinned. "Besides, I suspect you're downplaying what you did. Spies probably have to be secretive and can't reveal all the exciting details. But," he added, eyes twinkling with interest again, "you can tell us about being a police detective."

"Not when we're about to eat lunch," she said firmly. She had been a homicide detective, not a subject likely to improve the appetite.

"Speaking of which, lunch is on the way," Bricker said happily.

CJ turned to look around, her eyes widening slightly at what she saw. Their waitress was indeed on the way to their table, but three more were following her, each carrying a plate. That was some serious overkill. Even a non-waitress could manage to carry two plates. It seemed obvious this was simply a case of the other women wanting an excuse to approach the table. She hadn't missed the way the waitresses had all kept walking past and smiling at the men since they'd sat down.

Rolling her eyes, CJ sat back in her seat and simply waited for their food to be placed before them.

Conversation after that was light, with Bricker doing most of the talking. CJ was relieved because she was having trouble thinking about anything other than Mac's nearness. He had shifted closer to her along the booth to avoid the waitress's space-invading maneuvers earlier and hadn't moved back. It meant his knee was pressed lightly against her own and his arm occasionally brushed hers. Both of which made her aware of him in ways she wasn't completely comfortable with.

CJ knew she should ask him to give her some space now that the waitress was gone, but for some reason she didn't, which was just something she had no desire to question or think about. She also didn't want to think about the strange combination of relief and disappointment she experienced when they finished their meal and the waitress brought the check. The relief was expected. Soon they would get up and Mac would have no excuse to remain so close to her. The disappointment, however, was because soon they would get up and Mac would have no excuse to remain so close to her. It was a conundrum, CJ acknowledged to herself as she insisted on paying for her own meal and accepted the mobile handheld little gadget to pay using her debit card.

"Cowessess Jane Cummings," Bricker said suddenly, his gaze on her card.

CJ had to resist the urge to hide the bank card. It was too late anyway. Instead, she calmly finished the transaction and said, "You actually pronounced it correctly."

"I had a job in Saskatchewan a couple years ago and the Cowessess First Nation is there," Justin said with a shrug. "I first thought it was pronounced Cow-wessess, but soon learned it was actually Cow-sess."

CJ nodded as she finished and put her card away. She didn't ask what kind of job he had out in Saskatchewan, but did wonder.

"Were you named after the First Nation?" Mac asked with curiosity as Decker pulled out a credit card to pay for the other three meals.

"No," CJ said, and reluctantly admitted, "A social worker named me after the two officers who found me:

Officer Cowessess and Officer Cummings. They were partners."

"Found you?" Mac asked gently.

"Yes." The word was stiff and she gave him a nudge to get him moving so that she could get out of the booth. "We should head out. I have an appointment with Captain Dupree and Jefferson at 3 P.M. and I have to take you back to Mrs. Vesper's first to drop off your clothes. After my appointment, we should probably see about renting you boys a car so you don't have to constantly depend on me."

No one argued and the men quickly slid out of the booth once Decker had finished paying for their meals.

They were outside and walking to her car before Bricker asked, "What about the middle name Jane? Where did that come from?"

"It was the first name they gave me when I was found. Kind of a place saver while they looked for any family."

"Jane Doe," Mac said quietly, working it out without her having to explain.

"Yes," she said without emotion, and was searching for a way to change the subject when Bricker gave a sudden shout of warning. CJ instinctively stopped walking to look around for any threat, and had just spotted a red pickup barreling down on them from her left, when she was caught around the waist, slammed into Mac, and pretty much thrown forward with him by Justin Bricker.

CJ felt Mac's arms close around her as they flew through the air, was aware of his turning his body in an effort to shield her from impact as they crashed toward the tarmac, heard his grunt of pain, and saw the agony that flashed across his face as they hit the ground and slid. But she only caught a brief glimpse of it. The jolt of their rough landing had her head snapping forward over his shoulder. The next moment her forehead slammed into the tarmac so hard stars swam in front of her eyes . . . before they blinked out, leaving darkness.

Eleven

"CJ?" Mac asked with concern, worried by the way she'd suddenly gone limp against his chest. Rolling her under him, he lifted his weight from her body and peered down into her pale face, noting that her eyes were closed and blood was pouring from a wound on her forehead. "Dammit!"

"What is it? What happened?" Decker's growl drew his attention around to see him half carrying Bricker toward them. While the young immortal had basically tossed them out of the way like they were a couple of toddlers, Bricker obviously hadn't got out of the way in time himself. One arm was bloody and hanging limp, and one leg mangled and dragging behind as Decker helped him hop toward them. He also had a head wound. It looked much worse than CJ's, but he was still conscious so the flap of skin drooping down to reveal the skull beneath apparently wasn't as damaging as what CJ had received. At least his skull looked fully intact. It made Mac worry that CJ's wasn't.

"We have to get her to the hospital," Mac said grimly, scooping CJ up and getting to his feet.

"Bricker needs blood," Decker said with a frown, and then catching a glimpse of his back, added, "So do you."

Mac wasn't surprised at that news. He'd slid across the pavement on his back and probably had a serious case of road rash, third-degree friction burns where his skin had been scraped off by the tarmac. "CJ goes to the hospital first, then you can use her car to take Bricker back to the RV for blood while I wait at the hospital with her."

Decker didn't argue. As an immortal, Bricker would heal from any wound he'd sustained the moment he was given blood. But CJ was mortal, and much more fragile. Her head wound could be deadly, so as Mac expected, Decker merely nodded and scooped up Bricker to follow him to CJ's car. Mac had reached the vehicle and was shifting CJ in his arms to open the back door when he noticed that Decker wasn't with him anymore. Pausing, he glanced around and saw that the other man had stopped to deal with the restaurant workers and guests who had poured out of the Pub and Grill to hurry toward them. Mac watched as their faces turned blank and they began to return inside, and then—assured that Decker had handled it—he finished opening the back door and slid in with CJ, arranging her in his lap so that he could see her face.

"Do you know where the hospital is?" Mac asked Decker with concern a moment later as the other immortal settled Bricker in the front passenger seat. The injured immortal's eyes were closed now, his face slack. He'd obviously lost consciousness. No doubt due to the pain, Mac thought as Decker nodded in answer to his question.

"We passed it several times while trying to figure out where you were," Decker told him. "It's on the edge of town on the main street."

Decker had straightened and closed the passenger door, so Mac didn't comment; he merely grunted and lowered his head to peer at CJ. She was as still as death in his arms, her face much prettier in repose without her defenses tightening her features. But she was so pale.

"Did you see who was in the pickup?" Decker asked as he slid into the driver's seat a moment later and started the engine.

"No," Mac admitted grimly as the man steered them out of the parking lot. "You?"

"No. It all happened too fast," Decker said unhappily. "Bricker shouted, I started to turn, and then you two were flying through the air and he was disappearing under the pickup, and then the pickup was gone." He was silent for a minute and then added, "It was red. That's all I saw."

Mac hadn't even seen that, so could hardly complain that Decker hadn't got the license plate.

"I guess this means whoever set the fire knows you survived it."

Mac glanced toward Decker with surprise. "You think that truck deliberately tried to hit us?"

"Well, it sure as hell was no accident," Decker said grimly. "The guy came out of nowhere going eighty. No one goes eighty in a parking lot."

"Right," Mac said, thinking he must have sustained a little brain damage too if he hadn't considered that for himself. Sighing, he turned his gaze back down to CJ. She'd only been hurt because she was with him. And the hell of it was, he had no idea who was trying to kill him.

"I'll take care of Bricker and then bring back blood for you," Decker said as he turned into the hospital parking lot moments later.

"Right," Mac said, looking around impatiently as Decker drove them to the emergency entrance.

"Wait!" Decker barked, shifting into Park and jumping out of the car when Mac opened his door and got out with CJ in his arms.

"Put this on when you have the chance," Decker said as he yanked his T-shirt off and draped it over Mac's shoulders to hide his back. "It'll save you having to wipe the minds of the entire emergency room." He took a moment to tuck the top of the T-shirt into the back of the neckline of Mac's own ruined T-shirt and then stepped back. "I'll be back as quick as I can."

"Thanks," Mac said, and hurried toward the hospital's emergency doors.

He had been prepared to take control of the first emergency room worker he spotted and make them help CJ, but it wasn't necessary. The moment Mac strode into the busy waiting area with CJ in his arms, people came rushing to his side. It was the blood pouring from her forehead and her lack of consciousness that caused the stir, he supposed. Head wounds were a serious business and it apparently put her at the top of the queue for assistance.

"What happened?" the first woman to reach him asked, lifting CJ's eyelids to peer at her eyes even as she ushered him quickly through the milling people waiting to be seen.

"Hit-and-run," Mac said grimly as he was led

through a pair of double doors to a hall that led off in three directions. A woman pushing a wheelchair rushed up, but he ignored the chair and gave the woman a mental push to make her leave him alone as the first woman led him to a tiny room with a gurney. Mac carefully laid CJ on it. It was only when he straightened and glanced around that he realized that others had joined them. There were now four people in the small room besides CJ and himself: a doctor and three nurses.

Mac watched with concern as they converged on her, sure someone would try to make him leave. He prepared himself to take control of their minds and prevent it if necessary. He wasn't leaving CJ. She was his life mate. If worse came to worst and it looked like her life was in danger, he would turn her on the spot. Without her permission. That was something that was considered a no-no to his kind except in emergency situations, but if this head wound proved to be life-threatening, it would pass the emergency situation requirements. Actually, it would almost be a relief if he had to, Mac acknowledged. He would have to explain everything to her much more swiftly, of course, but once she was turned it would be easier to claim her as his life mate.

He'd barely had the thought when he heard the doctor say, "She's regaining consciousness."

"**Understand, Ms.** Cummings. I don't approve of this at all. I really think you should stay overnight for observation," the gentleman whose name tag read Dr. Pearson said firmly.

"I understand." CJ shrugged out of the gown they'd urged her into when she'd first woken up, and pulled on her blouse in its place. She'd stripped for so many doctors over the last three and a half years she felt no discomfort at all standing around in only her panties and bra in front of this one and the nurse with him. "But you've done tests and scans, and even an MRI for heaven's sake, and found nothing wrong. I'm sure I'm fine, but I'll return if I have any symptoms. Anything at all." Pausing in doing up her buttons, she frowned and lifted the collar of her shirt to get a closer look at the spot of blood there. "Damn."

"It'll wash out," Nurse Becca said reassuringly, and then smiled as she added, "Consider yourself lucky that a couple of splotches of blood is all you have to worry about. Had you not woken up when you did, you'd be without clothes at all. I was about to start cutting them off when you opened your eyes."

"Cutting them off?" CJ asked with surprise. "I hit my head. Why would you need to— Never mind," she interrupted her own question. She didn't really care, but supposed it made it easier to check for other injuries and probably to attach heart monitors and whatnot if necessary. Finishing with her top, she pulled on her pants next and then peered at her bare feet and said, "I had boots."

Nurse Becca was holding them out before CJ finished the statement and she wondered that she hadn't noticed her holding them.

"Thank you." CJ took her cowboy boots from the woman. Pulling out the socks she'd tucked into them a good seven hours earlier when they'd asked her to change into the hospital gown for the X-rays and myriad other tests they'd insisted on, she quickly donned them as well as the boots. Straightening once she was done, CJ glanced to Becca and asked, "My purse?"

"There was no purse when you were brought in," Becca said with a shrug.

"Oh," CJ said weakly, and then started toward the door.

"Ms. Cummings," Dr. Pearson said, following her. "I can't make you stay, but you will have to sign a release before you go, relieving us of any responsibility should your refusal to stay be detrimental to your health."

"Yes, fine, I'll sign a release form," CJ agreed.

"Good, good." He sounded relieved, but then added with a small frown, "Although I think you should really wait here at least until the police come to interview you. They've been notified and will want to question you about the vehicle that hit you."

"Waiting isn't necessary. I'm going straight to the police station from here anyway," CJ assured him, concentrating on keeping any sign of the headache she was suffering off of her face. She didn't want them to change their minds and insist on keeping her whether she wanted to stay or not. CJ had always hated hospitals and doctors and avoided them like the plague. Besides, she had things to do here in Sandford, and that didn't include lying around in a hospital bed being moni- tored when she was okay other than a skull-splitting headache that a couple of aspirin would no doubt fix. Which made her think of her purse, because she had a bottle of aspirin in it, but it wasn't here. Hopefully, Mac, Decker, and Bricker had it with them wherever they were. Her car was probably with them too. Which meant she'd need to call a taxi.

"Mrs. Vesper mentioned that there's a taxi service in town," CJ said moments later as she signed the release form Dr. Pearson had brought to the nurse's station.

"Yes," Becca agreed, looking a little confused as to why she'd bring that up.

"Do you think someone could call them for me? I'll need a ride to the police station."

"You don't wish to go with your man and his friends?" the nurse asked with surprise.

CJ glanced up sharply from the release form, her gaze sliding between Dr. Pearson and Nurse Becca. "My 'man' and his friends?"

"Yes. The handsome young fellow who carried you in," Dr. Pearson explained. "He was in the emergency room with you when you first woke up."

"Yes, he was very worried about you. Wouldn't leave your side until you ordered him out when we started to help you undress," Becca put in now, and then asked with concern, "Don't you remember?"

No, she didn't remember that at all. She did have a vague recollection of being made to undress and put on a hospital gown, though. At least, she remembered someone tugging at her clothes and helping her struggle into the gown, although those memories were kind of jumbled and fuzzy. She supposed she hadn't been totally with it yet at that point. But noting the concern on Nurse Becca's face and the narrowed-eyed look Dr. Pearson was giving her, CJ forced a smile and lied through her teeth, "Yes, of course. I just assumed he would have left by now. I've been here for hours."

"Oh," Becca said, and both she and the doctor relaxed. "No. His friends joined him a couple hours later and they've been in the visitor's waiting area ever since," Becca assured her earnestly, and then beamed and added, "He's been asking the nurses for an update every five minutes. He'll be relieved to see you up on your feet and moving around."

"I'm sure," CJ murmured, pushing the release form toward her. She turned then to find a wheelchair in her path, started to step around it, and then paused when Nurse Becca put a hand on her arm.

"The wheelchair is for you," she said gently.

"Oh, I don't need it. I'm fine," CJ said with dismay.

"Hospital rules," Nurse Becca said firmly. "All patients get wheeled out to their vehicles. Wouldn't want you to slip and fall on the way out and sue us." Her words ended on a grin, but CJ suspected she'd just given the true reason patients were released that way.

"Right," she sighed, and settled reluctantly in the wheelchair.

"Here we go," Nurse Becca said cheerfully, pushing her down the hall. "Let's go find your man and his friends so they can take you home and start pampering you and showing you some TLC."

CJ snorted at the suggestion. She could only think her "man" and his friends must be Mac and his bodyguards, Bricker and Decker. But none of those three were her "man," and there definitely wouldn't be any pampering or TLC coming her way. Fortunately,

Nurse Becca didn't hear—or chose to ignore—her derisive snort and chattered happily away as she wheeled her down the hall.

CJ let the woman's voice flow over her and wondered over which of the three men had carried her into the ER. The last thing she remembered was . . . well, it was crazy and couldn't possibly be true. She remembered Justin Bricker's shout of warning and looking around. She remembered spotting the red pickup barreling down on them, and then she had some crazy recollection of being scooped up, pressed against Mac, and basically tossed forward through the air with him like they were a couple of tiny tots rather than the full-grown adults they were.

She even remembered Mac's grunt of pain as they slammed into the ground, and the agony that had crossed his face before her head had slammed down into the pavement and she'd lost consciousness.

But none of that could have happened. She and Mac were not toddlers, and even the Rock couldn't have slammed them together and thrown them around like that. The Hulk maybe could have done it, but he wasn't real, and even if he had been, Justin Bricker, who had been the one behind them, was no Hulk. He must have just pushed them forward or something, out of the way of the vehicle, and the crazy memory she had was something her mind had dreamed up after she'd hit her head and been knocked out.

"Here we are."

CJ glanced up at that cheerful announcement from Nurse Becca to see that they'd arrived at a large open area filled with seats at the end of the hall. Movement drew her attention to Mac as he stood and moved toward them with Decker and Bricker following. Her gaze slid over the man, noting that he was wearing a black T-shirt now rather than the blue one she'd bought him, but otherwise he looked perfectly fine. There was no discomfort on his face, or any stiffness in his movements to suggest he'd taken on damage when they'd been pushed out of the way of the vehicle. The memory she had was obviously something she'd dreamt up while unconscious, CJ decided, and tuned in to what Nurse Becca was saying.

"—dizziness, confusion, sensitivity to light, memory issues, sleeping issues, or things like that. But that isn't just for the next twenty-four hours. Symptoms can show up later too, so please keep an eye on her, but definitely don't leave her alone for the first twenty-four hours."

"Of course not. We'll look after her," Mac said solemnly, and CJ gave him a grateful half smile. She wouldn't hold him to the promise, but appreciated his saying it. She wouldn't have put it past Nurse Becca to turn the wheelchair around and take her back to Dr. Pearson if she even suspected CJ might not have someone watching over her.

CJ had been rather hoping that Nurse Becca would leave her with the boys and go back to work, but the woman insisted on wheeling her to the elevator and seeing her down to the emergency room exit. She then stood, chatting idly with Mac and Bricker while Decker went off to retrieve the car.

CJ sighed with relief when her car finally pulled up. She would have liked to drive. It was her car, after all, but she wasn't given the choice. The moment Decker pulled up in front of them, Nurse Becca wheeled her to the front passenger door and held the wheelchair while Mac helped her up and into the front passenger seat. The nurse then wished her a cheery goodbye, admonished her once more to return immediately if she had any kind of symptoms at all, and then trundled off with the wheelchair.

While Decker had gone to collect her car, Mac was the one to get in the driver's seat once she was settled. CJ watched him put on his seat belt and muttered, "I was surprised you guys waited around for me at the hospital. I was there for hours. You should have just gone back to the bed-and-breakfast. I could have taken a taxi once they finished all their tests."

"Is that your way of saying thank you?" Mac asked with amusement as he shifted the car into gear and steered toward the road.

CJ felt herself blush with chagrin, and muttered, "Thank you."

"You're welcome," he said sincerely. "How is your head?"

"Sore," she admitted and—reminded of the pills in her purse—asked, "One of you didn't happen to grab my purse back at the— Oh, thank you," she breathed when it suddenly appeared next to her head. Turning, she grabbed it and offered Bricker a smile when she saw that he was the one passing it up to her.

"Do you need water?" Mac asked, glancing her way with concern when she dug out the small bottle of aspirin. "We can probably get you a bottle of water when we stop for Chinese takeout."

"No, I'm—Chinese takeout?" CJ asked with surprise.

"Well, I was not sure what time they would finish all their tests and release you."

"Or even if they *would* release you," Bricker put in. "They were talking about keeping you overnight when Decker and I got there, and right up until Nurse Becca wheeled you out."

"Yes," Mac said solemnly. "So I told Mrs. Vesper

not to trouble herself about dinner for the two of us, that we would pick up Chinese or something else on the way back."

"Oh," CJ murmured with a frown. Before she'd realized the men were at the hospital waiting on her, she'd planned to go straight to the police station. She'd obviously missed her afternoon appointment with Jefferson and she needed to arrange a new one. She also needed to make a report on the pickup that had nearly run them down, or give a statement if the men had already reported the incident, she thought, and said, "Have you guys talked to the police yet?"

"No," Mac said at once.

"But we probably should," Decker put in, which made surprise flash over Mac's face before the other man pointed out, "The hospital probably reported the incident to them . . . and CJ missed her afternoon appointment with Jefferson. I'm sure she'd like to reschedule that. Besides, I suspect if we do not stop with her, she'll just head back on her own after we get to the house. I don't really think she should be driving right now."

"No," Mac agreed.

Bricker immediately groaned. "I'm guessing that means a delay to eating."

"You guess right," Decker said dryly, and then shook his head. "Bricker, your relationship with food is really rather worrisome at times. You can't possibly be hungry. You ate three times while we were waiting at the hospital."

"Cafeteria food," Bricker scoffed. "And we were at the hospital forever."

"We were there for five hours," Decker corrected. "It was just after one when we got back to the RV after dropping Mac and CJ off at the office. We dropped off Mac's things, tended your wounds, and returned to the hospital at 3 P.M. It's now eight o'clock. You ate three times in five hours, and that doesn't include the lunch we'd just had before the incident with the truck. There is something wrong with you."

"Maybe he has a tapeworm," CJ suggested, leaning her head back and closing her eyes. Her skull was reverberating with pain and their squabbling was just aggravating it. She couldn't decide if they sounded more like fractious siblings or a quarreling husband and wife, but they weren't helping her headache any.

"We'll be at the police station in a few minutes and you can get water there," Mac said suddenly, his voice soothing but carrying an undertone of concern that told her she wasn't hiding her pain well.

His words also reminded her that she was still clutching the pill bottle in her hand, but hadn't done anything with it yet. Forcing her eyes open, she squinted down at the bottle, undid the lid, retrieved two pills, and dry-swallowed them. To hell with water, she needed pain relief now.

"How bad is your headache?" Mac asked with concern as she tucked the pill bottle back in her purse. "Maybe we should take you back to the hospital and—"

"Try it and I'll be kicking you guys out of *my* car and driving off without you," she growled, closing her eyes once more, but then snapped them open again as Decker's words finally penetrated the pain clouding her brain. "Tended his wounds? Bricker was hurt too?"

"Nothing serious," Decker assured her. "Just a bruise and a little road rash on his ass."

She thought she heard an annoyed growl from Bricker, saw Mac's lips twitch with amusement, but was scowling herself. "Why was I the only one to end up in the hospital? Bricker got off with just a little road rash, and you—" She glared at Mac. "What about your back?"

"My back?" he asked, his eyes going wide.

"Yes, I distinctly recall you skidding across the tarmac on your back with me on top of you after—"

She stopped abruptly, a frown claiming her expression. CJ had been going to say after Bricker scooped them up and tossed them out of the way of the pickup, but that was impossible. That couldn't have happened. Obviously, her memory was confused, or mixed up with maybe some dream she'd had. In which case, she didn't want to say anything about her mixed-up memory. The men might see it as another reason to try to convince her to return to the hospital, so she closed her eyes again and muttered, "Never mind."

Silence fell in the car then, but she ignored it and just concentrated on trying to breathe deeply as she waited for the pills to start working and her head to stop aching. She wasn't going to admit it to the men, but she was a little concerned about her headache. Not a lot. Certainly not enough that she'd been willing to admit to the doctor and nurses to having one, or to the severity of it, and risk being forced to stay in the hospital for observation. CJ hated hospitals. She wasn't keen on doctor visits either. Besides, her headache was probably a combination of hitting her head and dehydration. Maybe even a need to eat. She hadn't had anything since lunch.

She'd grab a glass of water at the police station and see if that helped. Maybe they'd have snacks there too. Something to bring her sugar up. If eating and drinking didn't help, and her headache persisted or got worse, she'd consider going back to the hospital. But she wouldn't like it.

A combination of the vehicle slowing down and the clicking of the blinker being utilized made CJ open her eyes. Much to her surprise, they were pulling into the parking lot of a Tim Hortons coffee shop with a drive-through.

"We can get you a bottle of water here," Mac said in explanation when she glanced his way.

"Thank you," CJ breathed.

Mac nodded as he maneuvered into the short line of cars waiting to place an order, and then asked, "Did they feed you anything in the hospital?"

CJ started to shake her head, but immediately stopped as the action sent pain shooting through her skull. Resisting the urge to clasp her head in her hands until the pain eased, she simply closed her eyes again and said, "No."

"You must be hungry, then. Do you want a sandwich or something?"

He didn't have to ask twice. "A chicken wrap, honey cruller, mocha latte, and the bottle of water please," CJ rattled off, her hand dipping blindly into her purse to pull her wallet out.

"Put that away," Mac said with exasperation. "I've got this."

CJ opened her eyes to scowl at him, but Mac ignored her and turned to the men in the back.

"Decker? Bricker? What do you guys want?"

"I'm good," Decker said, but Justin Bricker rattled off a list of items that was three times longer than what CJ had asked for.

She was grinning with amusement by the time he finished, and not at all surprised when Mac said, "Yeah, well, open your window and you can repeat all that to the speaker when the server asks what we want, 'cause I'm not going to remember it."

"Hell, Bricker, even you won't remember all that," Decker said with disgust.

"Will so," Bricker responded at once.

"Will not," Decker assured him.

"How much do you want to bet?" came Bricker's challenge.

"Have those two been partners for long?" CJ asked Mac as the pair continued to bicker in the back seat.

"A couple of years now, I think," Mac said, eyeing the two men in the rearview mirror.

"We aren't partners," Decker said, proving he had heard her question. "At least not all the time."

"Are so," Bricker countered.

"Not really," Decker said with a frown in his voice.

"When is the last time you worked with someone else?" Bricker asked, and when Decker didn't answer at once, said, "See? Partners."

"Damn," Decker muttered.

CJ smiled faintly and closed her eyes again. Keeping them closed seemed to ease her headache. Either that or the pills were kicking in. Although it seemed too soon for that to happen, so she kept her eyes closed and let the men's conversation drift around her until they were through the ordering process and receiving the food at the window. She opened her eyes and sat up then to take the food and drinks from Mac as he got it from the cashier and passed it over. Neither Decker nor Mac had ordered anything, so CJ took what she'd ordered from the selection and passed the rest back to Bricker.

She drank the water first, opening the bottle and chugging down the contents so swiftly even she was surprised. But once the cool liquid touched her tongue, CJ couldn't seem to stop drinking. It was lovely and so refreshing, and she had definitely been dehydrated.

Capping the empty bottle with a small satisfied sigh, she turned her attention to the chicken wrap. It went down almost as quickly, although she did take the time to chew her food so she wouldn't choke on it. She was slowing down, though, by the time she finished that and started on the latte and honey cruller. Even so, she finished it off fast enough that she was popping the last bite of the sweet, airy donut into her mouth when Mac turned into the police station parking lot.

Twelve

Captain Dupree was waiting in the reception area when they entered the police station. The older man grunted when he spotted them, his gaze zeroing in on CJ.

"You missed your appointment," he growled with irritation.

"I've been at the hospital," CJ growled back with just as much irritation.

"Doc Pearson said as much," Dupree admitted grudgingly. "Said you were the victim of a hit-and-run in the parking lot of the Sandford Pub and Grill."

"Hmm." CJ narrowed her eyes on him and pursed her lips before saying, "We must have missed the man you sent out to take a report on it."

"You did. Doc said he had a bunch of tests to do on you and not to bother sending anyone for a bit, so Dandridge only left a few minutes ago. He probably isn't even at the hospital yet. I'd best go call him and tell him to head back," he added, and turned away to disappear from view.

CJ rolled her eyes at the man's attitude and walked around the counter to follow him, aware that Mac, Decker, and Bricker stayed hard on her heels. CJ stepped into the bullpen and then paused. While it had been abandoned the night before with just Mrs. Dupree wandering the place like a ghost, tonight it was a hive of activity, with at least five officers that she could see, talking on the phone, doing paperwork, or moving around performing other tasks.

"Officer Jefferson doesn't appear to be here tonight," Mac commented. "I don't see Simpson either."

"They should be on shift, though. They're probably out on a call," CJ said, and then noted the captain standing in his office door, one hand holding a phone to his ear, the other waving them his way.

"Looks like Dupree is going to take our statements," CJ commented, gesturing for the men to follow her as she headed for his office.

Captain Dupree was hanging up the phone when CJ led the men in. Scowling when he saw that all four of them were there, he said, "You three boys wait in the bullpen. I'll take Ms. Cummings's statement first."

CJ frowned at the words. Not because he'd said them, but because she should have expected that he'd want to take their statements individually and suggested the men wait in the bullpen rather than having them accompany her. It was a common practice to interview witnesses separately, used to ensure one witness's statement didn't influence another's. She knew that, yet it hadn't occurred to her until just now. Which told her that her thinking processes weren't functioning properly yet.

"CJ?"

Her gaze flickered to Mac to see him watching her with concern, and supposed her expression was probably showing her own worry. She didn't like that her brain wasn't performing up to par. It was the one thing she'd always been able to count on. People? No. She'd learned years ago never to count on people. Her body? No. It had disappointed her as well. But her brain? That she had always depended on, and the possibility that she maybe shouldn't right now was extremely distressing to her.

"Will you be all right?" Mac asked quietly. "Do you need more water or—?"

"I'm good," she assured herself as much as him.

She'd hit her head. Of course she wouldn't be on her game at the moment. But once her headache was completely gone, and she'd had some rest, she'd be fine. She hoped.

"Out," Dupree said brusquely, shooing the men toward the door. "The sooner you're out, the sooner she can give her statement, and the sooner you all can get the hell out of my station." He'd managed to get them to the door by then, and as the men filed out of the room, the captain barked out, "Jamieson! Owens! Brown! Drop what you're doing and each of you take statements from these boys. They're the ones involved in the hit-and-run at the Pub and Grill."

He didn't wait for a response, but immediately closed the door and turned to cross the room.

"Sit down before you fall down," Dupree growled as he walked past her to take his seat.

Grimacing, CJ sat down in the chair in front of the man's desk. She didn't feel 100 percent and, pathetically enough, the walk in here had actually left her a bit weak-kneed, but surely she didn't look that bad?

Dropping into his chair, the captain assessed her grimly and said, "You look like hell."

"Well, that answers that question," CJ said dryly.

"What question?" Dupree asked with a frown.

"Never mind," CJ muttered. "Let's get this over with."

Dupree eyed her for another moment, and then nodded and opened a drawer to retrieve a tape recorder. Setting it on his desk, he said, "You don't look in any shape to write it all down, so we'll record it and have my secretary type it up for you to sign tomorrow."

CJ was surprised by the man's thoughtfulness, but merely nodded acquiescence, waited for him to turn on his tape recorder, and then began to list her name, address, and cell phone number. She didn't wait for him to ask questions after that, but immediately launched into describing the where, when, and how of what had taken place.

"Red?" Captain Dupree barked a couple of moments later, interrupting CJ at the point where she'd turned and spotted the pickup after Bricker's warning shout.

"Yes. Red," CJ said, eyeing him with curiosity. It wasn't the most popular color for a pickup. White seemed to be the top color choice, followed by black and silver. At least that was something she'd concluded on her travels. She passed tons of white pickups every day, a lot of black and silver too, but red pickups seemed much less popular. Which should make it easier to find, she supposed, and wondered if the captain might not already have a candidate in mind. If so, he certainly wasn't looking pleased about it at the moment.

Running a weary hand through his thinning hair, he grunted and said, "Go on."

CJ continued her witness statement, telling him about Bricker pushing her and Mac out of the way—she didn't mention the whole flying through the air thing, because that just wasn't possible. She ended with being knocked out when she hit her head on landing, and waking up in the hospital. There wasn't much else to tell after that. And frankly, her statement didn't have a lot of clues in it that she could tell other than the color of the truck. A license plate number or a description of the driver would have been more helpful.

"I'll make sure this is all typed up and ready for you to read and sign when you arrive tomorrow to interview Jefferson," Captain Dupree said as he turned the recorder off and stood. "I presume 3 P.M. is good for you? Same time tomorrow as it was supposed to be today?"

"Yes. Fine," CJ confirmed as she got to her feet as well. She was more than a little surprised that he was being so accommodating about the meeting. She hadn't even had to bring the subject up herself.

"Three o'clock, it is, then," Captain Dupree said as he walked her to the door. "I'll make sure Jefferson is here."

"Thank you," CJ murmured.

Dupree nodded as he opened the door for her, and as she walked past him to leave, he said, "Get some rest tonight, Cummings. You're pale as hell."

CJ glanced back with surprise at the concern in his voice, but he was already closing the door. Bewildered by the sudden show of concern from a man who had been nothing but a pain in her arse over the last two weeks, CJ gave her head a shake without thinking. Much to her relief, the pain pills were apparently doing their work. At least she wasn't suddenly overcome by excruciating pain at the headshake, just a mild throb. She thought that was a good sign.

Exhaling a relieved breath, she turned to peer around the bullpen. Decker and Bricker were seated at the two far desks, still talking to the officers taking their statements, but Mac was just getting up from his interview at the desk nearly next to her. She could also see the recorder the officer who sat at the desk was putting away. He'd chosen to record the statement and have it typed up like Captain Dupree had done, she realized. So had Decker and Bricker, but both men were still giving their statements.

"All done?" Mac asked, pausing in front of her and offering a smile.

CJ nodded and smiled back before she could catch herself, which in turn made her frown.

"Does your head still pain you?" Mac asked as she heard Captain Dupree's office door open behind her. "Do you want me to take you back to the bed-and-breakfast right away? I can come back for Decker and Bricker."

"No one's going anywhere just now," Captain Dupree announced grimly, moving past them and striding through the bullpen to the doorway to the reception area.

CJ blinked after him with surprise, and then followed. The man's voice and demeanor shouted trouble.

"What's going on?" CJ asked as she stepped into the reception area and saw the captain had gone around the counter and was headed for the entrance.

"We have a situation," Dupree said, locking the front door.

"What are you doing?" CJ asked with surprise. Police stations weren't like stores. They were always open for business, because there was always someone doing something they shouldn't. They did not lock their doors. At least not normally.

"We have a mob growing out front," Dupree announced. "There's going to be trouble."

Concern mounting within her, CJ walked to the door to peer out at the parking lot, aware that Mac had followed her, but her attention was on the crowd outside.

The sun had set while they'd been giving their statements, and either there was something wrong with the parking lot lights or they simply hadn't come on yet, but she had no problem seeing that there was indeed a crowd gathering. There had to be fifty people out there, and their numbers were increasing by the minute with others coming from all directions.

The most troubling thing to her was that they appeared to have parked somewhere else and walked to the police station. The only reason she could think of for that was to avoid having their license plates recorded by the cameras all over the parking lot, which had night vision capabilities. That didn't bode well. "Why are they here?"

Captain Dupree's mouth compressed with displeasure, but before he could respond something crashed through the large plate-glass window on the other side of the door.

CJ was moving before she was even thinking; grabbing Mac's arm, she rushed him back the way they'd come, and hurried him around the reception desk to take cover as another crash sounded, and then another. She ducked briefly behind the counter herself to get him there, then popped up for a quick look over the floor on the other side of the reception counter, her gaze sliding over the large rocks that had smashed through the glass and were growing in number on the tiled floor as they continued to fly through the now shattered windows.

"What the hell?" she exclaimed with amazement, and then whirled to where Captain Dupree was hunched down behind the counter on the other side of Mac. Stabbing him with accusing eyes, she demanded, "What have you done?"

"I haven't done a damned thing," he snapped back at once, but the guilt on his face suggested otherwise.

CJ's mouth tightened and she asked, "Why were you and Jefferson at the hospital last night?"

That brought a startled glance from the man before he quickly looked away toward the gaping holes where the windows used to be. The number of rocks flying in were slowing now. Either the crowd had expended their anger, or they'd simply run out of rocks.

Captain Dupree's mouth compressed and it was Mac who answered. "While at the hospital waiting for you I overheard some nurses saying that Jefferson beat the hell out of a couple of teenagers and put them in the hospital," Mac announced quietly. "One's in a coma with possible brain damage, and the other has a broken cheekbone, jaw, and clavicle."

"Christ," CJ growled, turning on Dupree. "Is this true?"

"Jefferson's a good cop," Dupree said, but she noticed that he didn't sound as certain of that as he'd been during her previous conversations with him about Jefferson. He'd been a staunch defender of the man during their phone calls, informing her that he'd come with the highest recommendation when he'd hired him and had never had an incident like this. But it seemed to her that some of his faith in the officer had been shaken by this latest incident. Still, he frowned and added, "Jefferson said those boys were looking for trouble, started wailing on him and he defended himself. He was injured too," he added defensively.

"He has a bump on his forehead and a black eye," Mac said when CJ turned to him in question. Grimacing, he then added, "The nurses were of the opinion that he gave it to himself to be able to claim they attacked him. Apparently, the kid who's still conscious said he hit him to get him off of the other kid before he killed him, but that he hit him in the kidneys, not the face."

CJ cursed, and said, "Oh, for—"

"What's happening?"

That question had CJ snapping her mouth shut and glancing around to see that Decker and Bricker had joined them in hunkering down behind the counter. So had the remaining police officers at the station. But while Mac's two bodyguards were behind her and

Mac, the officers were stretched out along the counter, crouched down, looking to their captain, their hands on their guns.

Eyeing them with concern, she said, "The citizens of Sandford are displaying their displeasure with their police captain."

"Me?" Captain Dupree said with amazement. "I haven't done a damned thing."

"No, you haven't," she agreed. "You should have relieved Jefferson of duty pending the investigation after the Keith Kaye incident. Instead, you kept him on and let him hurt two more people."

"You don't know that he hurt anyone," he insisted, but he was avoiding her eyes as he added, "Jefferson is a good cop."

"Your expression belies your words, Captain. So why are you defending him? What is he? Your illegitimate son?" she asked impatiently.

"Of course not," Captain Dupree snapped, but then grudgingly admitted, "He's my son-in-law."

CJ's head went back slightly at the words and her eyes widened with dismay. "Are you shitting me? Is your daughter okay?" When he looked startled by the question, she pointed out, "Cops who abuse their power and position on the job are usually abusive at home too, Captain. Surely you know that?" When he frowned but didn't respond, she asked, "Any changes in your daughter since the marriage? Sudden increase in bruises from supposedly clumsy accidents, black eyes from walking into open cupboard doors, stuff like that? Or does she wear long-sleeved shirts on even the hottest summer day? Flinch at sudden movements? That kind of thing?"

The captain didn't respond, but swallowed heavily, concern now wreathing his face.

"Yeah," CJ said grimly. "So, you're protecting a guy who's not only abusing the kids in this town, but probably your daughter too." She shook her head with disgust and turned to glance toward the broken windows as another rock crashed to the floor, sending the glass skittering across it. Sighing, she muttered, "Let's hope it doesn't have the townspeople voting to close the police station and contract the policing out to the OPP like most of the other small towns have done."

Ignoring his alarmed gasp, she stood abruptly and moved around the counter to approach the door.

"What are you doing?" Mac asked with dismay, hurrying to catch up to her as she unlocked the shattered door. Most of the glass in it was gone now and she'd have walked through it, but a bar across the middle meant she would have had to limbo out and she didn't have the energy for that just now.

"You aren't going out there?" Mac asked with alarm as she finished unlocking the door.

"Well, we can't sit cowering in here until one bold asshole decides to toss a Molotov cocktail in," she pointed out dryly. "Someone has to talk to these people."

"Let Dupree do it, then," Mac growled, catching her arm to stop her. "He's the police captain."

"Seeing him would just piss them off. I'm an out-of-towner, so less likely to raise their ire," CJ pointed out, shaking off his hold. She took another step, but when he stuck to her side like glue, she paused to turn a scowl on him and spotted Decker and Bricker behind her as well. "You should stay here with your bodyguards."

CJ didn't wait to see if he'd listen, but opened the shattered door and walked calmly outside and nearly into an oncoming rock. She saw it shooting toward her face, instinctively took a step back into someone's hard chest, and raised her hands to try to catch or deflect the missile, but a large, male hand was already there, snatching it out of midair before it reached her or her hands.

The sharp thwack as it hit flesh made her glad she wasn't the one who had caught it. It also made her worry about Mac, but she couldn't take the time to check on him just then. She had angry townspeople to deal with.

"I know you're all upset, and I don't blame you. That's the reason I'm here," she said quickly, but was relieved to see that no more rocks were flying toward the building. "My name is CJ Cummings. I'm an investigator with SIU, the Special Investigations Unit, and I'm here to investigate the incident involving Keith Kaye and Officer Jefferson."

"What about what that bastard did last night to Mark Loop and Mike MacDonald?" someone shouted angrily.

"Well, I just heard about that from Captain Dupree a few minutes ago," she admitted, deliberately making it sound as if he'd told her willingly. The man had been difficult and obstructive, but Jefferson was his son-in-law. He'd naturally been trying to protect his daughter's husband. She didn't think he'd do that anymore and didn't see any reason to ruin the man.

"Since that incident also involves Officer Jefferson," she continued, "it falls under my purview and I will be investigating that as well. But obviously I could use some help here," she said, letting her gaze run over the people in the crowd. "I plan to be at the diner on the corner tomorrow from noon until 2:45. Tell your friends and neighbors that I'll be there and that anyone who was a witness to either incident, and can help with my investigation, should come down and talk to me. In the meantime, I'd appreciate it if you all went home. No one will be charged or reported for this incident, but you have to go home now. Let me take care of this."

For a moment, no one moved or spoke, but then the people on the fringes of the crowd began to back away and turned to head off into the night to walk home, or at least to wherever their vehicles were parked. A moment later, the rest of the crowd turned almost as one and followed, and CJ let her breath out slowly. She hadn't been sure it would work, and she'd damned near had another head wound to add to the one she'd got in the hit-and-run.

That thought made her spin toward Mac. "Let me see your hand."

His eyebrows rose, but he held out his hand for her to take a look. The rock was gone, and his hand looked perfectly fine. There wasn't a mark on it. CJ stared at it blankly. From the sound when it had hit his hand, she'd been sure he'd at least have a bad bruise if not a terrible gash. Sighing, she released his hand and glanced around at the now empty parking lot.

"Well, I guess we should go back inside. I need to talk to Dupree before I leave, make sure he doesn't charge anyone for what happened here tonight," she said, moving around the three men and heading back inside.

A much-subdued Captain Dupree was alone in the reception room. He met her just inside the door, and spoke before she could. "Thank you for handling that."

"You're welcome," she said solemnly. "But—"

"I've called Steve—Officer Jefferson in," he interrupted solemnly. "He should be here in twenty minutes. I'm going to put him on leave until you finish your investigation and come to a decision. I also had my wife call my daughter over to our house. After I deal with Steve, I'm going home to talk to her and find out if the bastard has been beating her."

"That's good, but—"

"And myself and the men will cooperate fully with your investigation. I'll talk to them and make it clear that they're to answer all questions honestly."

"Good. Thank you. Now about the mob out here tonight. I told them no one would be charged for this," she said quickly, just wanting to get that subject out of the way and head back to the bed-and-breakfast before she collapsed where she stood. She was exhausted and the stress had brought her headache back. All she wanted at that point was to take a couple more painkillers and lie down.

"I heard you say that," Captain Dupree said, and grimaced as his gaze slid to the shattered windows and door. "They caused a lot of damage."

"So has Jefferson if what those boys are saying is true," CJ countered quietly. "And the townspeople are angry. The way they see it, he's misusing his authority. He's actually breaking the law, and from their perspective you've been letting him do it." She paused briefly to let that sink in and then glanced toward the glass and rocks covering the floor before adding, "If they'd hurt anyone I'd say throw the book at them, but since that didn't happen, I suggest you bite the bullet on this and just get the glass replaced and take this as a lesson learned. Your people expect you to keep them safe, even from your own men. Maybe *especially* from your own men."

"Yeah," he sighed unhappily, running a hand through his hair. "He used to be a good guy. I hope he still is and this is all just a mistake, but . . ." He shook his head.

CJ was silent. There was really nothing she could say to comfort the man. This was a mess, but she'd get to the bottom of it with her investigation. For now, though, she really just wanted to leave. Unfortunately, her brain was pounding and her thinking processes were slow and she didn't know how to end this and leave without seeming rude or uncaring. Fortunately, Bricker had no such problem.

"So," he said abruptly, clapping his hands. "Are we done here? Can we get some Chinese and go back to the bed-and-breakfast?"

CJ glanced to Captain Dupree in question. "Is there anything else before we go?"

"No, I guess not," the captain said, glancing around. "You're coming back tomorrow to sign your statement and interview Steve."

It was more a reminder than a question, but CJ treated it like a question. "Yes. I'll try to be here early to sign the statement, but if not, I can always sign it after the interview."

"Right," he muttered, frowning at the mess of glass on the floor. "I need to clean this up and call our window guy."

"All right, then," CJ said mildly. "We'll head out and leave you to it."

Grunting, Captain Dupree nodded and turned to make his way around the reception counter and into the back of the station without another word.

"I guess that means we're good to go," Bricker said cheerfully.

"I guess so," CJ agreed, relieved to be able to get out of there before Jefferson got back. Which was ironic, she supposed. She'd been trying to meet with the man for weeks, and now just wanted to avoid him.

"Awesome! Next stop: the Happy Wonton," Bricker said cheerfully, taking her arm in one hand and Mac's in the other and ushering them out of the station with Decker leading the way.

Thirteen

"I should probably check on CJ again and make sure that she's okay," Mac muttered, glancing toward the hall and the stairs beyond. They'd stopped to pick up Chinese food on the way back to the bed-and-breakfast, but CJ hadn't been interested in having any when they'd got there. She'd gone straight up to her suite for what she'd called a "lie down," leaving Mac and the others to feast on the Chinese food without her.

The minute she'd left the room, Mac had started to fret over her. He'd managed to restrain himself for twenty whole minutes before going up to check on her the first time. The second time had been twenty minutes after that. Now another twenty minutes had passed and he was anxious to check on her again. It was looking like he'd be running up to be sure she was still breathing three times an hour for the rest of the night. At least until Mrs. Vesper went to bed and he could just go up there and stay in CJ's suite. Unfortunately, the woman appeared to be enjoying the company at the table and was showing no signs of tiring.

Mac blamed that on Marguerite. His aunt and Julius had joined them to eat when they'd returned, and after hearing about their day and evening, she'd been chatting away with Mrs. Vesper, asking her all sorts of questions that Mrs. Vesper had happily answered. The woman was blooming under the attention, which Mac would have thought was nice if he wasn't so anxious about CJ. He knew damned right well that head wounds could be risky for mortals. Swelling on the brain could cause problems that weren't immediately evident but could kill them. And those problems might not be apparent while she slept, he thought now with a frown. Perhaps he should wake her up this time.

"Or you could go have a nap yourself," Decker suggested.

Mac blinked at the comment, somewhat confused by where it had come from. Deciding he must have missed part of the conversation, he merely shrugged and said, "I'm not tired."

His answer inspired dead silence for a minute, and

then Bricker pointed out, "It was just after nine o'clock when we got back and CJ went to lie down. She might sleep straight through the night rather than just nap . . . or enjoy *dream time* as my Holly likes to call it," he added pointedly.

"Dream time?" Mrs. Vesper said with a faint smile. "Isn't that sweet. It sounds much less lazy than 'nap.' I like it."

Mac heard Mrs. Vesper's comment, or at least the rumble of her voice, but his mind was on what Bricker had said. Dream time. Immortals were said to share dreams with their life mates when sleeping near each other. Usually they were shared sex dreams. If he went up and slept too . . .

Standing abruptly, he picked up the full glass of water Mrs. Vesper had fetched for him and said, "I'll just go look in on her and set this by the bedside table in case she's thirsty when she wakes up, and then I might just have a little nap myself. I wouldn't want her to be up by herself in the middle of the night."

"That's very kind of you, Mac," Mrs. Vesper said with a smile. "Well, if you don't get up until after I've gone to bed, I'll wish you good night now."

"Good night," Mac murmured, heading out of the kitchen.

He heard Marguerite's soft "Sweet dreams" as he left the room.

CJ was asleep in her own bed when Mac reached her suite. He supposed he shouldn't be surprised. She'd probably assumed that he'd be out in the RV with his bodyguards now that they were here, and if today hadn't gone as it had, he probably would have been. But her head injury meant she wasn't supposed to be left alone for twenty-four hours and he intended on watching her like a hawk. He wasn't risking losing his life mate to swelling on the brain, or anything else, before he could even claim her. Fortunately, sharing dreams with her would give him more of an idea of how her mind was working than waking her up and asking questions to judge whether she was suffering confusion or any of the other symptoms connected to such an injury.

Assured she was breathing fine and seemed well, Mac set the glass of water on the bedside table and then retreated to the salon. The cot was still there, but it had been stripped and closed. Rather than go to the trouble of setting it up and making it, he lay down on the couch. It was plush and overstuffed and a good size as couches went, but he was still too long for it. Mac was used to that, though, and simply rested his head on one arm of the couch and his ankles on the other, and closed his eyes.

CJ stroked through the silky water, enjoying the feel of it rushing over her body as she swam straight out from the cliff that her cottage sat on. She swam for several minutes before stopping and rolling over in the water. Floating on her back now, she stared up into the fiercely bright sun for a moment before closing her eyes against it and simply enjoying the feel of its heat kissing her skin where it wasn't submerged under the water.

CJ had always enjoyed the water. As a kid she'd spent more time in the lake than out of it when they were on the island. Her father used to say that it was because she was really a mermaid they'd found as a baby and taken in. He'd then caution her not to stay in the water too long or her legs would merge into a tail fin and she'd have to live in the water forever.

CJ smiled at the memory. She'd always laughed at that claim, never realizing how close to the truth it was. Oh, she wasn't a mermaid, but the man she'd always thought was her father *had* found her when she was young and he and his wife had taken her in, raising her as their own. They had been wonderful parents, and she had enjoyed a happy and loving childhood because of them.

Sighing, CJ rolled over in the water again and struck

out for shore. It didn't take her long to reach shallow water. The moment her fingers brushed over the sandy bottom as she stroked, CJ stopped swimming and stood up in the water to wade out. She stopped, though, after just a couple of steps when she spotted the man standing on the small patch of beach in the shade cast by the U-shaped cliff.

CJ stared at Mac Argeneau blankly for a moment, a little confused as to what he was doing there. He was wearing a black T-shirt and the blue jeans she'd picked out for him, the same clothes he'd been wearing when she'd seen him last . . . In Sandford where she was investigating Officer Jefferson, she recalled, and that's when CJ realized she was dreaming. Because she had no recollection of getting from Sandford to her cottage on Pelee Island.

This was a dream, and one she had a lot. Well, part of it was one she had a lot. CJ often found herself dreaming of her cottage and the peace and relaxation she found there. It was the place she'd been most happy in her life, so where she went in her sleep. But she'd rarely dreamed of anyone else being there with her. Mac's appearing here now was a new experience and a bit of a surprise, but not an unpleasant one, she decided. She might not be able to have him in real life, but this was a dream. Here she was safe and so was he. Here she could even experience and enjoy what she couldn't in reality. If she wanted, which wasn't something she was too sure about. Still, she was in control here in her dream.

Relaxing at the thought, CJ waded out of the water toward the large beach towel she'd left warming on a rock in the sun. Her path took her away from Mac, but she could feel him watching her as she moved, his gaze sliding down her body in the one-piece black bathing suit she wore, and then back up again with an appreciation that was almost a hum in the air. It made her hyperaware of her body, of the feel of the water running in rivulets down her chest and legs, of the warm sand under her feet, of the cool breeze on her skin.

"So, this is your cottage," Mac commented idly as he watched her pick up the towel and begin to dry herself off.

CJ smiled faintly, but took a moment to wrap the towel around herself and tuck the end in the top to hold it in place before saying, "This is my beach. That's my cottage."

He followed her pointing finger up toward the pretty white cottage on the cliff above them, taking in the board and batten siding, and the sliding glass doors with large windows on either side looking out over the lake. It was all there was to see from where they were.

"Would you like to see the inside?" she asked, and when he nodded, turned to lead the way toward the stairs on the other side of the outcropping of rocks that lay at the base of the cliff. She walked slowly, giving him the chance to catch up, but was almost sorry she had when he took her hand in his. The move caught her by surprise and made her steps falter briefly, but then she forced herself to relax and continue moving. It was a dream. Her dream. There was nothing wrong with holding hands.

CJ told herself that several times as she led Mac to the wooden stairs built into the face of the cliff. But it didn't help her to relax any. His hand was cool, his hold firm, and he didn't let her go when they started up the stairs so that they could mount them single file, but held on and walked a little to the side and one step below her, the back of his hand occasionally brushing against her hip as they moved. It was having a most disconcerting effect on her equilibrium and she found herself beginning to babble nervously as they ascended the stairs.

"This was a one-room cottage when my foster parents bought it," she told him. "They worked on it every summer for years, adding on two bedrooms, a loft, and even a bunkie out front."

"A bunkie?" Mac asked with curiosity.

"A small building with one long room and a bathroom. It's fitted out like a sitting room with two couches, some chairs, and a dartboard, but the couches pull out into beds for extra guests," she explained. "It's where my friends and I used to sleep when I brought them over from the mainland with us, or if one of the friends I had here on the island stayed overnight. Otherwise, I slept in the cottage."

They'd reached the deck by then and she led him to the sliding glass doors and used the need to open the door as an excuse to free her hand from his. Sliding it open, she waved him in and then followed and stopped just inside the door as the breeze from the ceiling fan brushed over her body. There was no air-conditioning in the cottage, but shade from the large trees around it, combined with the ceiling fan in the main room and the breeze off the lake blowing through the screens on the open doors and windows, kept it mostly cool. The only time she missed air-conditioning was on those really hot days when there was no breeze. That happened rarely, though, and when it did, relief could be found in the water.

CJ closed the screen on the sliding glass doors, and

then watched Mac look around her home away from home. She did too, her gaze sliding over white walls, hardwood floors, dark leather furniture. Half the large space was a living room with furniture that was over-stuffed and comfy, but definitely older and well used. A faux fur rug lay on the floor in front of the fireplace, a large coffee table to do jigsaw puzzles on sat in front of the sofa, and there were lamps by every seat for read-ing at night.

The other half of the room was the kitchen and dining area. Blue cabinets with white quartz counter-tops lined the wall facing onto the road and the side wall, while a long wooden table with eight chairs filled the rest of the space.

When she glanced back to Mac and saw that his at-tention had moved to the ladder leading up to the loft, she said, "All there is up there is a king-sized mattress. There wasn't enough height for a proper bed, but it's only used when there's lots of company . . . which hasn't happened for a long time," she added almost sadly. She used to love it when they had lots of com-pany on the island. She missed those days. She missed a lot of things. Having a family. Having . . . someone of her own.

"Where do those doors lead?" Mac asked, gesturing to the three doors in the wall on the right.

CJ hesitated, and then led him to the first door and opened it to the larger of the two bedrooms in the cottage. It was where her foster parents used to sleep. She'd taken it over after they'd died and left the cottage to her. It faced out on the lake, which eliminated the need for curtains. It was a beautiful view to wake up to in the morning, she thought, and watched him peer around at the pale silver-blue walls, the king-sized brass bed, and the pine bedside tables and dresser. When his gaze settled on the large white quilt with the red and blue star pattern on the bed, she shifted uncomfortably and turned to leave the room.

The middle room was a small bathroom. CJ opened the door and then moved aside so he could step in and look around. It wasn't a very impressive bathroom. Built when her parents first bought the cottage in the '80s, it was older than she was and it showed. The room was also tiny with just a small sink, a toilet, and a shower Mac would have trouble using without knocking his elbows black and blue. CJ had considered remodeling it a time or two, but she was also considering the possibility of somehow making it a little bigger too, and until she figured out a way to do that without taking too much room from one of the bedrooms on either side of it, she didn't want to remodel.

The last room was a smaller bedroom than the front

one. It was where CJ used to sleep as a child and still had a single white captain's bed with drawers, white end tables, and pink shaded lamps. Three of the walls were painted a creamy white, while the fourth wall was covered in wallpaper with pretty pink roses on it similar to the duvet on the bed. It was a young girl's room. Too young for a fourteen-year-old "almost woman," her mother had decided and had been planning on redecorating it before the car accident that had taken her life.

Pushing the thought away, she said, "My parents added on the two bedrooms. It was just the main room and the loft before that."

"No bathroom?" Mac asked with surprise.

CJ shook her head. "Outhouse. We were all grateful when the bathroom was done," she added dryly, and then turned to leave the room, heading for the kitchen.

"Would you like some iced tea or a soda?" she asked when she sensed him following her.

"Tell me about your childhood."

CJ stopped walking. This was her dream. She was supposed to be in control and that was not a subject she wanted to discuss. On the other hand, she was here, in a home where she'd spent some of the happiest weeks of her childhood every year, with her first foster parents, who had been more real parents than foster. Her life had been secure and happy with them until the last few months before they'd died. She often wished she could return to that time in her life and live everything after discovering she was a foster child again. She'd make so many different decisions if she could. But she wasn't the first person in history to regret decisions made in her past, or to learn the hard way that some mistakes could not be undone or fixed and had to be lived with, or eventually died with as the case may be.

"My childhood," she murmured, and then continued on into the kitchen and opened the refrigerator. There was a large pitcher of iced tea inside that looked much like one she'd seen in a magazine ad a while back. It was larger and prettier than any she'd made in real life, with slices of lemon floating in the ice cubes at the top of the pitcher. Nice.

CJ poured them both a glass, handed him one, and then leaned back against the counter and eyed him solemnly while she took a sip. As she'd noticed before, Macon Argeneau was a good-looking man. With thick, dark hair and attractive features, which included eyes the same silver blue as the walls in her bedroom here, she realized. He was also well-built, which was somewhat surprising considering he was a lab rat. She wasn't surprised to find herself dreaming about him. In real life, if she weren't sick, she'd have been interested in dating the man. She maybe even could have fallen in love with him. He had the kind of personality she liked. His sense of humor was killer.

"CJ?" he queried when she remained silent.

"Why do you want me to tell you about my childhood?" she asked instead of answering his question, and was actually curious about his response. What was her subconscious dredging up here?

"Because I'm attracted to you. I like you and I'd be interested in being in your life," he answered without hesitation.

CJ closed her eyes briefly, allowing the words to wash through her mind. He was attracted to her and he liked her and wanted to be in her life. Just the words every girl wanted to hear, she thought, and felt sadness slide over her. CJ was used to that sadness and usually soaked in it, allowing it to fill every corner of her mind and body, but she didn't want that now. She was tired of being sad and lonely and depressed. She was even more tired of the anger that rode with it like a dark shadow, a smoke that burned through her. Just this one time she wanted to fight it, to push it away, pretend she was the CJ she used to be and take what life, or in this case her dreams, were offering.

Opening her eyes, she met his gaze, and then reached back to set her glass on the counter before moving her hands up between them and pressing them to his chest. She watched Mac's eyes widen slightly as her hands grazed his chest, and then he reached past her to set his own glass down and closed his arms around her, drawing her nearer. His head started to lower as if he planned to kiss her, but she pulled back slightly to avoid it. She wanted to touch him first, to explore the wide, strong chest she'd been lusting after since meeting him.

Much to her relief, Mac stopped at her slight withdrawal and straightened again, simply waiting. It made her smile as she ran her hands over his chest, feeling and exploring its hard expanse. Her fingers glanced over firm pectorals, up to his deltoids, and then down his biceps. His shoulders were wider than hers, his biceps easily twice the size of her own toned upper arms, and she longed to see them without the T-shirt covering them.

CJ had barely had the thought when the soft cloth was suddenly gone, leaving him bare-chested before her. The shift made her blink in surprise, and then she grinned, thinking that dreams rocked as she shifted closer and pressed her face to all that male flesh, inhaling his scent before pressing her lips to the taut skin.

Mac sighed at the soft caress, his hands moving up and down her back now, urging her closer as she trailed her lips over his pectorals, brushing across one hardening nipple and then stopping to nip lightly at it. The teasing move had Mac sucking in a gasp of air, and then he gave up passively holding her, caught her face with his hands, and urged it up so that he could kiss her. CJ didn't fight the move this time. Curious, she willingly raised her head, offering her lips and closing her eyes as his mouth descended toward hers.

The first touch of his mouth on hers had CJ holding her breath as it moved gently back and forth. A languid heat slid through her body, warm and gentle. When he drew her closer and his tongue slid out to run along the seam where her lips met, she hesitated, but then opened for him, and in the next moment the whole tone of the kiss changed. Warm and gentle turned to hot and demanding and the languid heat turned to lava, bubbling up in her body to chase the excitement now pouring through her.

CJ had thought she'd experienced passion before, but this was beyond anything she'd ever encountered. It was hot and fast and overwhelming. Every nerve in her body seemed suddenly to be alive and on fire and she stopped being passive and joined in the kiss. Her own mouth was now demanding and her hands moved over him, trying to touch him everywhere. She explored his hard chest, clasped his wide shoulders, and then her hands slid along his strong arms before dropping down and around to clasp his hard butt cheeks, to squeeze and tug him closer even as her body pressed tighter to him.

His mouth was magic, his tongue talented as it thrust and laved the inside of her mouth, tangling with her own. His hands were moving as well, sliding up her body, pressing her hips tighter still to his before one slid between their upper bodies to find and cup the curve of a breast through her swimsuit.

CJ moaned into his mouth at the touch, her back arching into the caress as he palmed and squeezed her breast and then found and tweaked the pebbling nipple through the cloth. It was CJ who reached up to catch the shoulder straps of her swimsuit and tug them to the sides until they slid down her arms. Mac immediately turned his attention to helping to free her of the straps, and then his hands replaced the material now gathered around her waist. His kiss became even more hungry as he palmed the aching globes revealed, and then he slid one leg between both of hers and CJ gasped as it pressed against her core.

CJ didn't get a chance to feel disappointment when his hands suddenly left her breasts. Just as she realized they were gone, he was clasping her by the waist and lifting her to sit on the countertop. His hands dropped to her knees then, urging them open so that he could step between them. Only then did he finally break their kiss. CJ murmured a protest at the loss, but it ended on a sigh and she tilted her head back and to the side as his mouth blazed a trail down the length of her throat, licking and nipping along the way to the slope of one breast and continuing on until he found the nipple. CJ cried out and arched when his mouth closed over that. Her hands were on his shoulders now, digging into the skin there.

Realizing what she was doing, she forced herself to ease her hold and then retrieved one hand to glide it into his hair and cup his head to urge him on as he licked, nipped, and suckled at the excited bud until she was aching with need. She was vaguely aware of the sounds she was making—the sighs, the moans, the pleas for him not to stop—but those sounds ended on a choked gasp when he suddenly slid one hand up the inside of her leg to press it against her core through the swimsuit.

They were both completely still for a moment, until CJ realized he was waiting for her either to make him stop or give some indication that he should continue. Once she understood that, she didn't hesitate, but reached down to cover his hand and squeezed gently. That was all he needed to begin suckling at her breast again, even as his hand between her legs began to move.

CJ groaned, her arms sliding around his shoulders and tightening, her bare feet pressing into the front of the cupboard, and her hips sliding forward slightly on the countertop, pushing into his touch.

When Mac eased the cloth of her swimsuit aside so that he could touch her without it in the way, she cried out and threw her head back, her entire body clenching. Mac immediately let her nipple slip from his mouth and raised his head to claim the sound, drinking in her whimpers and excited cries as he caressed her. It was too much . . . and not enough and CJ wrapped her legs around his hips, urging him closer so that her sensitive nipples were rubbing against his chest, and then she reached down to find him through the front of his jeans, and began to rub his hard length through the thick cloth.

Mac groaned into her mouth in response, his hips bucking into the caress, and she felt her way to the button and zipper of his jeans, eager to open both. One moment she was struggling to get his pants undone, and the next his pants were gone, vanishing like his T-shirt had earlier. Free to touch him now, CJ closed her hand around his erection, marveling at how hard and soft it was all at the same time, like velvet over steel. She squeezed gently, and then stroked him once, twice . . . halfway through her third stroke, he caught her hand in his, forcing it away.

CJ was just thinking that this was her dream, and she should be able to do what she wanted, when Mac broke their kiss and suddenly dropped out of her hold. Blinking her eyes open, she glanced down with confusion to see that he'd dropped to his knees between her legs and was now—

Gasping, she reached back to brace her hands on the countertop as he caught her under the knees, drew her butt to the edge of the counter, and then buried his face between her legs. She'd barely recognized that her bathing suit was suddenly gone when his tongue rasped over her trembling flesh, pushing all thought from her mind and making her buck and cry out. Her legs instinctively tried to slam closed. His shoulders prevented that, but it was an instinct that she had repeatedly, though it was quickly followed by her feet pressing hard into the cupboard front as she lifted her hips into what he was doing as he used his lips and tongue to drive her crazy.

The man was teasing her, lashing the bud that was the core of her excitement lightly with his tongue and then shifting his attention to suckling on the protective lips around it before lashing her again. Just when CJ was ready to pull his hair and push his face more firmly against her, he suddenly shifted gears and began to suck hard on the bud even as he slid one finger into her.

CJ cried out then, a harsh guttural sound that seemed to be ripped from her very depths as her hips tried to buck on the countertop but were held in place by Mac. Gasping for breath now, every inch of her trembling with mounting excitement, CJ arched on the countertop, her body so stiff and tense she began to fear her back would snap under the pressure, and then the tension snapped instead and she convulsed, a long ululating cry sounding her release. Lost in the wash of pleasure, she didn't even notice when Mac straightened before her and spread her legs even farther as he stepped up to her. She did notice, though, when he thrust into her.

A long gasping groan slid from CJ's lips as he filled her, and she grabbed desperately for his shoulders, then pressed her forehead to his chest as she tried to catch her breath.

For one moment they remained like that, just holding each other with him deep inside her, but then Mac leaned his upper body back and bent to claim her mouth when she instinctively raised her head. This time it was a slow, languorous kiss, a luscious exploration that was almost soothing until he began to move his hips, slowly withdrawing himself from her and then just as slowly easing back in. His angle with each exquisite move resurrected the passion she'd just spent, stirring it languidly back to life with each stroke.

It was CJ who changed the tempo in the end. First, she deepened the kiss, tilting her head and thrusting her tongue out to tangle with his aggressively, and then she dug her heels into his behind, spurring him on. She got the exact response she'd hoped for; Mac began to surge into her more quickly, thrusting as deeply as he could over and over with mounting need and speed. Feeling her behind slip backward on the countertop, CJ gave up her hold on Mac to throw her hand back in search of the wall to brace herself, but pain startled a soft cry from her throat and had her opening her eyes . . . to darkness.

Fourteen

C J was not seated on the kitchen counter of her cottage on a sunny summer afternoon. Instead, she was horizontal on a soft surface in darkness. Her bed at Millie's bed-and-breakfast, she realized as her hands moved over the sheets tangled around her body. Good heavens! She must have been thrashing around like a fish out of water. The sheets had become a tight, cinching belt around her waist, her T-shirt was up under her armpits, leaving her chest bare, and where the hell had her panties gone?

Sitting up in bed, CJ felt around for the lamp, and nearly knocked it over. She had to grab the lampshade to keep it in place, but then felt her way to the stand and the switch to turn it on. Light immediately exploded into the room, leaving her blinking wildly as her eyes tried to adjust. Once she could see again, CJ glanced around. Her concern about her panties was immediately forgotten when she spotted the overturned glass and pool of water on the bedside tabletop. The sight made her recall the pain that had woken her up. Obviously, she'd hit the glass with her hand and knocked it over, and now water wasn't just pooling on the tabletop, but was running over the side and dripping onto the bedroom carpet.

Cursing under her breath, CJ lurched out of bed. She had to take a minute to untangle herself from the sheet that had a stranglehold on her waist, and then she tripped over the duvet lying on the floor, but she managed to keep her feet and get to the bathroom. Snatching up the first towel she saw, CJ then hurried back to mop up the mess on the table and soak up the water that had made its way onto the carpet. Once finished, she stood and surveyed both the wood and the carpet. The tabletop seemed fine; the water hadn't sat long enough to do damage, and she couldn't even see where the water had gathered on the carpet anymore. It seemed to have all come out, but she'd check both in the morning to be sure no damage had been done.

The thought made her frown slightly. The glass of water hadn't been there when she'd gone to sleep.

The obvious explanation was that either Mac or Mrs. Vesper must have been in to check on her and left it.

Mrs. Vesper, CJ decided. Mac was a man and, in her experience, men didn't think of things like that. Besides, the older lady seemed like the motherly sort and a worrier. She'd probably come to check on her on her way to bed and left the water in case she woke up in the night. A really sweet thing to do, CJ assured herself. But was disturbed at the thought of anyone creeping into her room while she'd been sleeping. Especially if she'd been thrashing around as it appeared she had been. She hoped she'd still had her panties on at the time.

Sighing, CJ briefly considered crawling back into bed and trying to return to sleep, hopefully to find her way back to the steamy dream she'd been enjoying. Unfortunately, now that she was up and had been rushing around, she was aware that her T-shirt and hair were damp and her skin clammy. She'd sweated up a storm while she slept, but knew that wasn't why they called them wet dreams.

On the other hand, she'd never experienced a wet dream quite like this one. Usually, she didn't remember her dreams when she woke. She might have some vague idea that she'd dreamed this or that, or have an image or two in her head, but she didn't usually remember every minute of what had happened as she did with this dream, and she'd absolutely never woken up drenched in sweat like this either.

Maybe she was going into menopause early and it had been a hot flash, she thought.

"Yeah, a hot flash named Mac," CJ muttered to herself. She was too young to be starting into menopause. She'd just had one hell of an intense wet dream inspired by a sexy, silver-eyed lab rat, which was the last thing she needed. It was hard enough being around the man without sex dreams taunting her with what she couldn't have.

Sighing, she considered the mess she'd made of the bed. Or the floor around it, she supposed, shifting her gaze to the bed missing everything but one pillow. The other pillow was on the floor along with the sheet, duvet, and her panties. Muttering under her breath, she quickly grabbed up the items on the floor and tossed everything but her underwear back on the bed, then checked the clock radio on the bedside table.

It was 4 A.M. She'd slept somewhere around seven hours. That was a bit long for her. She usually only managed six hours a night. Not because she stayed up late and was woken by her alarm clock. She just didn't seem to be able to sleep longer than five or six hours as a rule. Getting seven hours of sleep was actually an oddity for her. Probably something to do with the head injury, CJ thought as she headed into the bathroom.

Ten minutes later she was showered, and dressed. The plan was to go downstairs and make herself some coffee, but the sight of Mac asleep on the couch in the salon when she came out of the bedroom made her footsteps falter. She really hadn't expected to find him here. The arrival of Marguerite and the others with the RV had made her assume he would sleep there with his bodyguards, Bricker and Decker. In fact, that's where he should be.

CJ frowned and briefly considered waking him up to find out why he wasn't with his bodyguards, but memories of the dream she'd had prevented her doing that. Just seeing him lying there looking all sexy and manly with his way-past-five-o'clock shadow and bed-head had her wanting to run her fingers through his disheveled hair and kiss him to see if he was as good a kisser in real life as he had been in the dream.

Recognizing how dangerous those thoughts were, CJ forced herself to get moving again and tiptoed across the room, wondering why he was there in her salon. He should have been with his protection. That thought made her pause again as she reached the door. Glancing back at him, CJ suddenly worried that maybe she shouldn't be leaving him there alone. She debated the issue briefly, but frankly she didn't trust herself alone with the man after that dream. Besides, he wasn't really her responsibility. He hadn't been when Captain Dupree had asked her to look after him, and he wasn't now that his company had sent bodyguards to keep him safe . . . And dammit, she wanted a coffee.

Mouth tightening, she unlocked and opened the suite door and slid out. CJ did lock it, though, something she'd neglected to do when she came up to lie down last night. She wouldn't make that mistake again, she decided as she made her way to the stairs by the dim glow of the night-lights in the hall.

A lamp was on in the living room below, casting a pale glow out into the hall, and enough of it reached the stairs that she was able to descend them without breaking her neck. CJ glanced into the room as she passed and spotted Bricker in a chair facing the door. He looked alert and ready for action, and waved when he spotted her. She waved back, but continued on into the kitchen without stopping.

CJ wasn't a morning person. She'd need at least two cups of coffee before she could string words together to make sentences. Or maybe it was more appropriate to say before she'd *feel like* stringing words together. Most people in her life quickly learned to steer clear of her until she'd had a chance to wake up.

Mrs. Vesper had told CJ that she was free to make coffee or tea or eat anything she liked while here, and she took advantage of that now. CJ quickly made a pot of coffee and grabbed a mandarin from the bowl on the table to eat while she waited. She was peeling the orange when Bricker stuck his head into the room and announced, "I'm going up to stand outside the suite door."

CJ grunted an acknowledgment, but didn't even glance up from what she was doing. By the time she finished the orange, the coffee was done. She drank the first cup there at the counter, but took her second cup out to sit on one of the wicker chairs on the porch to enjoy the night air. That's where Mac found her some ten minutes later.

Sitting with coffee cup in hand, CJ was peering up at the stars trying desperately not to recall her wet dream when she heard the screen door open and close. Assuming it was Bricker, she turned sharply, her mouth already opening on a lecture about it being unprofessional for a bodyguard to leave his client alone in a situation like this. But the words stalled in her throat when she saw that it was Mac.

"How's your head?" he asked softly as he settled into the cushioned wicker chair next to hers.

CJ considered him briefly as her mind suddenly suffused with the memories from her dream that she'd been trying so hard not to recall. Mac naked, Mac kissing and touching her. Mac thrusting into her body. It had all felt so good, and so real, and those memories made it impossible for her to think clearly for a minute. They also annoyed the hell out of her. To her it was like Vegas. They said what happened in Vegas stayed in Vegas. Well, what happened in her dreams should stay there too, she thought grimly, and instead of answering his question, asked one of her own.

"What were you doing in my room?"

Mac's head went back slightly, almost as if she'd punched him, but then he straightened and reminded her, "The nurse said you shouldn't be left alone for the first twenty-four hours. She said that someone had to watch over you to make sure you were okay and there was no swelling on the brain." He paused and shrugged. "So I checked on you every twenty minutes for the first hour or so, and then decided just to stay in the room so I'd be nearby if you ran into difficulty and needed help. I fell asleep there."

CJ did recall the nurse telling the men that someone needed to keep an eye on her for the next twenty-four hours, but she hadn't expected any of them to listen. She wasn't their responsibility. Yet, Mac had taken it upon himself to keep an eye on her. Even checking on her repeatedly before taking up residence in her sitting room. It was really sweet and thoughtful, she acknowledged, and scowled at him for it. The last damned thing she needed was for him to be sweet and thoughtful on top of gorgeous and sexy. Was he *trying* to make her fall for him?

When he looked confused by her narrow-eyed glare, she realized how ridiculous she was being and allowed the expression to fall away before asking in a conciliatory tone, "Did Bricker wake you up, or was it my leaving the room?"

Mac relaxed a bit at her change in attitude and shook his head. "Neither. I just woke up on my own."

"Oh," she murmured, and took a sip of coffee, her gaze moving to the RV and the light shining from the windows. She'd expected everyone else would be sleeping at this hour other than her and Justin, so had been surprised to see that the lights were still on in the RV when she'd come out. It seemed like Mac and his sister weren't the only night owls in the family.

"Marguerite and Julius were late risers on the island," she said suddenly as she recalled that.

"They're night owls too," Mac said easily. "Most of my family is."

"Yeah. Your sister and brother-in-law work nights," she murmured. "And so do you."

"Yes," he agreed mildly.

"But you don't have to," she pointed out. "I mean, you work from home. Presumably you could work days instead of nights."

"I could," he acknowledged. "But I like working at night. It's quiet. Most of the rest of the world is sleeping. There are less distractions."

CJ nodded. She got that. In university, she'd preferred working on her papers and such at night exactly because it was quiet and her friends were less likely to call and interrupt, or drop by unexpectedly. She'd got a lot more done that way. She'd also preferred working the night shift when she was a police officer.

"You told Bricker you were off men," Mac said suddenly. "Why is that?"

CJ stiffened at the question.

"Is it your childhood that turned you off men?" he asked when she didn't respond. "An abusive foster father, or—"

"Why does no one believe me when I say I had a good childhood?" she interrupted him with sudden exasperation. "Honestly, anyone who's ever found out I was raised in the system immediately concludes I must be horribly damaged by it. That I had to have either been sexually abused, beaten, or misused in some way. Why is that?"

Mac hesitated briefly and then said with blunt honesty, "Probably because you're so closed off and prickly. People naturally assume a tough time in the foster care system would explain that."

CJ scowled at the words. "Well, you know what they say about assuming things and asses," she muttered with irritation, not liking that he saw her as closed off and prickly. She knew she was. Still, she didn't like hearing it.

Sighing, she shook her head. "It wasn't my childhood that did that. My early years were lovely. I was well-fed, never beaten or abused, and was given lots of attention and love," she assured him, and then fell into a brief silence before admitting, "I told you I was named after the officers who found me. One of them was Officer Johnathan Cummings. He and his partner, Ernie Cowessess, actually found me on the beat one day when I was less than a month old. I was lying in dirty rags next to my mother's body in an alley. Drug overdose," she explained. "They believed she was a teenage runaway living on the streets in Toronto. They never knew for sure. They didn't find any ID on her, or anything else that could tell them who she was or where she came from. Nothing to tell them my name or birth date either. There was no way for them to contact her family to come and get me."

"I'm sorry," Mac said solemnly.

"Don't be," she said at once. "It worked out for me. I mean, if she was a runaway there was probably a reason for it, so I may have been better off not being found by her family," she pointed out, because that was what she'd told herself for years. CJ knew kids didn't always run away because of problems at home. Sometimes it was the child who was the problem, or sometimes they were running away because of being bullied at school, or because they felt like a failure, or . . . there were myriad reasons. It wasn't always bad parents. But it made her feel better to think she might have been lucky to land where she had. Besides, she actually had enjoyed a really good childhood in the end. She'd had parents who had loved her and whom she'd loved. She'd been lucky.

Determined to convince Mac of that, she explained, "When I was found I was malnourished and sickly. They took me straight to the hospital. The doctors there guessed that I was about two and a half weeks old, which gave them a rough birth date, which ended up being my legal birth date in the end when they couldn't find out who I was."

When Mac nodded encouragingly, she continued, "I was in the hospital for a couple of weeks with that birth date and the name Baby Jane Doe. During that time, the police tried to find out my mother's identity, and if there was any family who could take me in—my grand-parents, etc. I guess they put the story on the news and everything. They had a sketch done of my mother, and took pictures of me that ran with the stories, hoping that someone would recognize one of us, but—" she shrugged "—no one ever came forward and they never figured it out. I guess they even tried questioning other runaways and shelters and stuff, but nothing came of it."

"So you went into the foster care system," Mac said solemnly.

CJ nodded. "I was placed in a home with several other foster kids at first, but the man who would become my father kept track of me and checked on me regularly. Good thing he did too, because apparently there was some problem with the people I was first placed with. No one ever told me what the problem was, but Johna-than Cummings raised a stink about it and then he and my mother—his wife, Marge—ended up fostering me themselves."

"And they adopted you and gave you their last name, and your father's partner's name as your first name," Mac said with a smile.

She wasn't surprised that he'd guess that. Her last name was Cummings, after all, but CJ shook her head. "No. The care worker gave me the last name Cummings while I was still in the hospital."

"What?" Mac exclaimed with surprise.

CJ nodded. "They had to get me a birth certificate and whatnot to put me in the system. She didn't want me to be stuck with Jane Doe, so she gave me the names of the officers who had found me."

"Cowessess Jane Cummings," he murmured her name. "Cowessess is an interesting name."

"It's Ojibway; my father's partner was Native American," CJ explained, and then smiled wryly as she added, "I guess the care worker thought Cowessess Jane Cummings made a better name than Cummings Jane Cowessess."

Mac looked dubious. "She obviously didn't know a thing about kids if she thought either version would pass muster."

"Yeah," she said on a slight laugh. "Having the first name Cowessess caused me no end of misery at school as a kid. But Cummings as a first name would have been just as bad."

"No doubt," Mac said sympathetically, and then pondered, "I wonder why she didn't just name you Jane Cowessess Cummings instead?"

CJ shrugged. She'd often wondered that herself, but the only thing she'd come up with was: "Maybe I was a colicky baby who drove her nuts when she had to deal with me."

"So she punished you with a horrible first name?" Mac asked with amusement.

"Maybe," she said with a faint smile, and then shrugged. "The truth is I prefer CJ to Jane anyway, so I guess it doesn't matter."

"Yeah, I like CJ better too," Mac admitted. They were both silent for a minute and then he asked, "Did Officer Cummings and his wife have kids of their own?"

"No," CJ said softly. "They'd apparently tried for years, but given up by the time I came along. They were older by then, in their late forties. But I think not being able to have children of their own, along with the fact that the care worker had given me his last name, is why he was so invested in my well-being at first. Most police officers would have handed me over to Social Services and forgotten all about me."

"But he didn't," Mac murmured. "And he and his wife ended up raising you."

"Yes. They were great parents, Mac," she told him solemnly. "Like I said, they were older, and had always wanted kids. They poured all that love they'd been saving up into me."

"Yet they never adopted you?" Mac said almost reluctantly, his confusion obvious.

CJ's smile dimmed and then she sighed. "You have to remember I already had their last name. Legally.

Everyone around us—teachers, the kids at school, and so on—all thought they already were my parents. Including me," she added quietly. Swallowing, she continued, "I gather they were advised not to adopt me at first, that it wasn't even likely the courts would allow it in case my mother's family popped up and wanted me. So my father, Johnathan Cummings," she added again to prevent confusion, "apparently spent a lot of his off-duty time the first four or five years of my life trying to identify my birth mother and locate her family. He was hoping they'd give him and Mom permission to adopt me.

"He said he gave up when I was six, and the courts probably would have allowed the adoption by then, but it would mean interviews with Social Services and the judge talking to me. They'd raised me as their own. I thought I was their daughter. They didn't want to confuse and upset me while so young. I already had their name, and they considered me their child. All that going through the courts would do is give them a piece of paper saying what they already felt in their hearts, that I was their daughter. So, they decided to wait until I was sixteen, and then planned to sit down and explain about my birth mother, and ask me if I'd let them adopt me and make me officially their daughter."

"But they died when you were around fourteen, you

said," Mac murmured with a frown. "Is that how you found out they weren't your real parents?"

"No," CJ admitted solemnly. "Unfortunately, I found out before that . . . by accident. I went poking around the attic in search of something to make a costume out of for Halloween when I was fourteen and found a stack of checks and a bunch of paperwork in the attic that told me before they could."

"Right," Mac murmured. "Foster parents get paid."

"They do," she agreed, and then added, "But mine didn't."

When he turned a confused expression her way, she smiled faintly. "These checks were uncashed. My parents never put them in the bank. They just stuck them in a box in the attic. They said they didn't want to be paid. Raising me was a labor of love. They considered me their daughter and always planned to adopt me, so there was no need to be paid." She peered down into her now empty coffee cup, and then admitted, "At least, they tried to tell me that, but in the end I didn't really accept or even hear what they were trying to tell me until I read their letter."

"A letter?" Mac echoed with surprise.

CJ nodded. "They wrote it when I was five or six and gave it to their lawyer to give to me along with their wills should anything happen to them."

"That's sweet, but why the hell didn't they just tell you everything themselves after you discovered the checks and paperwork about you being a foster kid?"

"They tried," she assured him. "Unfortunately, I wasn't in the headspace to listen while they were alive," she said regretfully. "I'm afraid finding out on my own as I did kind of rocked my world. I didn't even notice that the checks were uncashed, just that there were checks. And I just—" she shrugged helplessly "—spun out. It felt like my whole world was crumbling. Mom and Dad weren't my parents, their home wasn't my home . . . Basically, I was a guest there that they were paid to feed and clothe and keep out of trouble. And they'd lied to me all those years, calling me their daughter and letting me call them Mom and Dad." She shook her head.

"Of course I confronted them, and not delicately. I basically tore into them and demanded to know who my real parents were, which I know hurt them terribly, but Dad told me the story of him and his partner finding me. Only that just made things worse to my mind. Not only was I no longer their daughter, but I was some charity case they'd taken in. The garbage baby of a druggie runaway and some unknown man who might have been a john she'd sold herself to for drugs for all I knew. I imagined all sorts of horrible things," she admitted sadly. "And I blamed them for it."

Swallowing, she raised her head and peered up at the starry sky as she confessed, "I ran a little wild for a while, gave them a lot of trouble and attitude. They kept telling me they loved me, and nothing had changed—I was still their daughter and they wanted to adopt me and make it official—but I was so caught up in my own hurt and anger I wasn't hearing them . . ." CJ paused briefly and then blew her breath out. "I was a mess, and I made their lives hell those last couple of months."

"But eventually you came around and they adopted you," Mac said, and she heard the hope in his voice. He wanted a happy ending for her. CJ was more than sorry to have to disabuse him.

"No," she told him solemnly. "I mean, I did eventually come around and realize that they'd loved me, and had only not told me out of that love, but not in time for them to adopt me." She saw his confusion, and explained, "Like I said, I was acting up. That included skipping school and staying out late and stupid tricks like that. One night when I was out past curfew, they got in the car and came out to look for me, and they were T-boned by a drunk driver. Mom died in the ambulance on the way to the hospital. It was while sitting at Dad's bedside in the hospital, praying for him to survive, that I got over my anger and hurt and realized that they both had loved me and I had repaid them like a spoiled little brat. But it was too late. My father died the second day."

"And you went back into the foster system," Mac surmised.

CJ nodded. "I was never really out of it, but yes, I went to a new foster home. The Millers. They were nice people too. They specialized in teenagers like myself. There were six of us there. Two boys and three other girls. We all got pretty close and I stayed there until I went off to university."

"At seventeen," Mac said, obviously remembering their previous conversation on the subject. "An impressive accomplishment."

CJ shrugged. "As Mrs. Miller used to say, I was a girl with a mission," she told him with a faint smile. "And she was right, I suppose. I was determined to prove to myself and everyone else that my parents, Marge and Johnathan Cummings, hadn't wasted their time and love on me. I decided to be a police officer like my dad and started taking summer school every year to finish high school a year early, and then I did the same at university and got out of there with my degree early too. After that I was off to the Ontario Police College."

She paused briefly, and then smiled crookedly and admitted, "I was the youngest cadet they'd accepted at the college and the only reason I got in so young was because I had the support of all of my father's coworkers. Especially Uncle Ernie. Ernie Cowessess, my father's partner," she explained, and when he nodded, she continued, "He and Captain Hatford personally went to the college to talk to the administration about my getting in."

"They were still involved in your life?" Mac asked with interest.

CJ nodded. "Uncle Ernie was a family friend as well as Dad's partner. Our families used to have barbecues together and whatnot. He and his wife wanted to take me in when my parents died, and I did stay with them for a while, but he was older than my dad. He had heart issues and was retired and . . ." She shrugged. "I didn't want to be a burden to them.

"Anyway," she said, forcing herself to sit up a little straighter. "Like I said, I had a great childhood. And Marge and Johnathan Cummings were the best parents a girl could ask for. I was not damaged by my childhood."

"Then what damaged you?"

CJ stiffened at the question, myriad reactions flowing through her: indignation, anger, hurt. She opened her mouth, about to deny that she was damaged at all, but then closed it again without uttering a word. Because she was prickly and closed off for a reason. She *was* damaged.

In the end, she ignored the question and asked a bit truculently, "Why do you care?"

"Because . . ." He hesitated and then simply said, "I am just trying to understand you better."

CJ nodded and then repeated, "Why?"

She wasn't surprised when that seemed to take him aback. But after a moment he said, "It's what people do, CJ. They ask questions, get to know each other, and become friends . . . or something more."

CJ stiffened and then said firmly, "I have enough friends. I don't need new ones, and I definitely am not in the market for 'something more.'"

"Why?"

CJ scowled now with irritation. "Why are you asking?"

"Because I'm attracted to you. I like you, and I'd be interested in being in your life," he answered promptly.

CJ swallowed and turned away again. It was what her dream Mac had said too, but she'd never imagined hearing it in reality. She was shocked that he had, shocked by how much his words affected her, and even more shocked by how appealing the idea of having him in her life was to her. She hardly knew the man. Sure, he was obviously smart—the man was a doctor, after all, so had to be smart. He was also funny and made her laugh, sometimes even on purpose. And yes, he had apparently slept on her couch to keep an eye on her, showing concern and caring and thoughtfulness. He was also sexy as hell. And that dream! Good Lord it had been hot! Powerful hot and tempting.

But it had only been a dream, she reminded herself firmly. He probably sucked at sex in real life. Besides, she couldn't risk finding out, and he wouldn't want to be a part of her life if he knew—

Mouth tightening, she cut off her own thoughts and assured him, "You don't want to be in my life, Mac."

"I do," he responded promptly.

"You don't even know me," she pointed out with frustration. She'd been rather hoping he'd just take the hint and shut up about this, but it appeared persistence was another quality he had. That was something she normally would have appreciated. Not so much in this instance, though, since it meant she was having to talk him out of something she actually really wanted but couldn't have. Because CJ was more than interested in the man herself. She had been even before the dream sex that had left her so hot and bothered. But she could not have it.

"I'd like to," he responded. "I'd like to learn every-thing there is to know about you."

CJ's mouth tightened. "Everything, huh?" she asked bitterly, and then nodded. "Fine, then. You want to know everything? How about this? I like you too. You're good-looking, intelligent, funny, and consider-ate, and I find you incredibly hot and sexy. The fact is, I'd love nothing more than to drag you up to my room right now and jump your bones. Hell, I'd even happily jump your bones right here."

Mac reacted like a bull at the twitch of a red cape. He was out of his chair and pulling her out of hers so fast she didn't even really see him or even herself move; she was just suddenly upright in his arms with his face lowering toward her. Fortunately, he wasn't as quick at the lowering his head to claim her lips part and she was able to get her hand up between them at the last minute. Catching his nose and mouth with the palm of her hand, she closed her fingers on his face and forced his head back up, then pulled out of his arms as she said, "There's just one thing stopping me from doing that."

She didn't wait for him to ask what that one thing was, but simply let the word fall from her mouth like the stone it was. The huge honking boulder that had been lodged in her gut for three and a half years. "HIV."

Mac stiffened, his eyes rounding, and she nodded. "Yeah. I have HIV." Smiling bitterly, she added, "Bet I'm looking a lot less attractive now, huh?"

"No," he said solemnly. "I'm sorry you have HIV, but it doesn't change how I feel. I'm still attracted to you and I still want to know more about you and have you in my life."

"You mean as a friend," she suggested quietly.

"As a friend, a lover, a partner," he countered.

CJ's heart jumped at his words and her eyes widened. That wasn't at all what she'd expected and she wasn't sure how to handle it. She was tempted, but . . .

"You do know what HIV is, right?" she asked with a slight frown.

"I'm a hematologist, CJ. Of course I know."

"Well, how the hell could you want me after learning that?" she asked with disbelief. She found it hard to imagine anyone would want her knowing that. She herself had felt dirty and tainted since finding out she had it. Counseling had helped a bit, but she still felt like her ex-husband had marked her like a dog pissing on a hydrant, and couldn't believe Mac didn't now find her repulsive.

"CJ," he began soothingly, but she cut him off.

"You're going to try to sell me that business about safe sex. I mean, yes, I take my antiretroviral treatments, and my viral load is undetectable, and between that and condoms it should be safe," she said, sure that was where he was heading. "But I don't have tests every single day—what if the day we had sex was the day it was detectable? Condoms are supposed to protect you, but do you know how many babies are born each year because of faulty or broken condoms?"

"CJ—"

"No," she said grimly.

"You don't have to worry about giving me HIV."

"Of course I do. I hate the person who gave it to me. I don't want you to hate me! And hell, I'd hate myself if I was responsible for giving it to you."

"You can't," he assured her.

"What?" she asked with disbelief. "Of course I can."

"No," he said firmly. "You cannot."

"How do you figure that?" she asked at once.

Mac opened his mouth, closed it, and then frowned as if unsure he should say what he wanted to.

"Because he already has it."

CJ turned sharply on Justin Bricker as he stepped out onto the porch after making that announcement from the doorway. She stared at him blankly, then shifted her gaze back to Mac. He was looking back at Bricker, his face turned away. She couldn't see his expression. Not that she would have probably noticed what it was if she could see it. Her mind was taken up with her own reactions. The shot of shock, followed by quick sympathy and sadness that a man so virile and strong had HIV. But hope and even happiness quickly overwhelmed both of those reactions. If he had HIV it meant she wouldn't have to worry about giving it to him, and she had a chance of making her dream a reality and having a relationship with him. She might be able to have him as a partner and enjoy a more normal life.

CJ liked Mac. She was attracted to him, and she could have him . . . without guilt or worry. She could have sex, and that was a big one. It had been more than three and a half years since she'd had sex, and she was so damned attracted to the man that she was having wet dreams about him. She'd never even had those about her ex-husband, whom she'd had the hots for something terrible.

But those thoughts were quickly followed by guilt. She was quite sure she shouldn't be so happy about his misfortune. That was selfish and just kind of disgusting.

Feeling swamped by the combination of emotions, CJ shot past Mac and Justin and hurried into the house. She needed time alone to think over what this meant for her. What she wanted it to mean.

Fifteen

"Why the hell would you tell her that?" Mac asked Bricker the moment CJ had disappeared into the house.

"Because you'd boxed yourself into a corner saying she couldn't give you HIV," Bricker said with a shrug. "You couldn't explain why without telling her the truth about our kind, and doing that would have been a huge mistake at this point."

"How do you know?" Mac asked resentfully. "She might have taken it well."

"If you thought that, you wouldn't have hesitated," Bricker said quietly. "Besides, what if she had? Then you'd always have had that niggling worry that she turned to be free of HIV."

"We're life mates. It doesn't matter why she turns.

We are meant to be together," Mac argued impatiently.

"But wouldn't it be nice to have a chance to actually woo her?" Bricker asked. "To fall in love before she knows about our kind? You've got a chance to do that. Few immortals do. Holly was turned before we even met. She was in a state of confusion and married to a mortal, for Christ's sake. The start of our relationship was one hell of a mess," he said with regret. "And then there's Decker. Dani knew about us before he could try to woo her too. In fact, I can't think of an immortal who's had the chance to actually woo their mate. But you could. You could date her, woo her, win her love and trust, and tell her you want to spend your life with her, and if she sounds agreeable, then tell her about our people, that she could be immortal and never have to worry about illness again.

"It might not seem important but . . ." He hesitated and then admitted, "I realized a while back that I dated and romanced a lot of women in my life, but not the one I love and who deserved it the most: my wife. I wish I'd been able to. I wish we had those kinds of memories, instead of just a leap to life mates." Expression troubled, he added, "And I wonder sometimes if Holly doesn't wish that as well, and feel a bit cheated because she didn't get it."

Mac considered what Bricker had said, and silently debated the issue. Tell CJ everything now and use her illness to gain her, or win her in a more traditional way and then tell her about immortals and that he was one. The first way would be fast and dirty; the second way would take longer, but would mean he would never wonder why she was with him.

Part of him just wanted to claim her any way he could, even if it meant bribing her to be his with her health. The other part, though, wondered if Bricker wasn't right. Would he regret it later if he forced the leap to life mates by revealing what he was to her?

"You're both assuming that she'll see being an immortal as a cure. But what if she sees it as another disease? One even worse than HIV? I mean, having to consume blood isn't for everyone."

Mac turned to stare at the woman mounting the steps to the porch, his eyes widening as they slid over her blond hair and athletic build.

"Oh, by the way, your sister is here," Bricker said wryly. "She arrived shortly after you went up for your nap."

Mac gave him a speaking look for the delayed announcement, and then turned his irritation on Katricia. "I told you I didn't need help, Kat."

"Yes, you did," she agreed with amusement as she

stepped up to hug him, completely ignoring how stiff he was. Pulling back, she then added, "And if you were even considering telling CJ that you're immortal so early in the game, you were wrong. You do need my help."

"She's sick," he argued at once.

"She's mortal, Mac. Being sick is a part of the mortal condition. But it doesn't guarantee she will embrace becoming immortal. Or that she won't be horrified and try to stake you once she learns you aren't mortal."

"What?" he asked with amazement. "She wouldn't do that."

"Are you so sure? She hasn't known you long," she pointed out.

Mac frowned at that truth as he realized he had only met CJ the day before yesterday. The thought was somewhat staggering. It already felt to him like she had always been a part of his life. Which, thinking about it, was somewhat bizarre. The only explanation he could come up with for that was that the nanos coursing through his body were somehow behind it.

Could they cause a feeling of familiarity with someone? Did they do that when they settled on a life mate for their host? Make them feel close and comfortable with the other individual as well as extremely hot for them sexually? He had no idea. It didn't really matter if they did, though, or what he felt. The issue was CJ, and she was mortal, without the nanos to tell her he was her perfect life mate. She wouldn't be experiencing the same comfort and sense of closeness he was. At least he didn't think she would. Although mortal life mates were supposed to enjoy the same deep hunger and passion for their partner as the immortal did. The nanos had to cause that, sending out some kind of cocktail of hormones to arouse them both. Maybe they sent out a cocktail of soothing and comforting hormones at the appropriate times too and she did feel safe and familiar with him. He could only hope.

"Bricker is right," Katricia said now. "You need to woo CJ. Gain her trust. She's already attracted to you, and likes you. But that kind of scares her. The truth is she uses her illness to avoid entanglements. She knows she can have a relationship even with HIV, but she has some issues. Guilt over her parents' deaths, a bit of a trust issue because of her parents lying to her all those years, as well as thanks to her ex-husband. The combination has worn her down. She's been hiding out these last three and a half years and healing, coming to terms with everything."

"You read her," Mac said quietly.

Katricia nodded. "I was out here when she came outside. I was standing in the shadows of the trees and she didn't see me. I was reading her the whole time, even after you showed up. And like I said, Bricker is right, you need to woo her. But most importantly you need to not scare her off before you get the chance to win her trust, so stay out of her bed. Date her like a 1950s mortal."

"A 1950s mortal?" he echoed with uncertainty.

"Think *I Love Lucy*, *Leave It to Beaver*, and *Father Knows Best*," she suggested.

"Basically PG," Justin Bricker said helpfully, or not so helpfully as it turned out since Katricia immediately shook her head.

"G. Not PG. No nudity," she corrected. "Just keep your clothes on and get to know her. And let her get to know you and what kind of man you are. Go hold her and kiss her and let her feel cherished without the complication of sex, at least for a little while."

Mac's eyes widened incredulously. "She's my life mate." As far as he was concerned that was all he had to say. Life mates were infamous for not being able to keep their hands off each other at first. What his sister was asking was the impossible.

"Yeah," Katricia sighed, but then shrugged. "But I have faith in you, and I think it's what she needs."

"Thanks," Mac said dryly, and thought she had more faith in him than he did.

"You should maybe go comfort her now," Katricia said solemnly. "She was a bit stressed when she rushed back into the house. Confused by her feelings and her reaction to the news that you supposedly have HIV."

Mac nodded and straightened his shoulders, then marched back into the house, telling himself he could do this. He could woo her like a 1950s mortal. Take it slow, take her places, dinner, movies, dancing— No, not dancing. If he touched her . . . dear God, this was going to be hard, he acknowledged unhappily.

CJ wasn't in the kitchen, so he headed upstairs, trying to figure out how he was supposed to comfort her without touching her. Offering platitudes seemed kind of lame, but touching her would be dangerous. Maybe if he just encouraged her to talk, and listened attentively . . .

That was the best he'd come up with by the time he reached the door to her suite. He was so used to just walking in that he almost did it again this time, but then caught himself and knocked softly instead, very aware that the other guests were probably back from the wedding and sleeping now.

CJ must have been in the salon, because he'd barely finished knocking when the door opened and CJ filled the doorway. For a moment they just stared at each other, and then Mac cleared his throat and opened his mouth to speak. What came out was a startled grunt as she caught his hand, tugged him into the room, and closed the door. He then found himself pushed back against it and CJ was kissing him. Mac was so startled at the greeting that for one moment he just stood there, his hands hanging loosely at his sides thinking, *G. No nudity.* But he was beginning to think Katricia had got CJ all wrong when her tongue slid out to brush along the seam of his lips. That small action sent a zip of excitement through Mac and almost had him opening his mouth, but instead he pulled back and eyed her worriedly.

"What are we doing?" he asked when she peered up at him in question.

Uncertainty entered her expression then and she bit her lip. "I was thinking, and I'm sorry you have HIV, but as ashamed as I am to admit it, I'm kind of glad too, because I like you and find you really attractive, and I thought you wanted—I mean, on the porch you—"

"I want you," he interrupted, unable to bear the sudden anxiety on her face. "But I wasn't sure that you wanted to."

A wry smile curved her lips into a crooked smile. "Mac, I haven't had sex for three and a half years. Trust me, I want to, and it's safe with you. As long as you have condoms. I mean, I take my antivirals religiously and—"

"Let's go," Mac interrupted abruptly, catching her hand and heading for the door. She'd won the battle at "Trust me, I want to." Katricia had definitely got it wrong. Thank God.

"Wait!" CJ tugged at her hand, breaking free and making him stop and turn to face her. "Where are we going? If you don't want to, it's fine. I just—"

"I want to," he assured her. "But I don't have condoms. We need to go to a twenty-four-hour drugstore. They will have one here, won't they?" he asked with sudden concern.

"Oh. I don't know," CJ admitted, and then ran a weary hand through her hair and shook her head. "Maybe this is a sign that we aren't meant to—"

"It's not a sign," he assured her with alarm. "Definitely not a sign. It just means a nice romantic drive under a starry sky. Or maybe they deliver," he added thoughtfully, and asked, "If we order now, how long do you think it would take them to get here?"

"I have no idea." CJ frowned and he could feel that he was losing this opportunity even before she said, "Maybe this was a bad idea."

"No. It's a good idea," he assured her, grasping her upper arms. "Really, really good. I— We don't have to have sex," he said now. "Kissing is a start, and touching. We can save the good stuff for next time."

CJ's eyebrows rose at that and she said dryly, "Mac, kissing and touching *are* the good stuff. It's called foreplay."

"Really?" he asked with interest. He knew kissing and touching were good, but they hadn't had a name for it the last time he'd had sex. Of course, that had been centuries ago. Maybe a millennium. They might have called it foreplay and he'd just forgotten. Realizing that CJ was staring at him with disbelief and something like disappointment, Mac realized that his "Really?" may have led her to believe that he didn't indulge in what she called foreplay. He had to correct that assumption at once, of course, or he suspected she wouldn't even give him a chance. But what was he to do? Say, *Yes, of course, foreplay. I love foreplay. Let me show you.* The words sounded lame even just in his head. He doubted he'd get far spouting them, so he gave up on talk and simply kissed her.

Now it was CJ's turn to stand still and unresponsive, but it didn't last long. When he let his tongue run along the seam of her lips as she had done with him, she didn't pull away as he had, but relaxed a little in his arms and opened tentatively to him.

CJ let her mouth drift open out of curiosity more than anything at that point. She was curious to see if he was as good as her dream Mac had been. She quickly realized he was better. That was the last coherent thought she had as his tongue slid past her lips and set off an explosion of nuclear proportions in not just her mouth but her body. A spontaneous combustion of need flared through her, zipping from her mouth down and out to every nerve end she had. She felt her nipples instantly pebble; heat pooled low in her belly. Heck, her very skin tingled in response, all the way down to her damned toes, and CJ had the instant mad urge to rub herself all over him like a cat in heat. It was crazy insane. He hadn't even touched her yet except where he was grasping her arms.

She'd barely had the thought when Mac used the hold on her arms to urge her backward. She felt something against the backs of her legs and then he was lowering her to lie on it—the sofa, she realized as she sank into its cushions. He immediately came down on top of her, his weight a welcome full-body press that had her moaning into his mouth as he kissed her over and over.

They were making out like teenagers, but CJ didn't recall any of her juvenile make-out sessions being quite so desperately passionate. She was wrapped around him now and clinging like English ivy with both her arms and legs, her hips grinding instinctively up into his. They were both still fully clothed, and yet excitement was pounding through her like a bass drum in a cave, echoing out and back, crashing against her so that her entire body seemed to be vibrating with the need he was stirring to violent life in her.

His hand slid between them to find one of her breasts, squeezing almost painfully through the material separating them, and CJ cried out and arched into the touch, egging him on. What she really wanted was for him to tear her shirt off so he could touch her bare skin. Unfortunately, her clothes didn't suddenly disappear as they had in her dream, and she couldn't tell him what she wanted with his tongue in her mouth. Instead, she grasped a handful of his T-shirt and started dragging it up his back, hoping to at least be able to touch his skin.

It was all the prodding Mac needed; in the next moment he'd started to move, lifting upward. With her arms around him, CJ went with him, their mouths clinging as he shifted them so that she was sitting up and he was kneeling with his knees on either side of her legs. CJ felt air touch the skin of her back and midriff, and then he broke their kiss and her shirt was coming off over her head. The moment the cloth was out of the way, he was kissing her again as his hands slid around to undo and then remove her bra. While he tossed that aside, CJ reached for the hem of his shirt again and jerked it upward until Mac took over the task and removed his own shirt. It meant breaking their kiss again, but this time CJ lowered her head and, spotting his broad chest and the hard nipples on it, she zeroed in on one and claimed it with her mouth.

"Oh, Christ, yes," Mac growled, gliding one hand up into her hair to cup the back of her head as he tossed his shirt aside with the other hand.

CJ smiled against his chest, suckled lightly, and then flicked one finger over the excited bud only to still as she became aware of the way touching him caused her pleasure too. Stiffening, she raised confused eyes to him, but Mac kissed her at once, his mouth hard and demanding as he urged her to lie back on the couch again. By the time his chest covered hers, she'd forgotten what had troubled her, and luxuriated in the feel of his chest hairs rubbing against her nipples.

She moaned in disappointment when he began to shift down her body. But then he cupped one breast and closed his lips over the areola and the hard pebble at its center, and CJ murmured incomprehensibly as his warm, wet mouth encompassed her and began to suckle. The sensation was so intense, the excitement so overwhelming, it felt like he was drawing her soul out of her body. Clutching at the short hair at the back of his neck, she urged him on, her body twisting under his, and then she felt his other hand drift down to press between her legs and she bucked into the touch, wishing her jeans were gone too. In the next moment, she felt his hand at the button of her jeans and she could have wept with relief. But he didn't remove them; instead, once he had the button undone, and the zipper down, he slid one hot hand inside to snake inside her panties and slide down between her legs.

CJ's cry of pleasure was caught by his mouth as he began to caress her and she realized he'd released her nipple to kiss her again. She was beyond kissing, though, at that point, and merely sucked desperately on his tongue as his fingers continued rubbing, circling, and gliding over her hot, damp skin. He was making her wetter by the moment as her body wept for the release it needed and then he slid a finger inside her, pushing into her moist depths even as he continued caressing her with his thumb, and that was when CJ broke. Something snapped inside her, some fine string of tension that had been growing and stretching since he'd started kissing her, and pleasure slammed through her, a tornado demolishing everything in its path and leaving nothing behind but a welcoming darkness that closed over her.

"Seriously? Condoms? Didn't you hear a thing Katricia said?" Justin Bricker asked with exasperation.

"Keep your voice down," Mac growled, glancing back to where CJ was still unconscious on the couch. He didn't know how long she'd been out, because he'd been out too, and had only just awoken. He was hoping, though, that she'd stay asleep long enough for Justin to go get some condoms and get back.

"Think 1950s dating," Bricker reminded him. "G-rated."

Mac rolled his eyes and swiveled his head back around to glower at the man. He'd actually expected to have to go downstairs to talk to him so had been relieved to find him standing guard outside the door. What he hadn't expected was Bricker giving him trouble over his request.

"Just get me the damned condoms, Bricker."

"I'm supposed to be guarding you," the younger immortal said. "I can't do that from the drugstore. If they even have a drugstore in this town that's open at this hour."

"Bricker," Mac snarled in a warning tone, and then snapped his mouth shut abruptly when he noticed a man approaching—one of Mrs. Vesper's guests, he presumed. In his late twenties, with damp sandy colored hair and an athlete's physique, the guy looked like he'd just come from the shower. But Mac had no idea how long he'd been there; he hadn't noticed him until now and he was already just steps away. He was about to slip into the guy's mind to see who the hell he was when the other man suddenly swerved their way and held up a small foil square.

Mac's eyes widened with excitement on the condom package the man was holding up.

"Take them," the stranger said cheerfully. "I keep plenty on hand since the wife had to take a break from the pill. Happy to help out a brother."

"Thank you," Mac said, taking what had looked like one but was actually two condom packets. He felt like he'd won the lottery. "Seriously, thank you."

"My pleasure," the man said easily, and then grinning, added, "Have fun," as he continued down the hall toward the stairs.

"If Katricia finds out—"

Mac closed the door on the rest of Bricker's warning. He didn't care what his sister thought. Only what CJ wanted, and she'd wanted a condom earlier. He was happy to be able to supply one when she woke up. Not that he hadn't enjoyed their make-out session, or maybe petting session was a more fitting description, Mac thought. He watched the occasional movie and was sure petting session was more appropriate. But anyway, he'd enjoyed it a great deal. Life mates shared not only dream sex, but they shared their pleasure during actual sex. He'd experienced every twitch, swell, and explosion of pleasure that CJ had as he'd kissed and caressed her. He'd even climaxed with her when she had and then passed out with her, which was a side effect of the mind-blowing sex life mates enjoyed. It was the shared pleasure that did it. Being bombarded by the pleasure of both parties, building and echoing in the body and mind, was overwhelming and usually sent both partners into unconsciousness. In reality, it was just a faint, but unconsciousness sounded more manly.

Despite having enjoyed what they'd done, Mac would be pleased to present the condom and actually make love to CJ if that was what she wanted when she woke up. But not out here, he decided as he stopped next to the couch and peered down at CJ. She was sprawled on the sofa, topless, her lovely breasts on display, and her pants were undone and open still. They'd also ridden down her hips somewhat, pushed there by his hand as he'd fought for the room to pleasure her. She looked delicious, and he fervently hoped that they would go for another round when she woke up. He just didn't want to do it here in the salon with Justin Bricker outside the door.

Sticking the condom packets between his teeth, he bent to carefully scoop up CJ and headed for the bedroom with her.

As careful as he'd been, CJ blinked her eyes open and eyed him sleepily as he was setting her down. She smiled when she saw him, and then reached up and took the condom packets from his mouth. Her eyes widened as she realized what they were. "You've been out."

Mac grimaced and opened his mouth to explain, but then she grinned and added, "You're my hero," and he smiled and kissed her instead. He'd meant it to be a light *you're adorable, thanks for saying that* kind of kiss, but light kisses never happened with life mates. What started out as a light brushing of mouths ended in a full-on assault of lips and tongue, and they were both lost. All the plans Mac had come up with when he'd first woken up, the things he'd wanted to do, the pleasure he'd wanted to give her, flew out the window as he fell on her like a starving man on a feast. And like a starving man, he did his damnedest to taste everything. Her lips were sweet and still swollen from their last round. He licked and nipped and soothed them by turn before nibbling a path to her ear where he concentrated briefly before turning his attention to her neck, nipping and sucking and licking on his way down to her chest.

Her breasts came next, a scrumptious buffet that he licked and suckled and squeezed by turn, enjoying the pleasure it sent coursing through him until she recalled him to the fact that she wasn't his own private playground by flipping him onto his back and climbing onto him like he was a ride at the fair. Mac groaned and clasped her hips as she settled on his groin, rubbing against him through their jeans, but his eyes popped open with alarm when she then reached for the button of his pants and announced, "I got all the pleasure last time. Your turn."

This was when Mac realized why his sister had counseled him to woo her like a 1950s mortal. Shared pleasure. The moment CJ touched him in any way, she would experience his pleasure and that was not something that could be explained without telling her about immortals and the special little abilities they had. He couldn't allow this, he realized even as she popped his button open and started lowering the zipper.

"Wait!" he gasped, catching her hands.

CJ paused and met his gaze with question.

"I . . . er . . ." He stared at her helplessly for a moment, unsure what the hell to say to keep her from touching him, and then it came to him. A good excuse, but one that would surely be humiliating as hell. But it had to be done, so he bit the bullet and cleared his throat and then said, "If you touch me I— You said it's been three years for you?"

She nodded.

"Well, it's been longer for me," he told her, and that was definitely the truth. It had been better than a thousand years since Mac had bothered with sex.

"Okay," CJ said slowly, looking a little bewildered as to why he would bring that up at this point.

"So I'm afraid if you touch me, I'll blow like a geyser . . . immediately," he added with a wince. No man wanted to suggest he might be premature at such things. Especially when it wasn't true. That was the thing about life mates, when one blew, the other went with them. It made premature ejaculation impossible. Or maybe it made them both premature ejaculators since life mate sex was fast and furious for at least the first year after coming together.

CJ grinned at him widely. "I'll risk it; we can always work you up again after and try a second round."

Mac gaped at that announcement, his grip tightening on her hands to keep her from going back to work on his jeans. They struggled briefly, and then he rolled her on the bed, raising her hands over her head as he did and keeping them there as he kissed her.

CJ stopped trying to free her hands at once when his mouth covered hers. Opening to him like a flower to the sun, she took in his tongue, rasping it with her own, and then tilted her head slightly to a better angle. When he began to grind his hips into her, she wrapped her legs around him, urging him on, and when he finally released her hands, she reached for him, sliding the fingers of one hand around his head to tangle in his hair, while the other reached down to cup and squeeze his bottom and urge him closer still.

Mac couldn't get any closer with their clothes on. He would have liked to remedy that situation, and planned to, just as soon as he'd sufficiently distracted CJ from trying to pleasure him. Once he had her so wound up she couldn't think straight, he'd strip them both, pull on a condom, and finally sink into her depths. At least that's what he told himself. The problem was, getting her that wound up got him that wound up too. He didn't even get the chance to caress her more intimately; kissing her deeply, caressing her breasts, and tweaking her nipples along with grinding himself against her over and over again did the trick quite nicely. And before he could even consider stripping her or himself, CJ was tearing her mouth away to cry out as he pushed them both past that fine border between excitement and release and into the darkness that waited on the other side.

It was something cool and sweet smelling running back and forth over her mouth that woke up CJ. Opening sleepy eyes, she peered up into Mac's smiling face and then noted the slice of orange he was rubbing across her lower lip.

"Hungry?" he asked softly.

She opened her mouth to answer and he slid the orange in. Tangy juice exploded into her mouth as soon as she bit down, and she smiled at the burst of flavor. But that smile faded slightly as her eyes slid over his body and she saw that he'd peeled away his jeans and boxer briefs as surely as he'd peeled the orange and was now completely naked. He was also fully erect.

A cool slice of orange running lightly across her nipple reclaimed her attention from his rather impressive erection and CJ shifted her gaze to his face again as he said, "I hope you don't mind."

She wasn't sure if he was asking about the fact that he'd stripped while she slept, or about the orange he was rubbing her nipple with, but she didn't mind either, so simply shook her head and then peered down at her chest with confusion when she felt a drop of liquid run down her breast to pool on her sternum. The orange he was rubbing over her nipple was only a half slice and it was the open end he was using. He'd also squeezed it so that juice covered the darkened area and as she watched he bent his head to lick up the small spot between her breasts, then followed the sweet trail up to her nipple.

CJ moaned as his tongue swirled over the tight bud, licking it clean with lavish attention before sucking it into his mouth. Her hands moved of their own accord to his head and the one shoulder she could reach, and she arched into his caress, her legs moving restlessly as a throbbing ache started between them.

As if drawn by the movement, Mac slid one hand down her stomach and over her jeans to cup her there and CJ gasped, and let her back drop in favor of bucking her hips up into the touch. The moment she did, Mac let her nipple slip from his mouth and sat up on his haunches to quickly pull her jeans down. The man was as fast as lightning. She'd barely registered what he was doing when her jeans were off and being tossed aside, and then Mac was shifting to cover her, his hips resting between her legs, pressing against her hungry ache as he kissed her.

Kiss wasn't really a proper description for what he did. It was more like his mouth was making love to hers, and every time his tongue thrust into her, he shifted his hips, rubbing his hardness against her as well until she couldn't stand it anymore. Breaking the kiss on a gasp, CJ dug her nails into his shoulders and twisted her head on the pillow. She'd drawn her knees up without consciously realizing it and now braced her feet on the bed and lifted her hips into the slow rub, trying to angle herself so that he'd enter her. She wanted him inside her, she wanted to finally feel him fill her, and when he fulfilled that request and pushed into her, her eyes shot open and a choked sound of pleasure came from her throat. Dear God he felt so good, she thought, and then she stiffened, her eyes shooting open and to him with alarm.

"Condom," she gasped.

"On," he breathed, and then kissed her again, his tongue and penis in sync as he thrust, pushing the worry away, along with everything else except that mounting excitement and need between her legs. But it wasn't just between her legs. Her whole body seemed infused with it, hunger, excitement, need, want . . . It vibrated through her body, pulsing and echoing and pounding against every nerve, soaking every cell, until she was nothing but this, until she knew nothing but that she needed release before it drove her mad.

Mac was moving too slowly, almost torturing her with his slow steady thrusts as he tried to draw out their pleasure. Finally, she couldn't take it anymore and, catching him by surprise, turned them both on the bed so that she came up on top. She saw Mac blink in surprise, and then he smiled and reached for her breasts. CJ grabbed his wrists as he began to caress and squeeze, using the hold to keep her balance as she began to move. She went slow for the first couple of strokes, but once she felt comfortable in the saddle, she began to increase her speed, raising and lowering herself, shifting her hips first a little one way and then the other. Then she stopped thinking and just moved as she wanted, riding him fast and hard and using his body to find her pleasure. It didn't take long. To CJ it seemed like she'd just started when her release hit her like a freight train. She was vaguely aware of Mac's shout as she threw her head back on a cry, but mostly she was aware of the pleasure overwhelming her and then she wasn't aware of anything.

Sixteen

C J woke up with a smile on her face . . . and sunshine warming her naked skin. The bedroom curtains were open, she realized, and turned her head to look out the window at a beautiful sunny day. The sky was blue with fluffy white clouds and the sun was high in the— CJ jerked her gaze to the clock on the bedside table and bit back a curse. It was eleven thirty. She was supposed to be at the diner at noon.

Panic coursing through her, she rolled out of bed, snatched up her suitcase, and dashed into the bathroom. She'd already noticed that it seemed to take a long time for the water to warm up here at Mrs. Vesper's, but she didn't have the time to wait for it to heat up this morning. CJ jerked the shower curtain half-open along the tub, turned the water on, and then stepped away long enough to pull out clean clothes. She hung them from the hook on the bathroom door and then gritted her teeth and stepped into the tub and doused herself under the icy spray.

God in heaven it was cold! Setting her jaw, CJ resisted the urge to jump out and determinedly set to work cleaning and shampooing. She was in the midst of rinsing before the water warmed up. Grateful for it, she turned under the spray, allowing it to rinse away the soap and shampoo she'd just applied, and warm her at the same time. She was just finishing when she heard the bathroom door open.

"CJ?" The shower curtain twitched at the far end and Mac peered around it to offer her a wide smile. "Good morning, beautiful."

CJ smiled instinctively back, and then scrambled out of her end of the tub when he started to step in on the other side.

"What are you doing?" Mac asked with surprise, stopping half-in and pulling the shower curtain aside to peer at her with dismay. "I'm sorry, I didn't mean to scare you out of your shower. I just thought to join you."

"It's okay. I'm done," she assured him. "You go ahead."

"Won't you stay and join me?"

His voice was a velvet growl, his smile sexy as hell, and CJ actually took a step toward him before catching herself. A weak breath slipping from her lips, she gave her head a shake to try to clear away the lust suddenly fogging it and said, "Hell, no. If I join you, we'll end up back in bed and I have to be at the diner in twenty minutes."

That was a guess. She didn't have a handy clock or watch to check the time, and she suspected she hadn't been in the shower that long, but her estimate was probably pretty close, and she had to move.

"I forgot about that," Mac muttered, and then tugged the shower curtain closed and apparently went about taking his shower.

Grateful that he wasn't going to be a distraction this morning, CJ quickly dried herself and pulled her clothes on. She was brushing the tangles out of her hair, in preparation to pull it back into a ponytail, when the water suddenly shut off and Mac pulled the shower curtain open. CJ cast a glance his way and then stilled, her eyes sliding over his naked, wet body. The man was beautiful. If he had a tan, he'd be perfect, but even without it he was an Adonis.

"Diner," Mac reminded her, snatching a towel off the towel bar and quickly drying himself off as he walked out of the room.

CJ closed her mouth and inhaled another shaky breath as he took his perfect butt out of the room. Man, he was one potent mix of male, she thought as she returned to the effort to pull her hair back into a ponytail. But while her hands were working on her hair, her mind was in the other room with Mac. The bedroom where she'd had the most incredible sex of her life. CJ had thought her ex-husband, Billy, was a skilled lover. Honestly, she'd been pretty sure no one else could compare to Billy in that area, but Mac had surpassed him. The man had seemed to know just where to touch her, and exactly how much pressure to apply, what speed to use, the perfect angle . . . It was like he had a road map of her body and what she liked. It was mind-blowing. The man had given her such powerful orgasms she'd passed out, not once but every single time they'd—

"How are you doing in there? It's a quarter to and it takes ten minutes to get to the diner," Mac called out from the other room.

Cursing, CJ gave up her woolgathering, finished with her ponytail, and rushed out of the bathroom.

Mac was fully dressed when she entered the bedroom, wearing the jeans and black T-shirt he'd had on last night. He was also holding out her boots and purse.

"Thanks," CJ muttered, taking them from him. As he turned and headed into the salon, she dropped to sit on the end of the bed to tug the boots onto her bare feet. CJ knew it was a mistake even as she did it. Wearing the boots without socks would surely give her blisters. It wouldn't do much for the boots either to have her feet sweating in them all day, but she didn't have time to stop and look for socks so she yanked them on, stood, and headed into the salon where Mac was already waiting with the door open.

"Thank you," she murmured again as he ushered her out of the room.

CJ didn't bother to lock the door, but hurried to the stairs and rushed down them to the main floor.

"Morning, dears," Mrs. Vesper called as she rushed past the kitchen.

"Morning, Mrs. Vesper. I'm late. I'll see you later," CJ called out, hurtling toward the back door.

"Where are we going?"

CJ glanced around at that question in time to see Decker leading Bricker out of the kitchen to join Mac behind her as he answered, "CJ has to go to the diner."

"Right. The mob last night," Decker said with a nod as CJ pushed through the door and hurried across the porch.

"You guys don't have to come with me. I'm good," she told them as they followed her to the car.

"The doctor said you needed to be watched for

twenty-four hours," Mac reminded her. "Besides, I'm pretty sure the last time I stayed here Mrs. Vesper said something about the diner offering an all-day breakfast and I'm really hungry."

"I'm not surprised," Bricker said dryly. "It's nearly noon. You went up to lie down fourteen hours ago."

Shocked, CJ quickly did the math and worked out that Mac must have come up to her room to nap on the couch about an hour after she'd gone up. Deducting the amount of time she'd slept and her short stint downstairs for coffee, they'd basically been "rolling in the hay" for the last seven hours at least. Well, rolling in the hay and passing out, then waking up and rolling in the hay again. That had happened repeatedly. The first two times had merely been heavy petting; the next two after that they'd put the condoms to good use, though, and then they'd reverted to everything-but-sex after the condoms had been used up. And then Mac had been ready for some shower play this morning. If it hadn't been for her having to get to the diner for noon, she would have too. The man was a machine . . . or the Energizer Bunny. He just kept going and going and going. It was something CJ appreciated, since she was finding him incredibly addictive. Every time she'd woken up from one of her swoons, she'd found herself reaching for him again, if he wasn't awake first and already holding her. And she was really sorry she'd had to pass up the shower play. Maybe when they got back she could lure him there and—

I need to pick up more condoms, CJ thought suddenly. Lots and lots of condoms.

It was three minutes before noon when they walked into the diner. CJ relaxed a little when she saw that, but then tensed again when she saw that every seat in the place was taken. Fortunately, she'd barely recognized that when an older couple at a booth halfway along the outer wall stood and made their way to the till.

"So, do you think anyone will show up today?" Mac asked, ushering her to the newly emptied booth with a hand on her back.

CJ took a couple of deep breaths to try to control her response to his touch, and then cleared her throat and said, "I hope so, or it's going to be a long two hours and forty-five minutes."

"What happens in two hours and forty-five minutes?" Bricker asked as they slid into the booth, Mac and CJ on one side, Bricker and Decker on the other.

"I have that appointment with Jefferson at three, and told the captain I'd be there fifteen minutes early to look over and sign the statement I gave yesterday," she explained as she pushed the dirty bowl and glass in front of her toward the end of the table, even as Decker did the same on the other side. They'd sat down so quickly the waitress hadn't had a chance to clean it yet.

"Oh, yeah, the statements," Bricker said with a nod. "Mine will probably be ready for signing too."

"And mine," Mac murmured, even as Decker said the same.

"Good afternoon, folks. Sorry, let me get this out of your way first and then I'll bring you menus," said a cheerful, stick-thin woman with salt-and-pepper hair, quickly scooping up the dirty dishes. "Can I bring you something to drink with the menus?"

"Iced tea, please," CJ said when the men all deferred to her.

A chorus of three "me toos" followed and the waitress beamed at them as she balanced the stacked dishes in one hand and with the other whipped out a damp cloth to wipe down the table. "Well, I can see you're going to be an easy table to serve. I'll be right back with those menus and your drinks."

"I already like it here better than the Pub and Grill," Bricker said with a grin as the woman sailed off.

"You haven't even tried anything yet," Decker pointed out with amusement.

"Yeah, but at least our waitress didn't try to crawl into anyone's lap," Bricker responded.

CJ chuckled at the words, her gaze sliding to Mac and then quickly away as she thought she wouldn't mind crawling into his lap. Damn, she had it bad for the guy. He was sitting close enough that his leg and arm occasionally brushed hers, and every time it happened she had to clench her fingers into fists to keep from reaching out to touch him.

"What if someone does want to speak to CJ?" Decker asked suddenly, and when they all turned to him in question, said, "It's possible anyone who wants to speak to her might not be comfortable with all of us sitting here at the table."

"They couldn't even sit at the table," Bricker pointed out.

"Oh, yeah," CJ said with a frown, and glanced around the diner. While all the tables and booths were still taken, there were now a couple of stools empty at the counter.

"We'll sit at the counter," Decker announced suddenly, noting where she was looking. "Let the waitress know where we are when she brings the drinks."

"Thank you. I will," CJ assured him as he followed Bricker out of the booth.

The moment the two men were up and crossing the restaurant to the counter, Mac turned to her, smiled, and announced, "I'd like nothing better in this world than to lay you out naked on this table and feast on you."

CJ's jaw dropped open, snapped closed, and then she leaned toward him, only to catch herself and pull back.

"You're an evil man, Mac Argeneau," she said finally. "Now I'm going to be thinking of that all day."

"Only fair, since I will too," he said with a slow smile, his gaze moving down her body as if he could see through her clothes.

CJ shivered, her nipples going erect, and then blinked. "Your eyes."

Mac stiffened, and then his head turned the slightest bit and his eyes narrowed warily. "What about them?"

CJ was about to tell him that his silver-blue eyes had gone more silver than blue, but even as she opened her mouth, she realized that the silver had receded with the slight movement and narrowing. Now they were back to looking like normal and she ended up saying, "Nothing. It must have been a trick of the light."

It was what she'd told herself last night in her room. There had been several times then when his eyes had seemed to have turned a metallic silver, as if mercury had filled his irises, but she'd been too distracted to do much more than decide it must be a trick of the light. And of course, that had to be the answer. Unless the man was some kind of robot or something. Normal people's eyes did not go silver.

"Here we are."

CJ looked up to see that their waitress had returned.

"I saw your friends at the counter, so left their drinks and menus there with them," the woman announced as she set a tall glass full of ice, clear brown liquid, and lemons in front of each of them and then tugged the menus out from under her arm and set one before each of them too.

"Thank you," CJ murmured, and started to open her menu, only to pause when she realized the waitress hadn't left them, but was now sliding onto the opposite bench seat to join them. Closing the menu, she smiled at the woman and waited as she got herself situated in the center of the bench and set her clasped hands on the tabletop.

"I heard you say last night you'd be here for anyone who has information about the Keith Kaye case," she announced.

"Yes." CJ nodded encouragingly at the waitress, whose name tag read Laurie, before asking, "Is it all right if Mac stays? Or would you be more comfortable if he joined the boys?"

"Oh, no, he's fine," Laurie said quickly. "And I won't take up much of your time, I promise."

"That's fine. Take all the time you need," CJ said in her most soothing interviewing voice before asking, "And is it okay if I record our conversation?"

Laurie looked surprised by the question, and then a bit uncomfortable, but nodded reluctantly.

CJ quickly dug out the small recorder she always kept in her purse, switched it on, and set it on the table, then nodded at Laurie. "What did you want to tell me, Laurie?"

The waitress's eyes flicked up from the recorder to her face and anger settled on her expression. "I wanted to tell you that that asshole Jefferson is lying his face off about what happened the night Keith was beat up. Jefferson says he pulled Keith over because one of his back lights was out, but the lights were just fine."

"It was his father's car, wasn't it?" CJ asked, re-membering what Keith had told her in their phone interview.

"Yes, it was, and I live with Keith's daddy. I've pretty much been the boy's mama since he was twelve years old. I was at the sink rinsing out the coffee cups as he pulled out of the driveway, and the lights were working just fine. They were two big red eyes in the darkness. Jefferson is lying. He just pulled him over to bully him."

"I see," CJ murmured, and then asked, "Why do you think Jefferson would want to bully Keith?"

"'Cause that's what the bastard does," Laurie said grimly. "He struts around like his shit don't stink. Thinks he owns the town just because he's a cop and his wife's daddy is the police captain. Hell, he even does it in here. I don't know how many times he's come in when it's busy and kicked kids out of a booth just so he can have it. The girls tell me about it all the time. But he doesn't do it when I'm here," she said firmly. "No, ma'am. The first time he tried that shit while I was working I gave him hell. Told him those kids were here first, it was their booth, and he could just march his butt over to one of the stools at the counter, or leave. But I wasn't having him harassing my customers. He didn't like that, I can tell you," she said, nodding, and then grinned and added, "But the kids did. Thought I was a hero for putting him in his place. I got a real nice tip from those kids too and Lord knows teenagers are usually the worst tippers so you know they appreciated it."

CJ smiled faintly and nodded. "How long ago was that, Laurie?"

"About three, maybe four days before he beat the hell out of Keith," the waitress said grimly. "See, I only took this job about a month and a half ago. Used to work at the Dollar Store, but the manager kept grabbing my ass and I'd had enough. Quit and applied here. Got hired the same day. But that was the first time he'd come in while I was working."

"I see," CJ murmured thoughtfully.

Laurie shifted in her seat before asking with concern, "You don't think he beat up Keith 'cause he's like my stepson and I stood up to him, do you? I'd feel awful if it was my fault. The bastard really gave Keith a walloping."

"It's not your fault," CJ said at once, but then hesitated to say anything else. Fortunately, that seemed to be enough for the woman. At least she started talking again.

"Well, anyway, it's like I said, those rear lights were working fine that night when he left the house. Keith said Jefferson smashed one with his baton when he asked why he'd been pulled over when he hadn't been speeding or anything. Slammed his baton into it and said, ''Cause you have a light out.' All shit-eating grin while he said it too." She shook her head with disgust. "And then he turned the baton on Keith when he protested his doing that and said he was going to charge him with destruction of property or something."

CJ nodded. "Yes, he told me."

"Well, I can tell you that Keith don't lie. He's a damned good kid. Never been a lick of trouble. Truth is, we'd almost like to see him act up a bit. He doesn't go out with friends, girls, nor nothing. Mostly stays in and plays video games. That night he borrowed the car to drive to the city. Some game he wanted was out and he wanted to buy a copy. Instead, he ended up in the hospital with a broken arm, black eye, and fat lip."

CJ murmured sympathetically, but couldn't say what she really thought. She was supposed to be impartial, and she was trying her damnedest, but between Keith and this lady who was like a stepmother to the boy, Jefferson wasn't looking good. Finding out he'd put two more boys in the hospital the night before wasn't helping much with that impression either.

"Well, I got nothing else I can tell you. I wasn't there, though I wish I was. I just know his taillight wasn't out when he left the house." Sighing, she shifted back to her feet, and managed a smile. "You go on and look over your menus. I'll be back for your orders when you're ready."

"Thank you," CJ murmured.

"She was telling the truth," Mac said quietly as the waitress walked away.

CJ smiled faintly. "And how do you know that?"

"I can read people and tell when they're lying and she was telling the truth," he said.

CJ didn't tell him that she too could usually read people well and tell if they were lying, and that she felt Laurie had been completely honest with her. She merely turned her attention to the menu.

It didn't take them long to decide on what they wanted. The minute they closed their menus and set them down, Laurie was back, snatching them up and taking their order. The woman still had worry in her eyes, but her smile was firmly back in place and she was cheerful with them. CJ decided to give her a big tip.

CJ had ordered a Reuben and fries. So had Mac for that matter, and they were ready and on the table pretty quickly. But CJ was only halfway through her meal when a skinny fellow with black hair and a beard slid into the opposite side of the booth.

CJ set her sandwich back on the plate and used her napkin to wipe her hands as she watched the man and waited to see what he had to say.

"Are you that CSI lady?" he asked the minute her eyes met his.

"SIU," CJ corrected.

"Yeah, her," he said, and tilted his head, waiting.

It took her a minute to realize he was waiting for her to verify that she was indeed the SIU lady. Apparently, her correcting his abbreviation hadn't been enough. "Yes, I'm her."

"Good, good." He glanced around the restaurant nervously.

"And who are you?" CJ asked, pushing the button to start her mini recorder.

"Andy," he said abruptly.

"Andy what?" CJ asked, realizing then that she hadn't asked Laurie for her last name. She'd have to find out before she left.

"My last name doesn't matter," Andy said, his gaze jerking in every direction before sliding back to her. "I'm just here to do my duty and tell you what I know about Jefferson."

"Okay," CJ said easily. "Go ahead."

"He's a meth-head," he announced.

CJ's eyebrows rose and she sat back in her seat. "A meth-head?"

"Yeah. He started out just trying this and that—experimenting with pot, coke, molly, and stuff—but about ten months ago he tried crystal meth and he really liked that shit. Started hitting it hard. Now he's full-on hooked. And he's not a happy cranker either.

But he's worse now that his source has dried up. That's why he's losing it and beating the hell out of people when he used to be a pretty good cop," the man told her grimly.

"And how do you know his source dried up?" CJ asked, but suspected she already knew the answer. The man was twitchy as a cat's tail. To her, that screamed meth user who was in need of a fix.

"'Cause I'm his source, aren't I?" he said dryly, and then scowled at her. "But you can't use that against me since I'm your snitch now."

CJ ignored that and asked, "So why aren't you supplying him anymore?"

"Because *my* source dried up," he said with a combination of misery and anger. Shaking his head, he muttered, "Goddamned Allistair, packing up and moving to the city like some—"

"Allistair?" Mac interrupted. "Not Allistair Tremblay?"

"Yeah. You know him?" their guest asked.

"He's my landlord," Mac said with a frown. "He's a drug dealer?"

"Yeah, he used to cook in the basement of his farmhouse here before he— Oh, hey! You're not that guy who was living in his house, are you?"

"Yes, I am," Mac said slowly, his eyes narrowing

briefly on the man before he sat up straight and barked, "You're the one who set it on fire!"

"Oh, hey, man, that was an accident. Totally. I mean, it *was* deliberate. Allistair was supposed to pay me for doing it, but you weren't supposed to be there. See, moving to Toronto was more expensive than he expected and he said he didn't have the money to pay me what he owed me, but if I set the house on fire, he'd get the insurance and pay me back."

"He *what?*" Mac demanded with disbelief.

"Yeah, but see, then you rented the place, and he didn't remember about me burning it down. And then I set the house on fire and heard the next day that some guy was living there who nearly bought it in the fire and I called him up. I was like, 'What the hell, Allistair? You nearly made me a murderer, bro.' And he was all like, 'What the hell are you talking about, Skunk?'" He paused his story briefly to explain, "That's what my friends call me 'cause I sell the best skunk weed you'll ever enjoy. Or I used to before Allistair stiffed me. Now I can't get any of the good stuff in, not crystal meth for Jefferson or even skunk." He shook his head with disgust, and then continued, "Anyway, he claims he doesn't even owe me money and didn't agree to no insurance burn, but I'm sure he did. Mostly sure," he added with a frown. "I mean, I was tweaking at the time, so . . ." He paused, his expression dissatisfied as he disappeared into his thoughts.

"Well, that solves one crime."

CJ glanced around Mac to see Captain Dupree standing next to the booth with Dandridge on his heels. He took a moment to nod politely at her, then turned to Dandridge and said, "Take Andy over to the station, get his statement, and put him in a cell."

"Oh, no, no, no, man. I'm a snitch. I'm protected, right?" He turned desperately to CJ as Officer Dandridge stepped up to take his arm and urge him out of the booth. "Tell him."

"You're being arrested for the fire," CJ said with a shrug. "Not anything you told me about Officer Jefferson and your business relationship with him."

"But that fire was totally an accident. I didn't know anyone was in the house when I lit it up," Andy protested as Dandridge got him to his feet and started to urge him toward the exit. "This isn't fair, man."

"Yeah, cry me a river," Dandridge said with a roll of the eyes as he urged him out of the building.

Seventeen

"What did he tell you about Jefferson?" Captain Dupree asked CJ grimly as he took Andy's spot in the booth.

After a hesitation, CJ decided she might as well tell him and said, "He says Officer Jefferson is a meth-head. That he started ten months ago, and wasn't a 'happy cranker,' as he put it."

"What the hell does that mean?" Dupree asked with disgust.

"Probably that he gets argumentative and aggressive on it," she said with a shrug before adding, "He also says Jefferson's even worse now that his source has dried up, which may explain the two incidents the last three weeks."

"Yeah," Dupree said wearily, and then glanced around in search of the waitress.

Laurie was already on her way to the table with a cup of coffee for him. Although her smile was noticeably absent as she eyed the captain.

"Thank you," Dupree said as she set the coffee down with a snap. But when she turned to leave, he caught her arm to stop her. The moment she swung back to glare at him, the captain said, "I just want to apologize, Laurie. For what Jefferson did to Keith and for not acting on it as quick as I should have. He came with a high recommendation when I hired him, and was a good cop at first. I had no idea that he'd got into drugs and was going bad, so when this incident came up I mistakenly gave him the benefit of the doubt. But I'm on it now. We'll get this investigated properly and hold him responsible for whatever he's done, both to Keith and those other two boys."

Laurie was stiff for a minute, and then relaxed with a sigh and shook her head. "It's not all your fault. None of us were telling you what he was getting up to until he hurt Keith."

"What do you mean what he was getting up to?" Captain Dupree asked with concern.

"Just his throwing his weight around and bullying and stuff," she said with a shrug. "Nothing as bad as what he did to Keith and the other two, Mark Loop and Mike MacDonald."

"Oh." Captain Dupree relaxed a little with a sigh and released her arm. "Well, I'll make sure he's held responsible. I just wanted you to know how sorry I am that it's taken me so long to get to this point."

"Well, at least you got there," she pointed out wryly, and then turned to move away.

CJ had started to eat again as she listened to the captain talk to Laurie. When he turned back to the table, but merely picked up his coffee to take a sip, she swallowed the food in her mouth and asked, "Does Andy have a red pickup?"

Captain Dupree looked surprised at the question and then gave a small laugh. "Hell, no. He doesn't drive at all. Doesn't have a license. Rides a ten-speed all over town, even in winter."

"Oh," CJ murmured with disappointment. She'd hoped they might have resolved both incidences with Mac, but it seemed not.

"But Steve drives a red pickup," he announced quietly.

She was so used to thinking of him as Officer Jefferson that it took CJ a minute to realize Dupree was talking about his son-in-law. CJ set her sandwich down again and asked slowly, "Does he?"

"Yes. I looked it over this morning. There's a dent on the front driver's side, but you said that Bricker fella pushed you and Mr. Argeneau here out of the way."

"But Bricker took a hit," Mac said grimly.

"Is that how he was bruised and got road rash?" CJ asked, her gaze sliding to Justin Bricker with concern. He'd seemed fine to her since the accident, but then she'd been a bit preoccupied with first her own pain and then with Mac in her bed. However, if the truck had hit him . . .

"He's fine," Mac assured her, and then turned to Captain Dupree and said, "But the dent is probably from Bricker."

"Unfortunately, I need more than a 'probably' to do anything about it. You guys didn't even see the license plate or who was driving," he pointed out, and his mouth compressed with anger before he blurted, "The bastard's been abusing his power, bullying people, beating up the young men in this town, and even abusing my daughter, and I can't do a damned thing about any of it. My Lily refuses to press charges and says she'll deny he ever touched her if I do anything, and then for the rest of these cases it'll end up being his word against three young men who—" He shook his head. "Mark Loop has a record and a rep as a troublemaker. Mike Mac-Donald isn't much better and is one of his cronies. As for Keith—" He paused and frowned. "I don't know the kid. He's never been arrested for anything, but that doesn't mean that his word is enough to . . ."

When his voice trailed off into unhappy silence, CJ eyed him for a minute, and then asked, "How long was it after the night Keith claims Jefferson broke his arm that he complained to you?"

Captain Dupree considered her question briefly and then grimaced. "I'm not sure. He filed the complaint via email." A short laugh slipped from his mouth, and he admitted, "I didn't really take it seriously at first. I thought it was just some prank or something. I hadn't even heard that a kid's arm had been broken during an arrest attempt."

"You didn't get the arrest report?"

"He didn't arrest him in the end," Dupree told her. "Took him to the hospital and told him to consider himself lucky he wasn't taking him to jail, broken arm and all. He did write up an incident report to cover his ass, but kept it in his desk until Keith started making noises. Then he produced it and said he'd forgotten to file it."

"And you believed him?" she asked, trying not to sound judgmental.

"Lily, my daughter, had just miscarried their first child. We were all a mess, so it didn't seem odd that he might mislay a file."

"I'm sorry for your loss," CJ said quietly.

Dupree shook his head. "Turns out she lost it because he beat the hell out of her. The bastard."

CJ remained silent for a moment, thinking, and then asked, "So no one investigated the area where Keith was pulled over to see if there was proof that Officer Jefferson broke the taillight there?"

Dupree's head shot up at that, realization on his face, and then he started to get up. "No. I'll head out there right now and—"

"Sit down, Charles." A large woman in jeans and a patterned top appeared at his side, prodding at his waist to herd him back toward the booth. "I came to see Ms. Cummings, but you'll want to see this too."

The captain scowled at her prodding, but sat back down and shifted along the bench to make room for the newcomer.

CJ's eyes flickered with interest from the woman's dyed blond hair and spectacles to the portable computer she'd set on the table, and then she raised her eyebrows once she was settled in the booth.

"I'm Joan Wilson," the woman announced, her attention on the portable computer she'd set on the table and was now opening and starting up. "A friend of Millie's. Mrs. Vesper," she added in case CJ didn't know who she was speaking about.

"She's mentioned you," CJ told her, wondering why the woman was there.

"Yes, well, we've been best friends since high school. I'm retired now, but used to work with computers," she added as she sat back and eyed her portable, waiting for it to load. "Always loved computers and gadgets. Have them all over my house. Alexa, the Nest, security cameras," she rattled off, and then met her gaze firmly. "It's the footage from my security cameras you'll be interested in."

CJ raised her eyebrows with intrigue at that. "Do tell?"

"Nope. You have to see it," Joan said firmly, and then began to tap on the portable's keyboard . . . entering the password to log in to the computer, CJ realized when she leaned forward to get a look at the screen. She just caught a glimpse of the dark screen with the password box and then Joan hit Enter and it disappeared, revealing a mountain range background with blue files littering the screen and a dock filled with icons.

"Here we go," Joan said, running her finger around the trackpad and clicking on something. A moment later, she grunted with satisfaction and then turned her computer so they could all see the frozen scene of an empty street at night. She explained, "The incident with Officer Jefferson and those two young boys took place on the road right in front of my house. Unfortunately, I was asleep when it happened so didn't witness anything. But my security cameras did, and they have night vision," she announced with satisfaction. As she tapped the trackpad to start the video, she told them, "This is just before the boys' car comes on-screen."

For a moment, CJ didn't think it was playing, but then the nose of a car came into view, followed by the rest of the car. It wasn't moving very fast.

"Mark definitely wasn't speeding," Captain Dupree said grimly as they watched.

The car was about three-quarters of the way across the image when a police car came on-screen from the opposite direction and swerved into the first car's path, cutting it off. There was no sound on this footage, but CJ was pretty sure that if there had been, she'd hear squealing tires as Mark Loop brought his car to an abrupt halt. She didn't know how he'd managed to stop in time to prevent an accident.

"The boy must have stood on those brakes," Dupree said with a shake of the head as they watched a man get out of the police car and approach the other vehicle.

"Is that Jefferson?" CJ asked. She'd never met the man so had no idea if the tall, thin man with what appeared to be dark hair was the man she'd been trying to interview for weeks.

"Yes," Dupree answered, and they fell silent as they watched Jefferson bypass the window Mark Loop was rolling down and walk to the back of the vehicle. He paused several feet behind the old Chrysler and surveyed the back end, then stepped forward, whipped his baton out of his belt, and smashed the back right light.

"Son of a bitch," Dupree growled.

CJ didn't comment; she simply watched Jefferson strut back to the driver's side window. She knew he must be talking to Mark Loop, or more likely the teen was cussing him out for smashing his taillight, but he wasn't moving and she couldn't see movement inside the vehicle, and then Jefferson struck like a snake, throwing his fist into the car and presumably punching Mark Loop in the face. Then both hands went in and when they came out they were wrapped around Mark Loop's neck. Jefferson dragged the teenager out of the car like he weighed nothing at all. He then slammed him against the side of the car and started hammering on him with both fists. He did that until the kid started to slide to the ground, and then he had to use one hand to hold him up while he continued to pound on him with the other.

CJ felt Mac's hand close over hers on the table and realized that she'd clenched her fists, but she didn't ease her fingers and relax. Her eyes were glued to the screen as helpless rage poured through her. She wanted to jump through the screen and stop Jefferson, but the beating was long over with and both young men were in the hospital. She would guess that the driver, Mark Loop, was the one in the coma. He was obviously unconscious on-screen, yet Jefferson was holding him up by his arm and continuing to slam his fist into the boy's head.

"Here comes Mike," Dupree said as they watched another young man run around the back of the car and charge on Jefferson. He jumped on his back like a monkey jumping on a tree trunk and wrapped his arm around his throat, but when that had no effect, he slid off of him and punched him in the side. The kidneys, she recalled someone mentioning.

That got Jefferson's attention. Dropping Mark Loop like he was garbage, he turned on Mike and started laying into him, punching him in the head and upper chest until the younger man stumbled back and collapsed to the ground. Much to CJ's relief, Jefferson didn't continue wailing on the unconscious young men. He just stood there for a minute. It looked to her like he was trying to catch his breath and then he turned and slammed his own head into Mark Loop's car once, and then again. He raised a hand to feel his forehead as he turned to look from one boy to the other, and then reached for his radio and began to speak into it.

CJ sat back, finally allowing her fingers to unclench. She turned the hand Mac held so that she could hold him back, and squeezed gently in appreciation of the silent support.

"He doesn't do anything after that of much interest," Joan told them as she stopped the video. "He smokes a cigarette, gives Mark another kick or two, and then the ambulance arrives." Joan glanced at Captain Dupree and added, "You showed up a couple minutes after the ambulance."

Dupree nodded. "I'll need that footage."

Joan promptly held up two USB sticks. "I made copies for both of you."

Dupree took the one she held out to him, asking, "Does it have everything on it?"

"Everything including an hour before and an hour after," Joan assured him. She passed CJ the other USB stick with a wry grin and admitted, "I wasn't sure how much you'd need so I overdid it as usual."

"Better safe than sorry," CJ responded as she accepted the USB stick, and then added solemnly, "Thank you."

"My pleasure," Joan assured her as she shut down her portable. "I'm just glad my tech obsession might come in useful for a change."

CJ smiled and then shifted her gaze to Laurie as the waitress arrived at their table. "What can I get you,

Miss Joan?" she asked, and then told her, "I was going to come over sooner, but you all seemed busy with something and I didn't want to intrude."

"No worries, Laurie," Joan assured her, closing her computer and sliding out of the booth. "I don't need anything. I'm not staying. I just stopped in to show Ms. Cummings something. Now I have to go back to the bed-and-breakfast and show Millie."

"Now, Joan, that's evidence," Captain Dupree said with irritation. "You can't go around showing it to everyone."

"I won't," she assured him. "Just Millie. I promised," she added with a wry grin. "I stopped there first looking for Ms. Cummings and she directed me here. In return, I promised to go back for tea and show her the video."

Captain Dupree scowled and opened his mouth, probably to threaten to take her computer away, but Joan was no one's fool. She was already bustling away, the portable tucked under her arm.

Dupree heaved an exasperated sigh as he watched her go, then shifted out of the booth as well. "I need to call into the office and put out an APB on Steve. Then I want to go check the road where Keith Kaye was stopped. If he smashed the taillight there like he did Mark Loop's car, there should be a couple of pieces left at least. It was on a rural route and there are no sewers for the rain to wash them down," he added, and then asked, "Do you still want to interview him?"

CJ nodded. "I have to at least see what he has to say for himself to write my report."

"Do you want me to call you when they pick him up?"

CJ shook her head. "I'll come over at 2:45 as planned. I promised I'd be here until then for anyone who might have helpful information, so we may as well stick to the three o'clock appointment."

"I'll make sure to be back before that, then," Dupree said, and nodded to them before heading out.

CJ watched him go, and then glanced at the clock on the restaurant wall. It was only 12:45. She had two hours to wait until she could leave the diner, she realized, and frowned at the knowledge. Two hours was a long time. Squeezing Mac's hand, she smiled when he shifted his attention from the retreating captain to her.

"You don't have to wait here with me. Why don't you and the guys take my car and go check out any houses they have for rent or sale in the area. You'll need a new home base now."

"Actually," he said slowly, squeezing her hand and raising it to his lips to kiss, "I was thinking I might like to set up shop somewhere else . . . like Mississauga."

CJ's eyes widened with surprise. "You were?"

Mac nodded and then asked with concern, "Would you mind?"

"Heck, no, I'd love that," she admitted, and then realized that maybe she was being a little too honest, and glanced away with embarrassment.

But Mac caught her chin and turned her back to face him. Expression solemn, he said, "I'd love it too."

CJ smiled crookedly, and then leaned forward to press a light kiss to the corner of his mouth. At least that was her intention. However, he turned his head at the last minute, catching her lips with his, and she ended up giving him a proper kiss, that was just starting to deepen when Bricker said, "Oh, man, you two. Get a room."

CJ and Mac broke apart guiltily and turned to see that Bricker and Decker were sliding into the booth with them.

"So?" Bricker raised his eyebrows. "What's the news? It sounded like they got the guy who started the fire?"

"Yes. It was an insurance job, not a murder attempt," CJ told them.

"Which means you guys don't have to stick around anymore," Mac added.

Bricker feigned an injured expression and asked Decker, "Is it just me? Or does he sound kind of happy about that to you?"

"It's not just you. He sounds happy," Decker said with a sad moue that just looked ridiculous on the man.

"That's gratitude for you, eh?" Bricker asked.

"Oh, stuff it," Mac said with amusement. "No one's buying your poor wounded act. Besides, I'm just relieved to know no one wants me dead."

"Good, because if it was that Officer Jefferson in the red pickup, then he was probably aiming for CJ and that means we should stay until he's been arrested and no longer a threat to her," Decker said quietly.

CJ's mouth slipped open with surprise and she shook her head. "You don't have to stay for me. I mean, you guys work for Argentis and they have no responsibility to see to my safety." Even as she said the words, her mind was turning the information over in her head. Jefferson owned a red pickup. He might have been behind the wheel of the truck that had tried to run her down. He might have been trying to bring an end to her investigation. Jeez, he might have been trying to kill her, and he might try again. The idea shocked her. She'd never had anyone try to kill her before. It was hard to absorb and accept.

"The people we work for look after the well-being of not only our people but their partners," Decker told her solemnly. "And I gather you two are involved now."

CJ glanced quickly at Mac and away. She could actually feel her cheeks heating with a blush. Dang, she was reacting like a teenager with her first boyfriend, and he wasn't even her boyfriend. At least, they hadn't discussed anything having to do with whatever it was they were doing. Although he had just said he was moving to the Mississauga area in a way that made it seem like it was to be near her, so she supposed they were doing something, she thought, and then turned with relief to Laurie when the waitress appeared at the end of the booth.

"I'm sorry to bother you, but there are a small group of young folks here who want to talk to Ms. Cummings, but they aren't comfortable approaching with the rest of you here," she said apologetically.

"There are other tables open now. We'll move to one of them," Mac said at once, and leaned to the side to kiss her cheek before sliding out of the booth. "Just shout if you need us."

CJ stared after him, a little sigh slipping from her lips. That peck on the cheek had left her skin tingling like she'd rubbed tingling tanning lotion on her face, and it was moving out from there to the rest of her body. The man was crazy hot and sexy and thank goodness he'd moved to another table. It was the only chance she had to actually get some proper work done. It was hard to concentrate with him close.

Her thoughts were distracted when a trio of teenagers approached the table. Crowding close together, and eyeing her with a combination of fear and determination, they stood next to the table waiting politely.

CJ invited them to sit and turned on her tape recorder.

CJ hit Send, emailing the report to her boss. She then sat back and twisted her neck one way and then the other to try to ease the crick she had in it from sitting hunched at the computer for so long. It had been a busy few days. Once the men had moved to another booth in the diner, it had been nonstop people approaching her to pass on information they had about Jefferson. Very little of it had been something that could be used in a court of law, but she'd put most of it in her report to her boss. She'd gone to the police station after that, accompanied by Mac, Decker and Bricker. They'd all reviewed their statements and signed them, and then waited a good hour for Jefferson to show up, but he never had. He hadn't been arrested either. It seemed the man had disappeared. The captain suspected that Jefferson's wife being at her parents' and their refusing to let him speak to her when he'd called searching for her had tipped him off, but the man also had a radio at home and had most likely heard the APB called out on him. He'd been missing when the officers had gone to the house, and he hadn't shown up for his shift either. It was looking like he'd "done a runner."

CJ had waited around the station for a while, but after the captain had promised to contact her if they were able to find and arrest him, she and the men had returned to the bed-and-breakfast where she'd met Mac's sister, Katricia. She'd liked the woman, and fortunately his sister wasn't holding her job against her. They'd got along great and visited for a while, and then they all went out to dinner, dragging Mrs. Vesper along with them since the rest of her clients had cleared out now that the wedding they were attending was over.

After that they'd returned to the bed-and-breakfast and sat on the porch chatting, half the group spilling onto the lawn there were so many of them. It had been a blast. CJ had never laughed so much in her life as she did that night, although her week on the island with Marguerite and Julius had come close. It had been late when Katricia had left to drive back to Port Henry and CJ and Mac had gone upstairs. He'd said he'd walk her to her door, and he had, but he hadn't left until the next morning and then it was only long enough for him to shower and change in the RV. CJ had done the same in her room, and then met him downstairs to go interview

Keith Kaye, Mark Loop, and Mike MacDonald. She hadn't expected to be able to interview Mark Loop, but he'd regained consciousness during the night and was able to tell her what he recalled of what happened. It was exactly what they'd seen: Officer Jefferson had stopped him, smashed his back light, and then attacked Mark when he started cussing at the man and threatening to complain to the captain about his actions. Jefferson may have started out a good cop, but he had definitely turned into one of those bad cops she wanted to see off the streets.

CJ had spent the time since her interviews writing up her report. It was a really long report thanks to the number of people who had approached her at the diner. She'd worked on it all afternoon the day before yesterday, and all day yesterday, and, now, at noon on the third day, she was done and had sent it to her boss. Which meant she was free to do what she wanted. The moment she'd hit Send she was on vacation for two weeks. Her original plan had been to go to Pelee Island again, but now she wasn't sure.

"And that's what getting involved with a guy does to you," CJ muttered aloud with a little grimace. She didn't want to be one of those women, someone who changes their vacation plans for a man. But sex with Mac was so damned good. It was beyond addictive, and she'd had a terrible time trying to be responsible and concentrate on her work when she knew Mac was downstairs and all it would take was a smile or a come-hither look to get him into her bed. But she'd managed it, and now she was done.

CJ shut down her computer and closed it, stood to stretch, and then headed downstairs.

"How's it going?" Marguerite asked when she found them all out on the porch, chatting with Mrs. Vesper.

"All done," CJ said with satisfaction, settling on the arm of Mac's chair. He'd patted his lap, offering her a seat there, but she wasn't all that comfortable behaving so familiarly in front of his family.

"Bravo!" Marguerite grinned at her.

"Does that mean we're headed for Mississauga?" Mac asked, taking her hand.

CJ bit her lip and hesitated as she debated continuing with her original plan or staying and enjoying her time with Mac. Or, more likely, helping him look for a new home base in her area. The man had to get back to work sometime. As his fingers ran over hers, sending chills up her back, she almost said yes, it was time to head to Mississauga, and offered to help him look for a new home. But she managed to control herself and instead took a deep breath and said, "Actually, I'm on vacation now, and had plans to go to Pelee for a couple weeks."

"Oh!" Marguerite cried. "We should go too, Julius. I loved Pelee Island and had such a lovely time there with CJ. We should all go."

Before CJ could respond, Mac squeezed her hand, drawing her attention to him as he asked quietly, "Would you be all right with that? If we joined you on the island?"

"Yes, of course. That would be fine. The island is awesome, but it's much more fun with others there to play with," she said, not really considering her words.

"Good, because I'd enjoy seeing your cottage and playing with you," he assured her, his voice deep and sexy. He ran his thumb over her palm, sending a tingling up her arm that vibrated through the rest of her body.

"I meant—" CJ began, flustered, but then just stopped and shook her head as everyone chuckled. Clucking her tongue with irritation, she tugged her hand free of his tormenting fingers and asked, "Can you delay looking for a house for two weeks? Your boss won't be upset?"

Mac shook his head. "Bastien's the one who told me to take my time and sort out where I want to be first. Besides, he's not really my boss. Argentis Inc. is a family business. All Argeneaus have stock in it."

"That's true," Marguerite assured her when CJ looked surprised. "Bastien just heads up the different branches and organizes things and such. But we all have stock and we all have a say in what's what."

"Oh," CJ murmured, a little startled to learn that. She'd been thinking of Mac as a lab rat, with a salary similar to her own, or possibly a bit larger. Instead, the man was a stockholder in a company with so many branches she hadn't bothered to read the full list on the website. Cripes, he was like a Rockefeller, she thought with dismay.

"We have a large family," Marguerite said suddenly as if she'd just read the thoughts running through her mind. "So the money is spread around quite a bit."

CJ decided to let the subject drop in favor of announcing, "I'm hungry and thought I'd treat everyone to Chinese, or pizza or something if you guys don't want Chinese again. I know you had it the other night."

"I'm in for Chinese," Bricker said at once. "Those spring rolls were good."

The others chirped up one after the other in agreement. Even Mrs. Vesper was on board, and CJ pulled out her phone to make a memo on what everyone wanted and then went in to place the order for their last meal with Mrs. Vesper. They'd be checking out the next day and heading for Pelee Island. Just the thought of it made her smile. Two weeks on Pelee with Mac. And the others, of course. She couldn't wait,

CJ thought, and then frowned a little as she began to worry he'd find it too sleepy and countrified for his tastes like her ex-husband, Billy, had. She fretted over that briefly, but then decided that if he did, it would be a sign that they would never work out, and was a good thing to know, especially this early in the relationship. It could prevent heartache later. At least that's what she told herself. But the truth was, it would cause heartache now if he was like Billy that way anyway. Because CJ was afraid she was already half in love with the man.

How could she not be? He'd proven himself to be extremely considerate the last couple of days, leaving her alone for the most part while she was writing her report, but checking on her several times a day, bringing her coffee, or lunch and making her stop to eat it. He'd also come up to tell her when dinner was ready, and dragged her down to join the others for a meal before she'd escaped back to her room to continue writing. Then he'd come up at midnight, to lure her to bed where he helped her relax with crazy, passionate sex that had left her unconscious at the end. The man had been exactly what she'd needed. God, she really hoped he liked her little cottage retreat at Pelee Island.

Eighteen

"I think I love this place."

CJ finished pouring water into the coffeepot and turned to stare at Mac as he walked into the kitchen. The man was naked as the day he'd been born and completely comfortable with it as he crossed from the bedroom door to where she stood in her robe, with a coffeepot in hand.

It was their last morning on the island. Today they had to catch the 10 A.M. ferry and then ride back to Mississauga in Marguerite and Julius's RV where they would drop her off before continuing on to their own home. That had been Marguerite's idea. There was no sense her driving separately when they had so much room in the RV, she'd insisted. Since it had meant she wouldn't have to leave her car in the parking lot on the mainland for two weeks while she was on the island, CJ had allowed herself to be talked into it. She kept an old beater on the island for transportation to avoid the cost of ferrying her car back and forth every time she visited.

Of course, her riding in the RV with the others had meant a quick drive home to leave her car there, and a train ride back to Sandford where Marguerite and the others had been waiting to collect them. But Mac had accompanied her, and despite the inconvenience, it had been more fun riding with the others. The whole trip had been more fun with everyone there. It was the end of September, but they'd been lucky when it came to weather. The temperatures had been in the high seventies and had even hit the low eighties a couple of times. It had been two weeks of lazy days by the water, swimming or fishing, or walking the trails at the point with the others, evenings sitting around a campfire laughing and chatting, and nights of passion with Mac. Still, it hadn't been what her husband would have considered exciting. There was no clubbing or theme parks here. It had mostly been peace and quiet and nature, and Mac had lived in New York for ten years. CJ had really worried that he would find this all too bucolic.

"Really?" she asked, setting the carafe on the burner and turning on the coffee machine. Then she turned and let her gaze slide over his beautiful body. One she'd enjoyed a great deal over the last two weeks, and in various and sundry places. They'd made love on the beach, in her fishing boat, in the lake, and every room in the cottage. Actually, they'd made love every chance they'd got, which hadn't been much during the day unless it rained thanks to Marguerite, Julius, Bricker, and Decker living just next door in the RV. But she could only think that was a good thing, otherwise she suspected she and Mac would have spent the full two weeks in bed, and that wouldn't have been very helpful in finding out if he liked the island as he was now claiming. Clearing her throat, she asked, "You don't find it too slow and quiet?"

"Are you kidding?" he asked on a laugh as he stopped in front of her and drew her into his arms. Bending, he kissed the tip of her nose, and assured her, "After ten years in New York, this is heaven. No honking horns, no shouting, no crowds to try to navigate everywhere you go." Hugging her tight, he rested his chin on her head and murmured, "Just you and peace and quiet and sunshine every day."

"It's rained four times in the last two weeks," CJ pointed out with amusement, slipping her arms around his waist.

"Yeah, but then we got to read and do jigsaw puzzles

and make love. I liked the making love best," he admitted with a grin, pulling back slightly to tell her seriously, "I could live here year-round, I think, if I didn't worry that getting daily deliveries would be a pain."

"Oh," CJ breathed, and then admitted, "I'm glad. I was worried you wouldn't like it. Billy, my ex-husband, didn't."

"Your ex-husband was an idiot," Mac assured her. "As proven by the fact that he let you get away."

CJ didn't respond; she merely leaned her head against his chest and tightened her arms, hugging him closer.

"You never talk about him," Mac said quietly. "Did he hurt you terribly?"

CJ hesitated, and then instead of addressing that, said, "You've never asked me how I got HIV."

He could have pointed out that she'd never questioned him on the subject either, but instead said, "I just assumed that you got it on the job. Maybe getting stuck by a dirty needle while you were trying to subdue a drugged-out perp or something?"

"I wish," she said with a snort. "At least that way I'd be a wounded warrior rather than a pathetic idiot."

Mac leaned back again, his expression full of sympathy, then he said softly, "Tell me."

CJ wanted to refuse and tell him it didn't matter,

it was what it was. But more than that, she wanted to tell him the truth. CJ had no idea why. Normally, she didn't want to talk about it at all. In fact, she'd gone to counseling because of it exactly once, and hadn't been able to bring herself to talk about it, even to a therapist. But she wanted to tell Mac, and for once in her life she didn't question the why or whether it was the smart thing to do. Instead, she pulled out of his arms, poured coffee into the two cups she'd fetched earlier, and fixed them both before pushing his toward him. Claiming her own, she then led him to the small kitchen table.

"My father, Johnathan Cummings, was the best man I've known in my life," she stated quietly once they'd sat down across from each other. "I always felt loved and safe with him around. He was kind, caring, an amazing father, and he became a police officer because he wanted to make the world a better place. He was a good man. The best."

Mac didn't comment, but nodded encouragingly.

"I actually became a cop to honor him," she admitted. "So maybe it isn't surprising that I wanted to marry a man just like him."

"Of course," he said as if that were the most natural thing in the world.

CJ nodded. "Unfortunately, to me that meant marrying a police officer," she said unhappily, and when his expression turned quizzical, she explained, "In my mind, I equated all of his wonderful qualities with his being a police officer. I assumed all police officers must be good men trying to better the world like him."

"Ah," Mac breathed with understanding.

"Yeah. It was pretty naïve of me," she admitted. "I mean, a lot of them are like that. But not all of them, and being young and stupid, I fell for a police officer who was one of the ones who weren't, one who was the exact opposite of my father." CJ turned her coffee cup on the table, enjoying the heat emanating from the ceramic and warming hands that she suddenly noticed were icy cold. "William Carter, better known as Billy, was seven years older than me, good-looking, and worked undercover for the police drug squad. All the female officers were gaga after him, and the men liked him. He was really good at his job, broke up more drug rings than anyone else, and was always the life of the party."

Her gaze flicked up to his face and back down before she admitted, "I was shocked as hell when he turned his attention on me. It was like being noticed by a rock star. It was exciting, flattering, and raised me up in the eyes of my peers." She grimaced and then glanced up again as she added, "It was also a whirlwind. He'd be away on his undercover assignments and then blow back in once they were done and want to celebrate his win with parties and marathon sex sessions, and then be gone on the next assignment."

CJ saw Mac wince at that, but ignored it and continued, "We dated a year before he asked me to marry him, which sounds all right, but when I look back at that period, I realize I probably only saw him the equivalent of a month or two during that time. A night or two here, a night or two there, a whole week a time or three, and then he'd be off on assignment again. He was always volunteering for extra assignments. He said he wanted to buy a house to raise a family in, and house prices in Toronto were crazy expensive even back then so I understood. I even admired him for it despite the fact that it meant not seeing him as much as I'd like. Besides, he made up for it with loads of texts and emails."

Smiling grimly, CJ told Mac, "Billy gave really good email. They were romantic and passionate, going on about how he missed me. How I was the only thing that got him through his crazy dangerous assignments. I was beautiful and smart and he was so damned lucky to have me to come back to." Her mouth twisted. "Basically, everything a young woman wanted to hear. Or read as the case may be.

"We were trying to arrange the wedding, picking out invitations and venues and not really settling on anything because he was there so rarely. On top of that, I had just made it to homicide detective and was working crazy hours trying to prove myself, so didn't have a lot of free time to taste cakes and look over menus," she said, but didn't admit that maybe a good portion of the time she spent working was to avoid having to deal with the wedding details. It was a lot of work, and she hadn't felt right doing such things without him anyway. It was his wedding too, after all.

"Anyway, that went on for a while and then, about six months after proposing, he whisked me away for a weekend in Vegas. And in the midst of gambling and drinking and having a desperately good time, he convinced me to forgo all the fuss and stress and marry him there."

CJ blew her breath out and shook her head unhappily. "It was one of the biggest mistakes of my life, second only to agreeing to date him."

She paused to take a sip of her coffee and then cleared her throat and said, "It took twenty minutes to get the license and ten minutes to find a chapel he liked, and just like that, I was Mrs. CJ Carter. After that it was twenty-four hours of celebration and consummation and then we were on a plane back home. But we'd barely landed back in Toronto before he was off on another assignment, and I mean that literally," she added, meeting his gaze. "We landed, he turned on his phone while we were waiting for our luggage, and it immediately started to ring. He hung up two minutes later and left me to wait for our things while he ran off to the station to talk to his team. I rounded up the luggage and caught a taxi home, and he came back several hours later with the news that he was going undercover again the next day."

CJ shook her head at the memory. "And then it was the same as it had been while we were dating. He was away more than he was there, and I was working a lot. I didn't mind too much at first, but after the first year I . . ." She shook her head. "It was nothing like my parents' relationship," she said finally. "Oh, he was sweet and attentive when he was there, but he was there so rarely . . . In truth, I didn't really feel married," CJ admitted with some of the bewilderment she'd felt at the time.

Sighing, she waved that thought away as the self-pity it was, and continued, "Three years passed like that. Basically, I felt more like I was married to my job, and he was the mistress on the side. Then I started to develop a paunch and throw up in the mornings."

Mac sat up straight, his eyes wide. "You had a baby with him?"

CJ mentally gave him marks for sorting out what

those symptoms meant so quickly. She'd been slower to cotton on to the issue. At first, she'd just thought she had a stomach flu or something. But then she realized she'd missed a couple of periods and she'd put two and two together. She didn't say that, though; CJ simply went on with her story as if he hadn't spoken.

"I took a home pregnancy test, and damned near fainted when it turned out positive. We were both workaholics. He was hardly ever there. We weren't ready for a baby. But when I told Billy about it the next time he showed up, he was happy as hell. This was great to his mind. We could do this. We'd saved nearly enough money to put a down payment on a house and should be able to swing it before the baby was born. And he swore he'd work less and help out with the baby. Which I didn't believe for a minute," she assured him.

She might have been naïve when she got involved with Billy, but she wasn't stupid enough to think a baby would change his habits. Marriage hadn't, why would a baby? Besides, men weren't known for loving the diaper routine. But he'd seemed so happy, and by that time CJ had started to come around to the idea of having a baby. It would mean taking pregnancy leave from work, and then finding a good nanny, but . . . A baby of her own, she'd thought with wonder. A little CJ or a little Billy. She'd started thinking about names and decided if it was a boy she would name him Johnathan after her father. A girl would be named Marge for her mom.

CJ didn't tell Mac any of that. Instead, she said, "I went to my doctor to have it confirmed and get checked out, as you do."

Mac nodded, but CJ didn't speak again for a moment. Licking her lips, she thought about her next words and then said, "In Canada an HIV test is standard for pregnant women. In some provinces they don't even tell the mother she's being tested for it, but in Ontario they do tell you to be sure you don't have an issue with it and I think you can refuse it if you want, but I didn't care one way or another. I had been jabbed by a needle in a perp's pocket while I was frisking him about a year before I started dating Billy. The guy had HIV, and I had to take meds and go in to be tested for HIV, hepatitis B, and syphilis every month for a year after, and every time I was freaked and stressed while I waited for the results. But every test was clean.

"And boy did I celebrate after the last one," she admitted with a faint smile. "I went out with some cop friends and got pickled pink. That's the night I caught Billy's attention. He joined our party as just another member of the gang, but asked me out the following week and we started dating. I wouldn't sleep with him at first, though. Knowing I was clean, I insisted on him getting tested for sexually transmitted diseases, including HIV, before I'd take that step. His tests came back clean too and he was the only person I'd slept with since then so I knew that I didn't have HIV. But if it was standard procedure, and my doc wanted to check, that was fine.

"At least that's what I thought at the time," CJ said bitterly. "So, you can imagine how shocked I was when this test came back positive for HIV."

Mac slid his hand forward on the tabletop to cover hers, but CJ withdrew from his touch. She could not take it just then. Straightening her shoulders, she soldiered on. "I won't bore you with the drama that followed that revelation. Suffice to say that he was tested again and turned up positive too, and then there was a lot of denial on his part, and blaming me, saying it must have been because of that jab I got from the druggie's needle. That a year of testing obviously hadn't been enough, and I'd contracted it and probably given it to him. He made me feel so bad, so guilty, and so dirty. He acted like I'd tainted him, and told me I was lucky he loved me, or he'd divorce me for it."

She paused to take another sip of coffee, and then said, "Word got out around the station, and interestingly enough, some of the other female officers started freaking out and getting tested. I wondered about that, and suspected he might have had affairs or something, but then Wally, one of Billy's coworkers who oversaw the audio and video recordings of his undercover activities, came and told me that not only was it common knowledge that Billy had screwed half the female cops in our station, but when he was undercover he really 'lived the life.' Like *really* lived it: shooting up and screwing countless skanks and even prostitutes who hung out around the drug dealers. And he'd continued to do so after our marriage," she added bitterly. "Wally said he was pretty sure that at least one of the prostitutes he'd been messing with for the last six months had HIV or maybe even full-blown AIDS, because she'd started looking really rough and losing weight the last three or four months."

"Ah, Christ," Mac muttered angrily.

"Yeah," CJ breathed sadly. "Billy was nothing at all like my dad. He was just a really huge mistake."

She peered down at her coffee cup, and gave it a half turn on the tabletop and then added woodenly, "I lost the baby."

Mac started to reach for her hand again, but stopped when she stiffened. She hadn't meant to, but didn't think she could get through this if he touched her.

Acting as if that hadn't happened, she said, "I guess

my body didn't handle all the stress and revelations well. Wally finished telling me what he had to say and I thanked him politely, like he'd just given me a weather outlook. Then I turned and started to walk away. I hadn't taken three steps when these terrible cramps had me stopping and hunching over . . ."

"Oh, sweetheart," Mac said, his voice breaking. This time he didn't reach for her hand. Instead, he was suddenly out of his seat and standing in front of her. Before that could even register with her, he'd scooped her out of her seat, taken it himself, and settled her in his lap.

"I'm sorry," he said, rubbing her back soothingly. "So sorry you went through that."

"It was bad. The baby was far enough along that . . ." She paused and shook her head. It didn't matter. Every miscarriage was a loss and bad. Sighing, she said, "I quit my job. I just couldn't handle everyone knowing everything about me like that. Besides, the other detectives acted like they were afraid to be around me. Like just being in the same room might give them HIV. So, I quit and took a job at CSIS while I went through the divorce. I worked there a couple years, and then switched to the SIU and here I am," she finished wearily.

Mac cuddled her close and kissed the top of her

head, murmuring, "Thank God for that. I might never have met you otherwise."

For some reason that made CJ smile, and she quickly dashed away the tears now leaking down her face and cuddled into him, allowing him to comfort her. She felt like she was finally grieving for all that she'd lost: her baby, her marriage, the man she'd thought she was married to, and even her own innocence. It was the first time she'd allowed herself to cry since it had happened, and it actually made her feel better. She supposed his reaction helped. He wasn't acting like she was tainted or dirty or stupid, or anything else she'd been telling herself the last several years. In her head, CJ knew that having the illness didn't make her any of those things, but feelings didn't always listen to the rational part of your brain, and she had felt like she was. But with Mac holding her and comforting her, she felt a little less like she was.

"I think maybe I should try to go back for counseling," she said suddenly.

Mac loosened his hold and leaned back to peer at her. "If that's what you'd like."

She smiled wryly. "What I'd like is to be normal."

"What is normal?" he asked with amusement. "I've lived a long time and have yet to meet anyone that most people would consider fully normal."

CJ smiled at the "lived a long time" bit. He insisted that he was older than he looked and she wasn't dating a younger man, but he looked—and had the stamina— of a much younger man. Pushing that thought aside, she shrugged and said, "Maybe normal is the wrong word. But I'd like to learn to live with who I am more comfortably, and not let it affect my future choices. I don't want to carry my baggage from my marriage into my relationship with—" She cut herself off abruptly as she realized what she was saying and to whom. They still hadn't discussed what this was they were enjoying and she wasn't sure she had a right to call it a relationship.

But Mac nodded solemnly. "I personally feel that you are handling your baggage just fine, but I understand. I worry that something from my past might affect my future with you too," he assured her, and then added, "And I have to tell you, I am hoping for a long and happy future with you, CJ."

CJ had started out wondering how his past might affect their future, and then realized that he hadn't yet told her how he had caught HIV, but then the second part of his comment had caught her attention and she now stared at him wide-eyed. "You are?"

Mac nodded. "I'd like you to be my life mate, and I'm hoping eventually you'll feel that way too."

CJ smiled at the term *life mate*. It sounded so much more grown-up and serious than girlfriend.

"I know it's early in our relationship to mention that, and I'm trying to be patient," he said.

Relationship. Yes! It was actually a relationship. Awesome sauce! CJ thought, because she wasn't the type of person to be comfortable sleeping with someone she wasn't in a relationship with, but since they hadn't discussed it she hadn't been able to claim it was one even to herself. Now she could.

"But you should know that I think you're the most incredible woman I've ever met. You're smart, and brave and strong, and you make me laugh . . . I've known you were perfect for me from the start, but now I'm afraid I might be falling in love with you, CJ Cummings."

CJ's heart skipped a beat. He'd used the L word. Oh, God, the *L* word. It was too soon. Wasn't it? She thought it might be. How long did it take to start falling in love? They'd only met a few short weeks ago. On the other hand, they'd met under strenuous circumstances, and seen each other under pressure. The man had lost everything when she met him, and yet he hadn't been depressed, or all doom and gloom. In fact, he'd been ridiculously good-natured about everything. And now they'd had two weeks on the island, laughing and playing and loving and talking, always talking. They hadn't argued once, or even disagreed about anything. Their tastes seemed to be completely in sync, as did their values from all the conversations they'd managed to fit in, and they had managed to fit in a lot of conversations. Usually while with the others, but still . . .

If CJ were to describe Mac, she'd say he was almost a male version of herself. Oh, there were differences between them, not least of all physically, but they were complementary differences rather than conflicting. They worked well together and she knew without a doubt that she was falling in love with him too. Unlike him, she didn't have the courage to admit that, though.

So much for his belief that she was brave, CJ thought, and wondered why she was holding back. It didn't take a lot of soul-searching or even counseling to figure that out. She'd thought she was in love with Billy too . . . until she found out that he wasn't the man he'd presented himself to be. Now she didn't trust her own instincts and feelings when it came to love.

She'd need time to assure herself that he was who he seemed to be, CJ supposed, and found herself dissatisfied with that opinion. She didn't really want to wait to embrace her feelings. She didn't want to spend the next six months to a year watching him for signs that he wasn't who he seemed to be, and trying to catch him in lies. But she was scared. She wished there was some way to be sure he was right for her and that she wouldn't be making another huge mistake if she gave in to her desires, welcomed him wholeheartedly into her life, and admitted she loved him too. But there wasn't, and she was too scared to take that chance this soon in the relationship.

What she needed was more information, she decided, and considered what she should ask him. Since she'd just told him how she had come to have HIV, it probably shouldn't be surprising that the first question to come to her mind was, "Would you be willing to tell me how you came to have HIV?"

The words slipped from her lips in almost a whisper, one he apparently didn't hear. Not only did he not respond, but he didn't even look as if he'd realized that she had spoken. His gaze was fixed somewhere well below her chin, his eyes wide and hungry and again looking more silver than blue, she noted, watching with fascination as liquid mercury seemed to slide into his eyes to swamp the blue. She was so fascinated by the sight that she didn't see his hand move until she felt the backs of his knuckles brush over one nipple without cloth to protect it.

Gasping, CJ glanced down at once to see that her robe had gaped open, leaving most of both breasts on display, and the one he'd just touched was pebbling and darkening as blood rushed to it. Even as she noticed that, Mac bent his head to claim the nipple he'd aroused.

"Mmm," CJ moaned, her hands tangling in his hair as he began to suckle. But when his tongue flicked the hard bud, sending a frenzy of sensation through her body, she gasped and wiggled excitedly on the growing hardness under her bottom and then tugged at the hair she was clutching, trying to raise his head.

Much to her relief, he released her nipple then and lifted his lips to find hers. CJ kissed him with every drop of the mounting excitement he'd roused in her. It brought an eager response from him and within moments they were both breathless and desperate for more. Until CJ broke their kiss and gasped, "I need you."

Mac growled deep in his throat at the plea, caught her by the waist, and stood up. She thought he'd carry her back to the bedroom, but he apparently didn't have the patience to seek comfort. Instead, he set her on the table, pushed the robe off her shoulders, spread her legs, and stepped between them. But he didn't enter her right away as she wanted. Instead, he rubbed himself against her as he reclaimed her lips, his hard length gliding over the bud of her excitement repeatedly as he devoured her mouth. The move was ridiculously effective. CJ was ready to come apart within moments, but she didn't want to go alone. It was best when he was in her, then she at least knew he found satisfaction too.

Tearing her mouth away, she growled, "Love me. I need you inside me."

Mac opened his mouth, and then suddenly snapped it closed and grabbed her robe to draw it up around her shoulders. The sudden move bewildered her until she heard the knock at the screen door. Glancing sharply over her shoulder, she saw Bricker through the screen and quickly faced forward again, her gaze dropping over Mac's very naked, very obviously excited body. If he stayed right where he was, it would be fine, but if he went to answer the door, Bricker would have no doubt of what they'd been up to.

"What?" he called, staying right where he was.

Bricker opened the screen door and popped his head in, his eyebrows rising when he took in their position. "Marguerite sent me to remind you that we have to leave by nine thirty to put the RV on the ferry before they start letting foot traffic on."

"Got it. Thanks."

Bricker narrowed his eyes. "You two have an hour and a half to get ready."

"Okay," Mac said grimly.

"Yeah. I'll come wake you up and remind you of that in half an hour," Bricker said dryly, and retreated, letting the door close.

CJ was just turning from watching the man go when Mac scooped her up off the table and headed for the bedroom. Hiding her disappointment, she muttered, "I suppose we should close up the cottage and get ready to go."

Mac shook his head, carried her to the bed, and tossed her on it before turning to the bedside table. He was holding up a condom packet when he turned back. "You heard him," he said, and then paused to tear the packet open with his teeth, before saying, "We have half an hour before he comes to wake us up. We can get ready then."

"Oh," CJ breathed as she watched him quickly roll the condom on. It was an oddly erotic thing to see, she decided, and then opened her arms when he started to climb onto the bed. They had half an hour. They only needed probably three minutes before they'd both be orgasming and passing out like Victorian misses. CJ had never experienced such intense sex. It was amazing, but appallingly short-lived each time. She'd be embarrassed by their pitiful performance if it wasn't so damned hot. But seriously, if they were porn stars, the sex tapes would be about the length of a commercial. How pathetic was that?

"Not pathetic at all," she gasped as he took her into his arms and slid into her at once.

"What?" Mac gasped with confusion, stopping to raise himself enough to see her face.

"Nothing," she got out a little breathlessly. "Shut up and love me."

Mac smiled widely and began to move.

Nineteen

"We'll wait out here while you help CJ take her luggage in, Mac," Marguerite said as Julius parked the very large RV in the driveway. It made CJ glad she'd parked her car in the garage when she'd brought it back. Normally, unless it was snowing, she left it out rather than have to open and close the old-fashioned manual garage door. But because she was going to be away for two weeks, she'd put it away properly. She really needed to get an automatic garage door opener, but had been putting it off.

Realizing that Mac was already gathering up her luggage, CJ hurried to grab one of her suitcases and two of the bags of dirty laundry before he could take everything himself. She then led the way to the door Bricker was opening for them.

Murmuring "Thank you," CJ slipped past him and stepped down out of the RV. She couldn't resist looking toward the back of the vehicle to see if it was sticking out into the road as she feared, and found that, yes, the back two feet were in the road. But Julius had also parked almost against her garage door, so there wasn't much to be done about it except to get the luggage inside and send Mac on his way so they could leave and stop blocking the road. Not that he would be gone long. He was just going to pick up Julius's Corvette so he'd have something to drive around in.

From the day after tomorrow on, he was going to search for houses while she was at work. Well, if they didn't find a house for him tomorrow. They'd come back a day earlier than they really had to from the island. CJ always made sure to come back from the island two days before she had to work. It gave her a day to recover from the journey home and do her laundry before she had to go into the office, and there was a lot of laundry since she'd brought back the dirty linens and towels as well as two weeks' worth of clothes. But she'd have to do those at night. The next day she planned to ride around with Mac looking at houses, which was their excuse for his staying with her tonight. It was just more convenient than his staying with Marguerite and coming back early in the morning.

CJ suspected they'd be coming up with a lot of excuses for him to stay at her place over the next couple of weeks, or months, or maybe forever depending on how long they were together. Her vote was forever, or at least until death did they part. But she was trying to keep her head about this, take her time, and move slowly and cautiously. It was hard to do when she found herself wanting to throw caution to the wind and spend every waking moment with the man. She really wasn't looking forward to going back to work and not being able to see him for eight hours on end.

That thought told CJ just how addicted she was to Macon (sexy beast Mac) Argeneau. Yeah, she had it bad for the guy.

"Do you need me to take the bags so you can unlock the door?" Mac asked as CJ stopped on her front step.

"No. I'm good," she assured him, and began punching numbers into the digital lock. It was new and really handy at times like this. No matter how bogged down you were with bags, you could usually get one finger or knuckle free to push buttons. The lock hummed as the dead bolt retreated into the door, and CJ managed to work the doorknob despite everything she was carrying and led the way into her home.

"Nice," Mac murmured as he followed her through the foyer into the living room.

"Thanks. I renovated it last year. I like the results," she admitted as she dropped her bags and peered around the large room. It was decorated in warm earth tones, with overstuffed comfy furniture and large windows overlooking the backyard.

"You got the house in the divorce, then?" Mac asked. "Or did you buy it after?"

"Neither," she said with a wry smile. "This was my parents' home. Marge and Johnathan Cummings," she added solemnly. "They left it to me along with the cottage. But since I had to go live with Mrs. Miller, Uncle Ernie, Ernie Cowessess, my father's partner, arranged to rent it to a nice couple with kids. I considered moving in after police college, but the couple living here had been in residence so long I didn't want to just kick them out. Besides, I worked in a station downtown after graduation, so I rented an apartment in the city instead. The rent here more than paid for my apartment."

Mac nodded as he set down the bags he was carrying. He then crossed to the dining room at the end of the large living area to look into the kitchen. A soft whistle slid from his lips as he took in the white cupboards, dark granite-topped counters and island. "Nice job decorating."

"Thank you," CJ said, pleased at the compliment.

She'd agonized over every little thing she'd had done, so it was nice to know she wasn't the only one who liked it.

"When did you move back in?" Mac asked, returning to her side.

"A little over a year ago," she admitted. "The Eastbrooks—they were the family who rented the house for something like twenty-one years," she explained, "their kids were grown up and had moved out, so they decided to move to an apartment since it was just the two of them. I kept my apartment while this place was renovated and moved back in last June, so a year and three months ago."

Mac hesitated, but then asked, "If you had this house, why were you and your ex-husband saving to buy another one? Why not just move in here?"

"Like I said, the Eastbrooks had lived here a long time. I didn't want to just kick them out," she repeated, but acknowledged to herself that it was only part of the truth, and admitted, "Besides, even after so many years had passed, this place was . . . It made me sad to be here. I was so happy here with my parents until I found those papers in the attic. I didn't really want to live in the home where I'd been so happy with them. It would have been a daily reminder of what I'd lost," she admitted.

"But you didn't want to sell it either and give up your last connection to them," he guessed.

CJ nodded slowly, impressed that he'd worked that out. He really got her, she thought. "No, I didn't want to give it up. I guess that's why I never told Billy that I owned it. He would have suggested living here, or selling and buying somewhere else, and I didn't want to do either."

"He never knew about this place?" Mac asked with surprise.

"Not while we were together, but I had to put it in the financials for the divorce," she admitted with a grimace. "I half expected him to freak out when he saw that I'd owned a house all that time, but he didn't. Actually, I'm not even sure if he read the financials. He just signed the papers and walked away."

"So, he never even saw the house?" Mac asked, looking around the room.

"No," CJ admitted.

"And you moved back here, after all? It doesn't make you sad to be here?" he asked with concern.

CJ smiled faintly. "No. I thought it would, but after losing the baby and the divorce and everything, it felt kind of comforting to be here. I felt closer to my parents." A little uncomfortable and embarrassed at the admission, she straightened and said, "You should probably get going. They're all waiting in the RV."

"Yes. Besides, the sooner I leave, the sooner I'll be back," he said with a smile as he bent to pick up the bags he'd carried in. "Where do you want these? Laundry room, I'm guessing?"

"I can manage from here. You go ahead," she said at once, but he was already shaking his head before she'd finished speaking.

"It'll only take me a minute to take these to your laundry room, and that way I get to see a bit more of your house before I go," he added with a grin. "So, where is it?"

"At the end of the hall, in the walk-in closet off the master bedroom," CJ explained, picking up her own suitcase and bags.

"The walk-in closet?" he asked with surprise, heading down the hall.

CJ grinned at his tone of voice. "Yeah. It actually used to be the laundry room, but I took over the smaller closet in the master to make the master bathroom larger. So, I knocked out the wall into the laundry room next door to make it a walk-in/laundry combo. It makes it pretty handy for doing laundry," she pointed out. "And with just me here, it's not like anyone would be traipsing through my room to get to the washer and dryer in the walk-in."

"Smart," he decided as he turned into the master bedroom.

She saw Mac looking around the large bedroom with interest as he crossed to the open door to the walk-in. It made her look around too as she tried to see it from his perspective. Her gaze slid over the pale beige walls, wide-planked maple hardwood floor, an area rug in beige, with a rust and medium brown pattern, a rust and white colored duvet with a folded beige quilt on the end, and rust colored blinds covering the sliding glass doors and window. It was warm, but not too girly. She was not a girly type girl, CJ thought, and then grunted in surprise when she bumped into Mac, who had stopped abruptly.

Taking a step back, she glanced at him and then frowned as she noted that he'd gone stiff and still in the doorway to the walk-in. Unnaturally so, she realized, and dropped the suitcase and bags to free her hands.

"What is it?" CJ whispered, trying to look around his shoulder, but Mac moved protectively to the side, blocking her from view as well as blocking her view.

"Back up."

Now CJ stiffened. That hadn't been Mac's voice. It

was gruffer, and angry, and coming from inside her walk-in closet/laundry room combo.

Mac immediately started to back up, putting a hand behind to urge her to move with him. They shuffled backward until they were halfway to the door to the hall, and then the man said, "That's far enough."

CJ stopped at once and stepped to Mac's side to see the speaker. Her gaze slid over the tall, skinny, haggard-looking man with dark hair that was confronting them. She recognized him at once as the man in the video Mrs. Vesper's friend Joan had shown them. Officer Steve Jefferson had apparently not been caught and arrested. He'd been on the lam for two weeks and broken into her home, and he was pointing a gun at them, she noted just before Mac shifted in front of her again. CJ knew he was trying to protect her and scowled at him for it before simply moving around him. She was the ex–police officer here, as well as the man's target, and it was her house. She didn't need Mac to protect her. She also didn't want him hurt in her place because of some sense of chivalry.

Mac did not retreat under the look she cast him. Instead, he moved in front of her again, turning his back to the man and scowling down at her in return as he hissed, "CJ, let me handle this. I can't control him. The guy's all hopped up on something."

"Yeah, and he's waving a gun around too," she pointed out, barely noticing the odd bit about not being able to control him. "Which is exactly why I should handle it. I'm trained to deal with trash like this. I used to be a cop, remember?"

"You may be trained, but I am immort—" He snapped his mouth shut in the middle of whatever he'd been saying, and asked in a growl, "You know how I said I think you're brave and I might be falling in love with you?"

"Yes," she said warily.

"Well, you are brave, stupidly so, but I lied about the rest," he said firmly. "I'm not falling in love with you."

He might as well have stabbed her in the chest, because CJ felt those words like a physical blow. The pain was very real, and didn't ease until he added, "Because I already do love you."

CJ blinked at the admission. He did not seem pleased to make it. She, though, was overjoyed. He loved her! Damn, wasn't that awesome, she thought, and then realized he was still yammering at her. Like anything else in the world could be nearly as important as that he loved her, she thought. Still, she tuned back into the conversation to hear "—making love to you too, and I'd like to be able to do so for a long time, so step back and let me handle this. In fact, perhaps you should just leave the room, so I can—"

"She's not going anywhere," the intruder growled with irritation. "I'm the one in charge here, and I plan to settle this today."

"Like you tried to settle it at the Pub and Grill, when you did your best to run us down in the parking lot?" CJ asked sharply, glaring at him around Mac's arm. She knew it was the wrong tactic to take, but Mac had just told her he loved her, dammit, and this guy was ruining what should have been a perfect moment.

"You saw me? You knew it was me?" Jefferson's eyes were wide with alarm. "Does Dupree know? Hell! He'll never let me get near Lily again if he knows— Goddammit! You've screwed up everything, you dumb bitch!" he snarled furiously, and raised his gun.

Mac was moving even as Jefferson pulled the trigger and then pain slammed into CJ's chest and she went tumbling to her bedroom floor with Mac on top of her . . . only she wasn't sure how he'd got there. His back had been to her when he'd moved in front of her, but he was facing her by the time her back smacked into the floor. He landed on top of her hard. She had the vague thought that he must have been like a whirling dervish to get turned before they landed, and damn he was heavy. But most of her mind was taken up with the fact that her chest hurt and she couldn't breathe. She just wanted him off of her, but he wouldn't budge when she shoved at him.

Instead, he growled, "Stay still," and shifted to cover her more fully.

He was acting like a human shield, CJ realized, and wanted to kiss him and hit him for it all at the same time. But she did neither. She didn't even tell him that it was too late and she had already been shot, because she couldn't. She was gasping and struggling for breath, but couldn't take any in. It felt like her lung had collapsed. Had the bullet hit a lung? She wished she could look to see, but Mac was in the way, and then she became aware that someone was screaming and turned her head, trying to see where the sound was coming from. Her eyes widened with alarm when she spotted Marguerite by the door.

She was screaming for the men, shouting their names, CJ realized, and then it was like watching a film with pieces cut out. Julius, Decker, and Bricker were suddenly behind Marguerite as if appearing out of thin air. The men took in the situation at once and both Bricker and Decker charged on Jefferson, crossing the room in what seemed like a blink. But Julius stopped by his wife, and slid a supporting arm around her. Then CJ was distracted from what was happening in the room when Mac pushed himself up and to the side to get off of her.

"No!"

CJ's gaze shot back to Marguerite at that screech. She saw the horror and dismay on her face and was briefly confused at what had caused it . . . until she looked down and saw the large black hole between her breasts and the blood soaking her shirt around it. Dear God in heaven, no wonder she couldn't breathe, she thought faintly.

"Marguerite!" Julius's voice, full of alarm, drew CJ's attention again and she saw that Marguerite was hunched over now, clutching her large stomach, a grimace of pain on her face. Struggling to draw breath into her lungs, CJ eyed her worriedly for a moment, and then closed her eyes briefly before opening them again to gape down at her chest. There was so much blood, and the hole was huge. It— Wait, that wasn't a hole, she realized as she was finally able to take a breath. It was the button of her shirt. She'd pulled on a casual white shirt with black buttons as large as quarters on it that morning.

Managing another labored breath, CJ pulled the material of the top of the blouse away from her skin and peered down at her chest beneath the cloth. Blood had soaked through, and painted her bra and chest red, but there was no wound that could have caused it. No reason for her to have had trouble breathing even. She must have had the wind knocked out of her when she'd hit the floor, CJ thought.

"But then where did the blood come from?" she muttered, and then realization struck and she turned sharply to Mac. He was lying facedown next to her, completely still. She couldn't even see a hint of movement to suggest he was breathing.

Dragging herself upright, she grasped his shoulder and pulled him over onto his side and then onto his back and stared with dismay. Mac's face was pale, and like her, his chest was blood soaked, but with his own blood. Obviously, the large dark red stain on her top had been transferral, because he really did have a hole in the center of his chest and there was no mistaking it. T-shirts didn't have big black buttons on them.

Cursing, CJ staggered to her feet and stumbled into the bathroom for a towel and rushed back.

"Mac?" she said shakily as she dropped to her knees and pressed the towel to his wound. "Stay with me, honey. It's going to be all right. Mac?"

When he groaned, his eyelids flickering, CJ could have wept with relief. He looked so pale and there was so much blood that for a minute she'd feared she'd already lost him. Pressing more firmly down on his wound, she looked around.

Julius had shifted Marguerite out of the doorway and was on his haunches next to where she sat on the floor, leaning against the wall. Her knees were up and spread, the skirt of her dress draping between them as she leaned forward between her knees, clutching her stomach and panting.

Good Lord, it looked like Marguerite was in labor, CJ thought, but was quite sure it was too early for that. By at least three months, but possibly by as much as four months. Damn Jefferson! If Marguerite lost her baby because of him—

"Has someone called an ambulance?" she asked anxiously, her gaze moving back to Mac.

"On it." Decker's answer drew her attention to the fact that he was standing with a cell phone to his ear next to where Bricker had Jefferson flat out on the floor. With nothing to tie up the officer, Justin was sitting on the man, holding both of his hands in one of his and glancing from Mac to Marguerite with worry.

"Did you hear that, Mac?" CJ said, bending to press a kiss to his cheek. "Help is on the way. Please hold on. Don't die on me. Please," she begged, her voice cracking.

"Help is on the way, Aunt Marguerite," Decker said reassuringly a moment later. "Just hang in there."

CJ glanced around to see him putting his phone away, and then looked at Marguerite again when she moaned. The woman was clutching her stomach protectively and rocking where she sat, her face contorted with pain and worry.

"Just breathe and try to relax, *mi amata*. It is your upset causing this. It is too early for the baby to come. You need to try to relax," Julius said anxiously, brushing strands of her long hair off her face with the hand that wasn't clasping hers. "Breathe with me."

CJ watched with concern as Marguerite struggled to calm her breathing, and then turned her attention back to Mac and lifted the towel to see if the bleeding had slowed at all. But it was hard to see anything with the shirt in the way. Biting her lip, CJ hesitated, and then yanked his T-shirt up to get a better look at the wound. She had to wipe away the blood left behind from where it had soaked into the shirt, but a quick swipe of a clean portion of the towel did the trick, and then she found herself staring down at the hole in his chest. That was all there was to see. Blood did not bubble up to fill the hole and spill over the sides . . . which seemed odd to her. If it weren't for the fact that she could now see his chest rise and fall as he breathed, she'd think he was dead. But he was definitely breathing. Still, it seemed weird that no blood at all was filling the hole in his chest, she thought, and bent closer for a better look. CJ stiffened when she saw what she thought was metal just an inch or two inside the hole.

"What kind of gun does Jefferson have?" she asked suddenly, resisting the urge to prod the hole and feel if it was actually the bullet she was seeing.

"A Glock 35," Bricker answered. "Why?"

"Well, that can't be the bullet, then," she muttered. Glocks were powerful; the bullet would have gone deeper and— The bit of metal didn't seem as far down in the wound as it had a moment ago, she realized, and leaned forward again, trying to get a better look. She could hear Bricker and Decker talking quietly with Julius, but her attention stayed glued on whatever it was she was seeing in Mac's wound. She stared for the longest time and could swear she was actually watching it rising in the hole, though it was incredibly slow. Still, it was moving and was definitely metal. What the hell kind of bullet crawled back out of its victim? And why wasn't there more blood?

She peered around again, hoping for some help or answers, but only Decker, Julius, and Marguerite were there now. The two men had helped Marguerite to her feet and were half walking and half carrying her to the bed. CJ watched them get her situated and then searched the room for Bricker and Jefferson, but they were gone. Guessing that Bricker had taken the disgraced officer out of the room to wait for the police away from the trauma he'd caused, she turned back to Mac.

The bullet, if that's what the metal was, was only a quarter inch inside the wound now. If she'd had a pair of tweezers handy that were sterile, she could have plucked it out. CJ actually considered running to the bathroom for tweezers and alcohol to do just that, but wasn't sure it was a good idea. What if the bullet was like a cork? Maybe it was being pushed out by a fountain of blood that would gush out like a geyser when the bullet was removed. Mac could bleed out in minutes if that's what was happening. Maybe she should cover the wound and keep the bullet in instead. Dear God, she didn't know what to do. So, she did nothing. She simply held Mac's hand and prayed while she waited for help to arrive. She also did her best not to listen to the voice in her head that was telling her he would die, just as her parents had, just as her baby had . . . and she'd be alone again.

CJ had no idea how much time had passed when she heard Julius exclaim, "Oh, thank God. Dani."

Glancing around, CJ watched a curvaceous woman with long, wavy blond hair rush into the room and head straight for the bed. Dressed in navy blue dress slacks and a sharp white blouse, the woman looked every inch the professional, and CJ recalled Decker mentioning his wife, Dani, was a doctor, an ob-gyn if she remembered correctly. But her presence there was somewhat confusing. Where the hell was the ambulance Decker had called? And why was the woman rushing to Marguerite rather than Mac, who was bleeding out on the floor? She might be an ob-gyn, but that was still a doctor and Mac was in desperate need of a doctor right now.

"Uh, hey," CJ called out with a frown. "You're Decker's wife, the doctor, right?"

The blonde turned silver-blue eyes her way and smiled distractedly. "You must be the CJ Decker mentioned. Hi. Sorry, Marguerite needs me right now."

CJ nearly goggled at that, but snapped, "So does Mac. He's bleeding out here. Or he was," she added with a frown, glancing back to his wound. Still no blood, but the bullet was poking out of the wound now, already halfway out from the looks of it.

"Bricker's bringing blood. Mac will be fine," she assured her, and then glanced to an anxious Julius and added, "And so will Marguerite. She's just had a little upset. But her water hasn't broken, she's calming now and we'll give her lots of blood to distract the nanos so they don't attack the baby."

"Nanos," CJ breathed to herself with bewilderment, and wondered what she meant by Bricker was bringing blood? What the hell were they supposed to do with blood? Hook him up right here for a transfusion without tending the wound to stop the bleeding that wasn't really happening?

"Here we are!" Bricker announced, sailing into the room with a large cooler in hand. "The police took Jefferson away, and I brought the blood. It's all good."

CJ peered at the man blankly as he set the cooler down on the floor next to Mac, but her eyes widened with incredulity when he flipped it open and grabbed a couple of bags to toss to Decker. She had no idea why. But then, nothing he had said had made any sense to her. The police wouldn't have taken Jefferson away without coming in to review the scene and interview everyone, and she still had no idea what the blood was for or why he was throwing them to Decker who had turned back to Marguerite now, blocking CJ's view of the woman. Mac was the one who needed blood, but unless Bricker had an IV stand, needle, and rubber tubing in his pocket somewhere to hook Mac up it was useless. They needed to get him to the hospital; he needed to be operated on to remove the bullet, she thought, and glanced back just in time to see the bullet push out of his chest the last millimeter necessary for it to tumble to the side and roll off onto the bed.

Okay, maybe he didn't need an operation, she thought grimly, watching the hole that remained and expecting blood to either start bubbling or shooting out. Neither happened, though. Frowning, she leaned down to get a better look in the hole again. There was no blood rushing toward the surface. There was no blood at all that she could see, just flesh.

If it *was* flesh, CJ thought suddenly as she recalled seeing a movie once where bullets had ejected from a robot's chest just like this. One of the *Terminators* or something. Or maybe it had been a werewolf. She couldn't remember, but this wasn't the first time she'd likened Mac to a robot. That freaky silver that looked like liquid mercury filling his eyes had made her think of a robot, and his ability to perform sexually over and over and over again had made her think he was a machine. Now his body wasn't bleeding and was ejecting bullets. Dear God, she hadn't fallen in love with a robot or something, had she? Some kind of cyborg, or android, or—

"He's not a robot," Bricker said with amusement, and then shoved a bag of blood her way. "Here, hold this."

CJ automatically took the cold bag, but she was staring at Bricker with uncertainty, wondering just how he'd known what she was thinking.

"Because I can read your mind," he explained as he pulled a second bag of blood out of the cooler and then glanced toward the bed to ask, "Does Marguerite need more blood?"

"No," Marguerite muttered, sounding less breathless and pained, but more annoyed now.

"It's probably best to keep the nanos busy, Marguerite," Dani said gently. "We need to keep them from attacking the baby."

CJ did notice the use of that word again: nanos. But she was more concerned with Bricker's comment about reading her mind. He couldn't read her mind. Could he? And if so, how?

"Incoming," Bricker called, and CJ watched him toss another bag of blood toward the bed. Dani reached up and caught it in the air and then turned and slapped Marguerite in the face with it. At least that's what it looked like she was doing, but then she took her hand away and the bag stayed on Marguerite's face. Although it did begin to shrink, CJ noted, and stared with fascination as the liquid inside disappeared and the bag compressed and wrinkled as it emptied.

Bricker turned back, saw her expression, and grimaced slightly. "Right. So, explanation time."

CJ shifted her gaze to him, her mind rife with confusion.

He hesitated, and then asked, "I don't suppose you can wait until Mac wakes up to explain everything? He'd probably really rather do it himself," he pointed out, and when her expression didn't change, said, "No, huh? Okay, then, how do I— Oh! I know, so you've heard of Casper the Friendly Ghost, right?"

CJ's eyebrows rose, but she nodded.

"He was a good happy little ghost, not scary like the other ghosts?"

CJ nodded slowly again.

"Well, we're like that, only we're vampires, not ghosts. Happy Casper vampires."

"Oh, my God, Bricker!" Dani turned to scowl over her shoulder at Bricker, snapping, "What the hell are you trying to do? Scare her right out of the house? Mac is so going to kill you."

Bricker grimaced and turned back to CJ with a sigh. "Okay, so we're not really vampires, that just sounds sexier. We're actually immortals. We're human just like you with souls and all that other good human-y stuff like consciences and so on, but we have these little bioengineered nanos in us that use blood to heal injuries, fight disease, and keep us young. But it takes more blood than we can produce to do all that, so we have to top up the old red juice on a regular basis," he said, holding up the bag of blood between them. He then peered down at Mac and reached to open his mouth.

CJ had seen Mac's teeth and had never noticed fangs in his mouth before this, so wasn't surprised not to see them now either. But then Bricker opened his own mouth. Like Mac's, his teeth looked perfectly normal . . . until his canines shifted and dropped down. While she gaped at him, he punctured the end of one index finger on the tip of one of those fangs, bringing about a pearl of blood that he then waved under Mac's nose. It twitched as Mac caught the scent, and then his canines did the same shift and drop that Bricker's had, presenting very long, pointy-tipped fangs.

While CJ gaped, Bricker slapped the bag of blood to his mouth and released it and they both watched as it began to shrink like Marguerite's had, and then CJ murmured, "You said these nanos keep you all young." Raising her head, she eyed him with curiosity and asked, "Are you saying you're older than you look?"

"Oh, yeah," he said with a grin. "While you've been treating me and even thinking of me like a younger brother the last few weeks, I'm actually older than you."

"How much older?" she asked dubiously. He didn't just look younger than her, he acted younger too. It was hard to imagine he was older.

"I'm over a hundred years old, CJ," he said with a grin. "I'm just young at heart still."

"You are not!" she said at once.

"I am," he assured her. "I was born in 1910."

"No way."

"Way," he assured her.

"But that's—"

She'd snapped her mouth closed before the word *old* could slip out, but he laughed and said, "If you think that's old, Decker is at least twice that," he told her, and then glanced toward Decker to ask, "What are you now—260, 270?"

"I was born in 1750," Decker answered. The man was standing next to the bed, his eyes shifting between his wife and his aunt.

While CJ goggled at Decker, Bricker continued, "Dani is the youngest. She's only in her forties, and I know Marguerite was born in 1265, but I'm not sure about Julius. I think he's a lot older than her. He—"

"I was born in 534," Julius announced, and then added, "B.C."

CJ stared at the people around the bed. They all looked in their mid-twenties, just like Bricker, and just like— She turned to stare down at Macon.

"When was Mac born?" Bricker asked the room at large.

"1009 . . . B.C," Marguerite answered. Her voice sounded weary now, but at least the breathless panting had ended. It looked as if the pains or contractions she'd been suffering had stopped.

That had to be a good thing, CJ thought. She stared at Mac silently now, recalling thinking that he was lying about his age and was younger than her. She'd been right, he'd been lying, but if what Bricker said was true, he definitely wasn't younger than her.

But how could what Bricker said be true? she asked herself with a small frown. They didn't have the kind of technology he was talking about now let alone two, three, or even four thousand years ago.

"The Atlanteans did," Bricker said suddenly.

"Did what?" she asked with confusion.

"They had that kind of technology," he explained. "Atlantis was more advanced technologically than we are even now. The nanos were one of their last great discoveries or inventions before it fell. They were still working on fixing the flaws when earthquakes and whatnot destroyed it."

"The flaws?" she asked.

"Well, they hadn't intended it to be a fountain of youth, for one thing," he admitted with a wry smile. "It was just supposed to cure cancer and mend wounds."

"But isn't the 'keeping you all young and healthy' bit a good thing?" she asked, finding it odd that they would see something that men had searched for forever, the fabled fountain of youth, a bad thing.

"No society can exist if the people don't die," he pointed out, sounding suddenly older and more mature than he'd ever seemed. "Not with new babies born all the time. The earth couldn't support us all if we kept just having babies and no one died."

CJ supposed that was true.

"That's why we have the law that each immortal couple is only allowed to have one baby every hundred years. It's to help prevent our outgrowing our blood source."

CJ grimaced at the "blood source" bit, but asked, "So Marguerite can't have another baby for a century after this one?"

"Nope." He shook his head. "It's been a little over two hundred years since she had her last child, and will be another hundred before she can have her next."

"Marguerite and Julius already have another child?" CJ asked with surprise.

"Yep. They have a son, Christian, together," he told her. "And Marguerite has four other children besides that from her first husband: Lucern, Bastien, Etienne, and Lissianna."

CJ peered at Marguerite, amazed to know the woman had five children, soon to be six. At one hundred years apart, her oldest must be at least six hundred years old. But then, he'd said she was born in 1265, so the lovely younger friend she'd thought she'd made was actually well past seven hundred and fifty years old. Yet she didn't look over twenty-five. CJ shook her head. It was really quite amazing.

"So," she said slowly, "the nanos fight disease and keep you young, but the trade-off is you have to take in extra blood to power them."

Bricker nodded solemnly.

"But you don't bite people, you use blood banks to get that blood?" she asked.

"Usually, yes."

CJ stiffened. "Usually?"

"Well, emergencies crop up," he said with a shrug. "And if an emergency does crop up, say, a car accident or plane accident in the Alps or someplace far from blood banks, it's better for an immortal to feed carefully and judicially on a mortal than to lose his shit and attack them."

CJ supposed that was true. Still, it kind of rankled that they drank blood at all. Essentially, it sounded to her like mortals were cattle for these immortals or vampires, or whatever they were.

"Immortals," Dani said firmly from her position by Marguerite. "Vampires are dead and soulless. We aren't."

CJ frowned at the woman. It sounded like she was correcting the thought she'd just had. Bricker had said he could read her mind. Surely the woman hadn't done that?

"Yes. I'm just monitoring your thoughts to make sure Bricker isn't freaking you out," Dani said, sounding distracted, and then she straightened from clasping Marguerite's wrist and said, "Your pulse rate has gone back down. How is the pain? Are you still experiencing contractions?"

"Just barely. It's like they are fading away," Marguerite assured her, sounding relieved to be able to say it.

"Good," Dani said with a smile that didn't hide her own relief. "Just keep breathing deeply."

CJ turned to stare at Bricker. "You guys can really read my mind?"

He nodded, his gaze on the shrinking bag of blood on Mac's face. "Read, control, put memories in that aren't real. The nanos give us any skills we might need to survive."

"Control?" she asked with concern, and wondered if Mac had controlled her. Was she really so crazy attracted to him or had he controlled her and made her think she was?

"Mac can't read or control you," Bricker said, proving he could indeed read her mind. "That's why you'd be perfect for him. Actually, that's how we recognize possible mates. We can't read or control them and the sex is—" He licked a finger, held it up, and made a sizzling sound. "Sex is hot, hot, hot between life mates."

"Life mates?" she questioned sharply. Mac had mentioned the word a couple of times on the island. He'd like her to be his life mate, he'd said.

"Yeah, that's what we call our wives or partners. The belief is that the nanos somehow suss out the perfect mate when she or he is near, and once they do—" he shrugged "—that's it. We're off the market. See, we're like wolves and swans and stuff. We mate for life. So, you know, you wouldn't have to worry about Mac messing around on you like your first husband did if you agree to be his life mate. We're loyal to the end, and really good in bed because we experience what our mates are experiencing. We share the pleasure back and forth somehow."

CJ's eyes narrowed skeptically. While the sex with

Mac had been crazy hot, she hadn't noticed sharing his pleasure. It had just been crazy, extreme pleasure.

"Bet he didn't let you touch him, then, huh?" Bricker asked as he plucked the now empty bag from Mac's mouth and applied another.

CJ blinked at the question as she realized Mac never had let her touch him. Every time she'd tried he'd changed position, or taken her hands in his and held them over her head to discourage it.

"Yeah, see, he had to do that. If he hadn't and you'd stroked his shaft and felt his pleasure coursing through your body, you'd have wanted explanations," he pointed out. "And he couldn't risk explaining until he was sure you cared enough about him that you might be willing to be his life mate. Otherwise, he'd lose you."

"Lose me how?" CJ asked with a frown.

Bricker met her gaze solemnly. "The entire last three weeks or more since the two of you met would be wiped from your memory and replaced with some nice generic recollection of a boring case in a boring town, not worth thinking about."

CJ sat back on her heels at this news. So, if she and Mac didn't work out, he'd be erased from her memory? All of them would. The entire last few weeks?

"The only way it won't work out is if you refuse to

be his life mate," Bricker said quietly, grabbing another bag of blood in preparation of the next switch needed. "But that would be a shame since you both love each other."

"We do?" she asked, but her question really was, Does he?

"He loves you," Bricker told her firmly. "I normally wouldn't be able to read him because he's so much older than me, but even older immortals are easily read for a year or so after meeting their life mate and Mac's been an open book since meeting you. He loves you, and I know you love him . . . so, hopefully, you'll make the right decision."

CJ was silent, her gaze on Mac as Bricker switched blood bags again.

Twenty

Mac woke up thirsty. Rolling out of bed, he headed for the bathroom to get a glass of water and walked into what he was pretty sure was a wall. Cursing, he stepped back, put a hand to his head, and turned, smacking into what felt like a chair. That brought another curse and then the light turned on.

"Mac? Are you okay?"

The sudden light in the room left him blinking, but the sound of CJ's voice made him smile. "Sorry," he said, turning toward her voice. "When I first woke up I thought I was in my apartment in New York and walked into your wall."

"Oh." He could hear the smile in her voice, but also could actually see it now. His eyes had adjusted to the light.

"Good morning," he said, and then grimaced and said, "Or evening, I guess. What time is it?"

"About ten o'clock," she said softly, and then asked uncertainly, "How do you feel? Do you need more blood?"

Mac stiffened. "Blood?"

She shifted in the doorway and nodded. "Bricker left a lot here for you. He said you'd probably need more when you woke up. I'll get you some," she decided, and spun away to hurry off down the hall before he could say anything.

Mac stared at the empty spot where she'd been standing a moment ago, his mind whirling madly, and then glanced around in search of his phone. CJ had asked him if he needed blood. What the hell was going on? What did she know? And how did she know it? Now that he was fully awake, he remembered helping her bring in her luggage and finding Jefferson here. The bastard had tried to shoot CJ, he recalled, and he'd jumped in the way. That was pretty much the last thing he remembered other than using his last bit of strength to shift off of her when he realized she was having trouble breathing and that the others were there to keep her safe. He'd obviously passed out, but what the hell had happened after that? And where were his clothes? His phone should be in the pocket of his jeans, which he'd been wearing the last time he was conscious, but were now missing. He was standing around in his boxer briefs.

"I didn't know how much you'd want, so I brought a couple of bags."

Mac whirled toward the door at that announcement and watched her cross the room to set the bags on the bedside table. She started backing toward the door then, her gaze somewhere over his shoulder rather than on him. She was also talking a little fast and almost nervously as she said, "You must be hungry. I'll go see what I have to feed you. Come on out when you're ready."

She spun around, seeming eager to flee, and rushed from the room again.

Mac stood still for a minute, thinking that her reluctance to be in the same room with him didn't seem like a good thing, and then sighed and scanned the room again. His jeans weren't there. The only thing he could think was that perhaps she'd taken them to wash them, so he headed into her walk-in closet and nearly tripped over the duffel bag Julius had given him to put his clothes in. It was the one thing he hadn't thought of on the shopping trip to get clothes, something to keep them in.

Bending, he picked it up and set it on the center island to open, wondering who had brought in his things. CJ'd had so many bags that they'd both been bogged down and he'd decided to leave his own bag until he returned with Julius's car, but someone had obviously brought it in for him after he was shot.

Mac was tugging on a pair of jeans when he spotted his cell phone on one of the two tall chests of drawers that framed either side of the entry. Leaving his pants undone, he hurried over to pick it up and quickly found and hit Decker's number.

"You're awake! About time," was Decker's greeting when he answered the call.

Mac scowled at the "about time" bit, but said, "What the hell happened while I was unconscious?"

"A lot," Decker said, sounding mildly amused, and then began to list various events for him. "CJ kicked all our asses at Match Up. She and Dani bonded over a mutual love of hot chocolate and Reese's Pieces. Marguerite and Julius have decided to name their baby girl Benedetta when she's born because that means blessed, but I really don't think they thought that through," he added, sounding a bit agitated. "I mean, you know it's going to get shortened to Benny or something and she'll probably hate that. I mean—"

"Decker?" Mac interrupted his rant impatiently to ask, "How long have I been out?"

"Uh, let me see," he said thoughtfully. "We got to CJ's place at about four thirty on Saturday afternoon and it's ten o'clock on Tuesday night so you were out three days and five and a half hours."

"Dear God," Mac said with shock.

"Yes, it was a pretty long time," Decker said seriously, and admitted, "We were getting a little worried, but Marguerite said it was fine, that you'd wake up when you were ready. She said sometimes it just took longer to heal than others."

"Yes, but three days?" Mac asked with amazement. He was usually a fast healer. "I mean, I healed pretty fast after the fire, and my organs were all probably parboiled in that tub—why would a single gunshot wound take longer?"

"Maybe that's why," Decker suggested. "Maybe you still hadn't fully healed from the fire, and your nanos decided to shut you down until everything was healed up so you wouldn't go out and add another injury to the list of repairs to be made."

"You make it sound like the nanos can think beyond their programming," Mac said with a faint smile.

"You don't think they do?" Decker asked with surprise. "They aren't programmed to pick life mates, and yet they seem to do it."

"Right," he sighed, and shook his head, and then suddenly asked, "What the hell is Match Up?"

Decker chuckled at his bewildered tone. "It's a game where you shuffle the cards and set them all out face-down on the table and take turns flipping two cards over, trying to match up pairs. The one with the most pairs at the end wins," he explained. "CJ said it was the only game we couldn't cheat at by reading her mind."

Mac grinned widely. "That's my clever girl."

"Yeah. Bricker tried to convince her to play poker for Reese's Pieces first, but she's no one's fool. I like her," he added.

"So do I!" he heard Dani say, her voice a little distant but still he heard it.

He also heard Bricker call out, "Me too."

"Did you hear that? We've voted. She passes Argeneau and Bricker muster. You can keep her."

"I can, can I?" he asked with a smile.

"Yeah," Decker said lightly, and then in a more solemn tone, "Seriously, cousin. I'm glad you have her. She's perfect for you."

"Do I have her?" Mac asked with concern.

"You're asking the wrong person, Mac. Man up and go talk to your woman."

Mac bristled at the "man up" bit. He'd only wanted

to know what he was walking into, so he snapped irritably, "How do you know I haven't talked to her already?"

"Well, for one thing, because Dani, Bricker, and I
just left maybe ten, fifteen minutes ago," Decker said
dryly. "And for another, if you'd already talked to her
you wouldn't be asking me these questions, would you?
Go talk to her."

"I will," he assured him. "But first just tell me what
exactly she knows."

"I think Bricker pretty much covered everything,"
Decker said thoughtfully.

"Bricker?" Mac asked with alarm.

"Yeah, but he did okay," Decker assured him.

But Mac heard Dani snort in the background and
mutter, "Sure, once he got past that 'We're the Casper
the Friendly Ghost of vampires' stuff."

"What did Dani say?" Mac asked sharply. "Casper
the friendly what?"

"It's fine," Decker assured him. "I think he was
just going with that because of the whole bit about her
thinking you were a cyborg or a werewolf."

"What?" Mac squawked.

"It's all good," Decker said soothingly. "She's there,
isn't she? She didn't run off into the night screaming.
She's there waiting for you to talk to her. So go do it."

"But what—"

"Dani's telling me to hang up now, Mac. Gotta go," Decker said. The words were followed by dead air and Mac pulled the phone away to see that the call had been ended.

"Casper the Friendly Ghost of vampires?" he muttered with bewilderment as he slid the phone into the back pocket of his jeans. "And how the hell could she think I was a cyborg or werewolf?"

Shaking his head, he moved back to his duffle bag and pulled out a T-shirt that he yanked on as he moved back to the bedroom to claim the bags of blood CJ had brought him. He slapped the first one to his fangs and waited impatiently for it to empty, then switched it out for the second bag and waited again before heading out in search of CJ.

He found her in the kitchen, humming as she stirred a creamy orangey red soup in a pot and flipped some kind of sandwich in a frying pan. She appeared much more relaxed than she'd been in the bedroom, and that made some of his worries ease.

"Oh, hello," she said, offering him a smile when she spotted him.

"Hello." Mac paused just inside the kitchen and smiled in return. "You seem much better."

"Me?" She blinked in surprise and then laughed and pointed out, "You're the one who was shot. I'm fine."

"Yes, but you seemed anxious and eager to get away from me or something in the bedroom and I was worried . . ." He let the words trail off and shrugged.

"Ah." She nodded, and gave the soup a stir, then lifted first one sandwich and then the other to check their bottoms before saying, "Well, I've been waiting for you to wake up so that we could talk, and then I walked in to find you standing there in nothing but your boxer briefs and male glory and—" she paused to give him a crooked smile "—you and I both know that half-naked in close quarters usually leads to fully naked and no talking at all for us." She shrugged and shifted her attention back to her cooking as she ended, "So I was anxious and eager to be away. But now you're dressed and so long as you don't get too close, or touch or kiss me, we should be able to manage that talk."

Oddly enough, her words made him want to get closer and kiss and touch her, talk be damned. But the moment he started to move closer, CJ stopped cooking to face him and warned, "Don't even think about it, my love. I've got a spatula and know how to use it."

She waved the spatula at him threateningly to back up her words, but she needn't have bothered. Her words had stopped him cold.

"My love?" he asked.

CJ tilted her head in question. "Yes?"

"No." He shook his head on a soft laugh and explained, "You called me 'my love.'"

"Oh. I suppose I did," she admitted easily.

Mac hesitated and then asked point-blank, "Do you love me, CJ?"

She didn't hesitate or prevaricate. CJ simply nodded and said, "I do," as she turned back to her cooking. It left Mac standing there just gazing at her, wonder filling him. She loved him. He'd told her he loved her in the middle of the Jefferson mess, but she hadn't responded in kind then. This was the first time she'd spoken her feelings.

His feet started to take him toward her, but Mac stopped himself when she waved her spatula in his direction in warning, and said, "You are eating this food I made for you, Macon Argeneau, and then we are talking, so do not even think about moving a step closer to me. You will not be making love to me on this island counter—which is the perfect height for such endeavors by the way—and having my food burn and possibly set the house on fire while we're lying unconscious in our blissful satisfaction from an excess of the crazy hot pleasure you give me."

Mac was just envisioning the image she'd put in his head of having said pleasure on said island when she added, "By the way, in future you will not have to stop me from touching you. Bricker told me about the shared pleasure you've been trying to prevent my experiencing and possibly questioning you on. I know about it, so from now on it will be true mutual pleasure between us. There'll be no more of that not letting me touch you business."

"Yes, ma'am," Mac said with amusement, but his voice was almost growly from the new images she'd put in his mind. Her touching him, caressing him, running her warm hand down his—

"For instance," she continued, drawing him from his imaginings to see that she'd halved, stacked, and moved the sandwiches—grilled cheese, he thought—to a plate and was now pouring what he was guessing was cream of tomato soup into a bowl set between the two half stacks as she said, "If I want to push your pants down and take you in my mouth, you should let me."

Mac blinked at her, that image now life-size in his mind and making him instantly erect.

CJ set the pot down, picked up the plate holding the

bowl and two sandwiches, and turned to present it to him with a truly wicked smile.

Mac's eyes narrowed on that smile and his own mouth widened with amusement. "Witch," he accused. "You're driving me mad on purpose."

CJ shrugged with unconcern. "What are you going to do about it?"

It was a challenge. Mac had never been able to pass up a challenge. Sauntering forward, he pointed out, "You're not holding your spatula now."

"Oh, dear," she said with feigned dismay.

Mac chuckled and took the plate from her to set it on the counter with one hand, as his other slid around her waist.

When CJ immediately leaned into him with a little sigh and tipped her face up, offering her lips, he said, "I thought you wanted to talk?"

"I want you more," she answered, leaning up on tiptoe to press her mouth to his.

"God, I love you," Mac groaned, and kissed her, his hands gliding over her body even as hers slid over him.

He didn't try to stop her from touching him this time, and nipped at her lip when she broke their kiss, but she pulled back and gasped, "I love you too."

Smiling, he shook his head at his good fortune, but

when she tried to return to kissing, he held her off to ask, "And you'll be my life mate?"

"Yes, of course," she said without hesitation.

"Thank you," Mac said, pulling her into a tight hug. "I'll call Bastien about making arrangements for the turn. We'll schedule it for whenever you—"

"Wait. What?" CJ asked, pulling back. "The turn? What are you talking about?"

Mac eyed her with confusion. "I thought Bricker explained things to you?"

"He did," she agreed. "They all did. They told me all about Atlantis, and the nanos. How they keep you healthy and heal wounds, and keep you young. How they make you strong, fast, give you night vision and all that, but nobody mentioned anything about a turn. What is it?"

"How could they not tell you that part?" he asked with disbelief.

CJ frowned. "It isn't like a vampire turn, is it? Like you turning me into a bloodsucking immortal?"

Now it was Mac's turn to frown as he recalled her reaction to the knowledge that he worked with blood when they'd first met. She'd shuddered and made a face that seemed to suggest she found blood gross. Swallowing, he considered the matter briefly, but he couldn't lie about this. Blood was a necessity to his kind. She would need to consume it if she turned.

"Yes," he said finally.

"Oh." She grimaced with disgust. "That isn't necessary, is it? I mean, do I have to turn for us to be together? Can't we just . . ." She shrugged helplessly. "Be together?"

"We could," he said slowly. "But turning has all sorts of benefits, my love. Your HIV would be eradicated. You wouldn't have to take medicine every day as you do now. In fact, you would never have to take any kind of medicine again for anything."

Her eyebrows rose at that, but then she bit her lip briefly and pointed out, "But it's kind of taking medicine for you when you take blood, isn't it? I mean, it's necessary for you guys to live. You can't do without it."

Mac blinked in surprise at the suggestion. He'd never thought of it like that.

"Can't we just be together without my turning?" she asked, leaning into him.

"We could, but . . ."

"But?" she prompted when he hesitated.

"You're asking me to accept your death before we've even started," he said sadly.

CJ's eyes widened with amazement. "I'm not dying.

You're not getting rid of me that quickly. I've got a good thirty years left in me at least."

"Unless you're in a car accident, shot, or hit by a bus," he said dully.

"Accidents happen all the time, Mac. Surely even your nanos can't save you from accidents?"

"Unless my head's cut off and kept away from my body for an extremely long time, or I'm set on fire, yes, the nanos can save me from most accidents," he told her solemnly.

"Oh." She bit her lip again, but said, "Still, we'd have thirty or forty years together. That's nothing to sneeze at."

"CJ," he said gently. "I was born in 1009 B.C. I've lived more than three thousand years, and may live three thousand more. The human life span is a blink of an eye to me. Thirty or forty years is half a blink, and I'd spend it constantly worrying about you getting in an accident, or falling ill . . . and then I'd spend the next three thousand years mourning your passing." Mac frowned as he recognized the truth behind his words. Being with her while she was mortal would be a constant hell of worry, mixed with the constant highs of having her near. It would be a roller coaster ride, but worse, because he'd also have the constant knowledge that she would die soon and leave him alone.

Mac wasn't sure he could handle that. He'd have to, of course. He couldn't not take her any way she was willing to be with him, but he was afraid he'd be a moody son of a bitch because of it and started to say, "I'm not sure—"

He'd meant to say, "I'm not sure you'll like the man I'll become living like that," but CJ had covered his mouth, cutting him off.

"I'll turn," she said abruptly.

"Really?" he asked, hope thrashing around inside his chest.

"Yes. Really," she said, and managed a weak smile. "I love you, and if it will make you happy, I'll turn or let you turn me, or whatever it is."

Scooping her up off the floor, Mac swung her around and then hugged her tightly. "You won't regret it. I promise. I'll spend the rest of my life ensuring you don't. I'll bring you flowers every day. I'll buy you stock in Reese's Pieces. I'll—" His words died as she covered his mouth again, and Mac stopped spinning around and set her down. Since her hand was over his mouth, he simply tilted his head in question.

"You don't have to do any of that," she said quietly. "Just love me and that will be enough."

"I already do," he told her solemnly.

"Well, I know that," she said with exasperation. "I meant, take me to bed and make love to me so I don't have to think about this turning business anymore for now."

A laugh slipped from Mac's mouth before he could catch it back, and he scooped CJ up into his arms and headed out of the kitchen, saying, "My God, you're a demanding woman. Are you going to be ordering me to make love to you often now that we're life mates?"

"Every chance I get," she assured him, running her hand over his upper chest.

"A ballbuster and a sex fiend." Mac clucked his tongue and shook his head. "Damn, how'd I get so lucky?"

"Some drug addict was tweaking and set your house on fire," CJ said dryly as he carried her into the bedroom. "It was obviously meant to be."

"Obviously," Mac agreed on a laugh, kicking the bedroom door closed behind them.

HARPER
LARGE PRINT

We hope you enjoyed reading
our new, comfortable print size and found it
an experience you would like to repeat.

Well – you're in luck!

Harper Large Print offers the finest in
fiction and nonfiction books in this same larger
print size and paperback format. Light and easy to read,
Harper Large Print paperbacks are for the book lovers
who want to see what they are reading without strain.

For a full listing of titles and
new releases to come, please visit our website:
www.hc.com

HARPER LARGE PRINT

SEEING IS BELIEVING!